THE NIGHT FIRE

P9-AZV-358

ALSO BY MICHAEL CONNELLY

THE HARRY BOSCH NOVELS

THE LINCOLN LAWYER NOVELS

OTHER NOVELS

NONFICTION

E-BOOKS

THE
NIGHT
FIRE

MICHAEL
CONNELLY

GRAND CENTRAL
PUBLISHING

New York Boston

Copyright © 2019 by Hieronymus, Inc.
Preview of *Fair Warning* copyright © 2020 by Hieronymus, Inc.

Grand Central Publishing
Hachette Book Group
1290 Avenue of the Americas, New York, NY 10104
grandcentralpublishing.com
twitter.com/grandcentralpub

Originally published in hardcover and ebook by Little, Brown & Company in October 2019
First trade paperback edition: April 2020

Grand Central Publishing is a division of Hachette Book Group, Inc. The Grand Central Publishing name and logo is a trademark of Hachette Book Group, Inc.

The publisher is not responsible for websites (or their content) that are not owned by the publisher.

The Hachette Speakers Bureau provides a wide range of authors for speaking events. To find out more, go to hachettespeakersbureau.com or call (866) 376-6591.

Library of Congress Control Number: 2019946507

ISBNs: 978-1-5387-3372-1 (trade paperback), 978-0-316-45748-4 (ebook)

Printed in the United States of America

LSC-H

10 9 8 7 6 5 4 3 2 1

For Titus Welliver,
for breathing life into Harry Bosch.
Hold Fast.

BOSCH

1

Bosch arrived late and had to park on a cemetery lane far from the grave site. Careful not to step on anybody's grave, he limped through two memorial sections, his cane sinking into the soft ground, until he saw the gathering for John Jack Thompson. It was standing room only around the old detective's grave site and Bosch knew that wouldn't work with his knee six weeks post-op. He retreated to the nearby Garden of Legends section and sat on a concrete bench that was part of Tyrone Power's tomb. He assumed it was okay since it was clearly a bench. He remembered his mother taking him to see Power in the movies when he was a kid. Old stuff they would run in the revival theaters on Beverly. He remembered the handsome actor as Zorro and as the accused American in *Witness for the Prosecution*. He had died on the job, suffering a heart attack while filming a dueling scene in Spain. Bosch had always thought it wasn't a bad way to go—doing what you loved.

The service for Thompson lasted a half hour. Bosch was too far away to hear what was said but he could guess. John Jack—he was always called that—was a good man who gave forty years of service to the Los Angeles Police Department in uniform and as a detective. He put many bad people away and taught generations of detectives how to do the same.

One of them was Bosch—paired with the legend as a newly minted homicide detective in Hollywood Division more than three decades earlier. Among other things, John Jack had taught Bosch how to read the tells of a liar in an interrogation room. John Jack always knew when somebody was lying. He once told Bosch it took a liar to know a liar but never explained how he had come by that piece of wisdom.

Their pairing had lasted only two years because Bosch trained well and John Jack was needed to break in the next new homicide man, but the mentor and student had stayed in touch through the years. Bosch spoke at Thompson's retirement party, recounting the time they were working a murder case and John Jack pulled over a bakery delivery truck when he saw it turn right at a red light without first coming to a complete stop. Bosch questioned why they had interrupted their search for a murder suspect for a minor traffic infraction and John Jack said it was because he and his wife, Margaret, were having company for dinner that night and he needed to bring home a dessert. He got out of their city-ride, approached the truck, and badged the driver. He told him he had just committed a two-pie traffic offense. But being a fair man, John Jack cut a deal for one cherry pie and came back to the city car with that night's dessert.

Those kinds of stories and the legend of John Jack Thompson had dimmed in the twenty years since his retirement, but the gathering around his grave was thick and Bosch recognized many of the men and women he had worked with during his own time with an LAPD badge. He suspected the reception at John Jack's house after the service was going to be equally crowded and might last into the night.

Bosch had been to too many funerals of retired detectives to count. His generation was losing the war of attrition. This one was high-end, though. It featured the official LAPD honor guard and pipers. That was a nod to John Jack's former standing in the department. "Amazing Grace" echoed mournfully across the cemetery and over the wall that divided it from Paramount Studios.

After the casket was lowered and people started heading back to their cars, Bosch made his way across the lawn to where Margaret remained seated, a folded flag in her lap. She smiled at Bosch as he approached.

"Harry, you got my message," she said. "I'm glad you came."

"Wouldn't miss it," Bosch said.

He leaned down, kissed her cheek, and squeezed her hand.

"He was a good man, Margaret," he said. "I learned a lot from him."

"He was," she said. "And you were one of his favorites. He took great pride in all of the cases you closed."

Bosch turned and looked down into the grave. John Jack's box appeared to have been made of stainless steel.

"He picked it," Margaret said. "He said it looked like a bullet."

Bosch smiled.

"I'm sorry I didn't get over to see him," he said. "Before the end."

"It's okay, Harry," she said. "You had your knee. How is it doing?"

"Better every day. I won't need this cane much longer."

"When John Jack had his knees done he said it was a new lease on life. That was fifteen years ago."

Bosch just nodded. He thought a new lease on life was a little optimistic.

"Are you coming back to the house?" Margaret asked. "There is something there for you. From him."

Bosch looked at her.

"From him?"

"You'll see. Something I would give only to you."

Bosch saw members of the family gathered by a couple of stretch limos in the parking lane. It looked like two generations of children.

"Can I walk you over to the limo?" Bosch asked.

"That would be nice, Harry," Margaret said.

2

Bosch had picked up a cherry pie that morning at Gelson's and that was what had made him late to the funeral. He carried it into the bungalow on Orange Grove, where John Jack and Margaret Thompson had lived for more than fifty years. He put it on the dining room table with the other plates and trays of food.

The house was crowded. Bosch said hellos and shook a few hands as he pushed his way through the knots of people, looking for Margaret. He found her in the kitchen, oven mitts on and getting a hot pan out of the oven. Keeping busy.

"Harry," she said. "Did you bring the pie?"

"Yes," he said. "I put it on the table."

She opened a drawer and gave Bosch a spatula and a knife.

"What were you going to give me?" Bosch asked.

"Just hold your horses," Margaret said. "First cut the pie, then go back to John Jack's office. Down the hall, on the left. It's on his desk and you can't miss it."

Bosch went into the dining room and used the knife she had given him to cut the pie into eight slices. He then made his way again through the people crowded in the living room to the hallway that led back to John Jack's home office. He had been there before. Years earlier, when they worked cases together, after a long shift Bosch would often end up at the Thompson house for a late meal prepared by Margaret and a strategy session with John Jack. Sometimes Bosch would take the couch in the home office and sleep a few hours before getting back to work on the case. He even kept spare clothes in the office closet. Margaret always left a fresh towel for him in the guest bathroom.

The door was closed and for some reason he knocked, even though he knew no one should be in there.

He opened the door and entered a small cluttered office with shelves on two walls and a desk pushed up against a third under a window. The couch was still there, across from the window. Sitting on a green blotter on the desk was a thick blue plastic binder with three inches of documents inside.

It was a murder book.

BALLARD

3

Ballard studied what she could see of the remains with an unflinching eye. The smell of kerosene mixed with that of burned flesh was overpowering this close, but she stood her ground. She was in charge of the scene until the fire experts arrived. The nylon tent had melted and collapsed on the victim. It tightly shrouded the body in places where the fire had not completely burned through. The body seemed to be in repose and she wondered how he could have slept through it. She also knew that toxicity tests would determine his alcohol and drug levels. Maybe he never felt a thing.

Ballard knew it would not be her case but she pulled out her phone and took photos of the body and the scene, including close-ups of the overturned camping heater, the presumed source of the blaze. She then opened the temperature app on the phone and noted that the current temperature listed for Hollywood was 52 degrees. That would go in her report and be forwarded to the Fire Department's arson unit.

She stepped back and looked around. It was 3:15 a.m. and Cole Avenue was largely deserted, except for the homeless people who had come out of the tents and cardboard shanties that lined the sidewalk running alongside the Hollywood Recreation Center. They stared both wide-eyed and addled as the investigation into the death of one of their own proceeded.

"How'd we get this?" Ballard asked.

Stan Dvorek, the patrol sergeant who had called her out, stepped over. He had worked the late-show shift longer than anybody at Hollywood Division—more than ten years. Others on the shift called him "The Relic," but not to his face.

"FD called us," he said. "They got it from communications. Somebody driving by saw the flames and called it in as a fire."

"They get a name on the PR?" Ballard asked.

"He didn't give one. Called it in, kept driving."

"Nice."

Two fire trucks were still on scene, having made the journey just three blocks down from Station 27 to douse the burning tent. The crews were standing by to be questioned.

"I'm going to take the fire guys," Ballard said. "Why don't you have your guys talk to some of these people, see if anybody saw anything."

"Isn't that arson's job?" Dvorek asked. "They're just going to have to reinterview if we find anybody worth talking to."

"First on scene, Devo. We need to do this right."

Ballard walked away, ending the debate. Dvorek might be the patrol supervisor but Ballard was in charge of the crime scene. Until it was determined that the fatal fire was an accident she would treat it as a crime scene.

She walked over to the waiting firefighters and asked which of the two crews was first on scene. She then asked the six firefighters assigned to the first truck what they saw. The information she received from them was thin. The tent fire had almost burned itself out by the time the fire-rescue team arrived. Nobody saw anyone around the blaze or nearby in the park. No witnesses, no suspects. A fire extinguisher from the truck had been used to douse the remaining flames, and the victim was pronounced dead and was therefore not transported to a hospital.

From there Ballard took a walk up and down the block, looking for cameras. The homeless encampment ran along the city park's outdoor basketball courts, where there were no security cameras. On the west side of Cole was a line of one-story warehouses inhabited by prop houses and equipment-rental houses catering to the film and television industry. Ballard saw a few cameras but suspected that they were either dummies or set at angles that would not be helpful to the investigation.

When she got back to the scene, she saw Dvorek conferring with two of his patrol officers. Ballard recognized them from the morning-watch roll call at Hollywood Division.

"Anything?" Ballard asked.

"About what you'd expect," Dvorek said. "'I didn't see nothin', I didn't hear nothin', I don't know nothin'.' Waste of time."

Ballard nodded. "Had to be done," she said.

"So where the fuck is arson?" Dvorek asked. "I need to get my people back out."

"Last I heard, in transit. They don't run twenty-four hours, so they had to roust a team from home."

"Jesus, we'll be waiting out here all night. Did you roll the coroner out yet?"

"On the way. You can probably clear half your guys and yourself. Just leave one car here."

"You got it."

Dvorek went off to issue new orders to his officers. Ballard walked back to the immediate crime scene and looked at the tent that had melted over the dead man like a shroud. She was staring down at it when peripheral movement caught her eye. She looked up to see a woman and a girl climbing out of a shelter made of a blue plastic tarp tied to the fence that surrounded the basketball court. Ballard moved quickly to them and redirected them away from the body.

"Honey, you don't want to go over there," she said. "Come this way."

She walked them down the sidewalk to the end of the encampment.

"What happened?" the woman asked.

Ballard studied the girl as she answered.

"Somebody got burned," she said. "Did you see anything? It happened about an hour ago."

"We were sleeping," the woman said. "She's got school in the morning."

The girl had still not said anything.

"Why aren't you in a shelter?" Ballard asked. "This is dangerous out here. That fire could've spread."

She looked from the mother to the daughter.

"How old are you?"

The girl had large brown eyes and brown hair and was slightly overweight. The woman stepped in front of her and answered Ballard.

"Please don't take her from me."

Ballard saw the pleading look in the woman's brown eyes.

"I'm not here to do that. I just want to make sure she's safe. You're her mother?"

"Yes. My daughter."

"What's her name?"

"Amanda—Mandy."

"How old?"

"Fourteen."

Ballard leaned down to talk to the girl. She had her eyes cast down.

"Mandy? Are you okay?"

She nodded.

"Would you want me to try to get you and your mother into a shelter for women and children? It might be better than being out here."

Mandy looked up at her mother when she answered.

"No. I want to stay here with my mother."

"I'm not going to separate you. I will take you and your mother if you want."

The girl looked up at her mother again for guidance.

"You put us in there and they will take her away," the mother said. "I know they will."

"No, I'll stay here," the girl said quickly.

"Okay," Ballard said. "I won't do anything, but I don't think this is where you should be. It's not safe out here for either of you."

"The shelters aren't safe either," the mother said. "People steal all your stuff."

Ballard pulled out a business card and handed it to her.

"Call me if you need anything," she said. "I work the midnight shift. I'll be around if you need me."

The mother took the card and nodded. Ballard's thoughts returned to the case. She turned and gestured toward the crime scene.

"Did you know him?" she asked.

"A little," the mother said. "He minded his own business."

"Do you know his name?"

"Uh, I think it was Ed. Eddie, he said."

"Okay. Had he been here a long time?"

"A couple months. He said he had been over at Blessed Sacrament but it was getting too crowded for him."

Ballard knew that Blessed Sacrament on Sunset allowed the homeless to camp on the front portico. She drove by it often and knew it to be heavily crowded at night with tents and makeshift shelters, all of which disappeared at daylight before church services began.

Hollywood was a different place in the dark hours, after the neon and glitter had dimmed. Ballard saw the change every night. It became a place of predators and prey and nothing in between, a place where the haves were comfortably and safely behind their locked doors and the have-nots freely roamed. Ballard always remembered the words of a late-show patrol poet. He called them *human tumbleweeds moving with the winds of fate.*

"Did he have any trouble with anybody here?" she asked.

"Not that I saw," said the mother.

"Did you see him last night?"

"No, I don't think so. He wasn't around when we went to sleep."

Ballard looked at Amanda to see if she had a response but was interrupted by a voice from behind.

"Detective?"

Ballard turned around. It was one of Dvorek's officers. His name was Rollins. He was new to the division or he wouldn't have been so formal.

"What?"

"The guys from arson are here. They—"

"Okay. I'll be right there."

She turned back to the woman and her daughter.

"Thank you," she said. "And remember, you can call me anytime."

As Ballard headed back toward the body and the men from arson, she couldn't help remembering again that line about tumbleweeds. Written on a field interview card by an officer Ballard later learned had seen too much of the depressing and dark hours of Hollywood and taken his own life.

4

The men from arson were named Nuccio and Spellman. Following LAFD protocol, they were wearing blue coveralls with the LAFD badge on the chest pocket and the word ARSON across the back. Nuccio was the senior investigator and he said he would be lead. Both men shook Ballard's hand before Nuccio announced that they would take the investigation from there. Ballard explained that a cursory sweep of the homeless encampment had produced no witnesses, while a walk up and down Cole Avenue had found no cameras with an angle on the fatal fire. She also mentioned that the coroner's office was rolling a unit to the scene and a criminalist from the LAPD lab was en route as well.

Nuccio seemed uninterested. He handed Ballard a business card with his e-mail address on it and asked that she forward the death report she would write up when she got back to Hollywood Station.

"That's it?" Ballard asked. "That's all you need?"

She knew that LAFD arson experts had law enforcement and detective training and were expected to conduct a thorough investigation of any fire involving a death. She also knew they were competitive with the LAPD in the way a little brother might be with his older sibling. The arson guys didn't like being in the LAPD's shadow.

"That's it," Nuccio said. "You send me your report and I'll have your e-mail. I'll let you know how it all shakes out."

"You'll have it by dawn," Ballard said. "You want to keep the uniforms here while you work?"

"Sure. One or two of them would be nice. Just have them watch our backs."

Ballard walked away and over to Rollins and his partner, Randolph, who were waiting by their car for instructions. She told them to stand by and keep the scene secure while the investigation proceeded.

Ballard used her cell to call the Hollywood Division watch office and report that she was about to leave the scene. The lieutenant was named Washington. He was a new transfer from Wilshire Division. Though he had previously worked Watch Three, as the midnight shift was officially called, he was still getting used to things at Hollywood Division. Most divisions went quiet after midnight but Hollywood rarely did. That was why they called it the Late Show.

"LAFD has no need for me here, L-T," Ballard said.

"What's it look like?" Washington asked.

"Like the guy kicked over his kerosene heater while he was sleeping. But we've got no wits or cameras in the area. Not that we found, and I'm not thinking the arson guys are going to look too hard beyond that."

Washington was silent for a few moments while he came to a decision.

"All right, then come back to the house and write it up," he finally said. "They want it all by themselves, they can have it."

"Roger that," Ballard said. "I'm heading in."

She disconnected and walked over to Rollins and Randolph, telling them she was leaving the scene and that they should call her at the station if anything new came up.

The station was only five minutes away at four in the morning. The rear parking lot was quiet as Ballard headed to the back door. She used her key card to enter and took the long way to the detective bureau so that she could go through the watch office and check in with Washington. He was only in his second deployment period and still learning and feeling his way. Ballard had been purposely wandering through the watch office two or three times a shift to make herself familiar to Washington. Technically her boss was Terry McAdams, the division's detective lieutenant, but she almost never saw him because he worked days. In reality, Washington was her boots-on-the-ground boss and she wanted to solidly establish the relationship.

Washington was behind his desk looking at his deployment screen, which showed the GPS locations of every police unit in the division. He was tall, African-American, with a shaved head.

"How's it going?" Ballard asked.

"All quiet on the western front," Washington said.

His eyes were squinted and holding on a particular point on the screen. Ballard pivoted around the side of his desk so she could see it too.

"What is it?" she asked.

"I've got three units at Seward and Santa Monica," Washington said. "I've got no call there."

Ballard pointed. The division was divided into thirty-five geographic zones called reporting districts and these were in turn covered by seven basic car areas. At any given time there was a patrol in each car area, with other cars belonging to supervisors like Sergeant Dvorek, who had division-wide patrol responsibilities.

"You've got three basic car areas that are contiguous there," she said. "And that's where an all-night *mariscos* truck parks. They can all code seven there without leaving their zones."

"Got it," Washington said. "Thanks, Ballard. Good to know."

"No problem. I'm going to go brew a fresh pot in the break room. You want a cup?"

"Ballard, I might not know about that *mariscos* truck out there, but I know about you. You don't need to be fetching coffee for me. I can get my own."

Ballard was surprised by the answer and immediately wanted to ask what exactly Washington knew about her. But she didn't.

"Got it," she said instead.

She walked back down the main hall and then hooked a left down the hallway that led to the detective bureau. As expected, the squad room was deserted. Ballard checked the wall clock and saw that she had over two hours until the end of her shift. That gave her plenty of time to write up the report on the fire death. She headed to the cubicle she used in the back corner. It was a spot that gave her a full view of the room and anybody who came in.

She had left her laptop open on the desk when she got the callout on the tent fire. She stood in front of the desk for a few moments before sitting down. Someone had changed the setting on the small radio she usually set up at her station. It had been changed from the KNX 1070 news station she usually had playing to KJAZ 88.1. Someone had also moved her computer to the side, and a faded blue binder— a murder book—had been left front and center on the desk. She flipped it open and there was a Post-it on the table of contents.

Don't say I never gave you anything.

B

PS: Jazz is better for you than news.

Ballard took the Post-it off because it was covering the name of the victim.

John Hilton—DOB 1/17/66–DOD 8/3/90

She didn't need the table of contents to find the photo section of the book. She flipped several sections of reports over on the three steel loops and found the photos secured in plastic sleeves. The photos showed the body of the young man slumped across the front seat of a car, a bullet hole behind his right ear.

She studied the photos for a moment and then closed the binder. She pulled her phone, looked up a number, and called it, checking her watch as she waited. A man answered quickly and did not sound to Ballard as if he had been pulled from the depths of sleep.

"It's Ballard," she said. "You were in here at the station tonight?"

"Uh, yeah, I dropped by about an hour ago," Bosch said. "You weren't there."

"I was on a call. So where'd this murder book come from?"

"I guess you could say it's been missing in action. I went to a funeral yesterday—my first partner in homicide way back when. The guy who mentored me. He passed on and I went to the funeral, and then afterward at his house, his wife—his widow—gave me the book. She wanted me to return it. So that's what I did. I returned it to you."

Ballard flipped the binder open again and read the basic case information above the table of contents.

"George Hunter was your partner?" she asked.

"No," Bosch said. "My partner was John Jack Thompson. This wasn't his case originally."

"It wasn't his case, but when he retired he stole the murder book."

"Well, I don't know if I'd say he stole it."

"Then what would you say?"

"I'd say he took over the investigation of a case nobody was working. Read the chrono, you'll see it was gathering dust. The original case detective probably retired and nobody was doing anything with it."

"When did Thompson retire?"

"January 2000."

"Shit, and he had it all this time? Almost twenty years."

"That's the way it looks."

"That's really bullshit."

"Look, I'm not trying to defend John Jack, but the case probably got more attention from him than it ever would've in the

Open-Unsolved Unit. They mainly just work DNA cases over there and there's no DNA in this one. It would have been passed over and left to gather dust if John Jack hadn't taken it with him."

"So you know there's no DNA? And you checked the chrono?"

"Yeah. I read through it. I started when I got home from the funeral, then took it to you as soon as I finished."

"And why did you bring it here?"

"Because we had a deal, remember? We'd work cases together."

"So you want to work this together?"

"Well, sort of."

"What's that mean?"

"I've got some stuff going on. Medical stuff. And I don't know how much—"

"What medical stuff?"

"I just got a new knee and, you know, I have rehab and there might be a complication. So I'm not sure how much I can be involved."

"You're dumping this case on me. You changed my radio station and dumped the case on me."

"No, I want to help and I will help. John Jack mentored me. He taught me the rule, you know?"

"What rule?"

"To take every case personally."

"What?"

"Take every case personally and you get angry. It builds a fire. It gives you the edge you need to go the distance every time out."

Ballard thought about that. She understood what he was saying but knew it was a dangerous way to live and work.

"He said 'every case'?" she asked.

"'Every case,'" Bosch said.

"So you just read this cover to cover?"

"Yes. Took me about six hours. I had a few interruptions. I need to walk and work my knee."

"What's the part in it that made it personal for John Jack?"

"I don't know. I didn't see it. But I know he found a way to make every case personal. If you find that, you might be able to close it out."

"If *I* find it?"

"Okay, if *we* find it. But like I said, I already looked."

Ballard flipped the sections over until she once again came to the photos held in plastic sleeves.

"I don't know," she said. "This feels like a long shot. If George Hunter couldn't clear it and then John Jack Thompson couldn't clear it, what makes you think we can?"

"Because you have that thing," Bosch said. "That fire. We can do this and bring that boy some justice."

"Don't start with the 'justice' thing. Don't bullshit me, Bosch."

"Okay, I won't. But will you at least read the chrono and look through the book before deciding? If you do that and don't want to continue, that's fine. Turn the book in or give it back to me. I'll work it alone. When I get the time."

Ballard didn't answer at first. She had to think. She knew that the proper procedure would be to turn the murder book in to the Open-Unsolved Unit, explain how it had been found after Thompson's death, and leave it at that. But as Bosch had said, that move would probably result in the case being put on a shelf to gather dust.

She looked at the photos again. It appeared to her on initial read that it was a drug rip-off. The victim pulls up, offers the cash, gets a bullet instead of a balloon of heroin or whatever his drug of choice was.

"There's one thing," Bosch said.

"What's that?" Ballard asked.

"The bullet. If it's still in evidence. You need to run it through NIBIN, see what comes up. That database wasn't around back in 1990."

"Still, what's that, a one-in-ten shot? No pun intended."

She knew that the national database held the unique ballistic details of bullets and cartridge casings found at crime scenes, but it was far from a complete archive. Data on a bullet had to be entered for that bullet to become part of any comparison process, and most police departments, including the LAPD, were behind in the entering process. Still, the bullet archive had been around since the start of the century and the data grew larger every year.

"It's better than no shot," Bosch said.

Ballard didn't reply. She looked at the murder book and ran a fingernail up the side of the thick sheaf of documents it contained, creating a ripping sound.

"Okay," she finally said. "I'll read it."

"Good," Bosch said. "Let me know what you think."

BOSCH

5

Bosch quietly slipped into the back row of the Department 106 courtroom, drawing the attention of the judge only, who made a slight nod in recognition. It had been years, but Bosch had had several cases before Judge Paul Falcone in the past. He had also woken the judge up on more than one occasion while seeking approval for a search warrant in the middle of the night.

Bosch saw his half brother, Mickey Haller, at the lectern located to the side of the defense and prosecution tables. He was questioning his own witness. Bosch knew this because he had been tracking the case online and in the newspaper and this day was the start of the defense's seemingly impossible case. Haller was defending a man accused of murdering a superior-court judge named Walter Montgomery in a city park less than a block from the courthouse that now held the trial. The defendant, Jeffrey Herstadt, not only was linked to the crime by DNA evidence but had helpfully confessed to the murder on video as well.

"Doctor, let me get this straight," Haller said to the witness seated to the left of the judge. "Are you saying that Jeffrey's mental issues put him in a state of paranoia where he feared physical harm might come to him if he *did not* confess to this crime?"

The man in the witness box was in his sixties and had white hair and a full beard that was oddly darker. Bosch had missed his swearing-in and did not know his name. His physical appearance and professorial manner conjured the name *Freud* in Harry's mind.

"That is what you get with schizoaffective disorder," Freud responded. "You have all the symptoms of schizophrenia, such as hallucinations, as well as of mood disorders like mania, depression, and paranoia. The latter leads to the psyche taking on protective measures such as the nodding and agreement you see in the video of the confession."

"So, when Jeffrey was nodding and agreeing with Detective Gustafson throughout that interview, he was what—just trying to avoid being hurt?" Haller asked.

Bosch noticed his repeated use of the defendant's first name, a move calculated to humanize him in front of the jury.

"Exactly," Freud said. "He wanted to survive the interview unscathed. Detective Gustafson was an authority figure who held Jeffrey's well-being in his hands. Jeffrey knew this and I could see his fear on the video. In his mind he was in danger and he just wanted to survive it."

"Which would lead him to say whatever Detective Gustafson wanted him to say?" Haller asked, though it was more statement than question.

"That is correct," Freud responded. "It started small with questions of seemingly no consequence: 'Were you familiar with the park?' 'Were you in the park?' And then of course it moved to questions of a more serious nature: 'Did you kill Judge Montgomery?' Jeffrey was down the path at that point and he willingly said, 'Yes, I did it.' But it is not what could be classified as a voluntary confession. Because of the situation, the confession was not freely, voluntarily, nor intelligently given. It was coerced."

Haller let that hang in the air for a few moments while he pretended to check the notes on his legal pad. He then went off in a different direction.

"Doctor, what is catatonic schizophrenia?" he asked.

"It is a subtype of schizophrenia in which the affected person can appear during stressful situations to go into seizure or what is called negativism or rigidity," Freud said. "This is marked by resistance to instructions or attempts to be physically moved."

"When does this happen, Doctor?"

"During periods of high stress."

"Is that what you see at the end of the interview with Detective Gustafson?"

"Yes, it is my professional opinion that he went into seizure unbeknownst at first to the detective."

Haller asked Judge Falcone if he could replay this part of the taped interview conducted with Herstadt. Bosch had already seen the tape in its entirety because it had become public record after the prosecution introduced it in court and it was subsequently posted on the Internet.

Haller played the part beginning at the twenty-minute mark, where Herstadt seemed to shut down physically and mentally. He sat frozen, catatonic, staring down at the table. He didn't respond to multiple questions from Gustafson, and the detective soon realized that something was wrong.

Gustafson called EMTs, who arrived quickly. They checked Herstadt's pulse, blood pressure, and blood-oxygen levels and determined he was in seizure. He was transported to the County–USC Medical Center, where he was treated and held in the jail ward. The interview was never continued. Gustafson already had what he needed: Herstadt on video, saying, "I did it." The confession was backed a week later when Herstadt's DNA was matched to genetic material scraped from under one of Judge Montgomery's fingernails.

Haller continued his questioning of his psychiatric expert after the video ended.

"What did you see there, Doctor?"

"I saw a man in catatonic seizure."

"Triggered by what?"

"It's pretty clear it was triggered by stress. He was being questioned about a murder that he had admitted to but in my opinion didn't commit. That would build stress in anyone, but acutely so in a paranoid schizophrenic."

"And, Doctor, did you learn during your review of the case file that Jeffrey had suffered a seizure just hours before the murder of Judge Montgomery?"

"I did. I reviewed the reports of an incident that occurred about ninety minutes before the murder, in which Jeffrey was treated for seizure at a coffee shop."

"And do you know the details of that incident, Doctor?"

"Yes. Jeffrey apparently walked into a Starbucks and ordered a coffee drink and then had no money to pay for it. He had left his money and wallet at the group home. When confronted by the cashier about this, he became threatened and went into seizure. EMTs arrived and determined he was in seizure."

"Was he taken to a hospital?"

"No, he came out of seizure and refused further treatment. He walked away."

"So, we have these occurrences of seizure on both sides of the murder we're talking about here. Ninety minutes before and about two hours after, both of which you say were brought about by stress. Correct?"

"That is correct."

"Doctor, would it be your opinion that committing a murder in which you use a knife to stab a victim three times in the upper body would be a stressful event?"

"Very stressful."

"More stressful than attempting to buy a cup of coffee with no money in your pocket?"

"Yes, much more stressful."

"In your opinion, is committing a violent murder more stressful than being questioned about a violent murder?"

The prosecutor objected, arguing that Haller was taking the doctor beyond the bounds of his expertise with his far-reaching hypotheticals. The judge agreed and struck the question, but Haller's point had already been made.

"Okay, Doctor, we'll move on," Haller said. "Let me ask you this: At any time during your involvement in this case, have you seen any report indicating that Jeffrey Herstadt had any seizure during the commission of this violent murder?"

"No, I have not."

"To your knowledge, when he was stopped by police in Grand Park near the crime scene and taken in for questioning, was he in seizure?"

"No, not to my knowledge."

"Thank you, Doctor."

Haller advised the judge that he reserved the right to recall the doctor as a witness, then turned over the witness to the prosecution. Judge Falcone was going to break for lunch before cross-examination began, but the prosecutor, whom Bosch recognized as Deputy District Attorney Susan Saldano, promised to spend no more than ten minutes questioning the doctor. The judge allowed her to proceed.

"Good morning, Dr. Stein," she said, providing Bosch with at least part of the psychiatrist's name.

"Good morning," Stein replied warily.

"Let's now talk about something else regarding the defendant. Do you know whether upon his arrest and subsequent treatment at County-USC a blood sample was taken from him and scanned for drugs and alcohol?"

"Yes, it was. That would've been routine."

"And when you reviewed this case for the defense, did you review the results of the blood test?"

"Yes, I did."

"Can you tell the jury what, if anything, the scan revealed?"

"It showed low levels of a drug called paliperidone."

"Are you familiar with paliperidone?"

"Yes, I prescribed it for Mr. Herstadt."

"What is paliperidone?"

"It is a dopamine antagonist. A psychotropic used to treat schizo-phrenia and schizoaffective disorder. In many cases, if administered properly, it allows those afflicted with the disorder to lead normal lives."

"And does it have any side effects?"

"A variety of side effects can occur. Each case is different, and we come up with drug therapies that fit individual patients while taking into account any side effects that are exhibited."

"Do you know that the manufacturer of paliperidone warns users that side effects can include agitation and aggression?"

"Well, yes, but in Jeffrey's—"

"Just a yes or no answer, Doctor. Are you aware of those side effects, yes or no?"

"Yes."

"Thank you, Doctor. And just a moment ago, when you described the drug paliperidone, you used the phrase 'if administered properly.' Do you remember saying that?"

"Yes."

"Now at the time of this crime, do you know where Jeffrey Herstadt was living?"

"Yes, in a group home in Angelino Heights."

"And he had a prescription from you for paliperidone, correct?"

"Yes."

"And who was in charge of properly administering the drug to him in that group home?"

"There is a social worker assigned to the home who administers the prescriptions."

"So, do you have firsthand knowledge that this drug was properly administered to Mr. Herstadt?"

"I don't really understand the question. I saw the blood scans after he was arrested and they showed the proper levels of paliperidone, so one can assume he was being given and was taking his dosage."

"Can you tell this jury for a fact that he did not take his dosage after the murder but before his blood was drawn at the hospital?"

"Well, no, but—"

"Can you tell this jury that he didn't hoard his pills and take several at once before the murder?"

"Again, no, but you are getting into—"

"No further questions."

Saldano moved to the prosecution table and sat down. Bosch watched Haller stand up immediately and tell the judge he would be quick with redirect. The judge nodded his approval.

"Doctor, would you like to finish your answer to Ms. Saldano's last question?" Haller asked.

"I would, yes," Stein said. "I was just going to say that the blood scan from the hospital showed a proper level of the drug in his bloodstream. Any scenario other than proper administration doesn't add up. Whether he was hoarding and then overmedicating, or not medicating and took a pill after the crime, it would have been apparent in the levels on the scan."

"Thank you, Doctor. How long had you been treating Jeffrey before this incident occurred?"

"Four years."

"When did you put him on paliperidone?"

"Four years ago."

"Did you ever see him act aggressively toward anyone?"

"No, I did not."

"Did you ever hear of him acting aggressively toward anyone?"

"Before this…incident, no, I did not."

"Did you get regular reports on his behavior from the group home where he lived?"

"I did, yes."

"Was there ever a report from the group home about Jeffrey being violent?"

"No, never."

"Were you ever concerned that he might be violent toward you or any member of the public?"

"No. If that had been the case, I would have prescribed a different drug therapy."

"Now, as a psychiatrist you are also a medical doctor, is that correct?"

"Yes."

"And when you reviewed this case did you also look at the autopsy records on Judge Montgomery?"

"I did, yes."

"You saw that he was stabbed three times in close proximity under the right armpit, correct?"

"Yes, I did."

Saldano stood and objected.

"Your Honor, where is he going with this?" she asked. "This is beyond the scope of my cross-examination."

Falcone looked at Haller.

"I was wondering the same thing, Mr. Haller."

"Judge, it is somewhat new territory but I did reserve the right to recall Dr. Stein. If the prosecution wants, we can go to lunch and I will recall him right afterward, or we can just take care of this right here. I'll be quick."

"The objection is overruled," the judge said. "Proceed, Mr. Haller."

"Thank you, Judge," Haller said.

He turned his attention back to the witness.

"Doctor, there are vital blood vessels in the area of the body where Judge Montgomery was stabbed, are there not?"

"Yes, blood vessels leading directly to and from the heart."

"Do you have Mr. Herstadt's personal files?"

"I do."

"Did he ever serve in the military?"

"No, he did not."

"Any medical training?"

"None that I am aware of."

"How could he have known to stab the judge in the very specifically vulnerable spot under the judge's—"

"Objection!"

Saldano was back on her feet.

"Judge, this witness has no expertise that would allow him to hazard even a guess at what counsel was about to ask him."

The judge agreed.

"If you want to pursue that, Mr. Haller, bring in a wound expert," Falcone said. "This witness is not that."

"Your Honor," Haller said. "You sustained the objection without giving me a chance to argue the point."

"I did and I'd do it again, Mr. Haller. Do you have any other questions for the witness?"

"I don't."

"Ms. Saldano?"

Saldano thought for a moment but then said she had no further questions. Before the judge could tell the jury to take a lunch break, Haller addressed the court.

"Your Honor," he said, "I expected Ms. Saldano to spend most of the afternoon on cross-examination of Dr. Stein. And I thought I would take up the rest of it on redirect. This is quite a surprise."

"What are you telling me, Mr. Haller?" the judge asked, his tone already tinged with consternation.

"My next witness is my DNA expert coming in from New York. She doesn't land until four o'clock."

"Do you have a witness you can take out of order and bring in after lunch?"

"No, Your Honor, I don't."

"Very well."

The judge was clearly unhappy. He turned and addressed the jury, telling its members they were finished for the day. He told them to go home and avoid any media coverage of the trial and to be back in the morning at nine. Throwing a glare at Haller, the judge explained to the jurors that they would begin hearing testimony before the usual ten o'clock start in order to make up lost time.

Everyone waited until the jurors had filed into the assembly room and then the judge turned more of his frustration on Haller.

"Mr. Haller, I think you know I don't like working half days when I have scheduled full days of court."

"Yes, Your Honor. Neither do I."

"You should have brought your witness in yesterday so that she would be available no matter how things progressed in the case."

"Yes, Your Honor. But that would have meant paying for another night in a hotel and, as the court knows, my client is indigent and I was appointed to the case by the court at significantly reduced fees. My request to the court administrator to bring my expert in a day earlier was denied for financial reasons."

"Mr. Haller, that's all well and good, but there are highly qualified DNA experts right here in Los Angeles. Why is it necessary to fly your expert in from New York?"

That was the first question that had come to Bosch's mind as well.

"Well, Judge, I don't really think it would be fair for me to have to reveal defense strategy to the prosecution," Haller said. "But I can say that my expert is at the top of the game in her specialty field of DNA analysis and that this will become apparent when she testifies tomorrow."

The judge studied Haller for a long moment, seemingly trying to decide whether to continue the argument. Finally he relented.

"Very well," he said. "Court is adjourned until nine o'clock tomorrow. Have your witness ready at that time, Mr. Haller, or there will be consequences."

"Yes, Your Honor."

The judge got up and left the bench.

6

Where do you want to go?"

They were in the back of Haller's Lincoln.

"Doesn't matter," Bosch said. "Somewhere private. Quiet."

"You hear that Traxx closed down?" Haller asked.

"Really? I loved that place. Loved going to Union Station."

"I already miss it. It was my go-to place during trial. It was there twenty years—in this town that says something."

Haller leaned forward and spoke to his driver.

"Stace, take us over to Chinatown," he said. "The Little Jewel."

"You got it," the driver said.

Haller's driver was a woman and Bosch had never seen that before. Haller had always used former clients to drive the Lincoln. Men paying off their legal fees. He wondered what Stace was paying off. She was mid-forties, black, and looked like a schoolteacher, not someone drawn from the streets, as Haller's drivers usually were.

"So what did you think?" Haller asked.

"About the trial?" Bosch replied. "You scored your points about the confession. Is your DNA expert going to be that good? Her 'specialty field of DNA analysis'—how much of that was bullshit?"

"None of it. But we'll see. She's good but I don't know if she's good enough."

"And she's really coming in from New York?"

"I told you, none of it was bullshit."

"So what's she going to do? Attack the lab? Say they blew it?"

Bosch was tired of that defense. It may have worked for O. J. Simpson but that was a long time ago and there were so many other factors involved in that case. Big factors. The science of DNA was too good. A match was a match. If you wanted to knock it down you needed something other than to attack the science.

"I don't know what she's going to say," Haller said. "That's our deal. She'll never shill. She calls them like she sees them."

"Well, like I told you, I've been following the case," Bosch said. "Knocking down the confession is one thing. But DNA's another. You need to do something. You have the case file with you?"

"Most of it—all the trial prep. It's in the trunk. Why?"

"I was thinking I could take a look at it for you. If you want, I mean. No promises. Just that something didn't seem right in there when I was watching. Something was poking at me."

"With the testimony? What?"

"I don't know. Something that doesn't add up."

"Well, I've got tomorrow and then that's it. No other witnesses. If you're going to look, I need it today."

"No problem. Right after lunch."

"Fine. Knock yourself out. How's the knee, by the way?"

"Good. Better every day."

"Pain?"

"No pain."

"You didn't call because you've got a malpractice case, did you?"

"No, not that."

"Then what?"

Bosch looked at the driver's eyes in the rearview. She couldn't help overhearing things. He didn't want to talk in front of her.

"Wait till we sit down," he said.

"Sure," Haller said.

The Little Jewel was in Chinatown but it didn't serve Chinese food. It was pure Cajun. They ordered at the counter and then got a table in a reasonably quiet corner. Bosch had gone with a shrimp po'boy sandwich. Haller had ordered the fried oyster po'boy and paid for both.

"So, new driver?" Bosch asked.

"Been with me three months," Haller said. "No, four. She's good."

"She a client?"

"Actually, the mother of a client. Her son's in county for a year on possession. We beat an intent-to-sell package, which wasn't bad at all on my part. Mom said she'd work off the fees driving."

"You're all heart."

"Man's gotta pay the bills. We're not all happy-go-lucky pensioners like you."

"Yeah, that's me all right."

Haller smiled. He had successfully represented Bosch a few years earlier when the city tried to pull his pension.

"And this case," Bosch said. "Herstadt. How'd you end up being appointed? I thought you didn't handle murder cases anymore."

"I don't but the judge assigned it to me," Haller said. "One day I was in his courtroom minding my own business on another case and he tags me with it. I'm like, 'I don't do murder cases, Judge, especially high-profile cases like this,' and he's, 'You do now, Mr. Haller.' So here I am with a fucking unwinnable case and getting paid hamburger when I usually get steak."

"How come the PD didn't take it?"

"Conflict of interest. The victim, Judge Montgomery, was formerly the Public Defender, remember?"

"Right, right. I forgot."

Their numbers were called and Bosch went up to the counter to get their sandwiches and drinks. After he delivered the food to the table, Haller got down to the business of their meeting.

"So, you call me up in the middle of a trial and say you need to talk. So talk. Are you in some kind of trouble?"

"No, nothing like that."

Bosch thought a moment before continuing. He had set up the meeting and now he wasn't sure how to proceed. He decided to start at the beginning.

"About twelve years ago I caught a case," he said. "A guy up on the overlook above the Mulholland Dam. Two in the back of the head, execution style. Turned out he was a doctor. A medical physicist. He specialized in gynecological cancers. And it turned out that he had gone up to St. Agatha's in the Valley and cleared out all the cesium they use for treatment from a lead safe. It was missing."

"I remember something about this," Haller said. "The FBI jumped all over it, thinking it was a terrorist thing. Maybe a dirty bomb or something."

"Right. But it wasn't. It was something else. I worked it and we got the cesium back, but not before I got dosed pretty good with it. I was treated and then had five years of checkups—chest X-rays, the whole thing. I was clean every time and after the five years they said I was in the clear."

Haller nodded in a way that seemed to indicate he knew which way this was going.

"So, all is well and I go in last month to get my knee done and they take blood," Bosch said. "Routine stuff, except tests on it come back and I have something called CML—chronic myeloid leukemia."

"Shit," Haller said.

"Not as bad as it sounds. I'm being treated but—"

"What treatment?"

"Chemo. The modern kind of chemo. I basically take a pill every day and that's it. In six months they see where it's at and if they need to get more serious about treatment."

"Shit."

"You said that. There are some side effects but it's not bad. I just get tired easily. What I wanted to see you about is whether I would have any kind of case here. I'm thinking about my daughter. If this chemo stuff doesn't work, I want to make sure she's set up, you know what I mean? Taken care of."

"Have you talked to her about this?"

"No. You're the only one I've talked to."

"Shit."

"You keep saying that. But what do you think? Is there a workman's comp thing I can go back to the LAPD with? What about the hospital? This guy just waltzed in there in his white doctor's coat and name tag and then waltzed out with thirty-two pieces of cesium in a lead bucket. The whole incident exposed the lax security in the oncology lab and they made big changes afterward."

"But too late for you. So, forget workman's comp. We're talking about a major claim here."

"What about the statute of limitations? The exposure was twelve years ago."

"The clock on something like this doesn't start ticking until you're diagnosed. So you're all right there. The deal we made when you exited the police department gave you a million-dollar health-insurance cap."

"Yeah, and if I get sick from this—I mean like really sick—I'll burn through that in a year. I'm not going to tap into my 401K. That's going to Maddie."

"Right, I know. With the department, we'll have to go through arbitration and most likely we'll get a settlement. The hospital will be the way to go. Poor security led to this scheme, which led to your exposure. That's our A game."

They started eating and Haller continued with his mouth full.

"All right, so I wrap up this trial—we'll go to the jury in another day, two at the max—and then we file a notice. I'll need to take a video deposition from you. We schedule that, then I think we'll have everything we need to move on."

"Why the video—in case I die or something?"

"There's that. But it's mostly because I want them to see you telling the story. They hear the story from you, instead of read it in a pleading or a depo transcript, and they'll shit their pants. They'll know they're on the losing end of this thing."

"Okay, and you'll set it up?"

"Yes. I've got people who do these all the time."

Bosch had barely gotten one bite of his sandwich but Haller was halfway finished. Bosch guessed that a morning in trial made him hungry.

"I don't want this to get out," Bosch said. "You know what I mean? No media on it."

"I can't make that promise," Haller said. "Sometimes the media can be used to apply pressure. You're the one who got dosed with this stuff while carrying out your job. Believe me, public sympathy will be with you ten to one easy. And that can be a powerful tool."

"Okay, then look—I need to know ahead of time if this is going to break in the media, so I can talk to Maddie first."

"That I can promise. Now, did you keep any records from that case? Is there anything I can look at?"

"Give me a ride back to my car after this. I have the chrono and most of the important reports. I made copies back then just in case. I brought it all in my car."

"Okay, we go back and trade files. You give me that stuff, I'll give you what I have on Herstadt. Deal?"

"Deal."

"You just gotta be quick with Herstadt. I'm almost out of time."

BALLARD

7

The tent was warm and cozy and she felt safe. But then the fumes of kerosene invaded her mouth and nose and lungs and it suddenly grew hot and then it was melting around her and burning.

Ballard sat up with a start. Her hair was still damp and she checked her watch. She had only slept three hours. She thought about going back down but the edges of the dream were still with her, the smell of kerosene. She pulled a length of hair across her face and under her nose. She smelled the apple in the shampoo she had used after paddling.

"Lola."

Her dog shot through the tent's opening and to her side. Lola was half boxer and half pit. Ballard rubbed her wide, hard head and felt the horror of the dream receding. She wondered if the man in the tent the night before had woken at the end. She hoped not. She hoped he was so doped up or alcohol addled that he never felt pain or knew he was dying.

She ran her hand along the side of her tent. It was nylon and she imagined heat from a fire collapsing it on her like a shroud. Awake or not, the man had died a horrible death.

She pulled her phone out of her backpack and checked for messages. No calls or texts, just an e-mail from Nuccio, the arson investigator, saying he had received her report and he would send her his reports in turn when completed. He said that he and his partner had determined the death was accidental and that the victim remained unidentified because whatever ID he had with him in the tent had burned.

Ballard put the phone away.

"Let's take a walk, girl."

Ballard climbed out of the tent with her backpack and looked around. She was thirty yards from the Rose Avenue lifeguard stand but it looked empty. There was nobody in the water. It was too cold for that.

"Aaron?" she called.

The lifeguard poked his curly-haired head up over the sill of the stand and she wondered whether he had been up there sleeping on the bench. She pointed to her tent and the paddleboard on the sand next to it.

"You watch my stuff? I'm going to get coffee."

Aaron gave her the thumbs-up.

"You want anything?"

Aaron turned his thumb down. Ballard pulled a leash out of one of the zippered pockets on the backpack and snapped it onto Lola's collar, then headed toward the line of restaurants and tourist stores that lined the beach walk a hundred yards from the ocean. She carried the backpack over one shoulder.

She went to Groundwork on Westminster, got a latte, and grabbed a table in the back corner where she could work without drawing attention from other patrons. Lola slid under the table and found a comfortable spot to lie down. Ballard opened the backpack and pulled out her laptop and the murder book Bosch had left for her.

This time she decided not to jump around in the book. The first section was most important anyway. It was the chronological record. It was basically a case diary, where the detectives assigned to the case described all their moves and the steps taken during the investigation.

Before starting her read she opened the laptop and ran the names

George Hunter and his partner, Maxwell Talis, through the LAPD personnel computer and determined that both detectives were long retired, Hunter in 1996 and Talis the year after. It appeared that Hunter had since died but Talis was still receiving a pension. This was valuable information because if she decided to do a thorough reexamination of the Hilton murder, she should try to talk to him about what he remembered of the case.

She closed the laptop and opened up the murder book. She started reading the chrono from the first entry—the callout. Hunter and Talis were at their desks at Hollywood Detectives on a Friday morning when alerted that patrol officers had come upon a car parked in an alley behind a row of shops off Melrose Avenue and the 101 freeway overpass. The detectives responded along with teams from the crime scene unit and the coroner's office.

The victim was a white male tentatively identified as John Hilton, twenty-four years old, by the driver's license found in the wallet on the floor of the 1988 Toyota Corolla. The photo on the license appeared to match the face of the man lying on his right side across the front seats and center console of the car.

A computer check of the name and birth date on the DL determined that this Hilton was not the scion of a hotel family but an ex-con who had been released a year earlier from a state prison after serving thirty months for drug possession and burglary convictions.

As lead detective, George Hunter had composed all of the early entries of the chrono, signing each one with his initials. These gave Ballard a good insight into how the investigation was initially focused. As she had surmised on her first quick overview of the book, the investigation took its cue from the victim's prior history of drug abuse and petty crime. Hunter and Talis clearly believed that this had been a drug rip-off and that Hilton had been murdered for as little as the price of a single hit of heroin.

Ballard now handled all calls for a detective on the midnight shift, but her previous posting had been as a homicide detective working specialty cases out of the downtown police headquarters. While the department's look-the-other-way sexual politics and systemic misogyny had caused her transfer to the lesser assignment, her skills as a homicide investigator had not deteriorated. Bosch had recognized this and tapped into it when they had crossed paths on a case the previous year. They had agreed to work cases together in the future, even if off the record and below department radar. Bosch was retired and an outsider, no longer encumbered by LAPD rules and procedure. Ballard was not retired but she was certainly out of sight and out of mind on the midnight shift. That made her both an insider and an outsider. All of her homicide skills now told her this was most likely an impossible case: an eighty-dollar drug rip-off that had ended with a bullet nearly thirty years before. There might have been something here that stuck in John Jack Thompson's craw and lit his fire, but whatever that was would be long gone now.

She first began to suspect that Hilton was a snitch. Perhaps a snitch for Thompson, which was why the detective took an active interest in the case, even though he was not assigned to it. She took a notebook out of her backpack. The first thing she wrote down was a question for Bosch.

How many other murder books did JJT steal?

It was an important question because it went to the level of dedication to this case. Bosch was right. If she could figure out why Thompson took this particular murder book, she might be able to zero in on a motive and then a suspect. But as described in the early entries of the chronology, this was a pedestrian murder—if there was such a thing—that would have been nearly impossible to solve at the time, let alone twenty-nine years later.

"Shit," Ballard whispered.

Lola alerted, raised her head, and looked up at her. Ballard rubbed the dog's head.

"It's okay, girl," she said.

She went back to the chrono and continued to read and take notes.

The manual transmission of Hilton's car had been in neutral but the key was in the ignition and in the on position. The engine was dead because the gas tank was empty. It was assumed that Hilton had cruised into the alley to make a drive-through drug purchase and had been shot after stopping and putting the transmission in neutral. It could not be determined how much gas had been in the tank when Hilton entered the alley, but the coroner's investigators estimated that time of death had been between midnight and four a.m., which was four to eight hours before the body was discovered by one of the shop owners arriving for work and parking behind his business.

Both front windows of the car were open. Hilton had been shot point-blank behind the right ear. This led the detectives to surmise that they were possibly looking for two suspects: one who came to the driver's door and drew Hilton's attention and another—the true killer—who came to the passenger door, reached through the window with a gun, and executed Hilton as he was turned and looking out the window. This theory was supported by the location of the shell casing ejected from the murder weapon. It was found on the passenger floor mat, an indication that the gun had been fired from that side of the car. Hilton then most likely slumped against the driver's door but was pushed back over the center console when his pockets were searched. In the crime scene photos, both front pockets of his pants had been pulled inside out.

To Ballard, the theory of two killers and how they carried out the crime veered slightly from the idea of it being a robbery. It was colder, more calculated. It felt planned to her. A drug rip-off would have also been planned to some extent but usually not with this kind of precision. She began to wonder whether the original detectives had zeroed in on the wrong motive from the start. This could have led to tunnel vision on the investigation, with Hunter and Talis ignoring any clue that didn't fit their premise.

She also discounted the theory by the original investigators that two killers were involved—one to distract Hilton from the left, one to reach into the car from the right to shoot. She knew that a solo gunman could have easily carried out the killing. Hilton's attention to his left could have been drawn by any number of things in the alley.

She wrote another note, wanting to remind herself to bring all of this up with Bosch, and then went back to the chrono.

Hunter and Talis focused their search for suspects on the immediate neighborhood and among the dealers known to sell in the alley. They checked with the sergeant in charge of a street-level narcotics unit assigned to Hollywood Division who said his team had intermittently worked undercover buy-bust operations in the area, as it was a known drug market because of its proximity to the 101 freeway. Customers came to Hollywood, jumped off the freeway at Melrose, and made drug purchases before jumping back on the freeway and getting far away from the transaction. Additionally, the location was close to several movie studios, and employees picked up drugs on their way to or from work, unless they were upper-level creatives who had their purchases delivered directly to them.

The chrono noted that the drug clientele in the area was mostly white, while the dealers were exclusively black males who were supplied product by a street gang from South L.A. The Rolling 60s Crips gang had laid claim to this section of Hollywood and enforced its grip with violence. The murder of John Hilton was not good for business because it flooded the area with police activity and shut things down. One note on the chrono stated that a street informant had told a gang officer that members of the Rolling 60s were attempting to identify the killer themselves to eliminate and make an example of him. Business came first, gang loyalty second.

That note froze Ballard and made her wonder whether she was chasing a ghost. The Rolling 60s could have caught and executed the killer or killers of John Hilton decades earlier without the LAPD making the connection between the two cases.

Apparently undaunted by the same question, Hunter and Talis put together a list of known drug dealers who worked in the area and began bringing them in for questioning. None of the interviews produced suspects or leads on the case, but Ballard noticed that the roster was incomplete. A few people on the list were never found or questioned. Among them was a man named Elvin Kidd, a Rolling 60s Crips gang member who was at a street-boss level and ran the territory where the Hilton murder took place.

They steered completely clear of another dealer, Dennard Dorsey, when they were told he was on keep-away status because he was a valuable informant. The snitch's handler—a Major Narcotics unit detective named Brendan Sloan—did the interview and reported back that his man knew nothing of value in regard to the Hilton murder.

Ballard wrote all of the names down. She was bothered that the homicide detectives didn't interview all the dealers and had left questioning the snitch to his department handler. To her it meant that this angle of the investigation was incomplete. She didn't know whether laziness or something else had gotten in the way. The murder counts in the city back in the late '80s and early '90s were the highest in the city's history. It was likely that Hunter and Talis had other cases at the time, with new ones constantly coming in.

She finished going through the chronology an hour and one more latte later. The thing that struck her was that the document ended with an entry from Talis on the one-year anniversary of the murder:

No new leads or suspects at this time. Case remains open and active.

And that was it. No explanation as to how it was still actively being pursued.

Ballard knew it was bullshit. The case had ground to a halt for lack of leads and viable angles of investigation. The detectives were waiting for what in homicide was called a "miracle cure" in the form of someone coming forward with the killer's name. This would most likely have to be someone from the underworld—someone arrested and facing charges, looking to deal their way out of a jam. Only then would they get a name they could run with. So it was kept "open and active," but Hunter and Talis were on to other things.

What also struck Ballard as missing was the work of John Jack Thompson. During the years he had held the murder book, he had apparently added nothing to it. There was nothing from him in the chronology that indicated he had made any moves, conducted any interviews, or broken any new ground on the case. Ballard wondered whether he had kept notes of his private investigation separate so as not to change or taint the record of the original investigation. She knew she would have to talk to Bosch about it and possibly go back to Thompson's house and home office to see whether there was a second murder book or any record of Thompson's work on the case.

She moved on from the chronology to fuller reports filed by the investigators based on the evidence collected and witness interviews. In the victim section of the murder book she read a bio authored by Talis and drawn from interviews and official documents. The victim's mother and stepfather were still alive at the time of the killing. According to the written account, Sandra Hilton expressed no surprise at her son's demise and said he had come back from his stint at Corcoran State Prison a different person. She said he seemed broken from the experience and wanted nothing more than to get high all the time. She admitted that she and her husband kicked John out of the house shortly after he returned from prison and appeared to be making no effort to integrate into society. He said he wanted to be an artist but did nothing to pursue it as a career. He was stealing from them in order to support his drug habit.

Donald Hilton stood by his decision to evict John from the family home in the Toluca Lake area. He was quick to note that John was his adopted son but was already eleven when Donald met Sandra and the two got married. His biological father had not been a part of John's life for those first eleven years, and Donald said that behavioral problems were already deeply set in the boy. Lacking a blood relation to the young man he raised apparently allowed him to kick him out of the house later on without a guilty conscience.

A section of the report had been redacted with a black marker. Two lines in the middle of the interview summary were completely blacked out. This seemed odd to Ballard because a murder book was already a confidential document. The exception to this was when a case was filed and murder book documents became part of discovery and turned over to the defense. On some occasions redacting occurred to protect the names of informants and others. But this case had never resulted in charges, and it seemed odd to Ballard that an interview with the parents of a victim would contain any information that would need to be kept hidden or secret. She opened the binder's rings and removed the page, studying the back to see if any of the redacted words could be read. Unable to make anything out, she put the page at the front of the binder to remind herself of the anomaly every time she opened the book: What information had been redacted from the case file? And who did it?

Ballard's review of the other witness summaries produced only one notable question. Hilton had shared an apartment in North Hollywood with a man named Nathan Brazil, who was described as a production assistant at Archway Studios in Hollywood. Ballard knew the studio was on Melrose Avenue near Paramount—and near where Hilton was murdered. Brazil told the investigators that he was working the night of the murder on a film production and Hilton had dropped by the guarded entrance to the studio and asked for him. Brazil did not get the message until hours later and by then Hilton was gone. Presumably he left the studio and proceeded down Melrose to the alley where he was shot and killed. Brazil told investigators that it was unusual for Hilton to come to his workplace. It had never happened before and he didn't know why Hilton did so or what he wanted.

It was another mystery within the mystery that Hunter and Talis had not solved.

Ballard looked at her notes. She had written down the names of several people she would have to run down and interview, if they were still alive.

Maxwell Talis
Donald Hilton
Sandra Hilton
Thompson widow
Vincent Pilkey, dealer
Dennard Dorsey, dealer/snitch — protected
Brendan Sloan, narcotics
Elvin Kidd
Nathan Brazil, roommate

Ballard knew that John Jack Thompson's widow was alive, as well as presumably Maxwell Talis. Brendan Sloan was still around as well. Sloan, in fact, was well known to her. He had risen from narcotics detective to deputy chief in the twenty-nine years since the Hilton murder. He was in charge of West Bureau. Ballard had never met him but since Hollywood Division fell under West Bureau's command, Sloan was technically her boss.

Ballard's back was stiffening. It was a combination of a tough morning paddle into strong headwinds, a lack of sleep, and the hard wooden chair she had been sitting on for two hours. She closed the murder book, deciding to leave the remaining pages and reports for later. She reached down to ruffle Lola's scruff.

"Let's go see Double, girl!"

The dog's tail wagged violently. Double was her friend, a French bulldog being boarded at the day-care center where Lola spent most nights and some days when Ballard worked.

Ballard needed to drop Lola off so she could continue to work the case.

8

Ballard's first stop was Property Division, where she checked out the sealed evidence box marked with the John Hilton murder case number. She could tell right away that it was not a twenty-nine-year-old box and the sealing tape was not yellowed as would have been expected. The box had obviously been repacked, which was not unusual. The Property Division was a massive warehouse but still too small for all the evidence stored there. Consolidation was an ongoing project and old, dusty evidence boxes were often opened and re-packed in smaller boxes to save room. Ballard had the evidence list from the murder book that she could use to make sure everything was intact—the victim's clothes, personal belongings, etc. She was primarily looking for two things: the expended bullet retrieved from Hilton's body during autopsy and the casing retrieved from the floor of his car.

She checked the sign-out sheet on the box and saw that, other than the repackaging that had taken place six years earlier, the box had apparently not been opened since it was placed in Property by the original two detectives—Hunter and Talis—nearly three decades before. This would generally not be unusual because no suspects had ever been developed, so there was no reason to analyze collected evidence in regard to a potential killer. Hunter and Talis had collected the evidence and had a list of the box's contents in the murder book. They knew firsthand what they had. They had seen it and held it.

However, what Ballard did find curious was that John Jack Thompson, when he took possession of the murder book and apparently started working the case, had never gone to Property and pulled the box. He had never checked out the physical evidence.

It was literally the first move Ballard had made. Yes, she had the property list from the murder book, but she still wanted to see the evidence. It was a visceral thing, like an extension of the crime scene photos. It brought her close to the case, closer to the victim, and she could not see pulling and working a case without this necessary step. Yet Thompson, the mentor to two generations of detectives, had apparently chosen not to.

Ballard put the question aside and started going through the contents of the box, checking them off against the list from the murder book and studying each piece of clothing and every item gathered from the Corolla. She had seen something in the crime scene photos that she wanted to find: a small notebook that was in the console between the front seats of the car. An entry on the property list said simply *notebook,* with no description of its contents or any detail about why Hilton kept a notebook by his side in his car.

She found it in a brown paper bag with other items from the console. These included a lighter, a drug pipe, spare change amounting to eighty-seven cents, a pen, and a parking ticket issued six weeks before Hilton's death. The parking ticket had been explored by the original investigators and there was a report in the murder book on their efforts. The ticket appeared to be a dead end. It had been issued on a street in Los Feliz where a friend of Hilton's lived. The friend recalled that Hilton had visited to sell the friend a clock radio he said his stepfather had given him. But he ended up staying at the apartment for several hours when the friend shared a hit of heroin with him. While Hilton was nodding off in his friend's apartment, his car was being ticketed. Hunter and Talis deemed the ticket irrelevant to the investigation and Ballard saw nothing that made her think otherwise.

Now she opened the notebook and found Hilton's name and a number she assumed was his prisoner number at Corcoran written on the inside flap. The pages of the notebook were largely filled with pencil studies and full sketches of hard-looking men, many with tattoos on their faces and necks. Other prisoners, Ballard surmised. The finished drawings were quite good and Ballard thought Hilton had some artistic talent. Knowing that he had this other dimension beyond drug addict and petty thief humanized him to her. Nobody deserved to be shot to death in a car, no matter what they were doing, but it was helpful to get a human connection. It added fuel to the fire that the detective needed to somehow keep burning. She wondered if Hunter or Talis or Thompson had made a connection to Hilton through this notebook. She doubted it. If they had, it would have been kept in the murder book so that the detective could see it and open it when he needed to stoke the fire.

Ballard finished flipping through the pages. One sketch caught her eye and she held on it. It was of a black man with a shaved head. He was turned away from the artist and on his neck was a six-pointed star with the number *60* in its center. Ballard knew that all Crips gangs or sets shared the symbol of the six-pointed star, its points symbolizing the early altruistic goals of the gang: love, life, loyalty, understanding, knowledge, and wisdom. The *60* in the middle of the star was what caught Ballard's eye. It meant that the subject of the sketch was a Rolling 60s Crip, a member of the same set of the notoriously violent gang that controlled drug sales in the alley where Hilton was murdered. Was that a coincidence? It appeared that Hilton had sketched this man while in prison; less than two years after his release, he was killed on Rolling 60s turf.

None of this had been in any reports in the murder book that Ballard had read. She made a mental note to check again. It might be a significant clue or it might be purely coincidental.

She flipped farther into the notebook and saw another drawing, which she thought might be the same man with the Rolling 60s tattoo. But his face was turned away and shadowed. She couldn't be sure. Then she found what she believed was a self-portrait. It looked like the face of the man she had seen in the crime scene photos. In the drawing, the man had haunted eyes with deep circles beneath them. He looked scared, and something about the drawing punched Ballard in the chest.

Ballard decided to add the notebook to the items she checked out of Property. The drawings reminded her of a case that was cracked by the cold case unit a few years earlier, when Ballard had been assigned to the Robbery-Homicide Division. Detective Mitzi Roberts had connected three murders of prostitutes to a drifter named Sam Little. Little was caught and convicted, then from prison started confessing to dozens of murders committed over four decades and all over the country. They were all "throwaway" victims—drug addicts and prostitutes—whom society, and police departments, had marginalized and given little notice to. Little was an artist and he sketched pictures of his victims to help visiting investigators identify the women and the cases. He held their images in his head, but not so often their names. He was given a full set of artist supplies and his drawings were in color and very realistic, eventually matching up to victims in multiple states and helping to clear cases. But they didn't serve to humanize Sam Little, only his victims. Little was seen as a psychopath who showed no mercy to his victims and deserved no mercy in return.

Ballard signed out the bullet evidence and the notebook and left the Property Division. She called Bosch when she got outside.

"What's up?"

"I just came out of Property. I pulled the bullet and casing. Tomorrow is Walk-In Wednesday at ballistics. I'll go right after my shift."

"Sounds good. Anything else in the box?"

"Hilton was a sketch artist. He had a notebook in his car that had drawings from prison. I checked it out."

"How come?"

"Because I thought he was good at it. There are a few other things from my review that I want to go over. You want to meet?"

"I'm sort of in the middle of something today but I could meet for a few minutes. I'm close by."

"Really? Where?"

"The Nickel Diner, you know it?"

"Of course. I'll be there in ten."

9

Ballard found Bosch in the back with his laptop open and several documents spread on a four-top table. It was apparently late enough in the day for the management to allow him to monopolize the spot. A plate with half a chocolate-frosted donut was on the table, assuring Ballard that Bosch was a paying customer rather than a freeloader who bought nothing but coffee and monopolized a table for hours.

She noticed the cane hooked over one of the empty chairs as she sat down. Assessing the documents that Bosch had started stacking when he noticed her approach, Ballard raised her hands palms up in a *What gives?* gesture.

"You're the busiest retired guy I think I've ever seen."

"Not really. I just said I'd take a quick look at this and then that would be it."

Putting her backpack on the empty chair to her right, she caught a glimpse of the letterhead on one of the documents Bosch was clearing. It said "Michael Haller, Attorney-At-Law."

"Oh, shit, you're working for that guy?"

"What guy?"

"Haller. You work for him, you work for the devil."

"Really? Why do you say that?"

"He's a defense attorney. Not only that, but a good one. He gets people off that shouldn't get off. Undoes what we do. How do you even know him?"

"Last thirty years, I've spent a lot of time in courthouses. So has he."

"Is that the Judge Montgomery case?"

"How do you know about that?"

"Who doesn't? Judge murdered in front of the courthouse— that'll get some attention. Besides, I liked Judge Montgomery. When he was on a criminal bench I hit him up for warrants every now and then. He was a real stickler for the law. I remember this one time, the clerk let me go back to chambers to get a warrant signed and I go in there and look around and there's no judge. Then I hear him say, 'Out here.' He had opened his window and climbed out onto the ledge to smoke a cigarette. Fourteen floors up. He said he didn't want to break the rule about smoking in the building."

Bosch put his stack of files on the empty chair to his right. But that wasn't the end of it.

"I don't know," Ballard said. "I may have to reassess our…thing. I mean, if you're going to be working for the other side."

"I don't work for the other side or the dark side or whatever you want to call it," Bosch said. "This is a one-day thing and I actually volunteered for it. I was in court today and something didn't add up right. I asked to look at the files and, as a matter of fact, did just find something before you walked in."

"Something that helps the defense?"

"Something that I think the jury should know. Doesn't matter who it helps."

"Whoa, that's the dark side talking right there. You've crossed over."

"Look, did you come here to talk about the Montgomery case or the Hilton case?"

"Take it easy, Harry. I'm just busting your balls."

She pulled her backpack over, unzipped it, and pulled out the Hilton murder book.

"Now, you went through this, right?" she asked.

"Yes, before giving it to you," Bosch said.

"Well, a couple things."

She reached into the backpack for the envelopes containing the ballistic evidence.

"I pulled the box at Property and checked out the bullet and the casing. As you said before, maybe we get lucky."

"Good."

"I also found this in the box."

She went into the backpack again and came up with the notebook she had found in the property box. She handed it to Bosch.

"In the crime scene photos this was in the center console of the car. I think it was important to him."

Bosch started flipping through the pages and looking at the sketches.

"Okay," he said. "What else?"

"Well, that's it from Property," Ballard said. "But I think what I didn't find there is worth noting, and it's where you come into the picture."

"You want to explain that?"

"John Jack Thompson never pulled the evidence in the case," she said.

She read Bosch's reaction as the same as hers. If Thompson was working the case, he would have pulled the box at Property and seen what he had.

"You sure?" Bosch asked.

"He's not on the checkout list," Ballard said. "I'm not sure he ever investigated this case—unless there's more at his house."

"Like what?"

"Like anything that shows he was investigating. Notes, recordings, maybe a second murder book. There's no indication at all—not one added word—that indicates John Jack pulled this case to work it. It's almost like he took the book so no one else would work it. So, you need to go back to his widow and see if there's anything else. Anything that shows what he was doing with this."

"I can go see Margaret tonight. But remember, we don't know

exactly when he took the murder book. Maybe he took it on his way out the door when he retired and then it was too late to get into Property. He had no badge."

"But if you were going to take a book so you could work on it, wouldn't you plan it so you could get to Property before you walked out the door?"

Bosch nodded.

"I guess so," he said.

"Okay, so you go to Margaret and see about that," Ballard said. "I made up a list of names from the book. People I want to talk to. I'm going to start running them down as soon as we're finished here."

"Can I see the list?"

"'Course."

For the fourth time Ballard went into the backpack and this time pulled out her own notebook. She opened it and turned it around on the table so Bosch could read the list.

Maxwell Talis
Donald Hilton
Sandra Hilton
Thompson widow
Vincent Pilkey, dealer
Dennard Dorsey, dealer/snitch — protected
Brendan Sloan, narcotics
Elvin Kidd
Nathan Brazil, roommate

Bosch nodded as he looked at the names. Ballard took this to mean he was in agreement.

"Hopefully some of them are still alive. Sloan is still in the department, right?"

"Runs West Bureau. My boss, technically."

"Then all you have to do is get around his adjutant."

"That won't be a problem. Are you going to eat the rest of that donut?"

"No. It's all yours."

Ballard grabbed the donut and took a bite. Bosch lifted his cane from the back of the other chair.

"I gotta get back to the courthouse," he said. "Anything else?"

"Yes," Ballard said, her mouth full. "Did you see this?"

She put the rest of the donut back on the plate, then opened the binder, unsnapped the rings, and handed Bosch the document she had moved to the front of the murder book.

"It's redacted," she said. "Who would black out lines in the statement from the parents?"

"I saw that too," Bosch said. "It's weird."

"The whole book is confidential, why black anything out?"

"I know. I don't get it."

"And we don't know who did it—whether it was Thompson or the original investigators. When you look at those two lines in context—the stepfather talking about adopting the boy—you have to wonder if they were protecting somebody. I'm going to try to run down Hilton's birth certificate through Sacramento, but that will take forever because I don't have his original name. That was probably redacted too."

"I could try to run it down at Norwalk. Next time I go to see Maddie on a weekday."

Norwalk was the site of Los Angeles County's record archives. It was at the far south end of the county and with traffic could take an hour each way. Birth records were not accessible by computer to the public or law enforcement. Proper ID had to be shown to pull a birth certificate, especially one guarded by adoption rules.

"That'll only work if Hilton was born in the county. But worth a try, I guess."

"Well, one way or another we'll figure it out. It's a mystery for now."

"What's at the courthouse?"

"I want to see if I can get a subpoena. I want to get there before the judges all split."

"Okay, I'll let you go. So, you'll go see Margaret Thompson later and I'll run down these names. The ones that are still alive."

Bosch stood up, holding the docs and his laptop under his arm. He didn't have a briefcase. He hooked his cane back on the chair so he could reach into his pocket with his free hand.

"So, did you sleep yet today or just go right into this?"

"Yes, Dad, I slept."

"Don't call me that. Only one person can call me that and she never does."

He pulled out some cash and left a twenty on the table, tipping as though there had been four people after all.

"How is Maddie?" Ballard asked.

"A little freaked out at the moment," Bosch said.

"Why, what happened?"

"She's got one semester to go down at Chapman and then she graduates. Three weeks ago some creep broke into the house she shares near the school with three other girls. It was a hot prowl. Two of the girls were there asleep."

"Maddie?"

"No, she was up here with me because of my knee. Helping out, you know? But that doesn't matter. They're all freaked out. This guy, he wasn't there to steal shit, you know, no money or anything taken. He left his semen on one of the girls' laptops that was on the kitchen table. He was probably looking at photos of her on it when he did his thing. He's obviously bent."

"Oh, shit. Did they get a profile off it?"

"Yeah, a case-to-case hit. Same thing four months before. Hot prowl, girls from Chapman, and he left his DNA on a photo that was on the refrigerator. But no match to anybody in the database."

"So did Maddie and the girls move out?"

"No, they're all two months from graduation and don't want to deal with moving. We put on extra locks, cameras inside and out. Alarm system. The local cops put the street on twice-by a shift. But they won't move out."

"So that freaks you the fuck out."

"Exactly. Both hot prowls were on Saturday nights, so I'm thinking that's this guy's night out and maybe he's going to come back. So I've been going down and sitting on the place the last two Saturday nights. Me and this knee. I sit in the back seat with my leg up across the seat. I don't know what I'd do if I saw something but I'm there."

"Hey, if you want company, I'm there too."

"Thanks, that means a lot, but that's my point. Don't miss your sleep. I remember last year..."

"What about last year? You mean the case we worked?"

"Yeah. We both had sleep deprivation and it...affected things. Decisions."

"What are you talking about?"

"Look, I don't want to get into it. You can blame it on me. My decisions were affected, okay? Let's just make sure we get sleep this time."

"You worry about you and I'll worry about me."

"Got it. Sorry I even brought it up."

He picked up his cane off the chair and headed toward the door. He was moving slow. Ballard realized she would look like an ass if she walked quickly ahead of him and then out.

"Hey, I'm going to hit the restroom," she said. "Talk later?"

"Sure," Bosch said.

"And I really mean that about your daughter. You need me, I'm there."

"I know you mean it. Thanks."

10

Ballard walked to the Police Administration Building so she could use a computer to run down some of the names on her list. This would be a routine stop for most detectives from the outer geographic stations. There were even desks and computers reserved for "visiting" detectives. But Ballard had to tread lightly. She had previously worked in the Robbery-Homicide Division located in the PAB and had left for the midnight shift at Hollywood Station under a cloud of suspicion and scandal. A complaint to Internal Affairs about her supervisor sexually harassing her led to an investigation that turned the Homicide Special unit upside down until the complaint was deemed unfounded and Ballard was sent off to Hollywood. There were those still in the PAB who did not believe her story, and those who viewed the infraction, even if true, as unworthy of an investigation that threatened a man's career. There were enemies in the building, even four years later, and she tried to maintain her job without stepping through its glass doors. But to drive all the way from downtown to Hollywood just to use the department's database would be a significant waste of time. If she wanted to keep momentum, she had to enter the PAB and find a computer she could use for a half hour.

She made it through the lobby and onto the elevator unscathed. On the fifth floor she avoided the vast homicide squad room and entered the much smaller Special Assault Section, where she knew a detective who had backed her through all the controversy and scandal. Amy Dodd was at her desk and smiled when she saw Ballard enter.

"Balls! What are you doing down here?"

Amy used a private nickname derived from the stand Ballard had made during the past troubles in RHD.

"Hey, Doddy. How's it hanging? I'm looking for a computer to run names on."

"I hear there are plenty of open desks in homicide since they trimmed the fat over there."

"Last thing I want to do is set up in there. Might get stabbed in the back again."

Amy pointed to the workstation next to hers.

"That one's empty."

Ballard hesitated and Amy read her.

"Don't worry, I won't talk your ear off. Do your work. I have court calls to make anyway."

Ballard sat down and went to work, putting her password into the department database and then opening her notebook to the list of names from the Hilton case. She quickly located a driver's license for Maxwell Talis in Coeur d'Alene, Idaho, which was not a welcome piece of information. Yes, Talis was still alive, but Ballard was working this case on her own and with Bosch, not as an official LAPD investigation. An out-of-town trip was not in the equation. It meant she would have to reach Talis by phone. This was disappointing because face-to-face interviews were always preferable. Better tells and better reads came out of in-person sit-downs.

The news did not get any better as she moved down her list. She determined that both Sandra and Donald Hilton were dead. They had passed—Donald in 2007 and Sandra in 2016—without knowing who had killed their son or why, without any justice for his life and their loss. To Ballard it didn't matter that John Hilton had been a drug addict and criminal. He had talent and with that he had to have had dreams. Dreams of a way out of the life he was trapped in. It made Ballard feel that if she didn't find justice for him, no one ever would.

Next on the list was Margaret Thompson and Bosch was handling that. Vincent Pilkey was the next name and it was another dead end. Pilkey was one of the dealers whom Hunter and Talis never connected with to interview, and now she never would either: Pilkey was listed as deceased in 2008. He was only forty-one at the time and Ballard assumed he met an untimely death by violence or overdose, but she could not determine it from the records she was accessing.

Ballard's luck changed with the next name down: Dennard Dorsey, the dealer Hunter and Talis did not talk to because he was also a snitch for Major Narcotics. Ballard ran his name on the computer and felt a jolt of adrenaline kick in as she learned that not only had the snitch somehow survived the last thirty years, but he was literally two blocks away from her at that very moment: Dorsey was being held in the county jail on a parole violation. She checked his criminal history and saw that the last decade was replete with drug and assault arrests, the accumulation eventually landing him in prison for a five-year term. It seemed pretty clear from the history that Dorsey's usefulness as a snitch had long since ended and he was without the protection of his handlers at Major Narcotics.

"Hot damn!" she said.

Amy Dodd leaned back in her chair so she could see around the partition between their work spaces.

"Something good, I take it?" she asked.

"Better than good," Ballard said. "I found a guy and I don't even have to get in my car."

"Where?"

"Men's Central—and he's not going anywhere."

"Lucky you."

Ballard went back to the computer, wondering if the dice would keep tumbling her way. She pulled up the hold for parole violation and got a second jolt of adrenaline when she saw the name of the PO who had filed the violation and pickup order on Dorsey. She pulled her phone out of her back pocket and called Rob Compton on speed dial.

"You," Compton answered. "What do you want?"

It was clear from his brusqueness that Compton still hadn't gotten past their last interaction. They'd had a casual off-duty relationship that blew up on-duty when Compton and Ballard disagreed on strategy regarding a case they were working. Compton bailed out of the car they were arguing in and then bailed out of the relationship they'd had.

"I want you to meet me at Men's Central," Ballard said. "Dennard Dorsey, I want to talk to him and I might need you for leverage."

"Never heard of him," Compton said.

"Come on, Rob, your name's on the VOP order."

"I'll have to look him up."

"Go ahead. I'll wait."

Ballard heard typing and realized she had reached Compton at his desk.

"I don't know why I'm doing this," he said. "I seem to recall being left high and dry by you the last time I did you a favor."

"Oh, come on," Ballard said. "I seem to recall you pussied out on me and I got mad. You got out of the car and walked away. But you can make up for it now with Dorsey."

"*I* have to make up for it? You've got balls, Ballard. That's all I can say about it."

Ballard heard a peal of laughter from the other side of the partition. She knew Amy had heard Compton's comment. She held the phone against her chest so Compton would not hear, then turned the volume down before bringing it back to her mouth.

"You got him or not?" she asked.

"Yeah, I got him," Compton said. "No wonder I didn't remember him. I never met him. He never reported. Got out of Wasco nine months ago, came back down here, and never showed up. I put in the VOP and he got picked up."

"Well, now's a good time to meet him."

"I can't, Renée. I got paper to do today."

"Paperwork? Come on, Robby. I'm working a murder and this guy may have been a key witness."

"Doesn't look like the type who's going to talk. He's got a gang jacket. Rolling 60s going back to the eighties. He's hard-core. Or was."

"Not really. Back in the day he was a snitch. A protected snitch. Look, I'm going over there. You can help me if you want. Maybe give him some incentive to talk."

"What incentive would that be?"

"I figure you might give him a second chance."

"Nah, nah, nah, I'm not letting the guy out. He'll just shit all over me again. I can't do that, Ballard."

Compton going to her last name told her he was set on this.

"Okay, I tried," she said. "I'll try something else. See ya around, Robby. Or actually, I probably won't."

She disconnected and dropped her phone on the desk. Amy spoke teasingly from the other side of the partition.

"Bitch."

"Hey, he deserved it. I'm working a murder here."

"Roger that."

"Roger the fuck that."

Ballard's plan was to go over to Men's Central, but first she finished the rundown on the names on her list. After Brendan Sloan, whose whereabouts she already knew, came Elvin Kidd, the Rolling 60s street boss at the time of the murder, and Nathan Brazil, John Hilton's roommate. Both were still alive and Ballard got addresses for them from the DMV computer. Kidd lived out in Rialto in San Bernardino County and Brazil was in West Hollywood.

Ballard was curious about Kidd. Now nearly sixty years old, he had moved far away from Rolling 60s Crips turf, and his interactions with the justice system seemed to have stopped almost twenty years before. There had been arrests and convictions and prison time, but then it appeared that Kidd either started to fly below the radar with his continuing illegal pursuits or found the straight-and-narrow life. The latter possibility would not have been all that unusual. There were not that many old gangsters on the street. Many never got out of their twenties alive, many were incarcerated with life sentences, and many simply grew out of gang life after realizing only the first two alternatives awaited them.

In checking Kidd's record she came across a possible connection to Hilton. Both had spent time at Corcoran State Prison, with what looked like a sixteen-month overlap in the late 1980s when they were both there. Hilton was finishing his sentence while Kidd was starting his. His term ended thirteen months after Hilton was released.

The overlap meant they could have known each other, though one was white and one was black and groups in state prison tended to self-segregate.

Ballard went onto the California Department of Corrections database and downloaded photos of Kidd taken each year at the prisons where he was incarcerated. She was immediately hit with a charge of recognition when the photos from Corcoran came up. Kidd had shaved his head since his previous prison stint. And now she recognized him.

She quickly opened her backpack and pulled out John Hilton's notebook. She flipped through the pages until she came to the drawing of the black man with the shaved head. She compared the drawing to Elvin Kidd's photos from Corcoran. They were a match. John Hilton had been murdered in a drug alley controlled by a man he had obviously known and even sketched while at Corcoran State Prison.

After that, she reconfigured her list based on what she now knew about the names on it. She put them into two groups because of the angles from which she had to approach them.

Dennard Dorsey
Nathan Brazil
Elvin Kidd

Maxwell Talis
Brendan Sloan

Ballard was excited. She knew she was making progress. And she knew that the first three interviews, if she got the men to talk to her, would give context to the conversation she hoped to have with Talis, one of the original investigators on the case. She put Sloan in last position because, depending on whether Dorsey spoke with Ballard, he might not even be relevant to her investigation.

Ballard logged out of the system and returned all the case materials to her backpack. She stood up and leaned on the partition to look at Amy Dodd. She had always worried about Amy, who had spent her entire career as a detective working sexual assault cases. Ballard knew it could wear you down, leave you feeling hollow.

"I'm going to go," Ballard said.

"Good luck," Amy said.

"Yeah, you too. You all right?"

"I'm good."

"Good. How are things around here?"

"No controversies lately. Olivas seems to be lying low since he made captain. Plus I heard he's only got a year left before he plans to cash in and retire. Probably wants things to go smoothly till he's out. Maybe they'll even send him out as a deputy chief."

Olivas was the lieutenant-now-captain who had been in charge of Ballard's old unit, Homicide Special. He had been the one who drunkenly pushed her up against a wall at a unit holiday party and tried to stick his tongue down her throat. That one moment changed the trajectory of Ballard's career and barely left a bruise on his. Now he was captain and in charge of all of the Robbery-Homicide Division squads. But she had made her peace with it. She had found new life on the late-show beat. The department brass thought they were exiling her to the dark hours, but what they didn't know was that they were redeeming her. She had found her place.

Still, knowing Olivas planned to cash out in a year was good intel.

"The sooner the better," Ballard said. "Take care of yourself, Doddy."

"You too, Balls."

11

The Men's Central jail was on Bauchet Street, a twenty-minute walk from the PAB. But Ballard changed her mind and decided to drive it so she could hit the road after speaking to Dennard Dorsey and move on to the next interview.

She waited in an interview room for twenty minutes before a sheriff's deputy named Valens brought Dorsey in and sat him at a table across from her. Dorsey had a casualness about himself that indicated he was comfortable in his surroundings. He was far from a wide-eyed first-timer in Men's Central. He was African-American, with skin so dark that the complete collar of tattoos on his neck was unreadable and looked to Ballard like a set of old bruises. He had a full head of graying hair that was cornrowed and matched a goatee that was so long, it too was braided. His wrists were cuffed behind his back and he had to lean forward slightly in the chair.

According to the records Ballard had pulled up on the computer, Dorsey had turned fifty in jail just a few days earlier, making him just twenty-one at the time of John Hilton's murder. But the man in front of her looked much older, easily into his sixties. The aging seemed so extreme that at first Ballard thought there had been a mistake and Valens had brought the wrong man into the room.

"You're Dennard Dorsey?" she asked.

"That's me," he said. "What you want?"

"How old are you? Tell me your birth date."

"March ten, 'sixty-nine. I'm fifty, so what the fuck is this about?"

The date matched and Ballard was finally convinced. She pressed on.

"It's about John Hilton."

"Who the fuck is that?"

"You remember. The guy got shot in the alley off Melrose where you used to sell drugs."

"I don't know what the fuck you're talking about."

"Yes, you do. You talked to your handler at the LAPD about it. Brendan Sloan, remember?"

"Fuck Brendan Sloan, that motherfucker never did jack shit for me."

"He kept homicide away from you when they wanted to talk to you about John Hilton."

"Fuck homicide. I never killed nobody."

Dorsey turned around to see if he could get a guard's attention through the glass door behind him. He was going to get up and go.

"Stay in your seat, Dennard," Ballard said. "You're not going anywhere. Not till we have a conversation."

"Now why would I have a conversation with you?" Dorsey asked. "I talk to anybody I talk to my lawyer, that's it."

"Because right now, I'm talking to you as a possible witness. You bring a lawyer into it, then I'll be talking to a suspect."

"I tol' you, I never killed nobody ever."

"Then I'll give you two reasons to talk to me. One, I know your parole officer—the one you never showed up to meet after you got out of Wasco. We've worked cases together. You help me here and I'll go talk to him. Maybe he lifts the VOP and you're back on the street."

"What's the other reason?" Dorsey asked.

Ballard was wearing a brown suit with chalk pinstripes. She reached into an inside pocket of her jacket for a folded document, a prop she had pulled out of the murder book in prep for the interview.

She unfolded it and put it down on the table in front of Dorsey. He leaned further forward and down to read it.

"I can't read this," he finally said. "They don't give me glasses in here. What is it?"

"It's a witness report from the John Hilton murder case from 1990," Ballard said. "The lead investigator says there that he can't talk to you because you're a high-value snitch for the narco unit."

"That's bullshit. I ain't no snitch."

"Maybe not now, but you were then. Says it right there, Dennard, and you don't want that piece of paper getting into the wrong hands, you know what I mean? Deputy Valens told me they got you in the Rolling 60s module. How do you think the shot callers in there will react if they see a piece of paper like that floating around?"

"You just messing with me. You can't do that."

"You don't think so? You want to find out? I need you to tell me about that murder from twenty-nine years ago. Tell me what you know and what you remember and then that piece of paper disappears and you don't have to worry about it ever again."

"Okay, look, I remember I talked to Sloan about it back then. I tol' him I wudn't there that day."

"And that's what he told the detectives on the case. But that wasn't the whole story, Dennard. You know something. A killing like that doesn't go down without dealers on that street knowing something or hearing something before or after. Tell me what you know."

"I can't hardly remember that far back. I done a lotta drugs myself, you know."

"If you 'hardly' remember, that means you remember something. Tell me what you remember."

"Look, all I know is we was told to get away from that location. Like we thought we had a tip that a bust was coming down or something. So I wudn't there, man, like I tol' Sloan back then and tell you now. I didn't see nothin', I don't know nothin', 'cause I wudn't there. Period. Now rip up that paper like you said."

"Is that what you told Sloan, that you were told to clear out?"

"I don't know. I tol' him I wudn't there that day and it was no lie."

"Okay, who told you to clear out of that alley?"

"I don't know. I can't remember."

"Had to have been a boss, right?"

"I guess maybe. It was a long time ago."

"Which boss, Dennard? Work with me. We're almost there."

"I ain't working with you. You get me outta here, then I tell you who it was."

Ballard was not happy that Dorsey was now trying to write the rules of the deal.

"Nah, that isn't how it works," she said. "You help me, then I help you."

"I *am* helping you," Dorsey protested.

"No, you're not. You're just bullshitting. Tell me who gave the clear-out order and then I talk to your PO. That's the deal, Dennard. You want it or not? I'm just about out of here. I hate being in jail."

Dorsey sat quietly for a moment, then nodded his head as though he had convinced himself internally to make the deal.

"I think he dead now anyway," he said.

"Then giving him up won't be a problem, will it?" Ballard said. "Who was it?"

"An OG name a Kidd."

"I want a real name."

"That was his name."

"What was his first name?"

"Elvin. Almost like *Elvis*. Elvin Kidd. He had that alley and he was the boss."

"Did he tell you to clear out for the day or what?"

"No, he just said like take the day off. We were like already out there and he came up and said you all scram outta here."

"Who is 'we'? You and who else were already out there?"

"Me and V-Dog—but that motherfucker dead too. He not going to help you."

"Okay, well, what was V-Dog's real name?"

"Vincent. But I don't know his last name."

"Vincent Pilkey?"

"I just tol' you I don't know. We just work together back then. I don't know no names."

Ballard nodded. Her mind was already going back to that alley twenty-nine years ago. A picture was forming of Dorsey and Pilkey running dope in the alley and Elvin Kidd driving in and telling them to clear out.

It made her think Elvin Kidd knew what was going to happen in that alley to John Hilton before it happened.

"Okay, Dennard," Ballard said. "I'll call your PO."

"Talk to him good."

"That's the plan."

BOSCH

12

Bosch parked his Jeep Cherokee on the north side of Fremont close enough to walk without his cane to Station 3 of the Los Angeles Fire Department. The station was of modern design and sat in the shadow of the towering Department of Water and Power Building. It was also less than six blocks from the Starbucks where Jeffrey Herstadt had suffered a seizure and had been treated by Rescue 3 EMTs on the day of the Judge Montgomery murder.

As he approached, Bosch saw that both of the double-wide garage doors were open and all of the station's vehicles were in place. This meant nobody should be out on a call. The garage was two rows deep. A ladder truck took up one whole slot while the other three contained double rows of two fire engines and an EMT wagon. There was a man in a blue fireman's uniform holding a clipboard as he inspected the ladder truck. Bosch interrupted his work.

"I'm looking for a paramedic named Albert Morales. Is he here today?"

Bosch noticed that the name over the man's shirt pocket was SEVILLE.

"He's here. Who should I tell him wants to see him?"

"He doesn't know me. I'm just passing on a thank-you from someone he took care of on a call. I have..."

From an inside coat pocket Bosch produced a small square pink envelope with Morales's name written on it. Bosch had bought it at the CVS in the underground mall by the federal building.

"You want me to give it to him?" Seville asked.

"No, it sort of comes with a story I need to tell him," Bosch said.

"Okay, let me see if I can find him."

"Thanks. I'll wait here."

Seville disappeared around the front of the ladder truck and went into the station house. Bosch turned and looked out from the station. There was an embankment supporting the 110 freeway and Bosch could hear the sound of traffic from above. He guessed that it was not moving very quickly up there. It was right in the middle of rush hour.

He raised his foot and bent his knee a few times. It was feeling stiff.

"You wanted to see me?"

Bosch turned and saw a man in the blue LAFD uniform, the name MORALES above his shirt pocket.

"Yes, sir," Bosch said. "You're Albert Morales, Rescue Three?"

"That's right," Morales said. "What is—"

"Then this is for you."

Bosch reached into an inside pocket of his jacket and pulled out a folded piece of paper. He handed it to Morales. The paramedic opened and looked at it. He seemed confused.

"What the hell is this?" he asked. "Seville said it was a thank-you note or something."

"That's a subpoena signed by a judge," Bosch said. "You need to be in court tomorrow morning at nine sharp. Jeffrey Herstadt thanks you in advance."

He offered the pink envelope to Morales, but he didn't take it.

"Wait, these are supposed to be served at headquarters, across the street from City Hall," Morales said. "Then they come to me. So take it over there."

Morales held the subpoena out to Bosch.

"There was no time for that," Bosch said. "Judge Falcone signed it today and he wants you there first thing tomorrow. You don't show, he'll issue a warrant."

"This is bullshit," Morales said. "I'm off tomorrow and going up to Arrowhead. I've got three days."

"I think you'll be in and out. You'll still get to Arrowhead."

"What case is this? You said Herstat?"

"Jeffrey Herstadt. Spelled H-E-R-S-T-A-D-T. You treated him for seizure at the Starbucks by Grand Park seven months ago."

"That's the guy who killed the judge."

"Allegedly."

Bosch pointed to the subpoena, still clutched in Morales's hand.

"It says you need to bring any documentation of the call you have. And your rescue kit."

"My kit? What the fuck for?"

"I guess you'll find out tomorrow. Anyway, that's all I know. You've been served and we'll see you at nine a.m. tomorrow."

Bosch turned and walked away, heading back toward his car and trying not to limp. Morales threw one more "This is bullshit" at his back. Bosch didn't turn around when he responded.

"See you tomorrow."

Bosch got back to his car and immediately called Mickey Haller.

"You get the subpoena?" Haller said.

"Yep," Bosch replied. "In and out—thanks for greasing it."

"Now tell me you served Morales."

"Just did. He's not too happy about it but I think he'll be there."

"He better or my ass will be in a sling with Falcone. You tell him the subpoena includes his kit?"

"I did, and it's on the subpoena. Are you going to be able to get him on the stand?"

"The prosecutor is going to carp about it, but I'm not counting on any pushback from the judge."

Bosch unlocked the Jeep and got in. He decided not to attempt the freeway at this hour. He would turn on First and take it to Beverly and ride that all the way into Hollywood.

"Your DNA lady get in?" he asked.

"Just got the word," Haller said. "She says she's in the car with Stace and heading to the hotel. She'll be good to go tomorrow."

"You talked to her about this? She knows the plan?"

"Ran it all by her. We're good. It's funny—today I was semi-bullshitting about her having a specialty and it turns out this *is* her specialty. She's been doing transfer cases for five years. It's like the gods of guilt are smiling on me today."

"That's great. But you've got nothing to smile about yet. Morales has to answer the way we think he'll answer. If he doesn't, we're cooked."

"I've got a good feeling. This is going to be fun."

"Just remember, Morales has to go first, then your DNA lady."

"Oh, I got it."

Bosch turned on the Jeep's engine and pulled away from the curb. He turned right on First Street and headed under the freeway. He changed the subject matter slightly.

"You told me that when you were prepping the case you had Cisco look into third-party culpability," Bosch said.

Cisco Wojciechowski was Haller's investigator. He had helped prep the Herstadt case but had to stop when he had an emergency appendectomy. He wasn't due back on the job until the following week. Third-party culpability was a standard defense strategy: someone else did it.

"We took a look at it," Haller said. "But to get it into court for the defense you need proof and we didn't have any proof. You know that."

"You focus on one subject?" Bosch asked.

"Shit, no. Judge Montgomery had lots of enemies out there. We didn't know where to start. We came up with a list of names—mostly out of the murder book—and went from there but never got to where we could point a finger in court. Just wasn't there."

"I didn't see any list in the material you gave me. And did you get a copy of the murder book?"

"Cisco had the copy we got in discovery. But if this thing goes down the way we think it will tomorrow, we won't need to prove third-party culpability. We won't even need it. We'll have big-time reasonable doubt already."

"You might not need it, but I will. See if you can get it from Cisco. I want to look at other avenues of investigation. The LAPD has to have looked at other persons of interest. I want to know who."

"You got it, Broheim. I'll get it. And thanks for today."

Bosch disconnected. He felt uncomfortable being thanked for a ploy that might set an accused murderer free. He felt just as uncomfortable being an investigator for the defense, even if the defendant in this case was possibly an innocent man.

13

Bosch parked right in front of Margaret Thompson's house. He thought about making the short walk to the house without his cane but he looked at the six steps leading up to the porch. His knee was aching from a full day of movement, with and without the cane. He decided not to push it, grabbed the cane off the passenger seat, and used it to amble up the front walk and stairs. It was getting dark now but there were no lights on that he could see. He knocked on the door but was thinking that he should have called ahead and avoided wasting time. Then the porch lights came on and Margaret opened the door.

"Harry?"

"Hello, Margaret. How are you doing?"

"I'm fine. What brings you here?"

"Well, I wanted to see how you were doing and I wanted to also ask about the case—the murder book you gave me. I was hoping I could get a look at John Jack's office, see if there were any notes relating to his investigation."

"Well, you're welcome to look but I don't think there is anything there."

She led him into the house and turned on lights as they went. It made Bosch wonder whether she had been sitting in the dark when he had knocked on the door.

In the office Margaret signaled toward the desk. Bosch paused and studied the whole room.

"The murder book was sitting on top of the desk when I retrieved it," he said. "Is that where it was, or did you find it somewhere?"

"It was in the bottom right side drawer," Margaret said. "I found it when I was looking for the cemetery papers."

"Cemetery papers?"

"He bought that plot at Hollywood Forever many years ago. He liked the name of it."

Bosch moved around the desk and sat down. He opened the bottom right drawer. It was now empty.

"Did you clean this out?"

"No, I haven't looked in there since the day I found the book."

"So there was nothing else in the drawer? Just the murder book?"

"That was all."

"Did John Jack spend a lot of time in here?"

"A day or two a week. When he did the bills and the taxes. Things like that."

"Did he have a computer or a laptop?"

"No, he never got one. He said he hated using computers when he worked."

Bosch nodded. He opened another drawer while talking.

"Had you ever seen the murder book before you found it in the drawer?"

"No, Harry, I hadn't. What's going on with it?"

The drawer had two checkbooks and rubber-banded stacks of envelopes from DWP and the Dish Network. It was all household billing records.

"Well, I gave it to a detective and she started checking into it. She said there was nothing added to it by John Jack. So we thought maybe he kept notes separate from it."

He opened the top drawer and found it full of pens, paper clips, and Post-it pads. There was a pair of scissors, a roll of packing tape, a mini-light, and a magnifying glass with a bone handle with an inscription carved in it.

To my Sherlock
Love, Margaret

"It's like he took the book with him when he retired but never worked it."

From the desk Bosch saw a door on the opposite wall.

"You mind if I look in the closet?"

"No, go ahead."

Bosch got up and walked over. The closet was for long-term storage of clothes. There was a set of golf clubs that looked like they had barely been used and Bosch remembered that they had been presented to John Jack at his retirement party.

On the shelf above the hanging bar Bosch saw a cardboard file box next to a stack of old LPs and a bobby's helmet that had probably been given to John Jack by a visiting police officer from England.

"What's in the file box?"

"I don't know. This was his room, Harry."

"Mind if I look?"

"Go ahead."

Bosch pulled the box down. It was heavy and it was sealed. He carried it over to the desk and used the scissors from the drawer to cut the tape stretched across the top of the box.

The box was filled with police documents but they were not contained in files or murder books. At first glance they appeared to be haphazardly stored, from multiple cases. Bosch started taking out thick sheaves of documents and putting them on the desk.

"This might take a while," he said. "I need to look through these to see what they are and if they're connected to the murder book."

"I'll leave you here so you can work," Margaret said. "Would you like me to make some coffee, Harry?"

"Uh, no. But a glass of water would be good. My knee is swelling and I have to take a pill."

"Did you overwork it?"

"Maybe. It's been a long day."

"I'll go get your water."

Bosch finished taking the documents out of the box and started going through them from what would have been at the bottom. It quickly became clear they had nothing to do with the John Hilton case. What Bosch had in front of him were copies of partial case records and arrest reports as well as state parole-board notifications. John Jack Thompson had been keeping tabs on the people he had sent to prison as a detective, writing letters of opposition to the parole board, and keeping track of when prisoners were released.

Margaret came back into the room with a glass of water. Bosch thanked her and reached into his pocket for a prescription bottle.

"I hope that's not that oxycodone that's in the paper all the time," Margaret said.

"No, nothing that strong," Bosch said. "Just to help with the swelling."

"Are you finding anything?"

"In this? Not really. It looks like old records of the people he put in prison. Did he ever say he was afraid that one of them might come looking for him?"

"No, he never said that. I asked him about it a few times but he always said we had nothing to worry about. That the baddest people were never getting out."

Bosch nodded.

"Probably true," he said.

"Then I'll leave you to it," Margaret said.

After she left the room, Bosch considered the documents in front of him. He decided he wasn't going to spend two hours looking at every piece of paper from the box. He was confident that the contents were unrelated to Hilton. He started checking through a final sampling of papers just to make sure and came across a copy of a sixty-day summary report on a murder case that he recognized.

The victim was a nineteen-year-old student at Los Angeles City College named Sarah Freelander. She was found raped and stabbed to death in the fall of 1982. She had disappeared somewhere between the school on the east side of the 101 freeway and her apartment on Sierra Vista on the west side of the freeway after attending a night class. Her apartment was thirteen blocks from the school and she commuted by bike. Her roommate reported her missing but she was young and there was no indication of foul play. The report was not taken seriously.

Thompson and Bosch were called in when her body and bike were found beneath a stand of trees that lined the elevated freeway beyond the outfield fence of a ballfield at the Lemon Grove Recreation Center.

The small park ran along Hobart Boulevard on the west side of the freeway and was equidistant from Melrose Avenue to the south and Santa Monica Boulevard to the north, the two streets with freeway underpasses that Sarah likely would have chosen between for her ride home from school. They worked the case hard and Bosch remembered coming to Jack's home office to get away from the station to discuss ideas and possibilities. John Jack had the internal fire going. Something about the dead girl pierced him and he had promised her parents he would find the killer. That was when Bosch first saw the fierceness his mentor brought to the job and to his search for the truth.

But they never cleared the case. They found a credible witness who saw Sarah on her bike riding toward the Melrose underpass but never were able to pick up her trail on the other side. They keyed on a fellow LACC student who had been rejected a month before when he asked Sarah for a second date. But they never broke him or his alibi, and the case eventually went nowhere. Yet John Jack always carried it with him. Even when their partnership was long over and Bosch would run into him at a retirement party or a training session, John Jack would bring up Sarah Freelander and the disappointment of not finding her killer. He still thought it was the other student.

Bosch put the summary back in the box and used the packing tape from the desk drawer to reseal it. He returned it to its place in the closet and left the room. He found Margaret sitting in the living room staring at the flames of a gas-powered fireplace.

"Margaret, thank you."

"You didn't find anything?"

"No, and there's no other place in the house where he would have kept anything regarding the murder book, right? Anything in the garage?"

"I don't think so. He kept tools in the garage and fishing poles. But you're welcome to look."

Bosch just nodded. He didn't think there was anything here to find. Ballard might have been right: John Jack hadn't taken the murder book to work it. There was something else.

"I don't think I need to," he said. "I'm going to go but I'll circle back if anything comes up. Are you okay?"

"I'm fine," Margaret said. "I just get a little wistful and a little teary at night. I miss him."

She was all alone. John Jack and Margaret had not had children. John Jack had once told Bosch he could not bring a child into the world he saw as a law officer.

"Of course," Bosch said. "I understand. If you don't mind, I'll check in on you from time to time, see if you need anything."

"That's nice, Harry. In a way, you're the closest we got to having a son. John Jack didn't want us to have our own. Now I'm left alone."

Bosch didn't know what to say to that.

"Well, uh, if you need anything, you call me," he mumbled. "Day or night. I'll let myself out and lock the door."

"Thank you, Harry."

Back in his car, Bosch sat there and decompressed for a few minutes before calling Ballard to tell her that Thompson's home office was a dead end.

"Nothing at all?"

"Not even a scratch pad. I think you're right: he didn't take the book to work it. He just didn't want anyone else to work it."

"But why?"

"That's the question."

"So, what are you doing tomorrow? Want to go with me out to Rialto?"

"I can't. I have court in the morning. I might be able to go later. But what's in Rialto? That's a drive."

"Elvin Kidd, the Rolling 60s street boss who told his dealers to clear the alley on the day Hilton got killed."

"How'd you get that?"

"From the snitch Hunter and Talis didn't get the chance to interview back in 1990."

"Wait till I'm clear, then we go see him."

There was a hesitation.

"You shouldn't go out there without backup," Bosch said.

"The guy's like sixty and out of the game," Ballard said. "Rialto's two hours and a world away from South L.A. It's where bangers go when they quit the streets."

"Doesn't matter. I'll call you when I clear, then we go out. Maybe you should get some sleep until then."

"Can't. I'm going to check out the ballistics first thing tomorrow."

"Then go home, wherever and whatever home is, and sleep."

"Yes, Dad."

"I told you about that."

"I'll make a deal with you. I'll stop calling you 'Dad' and you stop telling me to 'get some sleep.'"

"Okay, deal."

"Have a nice night, Harry."

"You too. Let me know about the ballistics tomorrow."

"Will do."

She disconnected. Bosch started the Jeep and headed home.

BALLARD

14

Ballard sat in on the third-watch roll call but there was no requirement for her skills at the start of her shift. No follow-ups, no interviews, no subpoena deliveries, not even a wellness check. Afterward, she went down to the empty detective bureau, picked a desk, and set up her radio, leaving it on the jazz station Bosch programmed. She settled in for some computer work, and started running deep background checks on Elvin Kidd and Nathan Brazil.

She learned that Kidd owned a home valued at $600,000 and ran a building business called Kidd Construction, specializing in commercial renovation projects. The contractor's license was in the name of Cynthia Kidd. Ballard guessed this was his wife, whose name was used to get around the fact that he had a criminal record.

It looked to Ballard, at least on the surface of things, that at some point Kidd had broken away from gang life and had chosen the straight life. Kidd Construction was first licensed by the state in 2002, twelve years after the murder of John Hilton.

Ballard pulled up a photo of Kidd's home on Google Maps and studied it for a few moments. It looked like the ideal picture of suburban life: gray with white trim, two-car garage. The only thing missing was a white picket fence out front. She noticed a pickup in the driveway with an equipment trailer hooked to it. The name of a business was painted on the side of the trailer, but it had been blurred out by Google. Ballard had no doubt that it said KIDD CONSTRUCTION.

This made her pull up the address on the contractor's license and she determined that it was a single-bay storage unit. So maybe Kidd ran his business out of his home and his business wasn't killing it financially. But he still had the house that had a single mortgage on it, and the pickup truck looked like it was only a year or two old. It wasn't bad for a guy who had spent two stints in state prison before he was thirty years old. Now sixty-two, he was one of the lucky few who had made it out alive.

Nathan Brazil was another story. Ballard found two bankruptcies on his record and a string of eviction actions taken against him over the prior twenty-five years. She also found a rental application online that listed him as working in the food service industry, which she took to mean he was most likely a waiter, a bartender, or maybe a chef. A reference on the application — which was from 2012 — was the general manager of a Tex-Mex restaurant in West Hollywood called Marix. Ballard had dined there frequently when, years earlier, she had lived in the area. It was the place to go for margaritas and fajitas. She wondered if she had ever been served by Brazil, even though she did not recognize him in the driver's license photo she had pulled up.

The Google Maps photo Ballard found for what she believed was Brazil's current address was of a '50s postmodern apartment house on Sweetzer. A single level of apartments over an open parking garage, the place looked worn and long out of style, its facade blemished by tenant-only parking signs slapped on the yellowed plaster.

As she was printing out screenshots of her search, Ballard's cell phone buzzed. The screen said UNKNOWN CALLER. She took the call.

"This is Max Talis. You left me a message."

Ballard checked the wall clock and was surprised. She had left the message for Talis four hours earlier. She wasn't sure if there was a time difference between L.A. and Idaho, but his calling back after midnight seemed strange for a retired man.

"Yes, Detective, thank you for calling me back."

"Let me guess, this is about Biggie?"

"Biggie? No, it's not. I—"

"That's what I get called about most of the time. I only had the case twenty minutes and then the big boys took over. But I still get calls 'cause I'm in the files."

Ballard assumed he was talking about Biggie Smalls, the rapper whose murder in the '90s was still officially unsolved but had been the subject of countless media reports, documentaries, and based-on-a-true-story movies. It was one of a long line of L.A. murders that captured the public imagination, when in reality it had been a street killing not that much different from the killing of John Hilton: a man shot to death in the front seat of his car.

In her message, Ballard had not mentioned the case she wanted to talk to Talis about because it might have given him a reason not to call.

"Actually, I want to talk to you about John Hilton," she said now.

There was a pause before Talis replied.

"John Hilton," he said. "You need to help me out with that one."

Ballard gave the date of the murder.

"White male, twenty-four, shot once in his Toyota Corolla in a drug alley off of Melrose," she added. "One behind the ear. You and Hunter caught it. I just inherited it."

"Wow, yeah, 'Hilton' like the hotel. I remember now we got that ID and thought, *I hope this guy isn't related,* you know? Then we'd have a media firestorm on our hands."

"So you remember the case?"

"I don't remember everything but I remember that we never got anywhere with it. Just a street robbery gone bad, you know? Drug-related, gang-related—hard to clear."

"There are aspects of it that make it look different to me. Are you okay to talk now? I know it's late."

"Yeah, I'm at work. I got plenty of time."

"Really? What do you do?"

"You said on the message you work the midnight shift. We used to call that the late show. Anyway, I'm the same. Night watchman. The late show."

"Really. What kind of place is it?"

"It's just a truck stop. I got bored, you know? So I'm out here three nights a week, keepin' the peace—and keeping the piece, if you know what I mean."

He was an armed security guard. To Ballard it seemed like a steep fall from LAPD homicide detective.

"Well, I hope you stay safe," she said. "Can I ask you about the Hilton case?"

"You can ask," Talis said. "But I'm not sure I'm going to remember anything."

"Let's see. My first question is about the murder book. The summary report with the victim's parents has a couple lines blacked out. I'm wondering why that happened and what was blacked out."

"You mean like on the page, somebody blacked it out?"

"That's right. It wasn't you or Hunter?"

"No, why would we do that? You mean redacted like the feds did with the Russia thing?"

"Yes, redacted. It's only two lines but it stood out, you know? I'd never seen that before. I could read you the page or maybe fax it to you. Maybe it would help you—"

"No, that won't help. If I can't remember, I can't remember."

Ballard detected a tonal change in Talis's voice. She thought maybe he had just recalled something about the case and he was shutting down.

"Let me pull the book and read it to you," she said.

"No, honey, I just told you," Talis said. "I don't remember the case and I'm kind of busy here."

"Okay, let me ask you this. Do you remember John Jack Thompson?"

"Sure. Everybody knew John Jack. What's he got—"

"Did you ever discuss this case with him?"

"Why would we do that?"

"I don't know. That's why I'm asking. He ended up with the murder book on this. When he retired he took it home with him—he stole it—and I'm trying to figure out why."

"You gotta ask him about that, then."

"I can't. He died last week and his wife turned in the murder book. Now I have it and I'm trying to figure out why he took it."

"I'm sorry to hear John Jack is gone, but I can't help you. I have no idea why he had the book. Maybe he talked to my partner about it, but he never talked to me."

Ballard instinctively knew that Talis was dissembling. He knew something but wasn't sharing it. She took one last try at digging it out.

"Detective Talis, are you sure you can't help me?" she asked. "It sounds to me like you do remember this case. Are you protecting somebody or some secret? You don't need—"

"Hold it right there, girl," Talis said, his voice angry. "You're saying I'm protecting somebody, keeping secrets? Then this is where I say fuck you. Nobody talks to me like that. I gave the department and that city—"

"Detective, I am not trying to insult you."

"—twenty-five years of my life and I was putting people in jail when you were giving boys blow jobs under the bleachers. You insult me and you insult everything I ever did down there. Goodbye, Detective Ballard."

Talis disconnected.

Ballard sat there, her face turning red with anger and embarrassment.

"Then fuck you," she said to the empty room.

She was saved from the moment when she heard her name come from the ceiling speaker. It was Lieutenant Washington requesting her presence in the watch office.

She got up to go.

15

Some calls come with a deep feeling of dread that hits long before any crime scene is viewed or question asked. This was one of those. Lieutenant Washington had sent Ballard out to a house in lower Beachwood Canyon, where a suicide had been reported. Patrol wanted a detective to confirm and sign off on it. The L-T told Ballard that it was a kid.

The house was a block north of Franklin on Van Ness. It was an old Craftsman that looked like its wood siding was being chewed up from the inside out by termites. There were two patrol cars out front and a white van with a blue stripe down the side that belonged to the coroner's office. Ballard pulled behind it and got out.

Two officers were waiting on the front porch. Ballard had seen them earlier at roll call and knew their names were Willard and Hoskins. They had long-distance looks in their eyes and had been horrified by whatever the scene was inside.

"What have we got?" Ballard asked.

"Eleven-year-old girl hung herself in the bedroom," Willard said. "It's a bad scene."

"Her mother found her when she came home from work around eleven," Hoskins added.

"Anybody else in the house?" Ballard asked. "Where's the father?"

"Not here," Hoskins said. "We don't know his story."

Ballard walked past them and opened the front door. Immediately she heard a woman crying. She stepped in and to her right saw a female officer named Robards on a couch next to a woman whose face was buried in her hands as she wept. Ballard nodded to Robards and pointed to the stairway in the front hall. Robards nodded—the body was upstairs.

Ballard went up the stairs and heard a commotion from the open door on the right of the landing. She entered a pink-walled bedroom and saw the body of a girl hanging from a noose made of neckties looped over a crossbeam. On the floor in front of a queen bed was a kicked-over chair that came from a small homework desk. There was urine on the rug beneath the body and the odor of excrement in the room.

An officer named Dautre was in the room, his hands in his pockets to make sure he didn't touch anything, as well as a forensic criminalist named Potter and two coroner's investigators whom Ballard did not know. They had stuck a thermometer into the body through an incision to take liver temperature and determine an estimated time of death.

"Ballard," Dautre said. "This is fucked up. She's just a girl."

Ballard had been at death scenes before with Dautre—she had told him the trick of keeping his hands in his pockets—and he had never seemed fazed by what he saw. But he did now. He was of mixed race but his face was blanched nearly white and his eyes were wide. She nodded and started to move in a circle around the room. She didn't want to look at the dead girl's face but knew she had to. It was contorted, her eyes slits. Ballard's gaze moved down the body looking for any sign of a struggle, getting to the fingers last. Many times suicides changed their mind and grappled with the rope or strap around their neck, breaking fingernails or leaving lacerations. There was no sign of this. The girl apparently never wavered in her decision.

The girl was wearing a plaid green skirt and a white blouse. There was an insignia from a private school on the blouse's pocket. She was overweight by about thirty pounds and Ballard wondered if she had been bullied because of it.

She also noticed that two men's ties had been knotted together to loop over the crossbeam and make the noose the girl had put around her neck. Ballard assumed that the girl had to go into her parents' bedroom to get the ties and wondered if that was significant.

"All right if we take her down now?" one of the coroner's investigators said.

Ballard nodded.

"Are you calling it?" she asked.

"Yes," the same man said. "We don't see any indication of a setup. Do you confirm?"

"Did you find a note?"

"No note. But her cell phone's on the dresser. Looks like she made a call to her dad about nine last night. That was it."

"I want a full tox screen, fingernail scrapings, and a rape kit, just to cover the bases."

"I'll put it in. You confirming suicide?"

Ballard paused. Her hesitation was that the mother didn't cut her down. She found her daughter hanging and didn't hold her up and cut her down just in case.

"I confirm. For now. Send me those reports, okay? Detective Ballard, Hollywood third watch. And nobody talks to the mother and father about that."

"You got it."

Ballard and Dautre stepped back as one of the coroner's men opened a stepladder while the other unfolded a body wrap on the floor. Then one man climbed up to cut the upper tie at the beam so as to have the entire ligature in one piece. The other man stood behind the body, spread his feet to brace himself, and then wrapped his arms around the dead girl. The ligature was cut and the man on the floor held the body until his partner came off the ladder and helped lower it onto the body wrap. They did the burrito wrap and then moved the body into a yellow bag that was zipped up around the package. Because of the unwieldiness of the house's stairs they had not brought in a stretcher. The two men lifted the yellow bag at either end and took it out of the room.

Ballard stepped over to the dresser and searched for a note. She gloved up and started opening drawers and a jewelry box. No note.

"You need me here, Renée?" Dautre asked.

"You can go downstairs," Ballard said. "But don't clear the scene just yet. Tell Willard and Hoskins they're clear."

"Roger that."

That left Ballard and Potter in the room.

"You want the full workup?" Potter asked.

"I think so," Ballard said. "Just in case."

"You see something?"

"No, not yet."

Ballard spent another twenty minutes in the room looking for a note or anything else that would explain why the eleven-year-old girl would take her life. She checked the girl's phone, which was not password protected—probably a parental rule—and found nothing of note in it other than the record of a twelve-minute call to a contact labeled DAD.

She finally went downstairs and entered the living room. Robards stood up immediately, obviously eager to pass this nightmare call on to Ballard.

"This is Mrs. Winter," she said.

Robards stepped around a coffee table to get out of the way so Ballard could move in and sit on the couch in her stead.

"Mrs. Winter, I'm very sorry for your loss," Ballard began. "Can you tell us where your husband is right now? Have you tried to reach him?"

"He's in Chicago on business. I haven't tried to talk to him. I don't even know what to say or how to tell him this."

"Do you have any family in the area, someplace you can stay tonight?"

"No, I don't want to leave. I want to be close."

"I think it's better for you to leave. I can call out a counselor to help you too. Our department has a crisis—"

"No, I don't want any of that. I just want to be left alone. I'm staying here."

Ballard had seen the child's name on the jewelry box and school-books she had looked through upstairs.

"Tell me about Cecilia. Was she having trouble at school or in the neighborhood?"

"No, she was fine. She was good. She would have told me if there was a problem."

"Do you have any other children, Mrs. Winter?"

"No, only her."

This brought a fresh burst of tears and a wrenching moan. Ballard let her slide into it while addressing Robards.

"You have any pamphlets on counseling we could give her? Numbers to call to talk to somebody?"

"Yes, in the car. I'll be right back."

Ballard turned her attention back to Mrs. Winter. She noticed that she was barefoot but the bottom edges of the one exposed foot were dirty.

"Are you sure your daughter didn't leave a note or send a text about what she was planning to do?"

"Of course not! I would have stopped it. What kind of horrible mother do you think I am? This is the nightmare of my life."

"I'm sorry, ma'am. I didn't mean to imply that. I'll be right back."

Ballard got up and signaled Dautre to follow her. They went through the front door and stopped on the porch, just as Robards was coming up the steps with a pamphlet. Ballard spoke in a low voice.

"Look around the neighborhood and check the trash cans for a note. Start with this house and do it quietly."

"You got it," Dautre said.

The two cops headed down the porch steps together and Ballard went back inside and returned to the couch. Mrs. Winter spoke before she could sit down.

"I don't think she killed herself."

The statement didn't surprise Ballard. Denial was part of the mourning process.

"Why is that?"

"She wouldn't have killed herself. I think it was an accident. She made a mistake. She was playing around and things went wrong."

"How was she playing around?"

"You know, the way kids do in their rooms. When they are alone. She probably was waiting for me to come home and catch her in the act. You know, to get attention. I would catch her and rescue her just in time and then it would be all about her."

"She was an only child and she didn't think she got enough attention?"

"No child thinks she gets enough attention. I didn't."

Ballard knew that people beset by trauma and loss processed grief in myriad ways. She always tried to reserve judgment on what people said in the throes of a life catastrophe.

"Mrs. Winter, here is a pamphlet that outlines all the services available to you at this difficult time."

"I told you. I don't want that. I just want to be left alone."

"I'll leave it on the table in case you change your mind. They can be very helpful."

"Please leave now. I want to be alone."

"I'm concerned about leaving you by yourself."

"Don't be. Let me grieve for my daughter."

Ballard didn't respond or move. Soon the woman looked up from her hands and fixed her with red and watery eyes.

"Leave! What do I have to do to make you leave?"

Ballard nodded.

"Okay. I'll leave. But I think it would be good to know why Cecilia did what she did."

"You can't ever know why a child decides to do something."

Ballard walked through the living room to the entranceway. She looked back at the woman in the chair. Her face was again cradled in her hands.

Ballard left the house and joined Robards and Dautre at their car.

"Nothing," Dautre said.

"We checked her cans and the neighbors on all sides," Robards said. "You want us to do more?"

Ballard looked back at the house. She saw the light behind the living room curtains go out. She knew that some mysteries never get solved.

"No," she said. "You're clear."

The officers moved quickly to their patrol car as though they couldn't wait to get away from the scene. Ballard didn't blame them. She got in her own car and sat there for a long moment watching the now-dark house. Finally, she pulled her phone and called the number Cecilia had labeled DAD in her contact list. Ballard had written it down. A man answered the call right away but still seemed startled from sleep.

"Mr. Winter?"

"Yes, who is this?"

"Detective Ballard, Los Angeles Police De—"

"Oh god, oh god, what happened?"

"I'm sorry to tell you, sir, but your daughter, Cecilia, is dead."

There was a long silence, broken only by sounds of the man on the other end of the line beginning to cry.

"Sir, can you tell me where you are? Is there someone you can be with?"

"I told her. I told her this time it felt real."

"Told Cecilia? What did you tell her?"

"No, my wife. My daughter—our daughter is…was…troubled. She killed herself, didn't she? Oh my god I just can't…"

"Yes, I'm afraid she did. You spoke to her earlier tonight?"

"She called me. She said she was going to do it. She's said it before but this time it felt…is my wife there?"

"She's at the house. She asked us to leave. Is there a family member or friend I can call to be with her? That's really why I'm calling. We had to respect her wishes for us to leave but I don't think she should be alone."

"I'll get somebody. I'll call her sister."

"Okay, sir."

There was more whimpering and Ballard let it go for a while before interrupting.

"Where are you, Mr. Winter?"

"Naperville. The company I work for is based here."

"Where is that, sir?"

"Outside Chicago."

"I think you need to come home and be with your wife."

"I am. I'll book the first flight out."

"Can you tell me what your daughter said on the phone call?"

"She said she was tired of having no friends and being overweight. We tried different things with her. To help her. But nothing worked. It felt different this time. She seemed so sad. I told Ivy to watch her because I had never heard her so sad before."

His last few words came out in bursts as he started to cry loudly.

"Mr. Winter, you need to be with your wife. I know that won't happen until tomorrow, but you should call her. Call Ivy. I'll hang up now and you can call."

"Okay…I'll call."

"This is your cell, right?"

"Uh, yes."

"So you should have my number on your call log. Call me if there are any questions or there is something I can do."

"Where is she? Where is my baby?"

"They took her to the coroner's office. And they will be in touch with you. Good night now, Mr. Winter. I'm sorry for your loss."

Ballard disconnected and sat unmoving in her car for a long moment. She was torn between accepting that an eleven-year-old girl would take her own life and being suspicious because the mother left her hanging and the father never asked how she had killed herself.

She pulled her phone and hit redial. Winter answered immediately.

"Mr. Winter, I'm sorry to call back," she said. "Were you talking to your wife?"

"No," Winter said. "I couldn't bring myself to call her yet."

"Is this an iPhone you are on, sir?"

"Uh, yes. Why would you ask that?"

"Because for the report I'm going to have to write, I need to confirm your location. This means I need to contact the Naperville police and have an officer come to your hotel, or you could just text me your contact info and share your location with me. It would save time and you wouldn't be intruded on by the police up there."

There was silence for a long beat.

"You really have to do that?" Winter finally asked.

"Yes, sir, we do," Ballard said. "Part of the protocol. All deaths are investigated. If you don't want to share your location on the phone, just tell me where you are and I'll have a local officer run by as soon as possible."

Another silence went by and when Winter spoke, his voice had a coldness to it that was unmistakable.

"I'll text my contact info and share my location with you," he said. "Are we done now?"

"Yes, sir," Ballard said. "Thank you once again for your cooperation and I'm sorry for your loss."

16

On the way back to the station Ballard detoured down Cahuenga and then over to Cole. She drove slowly by the line of tents, lean-to tarp constructions, and occupied sleeping bags that ran the fence line of the public park. She saw that the spot previously used by the man who had been immolated the night before was already taken by someone with an orange-and-blue tent. She stopped in the street—there was no traffic to worry about impeding—and looked at the blue tarp where she knew the girl named Mandy slept. All seemed quiet. A slight gust of wind flapped the dirty tarp for a moment but soon the scene returned to a still life.

Ballard thought about Mandy and the prospects of her life. She then thought about Cecilia and wondered how she had lost any sort of prospect for happiness. Then Ballard thought about her own desperate beginnings. How did one child retain hope in the darkness and another come to believe it was gone forever?

Her phone buzzed and she answered. It was Lieutenant Washington and she immediately looked at the radio charger to see if she had left her rover behind somewhere. But it was there in its holder. Washington had chosen to call her rather than use the radio.

"L-T?"

"Ballard, where are you?"

"Headed to the house. About three blocks out. What's up?"

"Dautre and Roberts were just in here. They told me about the girl."

He had managed to mispronounce *Dautre,* making it sound more like *doubter* than *daughter,* and had missed Robards's name altogether.

"What about her?" she said.

"I heard it was bad," Washington said. "You confirm it was suicide?"

"I signed off on it. The parents were kind of hinky. The father is out of town. But I confirmed that. He's where he said he was. I'll turn it all over to West Bureau homicide for follow-up."

"All right, well, I want to get you back here and get BSU out to talk to you three."

Behavioral Science Unit. It meant psychological counseling. It was the last thing Ballard would want from the department. Half the department already thought she had fabricated sexual harassment allegations against a supervisor. That "unsubstantiated" investigation had resulted in her being forced into BSU sessions for a year. Adding another shrink sheet to her file would bring the other half in line with the popular belief. And that was before you even got to the double standard involving female cops. A male officer asking for counseling was courageous and strong; a female doing the same was just plain weak.

"Fuck that," Ballard said. "I don't want it."

"Ballard, it was a bad scene," Washington insisted. "I just got the details and it's a fucking horror show. You gotta talk to somebody."

"L-T, I don't want to talk to anybody, I don't need to talk to anybody. I've seen worse, okay? And I have work to do."

The tone of her voice gave Washington pause. There was silence for several seconds. Ballard watched a man crawl out of a single tent, walk to the curb, and openly start to urinate in the gutter. He hadn't noticed her or heard her idling car.

"All right, Ballard, but I made the offer," Washington said.

"Yes, you did, L-T," Ballard responded in a gentler tone. "And I appreciate it. I'm going to go back to the bureau and write this up, then I'll be done for the day. I'll hit the beach and all will be beautiful again. Salt water cures everything."

"That's a roger, Ballard."

"Thank you."

But Ballard knew she wouldn't be going west to the beach at the end of her shift. It was Walk-In Wednesday at the ballistics unit and she planned to be first in line.

BOSCH

17

It was 9:05 a.m. in Department 106 and there was no sign of EMT Albert Morales. Bosch stood in the back of the courtroom so that he could step out and search the hallway, as he had been doing every five minutes. Haller was at the defense table, busying himself with paperwork and files to make it appear he was prepping for the day of court.

"Mr. Haller," the clerk said. "The judge is ready."

The clerk's voice conveyed the impatience the judge had most likely imparted to her on the phone from his chambers.

"Yes, I know," Haller said. "I'm just looking for a witness sheet and then I'll be good to go."

"Can we bring in your client?" the clerk asked.

Haller turned and glanced back at Bosch, giving him a you-fucked-me stare.

"Uh, not quite yet," he said. "Let me confer with my investigator a moment."

Haller got up from the table and charged through the gate, striding toward Bosch.

"I'm not your investigator," Bosch whispered.

"I don't give a fuck," Haller said. "That was for her, not you. Where the fuck is our witness?"

"I don't know. The subpoena said nine and I told him nine and he's not here. I have no way to contact him other than calling the firehouse and I know he's not there because he's off today."

"Jesus Christ!"

"See if the judge will give you an hour. I'll go out looking for—"

"The only thing the judge is going to give me is a citation of contempt. He's probably in chambers writing it up right now. I can keep my finger in the dike maybe five more minutes. After that, I'll have to bring in my DNA witness and do this in reverse—"

He stopped when the door opened. Bosch recognized Morales in street clothes, looking as put out as Haller. His forehead was peppered with sweat. He was carrying his med kit, which looked like a large fishing tackle box.

"That's him."

"Well, it's about fucking time."

Bosch left Haller and went to Morales.

"The subpoena said nine," he said.

"I couldn't find parking," Morales said. "So I parked at the fire station and walked over, carrying this thing. It's thirty pounds. Then the fucking elevators take forever."

"All right, go back out in the hallway and take a seat on a bench. Don't talk to anyone. Just cool down and don't move till I come out and get you."

"I'm sweating, man. I have to hit the head and towel off or something."

"It's down the hall past the elevators. Do what you have to do but do it quick and get back here. You want me to watch your kit?"

"Don't do me any favors, man. I don't want to be here."

Morales left the courtroom and Bosch walked back to Haller.

"He'll be good to go in five minutes. He walked over from the station and is sweating, wants to clean up a little."

"He's got the gizmo in his box?"

"He should. I didn't ask."

"He'd fucking better."

Haller turned and headed back through the gate. He waved to the clerk.

"You can bring my client out and you can get the judge," he announced. "The defense is ready to proceed."

Bosch noticed Saldano, the prosecutor, eyeing Haller suspiciously. She had no idea what was going on.

Ten minutes later court was in session, with Herstadt seated next to Haller. Judge Falcone was on the bench but the jury box was empty. Bosch was watching from the back row of the gallery, near the courtroom door.

The judge was angry. He had told the jurors to come in early and they had done so. But now they sat in the assembly room while the lawyers argued over the inclusion of the unexpected witness. Morales was not on the witness list provided by the defense to the court and the prosecution at the start of the trial. Saldano had now blindly objected to him testifying, on principle, without even knowing who he was or what he would say.

It all made for a bad start to the day.

"Mr. Haller, in granting you the subpoena late yesterday I was not guaranteeing you that this witness would testify," the judge said. "I was anticipating the objection from the state and that you would supply solid grounds for his inclusion at this late moment in the trial."

"Your Honor," Haller said, "the court has granted the defense wide latitude and it is certainly appreciated. But as you told the jurors at the start of these proceedings, this trial is a search for truth. My investigator located a witness yesterday evening who could change the course of this search for truth. It is unfair not only to my client, but to the people of California to not let him be heard by the jury."

Falcone glanced out at the gallery and his eyes found Bosch. For a split second Bosch thought he saw disappointment, and once again he wished Haller would stop calling him his investigator.

"But you see, Mr. Haller, you have created a circumstance with your investigator and this witness that is patently unfair to the prosecution," the judge said. "Ms. Saldano has had no time to prepare for this testimony, to have her investigator vet and background this witness, or to question him on her own."

"Well, welcome to my world, Your Honor," Haller replied. "I have never met or spoken to this witness myself. As I said before, his importance was discovered late yesterday—I believe you signed the subpoena at five-fifteen. He is now here to testify. We will all learn what he has to say as he says it."

"And what exactly will you be asking him?"

"I will ask him about the events he was involved in on the day of the murder. He is the emergency medical technician who treated my client when he went into seizure in the coffee shop a little more than an hour before the murder of Judge Montgomery."

The judge turned his attention to the prosecutor.

"Ms. Saldano, do you want to respond?"

Saldano stood up. She was in her late thirties and a rising star in the D.A.'s Office, assigned to the Major Crimes Unit. Where she went, the media followed. Bosch had already noticed the reporters lining the front row of the gallery.

"Thank you, Your Honor," she said. "The state could simply object on the basis the court has already outlined: lack of notice, lack of inclusion of this witness on the defense's witness list, lack of discovery in regard to his testimony. But since Mr. Haller has decided to throw the old search-for-the-truth trope into his plea for special dispensation, the state would argue that this witness has nothing to add to the testimony in this case that will in any way get us closer to the truth. We have already had testimony from Mr. Haller's own expert witness on the seizure his client allegedly had in the coffee shop. The state did not object to that testimony. This new witness can only provide the same information."

She paused for a breath before wrapping her argument up.

"So, clearly, Your Honor, this is some kind of a stall," she said. "A waste of the court's time. More smoke and mirrors from a courtroom magician who has nothing left in his bag of tricks."

Bosch smiled and saw that Haller, who was leaning back in his chair and turned toward the prosecution's table, had to hold back a smile himself.

As Saldano sat down, Haller stood up.

"Your Honor, may I?" he asked.

"Please make it brief, Mr. Haller," Falcone said. "The jury has been waiting since nine."

"'Smoke and mirrors,' Your Honor? A 'bag of tricks'? A man's life is at stake here and I object to the characterizations by the deputy district attorney. It goes to—"

"Oh, come now, Mr. Haller. I have heard you called worse in this courtroom alone. And let's not kid ourselves: we both know Ms. Saldano has just given you the next slogan for the ads you place on buses and bus benches all over this city. I can just see them now: "'A courtroom magician,' says the District Attorney's Office.'"

There was a murmur of laughter in the courtroom and Bosch saw Saldano lower her head as she realized what she had done.

"Thank you for the promotional advice, Judge," Haller said. "I'll get right on that after this trial is over. But what matters right here, right now, is that my client's life and liberty are at stake, and there is a witness sitting on a bench in the hallway who wants to testify and who I believe will bring clarity to what happened—not only at the coffee shop but an hour later in Grand Park to your friend and colleague Judge Montgomery. The evidence the witness is expected to give is relevant and material to the central issue of whether the prosecution's evidence is reliable. And finally, I would add that the existence of this witness and his testimony was or should have been known to the prosecution—my investigator got his name from the state's own discovery materials. I ask the court's indulgence in allowing me to bring this new witness into the courtroom to testify."

Haller sat down and the judge looked at Saldano, who made no move to stand.

"Submitted," she said.

Falcone nodded.

"Okay, let's bring the jury in," he said. "Mr. Haller, I am going to allow you to put your witness on the stand, but then I am going to allow Ms. Saldano whatever time she'll need to prepare her cross-examination, if she indeed wishes to question the witness at all."

"Thank you, Your Honor," Haller said.

He turned and looked back at Bosch and nodded. Bosch got up to get Morales.

18

From the start, Albert Morales seemed like a man with a chip on his shoulder. He clearly did not want to be in court on his day off and showed this by acting uninterested and giving clipped answers to every question. This was a good thing, in Bosch's eyes. He believed that the EMT's obvious dislike of Haller would give more credence to anything the defense lawyer managed to extract from him that was beneficial to his client.

Bosch was again watching from the last row. This was not because he had to be near the exit, but because the last row gave him cover from the eyes of the courtroom deputy, who was posted at a desk in front of the door to the courthouse holding pens. The use of electronic devices was prohibited in all but the hallways of Superior Court. The deputies often cut law enforcement officers and prosecutors slack, but never the defense. And Bosch needed to be able to communicate with Haller as he conducted his examination of Morales without having previously questioned him. It was a high-wire act without a net and Haller wanted all the help he could get. He wore an electronic watch that received texts from his phone. As long as Bosch kept his messages short, Haller would be able to get them on the watch and check them as though he was checking the time.

After the preliminaries of name, occupation, and experience were out of the way, Haller got down to business, asking Morales if he had received a call regarding a man down at the Starbucks on First Street on the day of the Judge Montgomery murder.

"I did," Morales said.

"And did you have a partner with you?" Haller asked.

"I did."

"Who was that?"

"Gerard Cantor."

"And you two treated the man who was on the floor of the Starbucks?"

"We did."

"Do you recognize that man in the courtroom today?"

"Recognize? No."

"But you know he is in the courtroom?"

"Yes."

"And how is that?"

"It's been all over the news. I know what this trial's about."

He said it in an exasperated tone that Haller ignored as he pressed on.

"So you know that the defendant in this case, Jeffrey Herstadt, is the man you treated on the floor of the Starbucks that day?"

"Yes."

"But you don't recognize him?"

"I treat a lot of people. I can't remember them all. Plus, he looks like he got cleaned up while in jail."

"And because you can't remember all the people you treat, you write reports detailing what you did on each call for help, correct?"

"Yes."

Foundation laid, Haller asked the judge for permission to bring a copy of the Fire Department incident report that was filed by Morales after the incident with Herstadt. Once that was okayed, Haller put a copy down in front of Morales and returned to the lectern.

"What is that document, Mr. Morales?"

"The incident report I filled out."

"After treating Jeffrey Herstadt at the Starbucks."

"That's right. It's got his name on it."

"Can you read the summary to the jury?"

"Yes. 'Subject fell or seized on floor of business. All vitals good. Oxygen levels good. Refused treatment or transport for minor head laceration from fall. Subject walked away.'"

"Okay, what does that last part mean? 'Subject walked away.'"

"It means exactly what it says: the subject refused any help from us and just got up and walked away. He went out the door and that was that. I don't know why it's so important."

"Well, let's try to make it clear to you. What does—"

Saldano stood up and objected.

"Your Honor, he's badgering his own witness when the witness has legitimate concerns about what he is doing here. As do I."

"Mr. Haller, you know better," Falcone said.

"Yes, Your Honor," Haller said.

"And I join the witness and the prosecutor in questioning how we are advancing the search for truth with this witness," the judge added.

Morales looked out into the gallery and found Bosch. He gave him a fuck-you look.

"Judge," Haller said, "I think it will become clear to all concerned very quickly if I am allowed to proceed with my witness."

"Then please do," Falcone said.

Haller checked his watch as if noting the time and read Bosch's first text:

Get to the gizmo.

"Mr. Morales, the summary on your incident report says 'All vitals good. Oxygen levels good.' What does that mean?"

"His pulse and blood pressure were measured and within acceptable levels. His blood was oxygenated. Nothing was wrong."

"And how did you arrive at that conclusion?"

"I measured his pulse and my partner took his blood pressure. One of us put an oximeter on his finger."

"Is all of that routine?"

"Yes."

"What does the oximeter do?"

"It measures the oxygen content in the blood. You get a good idea about how the heart is working in terms of circulating oxygenated blood."

"Is that why it is clipped to the finger? You want the measurement from an extremity?"

"Exactly."

"Now I noticed today that you brought your EMT kit with you, is that correct?"

"Yes, because the subpoena told me to."

"This oximeter you just mentioned, is it in your kit?"

"Should be."

"Can you open your kit and show the oximeter to the jury?"

Morales reached down to the floor next to the witness stand and unsnapped the latches on his kit. He flipped the top open and grabbed a small device out of a tray. He held it up to Haller, then turned and displayed it to the jury.

"How does that work, Mr. Morales?" Haller asked.

"Simple," Morales said. "Turn it on, clip it to the finger, and it shoots infrared light through the finger. From that it can measure the oxygen saturation of the blood."

"And you just clip it to any finger?"

"The index finger."

"Either hand?"

"Either hand."

"How long did you treat Jeffrey Herstadt that day?"

"Can I look at the report?"

"You may."

Morales looked over the report and then answered.

"From beginning to end, when he walked away, it was eleven minutes."

"Then what did you do?"

"Well, first we realized he walked away with our oximeter still on his finger. I chased him down and grabbed that. Then we packed up, bought a couple lattes, and left."

"You returned to the station?"

"Yes."

"Where is that station?"

"On Fremont and First."

"Quite close to here, correct?"

"Yes."

"In fact you walked here from the station, with your kit, to testify today, isn't that correct?"

"Yes."

"Did you walk through Grand Park?"

"Yes."

"Had you ever been in Grand Park before?"

"Yes."

"When was that?"

"Many times. It's part of Station Three's coverage area."

"Going back to the day you treated Jeffrey Herstadt at Starbucks, did Rescue Three receive another emergency call soon after your return to the station that morning?"

"Yes."

"What was the call?"

"It was a stabbing. It was this case. The judge that got stabbed."

Bosch glanced away from Morales to Saldano. She had leaned toward the junior prosecutor, who was sitting next to her, and whispered in his ear. He then got up and went to a cardboard file box that was on a chair by the courtroom rail. He started going through documents.

"Do you remember how soon you got the call after returning from treating Mr. Herstadt and checking his vitals?" Haller asked.

"Not offhand," Morales said.

Haller went through the same procedure of asking the judge's permission to give Morales an incident report, this one from the Montgomery stabbing.

"Does that shed light on things, Mr. Morales?" Haller asked.

"If you say so," Morales countered.

"If you compare it to the first incident report, does it not say that the calls were one hour and nine minutes apart?"

"Looks like it."

"So let's keep going with this. You said you were with Herstadt for eleven minutes, then got a latte. How long did that take?"

"I don't remember."

"Do you remember if there was a line?"

"It was a Starbucks. There was a line."

"Okay, so at least a few minutes there. Did you and your partner sit down with your lattes or take them to go?"

"Took them to go."

"And you returned directly to the station?"

"Yes, direct."

"Is there some sort of protocol or procedure you follow after returning from a rescue call?"

"We replenish supplies, write the reports."

"Finish your latte first?"

"I don't remember."

"But then you get this call, a stabbing in Grand Park, correct?"

"Yes."

"And you roll on it."

"Yes."

"How long did it take you and your partner to get there?"

Morales looked at the incident report.

"Four minutes," he said.

"Was the victim, Judge Montgomery, alive when you got there?" Haller asked.

"He was circling the drain."

"What does that mean?"

"He was dying. He'd lost too much blood and was unresponsive. No pulse. There was nothing we could really do for him."

"You just said 'no pulse.' So you checked his vitals despite the fact that, as you say, 'he was circling the drain'?"

There it was, Bosch knew. The trial came down to this question.

"We did. It's protocol. No matter what, you do that."

"With the oximeter?"

Morales didn't answer. It looked to Bosch like he had finally tumbled to the importance of his testimony and realized that everything could shift on his answer.

"With the oximeter?" Haller asked again.

"Yes," Morales finally said. "Part of the protocol."

"Was that the same oximeter used less than an hour earlier to check the vitals of Jeffrey Herstadt?"

"It would have been."

"Is that a yes?"

"Yes."

"A moment, Your Honor."

Haller let that last answer hang out there in front of the jury. Bosch knew that he was trying to make a decision about the next question. He fired off a quick text:

Ask the ?

He saw Haller check his watch and read it.

"Mr. Haller?" Falcone prompted.

"Your Honor," Haller said. "May I have another moment to confer with my investigator?"

"Make it fast," Falcone said.

Bosch got up, slid his phone into his pocket, and walked up the aisle to the rail. Haller came over and they whispered.

"This is it," Haller said. "I think I leave it here."

"I thought you were rolling the dice," Bosch said.

"I am. I did. But I go too far and I blow the whole thing."

"If you don't ask, the prosecutor will."

"Don't be so sure about that. Cuts both ways for her too. She might not ask him a thing."

"It's a search for truth. The judge said so; you said so. Ask the question. Or I'm not your investigator."

Bosch turned to go back to where he had been sitting. For the first time he noticed Renée Ballard was in the courtroom, on the other side of the gallery. He had not seen her come in and had no idea how long she had been there.

Once seated, he turned his attention back to the front of the room. Haller was staring at Morales, still deciding whether to quit while he was ahead or ask the question that could win or lose the day—and the trial.

"Mr. Haller, do you have another question?" the judge prompted.

"Yes, Your Honor, I do," Haller said.

"Then ask it."

"Yes, Your Honor. Mr. Morales, between the two rescue calls you went out on, where was the oximeter?"

"In my kit."

Bosch saw Haller ball his hand into a fist and bounce it lightly on the lectern like he was spiking a ball after a touchdown.

"You didn't take it out?"

"No."

"You didn't clean or disinfect it?"

"No."

"You didn't sterilize it?"

"No."

"Mr. Morales, do you know what DNA transfer is?"

Saldano jumped to her feet and objected. She argued that Morales was not a DNA expert and should not be allowed to give testimony regarding the transfer of DNA. Before the judge could respond, Haller did.

"I withdraw the question," he said.

It was clear Haller knew the objection would come. He had just wanted to get the phrase *DNA transfer* into the record and the jury thinking about it. Haller's next witness would close the deal on that.

"Then do you have another question, Mr. Haller?" the judge asked.

"No, Your Honor," Haller said. "I have nothing further."

Haller returned to the defense table, glancing back at Bosch and giving a nod as he went. Bosch checked the row of reporters. They seemed frozen. There was a stillness to the courtroom that underlined what Haller had just done with his questioning of Morales.

"Ms. Saldano, do you wish to cross-examine the witness or take some prep time?" the judge asked.

Bosch expected the prosecutor to ask for a 402 hearing—to tell the judge without the jury present how much time she would need to prepare for her cross-examination of Morales. The judge had already said he would give her wide latitude.

But the prosecutor surprised Bosch and probably everybody in the courtroom by rising and going to the lectern.

"Briefly, Your Honor," she said.

She put a legal pad on the lectern, checked a note on it, and then looked up at the witness.

"Mr. Morales, do you carry only one oximeter in your EMT kit?" she asked.

"No," Morales said. "I carry a backup. You know, in case the battery dies on one of them."

"No further questions," the prosecutor said.

Now in the silence, it felt like the momentum had switched. With a single question, Saldano had been able to undo much of what Haller had accomplished.

"Mr. Haller, anything further?" the judge asked.

Haller hesitated and asked the judge for a moment. Bosch tried to think of a question he could text him. It seemed as though any question asked might offer another opening to the prosecutor. He typed quickly and didn't bother to correct typos:

Tel him open the kit.

He watched Haller check his watch. The judge noticed as well.

"I'll stop you before you ask, Mr. Haller," he said. "We are not taking the morning break until we are finished with this witness."

"Thank you, Your Honor," Haller said before turning his attention back to the witness. "Mr. Morales, can you open your kit again for us and show us where you keep both oximeters?"

Morales did as requested. The oximeter he had displayed to the jury was in the top tray of his kit. He then lifted the tray up, moved his hands over the contents of the deeper box until he found the other oximeter, and held it up.

"Thank you, you can close that up now," Haller said.

He waited while Morales closed up his kit. He glanced back at Bosch and gave a slight nod. The momentum was about to switch again.

"So, Mr. Morales, when you said you had a backup oximeter, you are talking about having an extra one stored in the bottom of your kit, to use if the device you currently have in the top tray of your kit happens to have a malfunction or the battery dies on you, is that correct?"

Morales clearly knew that he was providing pivotal information to the jury, and his loyalties were to the state. He hesitated and then tried to fashion an answer that would not give Haller what he wanted.

"You never know," he said. "We can use either one, depending on the situation."

"Then why is one on the top of your box and the other beneath the tray and in the bottom?" Haller responded.

"That just happens to be how I packed the kit."

"Really. So let me ask you a hypothetical question, Mr. Morales: Rescue Three gets a call. A man has been hit by a car on First Street. You respond. He is on the street, bleeding, unconscious. He's 'circling the drain,' if you will. You open your kit. Do you grab the oximeter on the top tray, or do you lift that tray out and dig the other oximeter out of the bottom?"

As if on cue, Saldano objected, saying that Haller was again badgering his own witness. Haller withdrew the question because he knew the jury didn't need to hear the answer. Common sense dictated that Morales would grab the oximeter in the top tray, and that he had done the same when he treated the fatally wounded Judge Montgomery.

"I have no further questions," Haller said.

Saldano demurred, not wanting to dwell on the oximeter any longer. The judge asked Haller if he had any more witnesses.

"Yes, Your Honor, one final witness," Haller said. "The defense would like to call Dr. Christine Schmidt to the stand."

"Very well," Falcone said. "We will take the morning break now and come back to hear from your last witness. Jurors, now is the time to use the restroom, get a cup of coffee. But be back in the assembly room and ready to go in fifteen minutes. Thank you."

The judge made no move to leave the bench as the jurors got up and filed through the door at the end of the jury box. This meant court was not adjourned and Falcone would have more to say to the lawyers once the jurors were gone.

He waited until the last one went through the assembly room door before speaking.

"Okay, the jury is no longer present and we're still on the record," he began. "I don't want to tell the lawyers here what to do, but it does seem to me that it would be a prudent use of the break if Ms. Saldano and Mr. Haller joined me in chambers to discuss the viability of this case going forward. Any objection to that?"

"No, Your Honor," Haller said immediately.

"No, Your Honor," Saldano echoed hesitantly.

19

After the lawyers filed back into the judge's chambers, Bosch went out into the hallway. Christine Schmidt was sitting on a bench there, waiting to be called to testify. Witnesses were not allowed to hear other testimony in a trial, and therefore she was unaware of the testimony Morales had just given or the seismic change it had brought to the case. Bosch crossed the hallway to speak to her and simply explained that the lawyers were meeting with the judge and she could expect to testify afterward.

He then walked back across the wide hallway to another bench where Ballard was waiting. He sat down and she put her backpack between them.

"So, what just happened in there?" she asked.

"I think Haller just got a directed verdict of acquittal," Bosch said. "At least that's what I bet they're talking about in chambers."

"That testimony. He knocked down the DNA?"

"More like he set up a way to explain how the defendant's DNA got under the judge's fingernail. It was transferred."

He nodded across the hall to the bench where Dr. Schmidt sat.

"That's his DNA expert," Bosch said. "She comes in next to talk about touch DNA, DNA transfer. Herstadt's DNA was found under Judge Montgomery's fingernail. One fingernail. The oximeter could have transferred it. It's reasonable doubt right there. It will hang up the jury if not get the outright acquittal."

"But wait," Ballard said. "What about the guy's confession? He admitted to the crime."

"Haller blew that up yesterday. Herstadt's schizophrenic. His doctor was on the stand saying he's got the kind of psychosis that would lead him to agree to anything while under stress, say yes to anything, including murdering a judge in the park. I think Haller's got this won. I think the judge thinks so too. That's gotta be what they're in chambers talking about."

"And you gave him all of this?"

She said it in a tone that Bosch heard as distrustful, as if what he had done was part of a contrived scheme by the defense. It offended him.

"I gave him facts," he said. "No tricks. I think what he laid out in there is what happened. Herstadt didn't do it."

"Sorry," Ballard said quickly. "I didn't mean to suggest…I liked Judge Montgomery. I told you that."

"I liked him, too. I just want to make sure the right guy goes down for killing him, that's all."

"Of course. Of course. We all do."

Bosch didn't respond further. He still felt the heat of being unjustly accused of something. He turned and looked down the hallway at people going in and out of courtrooms, waiting on benches, wandering aimlessly in the halls of justice. He saw some of the jurors from the Montgomery case coming back from the restrooms.

"So why are you here?" he finally asked. "You get something at ballistics this morning?"

"Actually, no," Ballard said.

Her tone had shifted. Bosch thought she was probably happy to change the subject after stepping into the shit with him on the trial.

"There was nothing in the data bank that matched the projectile or shell from Hilton," she continued. "But at least it's in there now should anything come up down the line."

"Too bad," Bosch said. "But we knew it was a long shot. What's next? Rialto?"

"The more I find out about Elvin Kidd, the more I think the answer is out there."

"What did you find now?"

Ballard pulled her backpack over and removed her laptop. She opened it and drew up side-by-side mug shots of a black man facing front and turned to the right.

"These are mug shots of Kidd from Corcoran, taken in 1989, the year he and John Hilton were both there. Now look at this."

She pulled Hilton's sketchbook out of the backpack. She opened it to a specific page and handed it to Bosch. He compared the drawing on the page to the man in the mug shots.

"It's a match," he said.

"They knew each other up there," Ballard said. "I think they were lovers. And then when they both paroled out and came back to L.A., that was a problem for Kidd. He was a Crip OG. Any gay vibe and that could be fatal."

"That's a big jump. You nail down that he was gay?"

"Not at the moment, it's just a guess. There's something about the drawings in the sketchbook...then the whole drug addiction thing, the coldness of the parents in their statement. I'm still working that. Why—what do you know?"

"I don't know anything about that. But I do remember that John Jack and I worked a few gay murders, and John Jack never got too motivated about them. It was his one flaw. He could never get the fire burning if it was a gay victim. I remember this one case— a one-nighter gone bad. An old guy picked up a young guy in West Hollywood, took him back to his place in the hills off Out- post. The kid robbed him, then beat him to death with his belt. It had a big rodeo buckle and it was a bad scene. And I remember John Jack said something that bothered me. He said, 'Sometimes people deserve what they get.' I'm not saying that's wrong all the time—I've had cases where I believed that. But in that case it was wrong."

"Everybody counts or nobody counts."

"You got it."

"So again we come to why did John Jack take the murder book? Was it because he hated gays and didn't want it solved?"

"That seems extreme. I don't think we're there yet."

"Maybe not."

They sat in silence for a few moments. More jurors were returning to the assembly room. Bosch knew he had to get back into the court-room. More out of curiosity about what was happening than any duty to be in there.

"Doesn't matter what Thompson did or didn't do with the case," Bosch said. "Or Hunter and Talis."

"We're still going to solve it," Ballard said.

Bosch nodded.

"We are," he said.

He stood up and looked down at Ballard.

"I need to get back in there. Are you going to Rialto?"

"No. West Hollywood. To see Hilton's old roommate, see if I can confirm some of this."

"Let me know how it goes."

20

Bosch entered the courtroom as the last few jurors were returning to their places in the box and the judge turned in his high-backed chair so he could look directly at the panel when he spoke. Bosch slipped into his familiar spot in the last row of the gallery. He saw that both Haller and Saldano were in their seats and looking directly ahead, so Harry got no read from them on what was happening. Just as the judge was about to begin, the courtroom door opened and Jerry Gustafson, the lead LAPD detective on the case, hurried in and up the center aisle, then sat in the first row directly behind the prosecution table. Gustafson had been in and out of the courtroom during the days Bosch had attended trial sessions.

"Ladies and gentlemen," Falcone began. "First of all, I want to thank you for your public service on this case. Jury duty can be time consuming, difficult, and sometimes even traumatic. You all have been troupers these past ten days and I and the state of California commend you and thank you.

"However, there has been a change and this case has come to an end. The District Attorney's office has elected to drop all charges against Mr. Herstadt and not proceed further with the case at this time."

There was the required buzz of whispers in the courtroom as a scattering of observers and the row of reporters reacted to the news.

Bosch watched Haller's back. He did not move and he made no motion toward his client to clap him on the arm or shoulder, no visual indication of victory.

Bosch did see Gustafson, who was leaning forward, arms on the courtroom rail, drop his head like a man kneeling in church, beseeching his god for a miracle.

But what confused Bosch was the judge's last three words: *at this time.* What did that mean? He knew, as assuredly as the judge did, that to drop all charges at this point was tantamount to an acquittal. There were no comebacks. In California a trial is considered engaged the moment a jury is selected. To go after Herstadt again after this would invoke his double-jeopardy protections. Bosch had no doubt: the case against Jeffrey Herstadt was over.

Following his unclear explanation the judge thanked the jurors one more time and asked them to return to the assembly room and wait. He said the prosecution team wanted to talk to them. Bosch guessed that Saldano wanted to survey them to see where they stood on a verdict. The conversation might tell her whether she had made a critical mistake in dropping the case. It could also confirm she had made the right decision.

Falcone adjourned court and left the bench. Haller stood for the exit and finally looked around to see Bosch in the last row. He smiled and shot a finger at him, then blew on his finger as though it was the imaginary barrel of a gun. Finally, he reached down and squeezed his seated client's shoulder. He bent down and started whispering in his ear.

Saldano and her second got up from the prosecution table and started making their way toward the jury assembly room door. Gustafson stood up and headed back down the aisle toward the courtroom exit. He stopped to look at Bosch. Years back they had worked together in the massive Robbery-Homicide Division squad room, but did not know each other well.

"Happy, Bosch?"

"What exactly happened?"

"Saldano dropped the case to keep her perfect record clean. Herstadt walks and whatever happens, that's on you, asshole. I know you teed this up for Haller."

"You still think he did it."

"Fuck you, man. I know he did it and so do you."

"What about the other five, Gustafson?"

"What five?"

"We got the murder book in discovery. You and your partner, you were chopping wood on five other people who would've been happy to have Montgomery dead, but you just dropped it when you got the DNA hit on Herstadt. You going to go back to them?"

Gustafson pointed to the front of the room where Haller was still whispering in Herstadt's ear.

"There's your killer right there, Bosch. I don't have to go back to anybody. It was him, we had him, and then you blew it up. Good job. You should be proud. You just undid everything you ever did with a badge."

"So that's a no?"

"Bosch, as far as I'm concerned, this case is CBA. And that's on you."

Gustafson walked out of the courtroom.

Bosch remained seated, his face burning with indignation. He tried to calm himself while Haller finished with his client and allowed the courtroom deputy to take Herstadt back into the courthouse jail so he could be processed out and released. Haller quickly gathered his files and legal pads and threw them into his briefcase. He then snapped its two brass locks closed and came through the railing, where four reporters were waiting for him. Talking over one another, they peppered him with questions about exactly what had just happened in the judge's chambers.

Haller told them he would answer their questions in the hallway. He led them out of the courtroom, winking at Bosch as they passed by his row. Then Bosch got up and followed them through the doors. Haller took a position in the middle of the hallway and the reporters gathered around him in a semicircle. Bosch stood outside the circle but close enough so he could hear what was said.

The reporters started shouting variations on the same questions.

"All right, all right, listen instead of talking and I shall enlighten you," Haller said, his voice almost giddy from the courtroom win.

He waited for them to quiet before he continued.

"Okay, ready?" he said. "Faced with more than reasonable doubt about the evidence it presented to the jury, the state took the high road today and withdrew the flimsy case it had against my client. Mr. Herstadt is currently being processed out of holding and will be a free man shortly."

"But this case started as a slam dunk," said a reporter Bosch knew was from the *Times*. "They had a confession and a DNA match. What happened?"

Haller spread his arms and smiled.

"What can I tell you? Reasonable doubt for a reasonable fee," he said. "What happened here was that they didn't do their homework. The confession was bogus—it came from a man who would have confessed to killing the Black Dahlia if he had been asked. And there was a perfectly reasonable explanation for the DNA match. The judge saw that, knew this case was a duck without wings, and called the prosecution on it. Ms. Saldano made a call to her boss and reasonable minds prevailed. She did what any prudent prosecutor would do: she folded her tent."

"So the case was dismissed?" asked another reporter.

"It was withdrawn by the D.A.'s Office," Haller said. "They dropped all charges."

"So that means they could still refile," said a third reporter.

"Nope," Haller said. "This case already went to trial. To charge my client again would be to submit him to double jeopardy. This case is over, folks, and an innocent man was proved so today."

"Who did Saldano call to get approval to drop the case?" the *Times* reporter asked.

"I don't know," Haller said. "She stepped out of chambers to make that call. You'll have to ask her."

"What happens to your client now?" the *Times* reporter asked.

"He's a free man," Haller said. "I am going to see if I can get him a place to stay and back into therapy. I'm thinking of starting a GoFundMe page to help with his expenses. He's got no home and no money. They've held him in jail for seven months."

"Are you going to ask the city and county for reparations?" a reporter asked.

"Maybe," Haller said. "I think amends have to be made. But that's a question for another day. Thank you all. Remember, that's a double *el* in *Haller*. Get it right."

Haller stepped back from the semicircle and raised his arm in the direction of the elevators, dismissing the journalists. As she walked by him, the *Times* reporter handed him a business card and said something in a low voice Bosch didn't hear. Haller took her card and slid it into the breast pocket of his suit jacket, behind the red-white-and-blue pocket square. He then sauntered over to Bosch, the smile seemingly a permanent feature of his face.

"You don't get many days like this one, Harry."

"I don't suppose you do. What really happened in chambers?"

"Pretty much what I just told them. I left out the part about the judge telling Saldano that it looked to him like there was no way a jury could return a verdict of guilt beyond a reasonable doubt. He did give her the option of continuing and hearing my DNA expert and then my very persuasive motion to dismiss. That was when she stepped out and made her call to the powers that be. The rest is just like I told it. Maybe now they'll go out and get the right guy for this."

"I doubt it. Gustafson still thinks your client did the deed. He stopped by on his way out to tell me."

"Wounded pride, that's all that is. I mean, what else is he going to say?"

"Yeah, but don't you see? He's not going to go after the real killer. He said it himself as he was leaving: 'CBA'—the case is closed."

"Meaning?"

"Cleared By Arrest. It means no further investigation. Meantime, whoever really did this is still out there."

"But that's not our problem, is it? We work for Herstadt and Herstadt is free."

"Maybe it's not *your* problem."

Haller stared at Bosch for a long moment before responding.

"I guess you gotta do what you gotta do."

Bosch nodded.

"I'm going to hang on to the discovery files and the copy of the murder book."

"Sure. Be my guest. I'll be in touch soon about that other thing we talked about. The medical thing."

"I'll be around."

BALLARD

21

Ballard woke with a deep soreness between her shoulder blades and pins and needles in her left foot. She sat up in the tent groaning and found that Lola had decided to sleep with all thirty-five pounds of her body across Ballard's foot. She pulled her foot free, waking the dog, who looked at her with betrayal in her eyes.

"You crushed my foot," Ballard said.

She began massaging and working her ankle until the burning feeling started to recede. Once she brought it back to life, she started rolling her shoulders, trying to loosen her back muscles. Before sleeping she had pushed herself on the board, paddling all the way down to the rock jetty at the inlet and then back up, the return being a battle against a strong wind coming down from Malibu.

Lola's eyes were now expectant and Ballard read the message.

"A short one, Lola. I've got work."

Ballard crawled out of the tent on her knees and looked around. The beach was deserted. Aaron was in the lifeguard stand, slouched so low only the top of his head was visible. Ballard picked the leash up off the sand and Lola heard its metal clip jingle. She shot out of the tent, pushed through Ballard's legs, and took a seated position in front of her. She looked back over her shoulder at Ballard, ready for the leash to be clipped to her collar.

"Don't be so pushy. It's only a short one."

Ballard put her feet in the sandals she had left outside the tent and they went up toward the boardwalk, where Lola liked to walk and observe the world. Ballard decided to walk north since she had paddled south earlier. They went all the way up to Rose Avenue and then turned around, Lola unsuccessfully tugging against the turn back.

After a half hour it was time for Ballard to get ready. It was almost four and she wanted to get back into the city before the crush of traffic moving east got into full swing. She went to her van, opened a can of food for Lola, and put it in her bowl on the ground in the parking lot. While the dog ate, Ballard looked through the work clothes she had on a hanging bar in the van to make sure she had a clean suit for the night.

After dropping Lola at night care, Ballard avoided the freeways and took surface streets toward Hollywood. She got there by 5:30, parked in the Hollywood Station lot, and changed clothes in the locker room before returning to the parking lot and switching to her city-ride. She then drove to West Hollywood, cruising by the apartment building she believed was the home of Nathan Brazil, John Hilton's roommate at the time of his murder.

She found parking on Willoughby and walked back to the apartment. There was no security gate, another indication that the building was not a sought-after address. She was able to approach apartment 214 directly and knock. Almost immediately the door was opened by a man with short black hair and a neatly kept beard. Ballard didn't recognize him from the four-year-old driver's license photo she had previously pulled up on the computer.

She had unclipped her badge from her belt and was holding it up.

"Mr. Brazil?"

"Yes, what is it?"

"I'm Detective Ballard with the LAPD. I'd like to ask you a few questions."

"Well, what's it about? This is West Hollywood, not L.A."

"Yes, I know it is West Hollywood. I'm investigating the murder of John Hilton in Hollywood and I know it's been a long time but I'd like to ask you about him and about his life back when you lived together."

"I don't know what you're talking about. I never lived with anyone named that."

"You are Nathan Brazil, right?"

"Oh, no. I'm Dennis. Nathan's my husband—I took his name. But I'm sure he doesn't know anything about a murder. What was—"

"Is he here?"

"No, he's at work."

"Where is work?"

Dennis started getting cagey.

"He works at a restaurant, so you can't just go barging—"

"He still works at Marix?"

His eyes confirmed this by widening slightly in how-do-you-know-that surprise.

"Do you have a card?" he said. "I'll have him call you."

"Or you could just text him now, tell him I'm on my way and to be ready. This is a homicide investigation, Mr. Brazil. We don't make appointments at people's convenience. You understand?"

"I guess I do now."

"Good. Thank you for your time."

Ballard walked back to her car. Marix was around the corner on Flores and it might have been faster to walk but she wanted to park the city-ride out front as part of her show of authority. If Nathan Brazil had the same attitude as his husband, he might need to be reminded of the power and might of the state.

She parked in the red zone in front of the three-step walk-up to the restaurant. Before she got to the first step, the glass door opened, and a man in his mid-fifties and unsuccessfully fighting baldness stepped out and positioned himself on the top step with his hands on his hips. He wore black jeans, white shirt, black tie, and black apron.

"Table for one cop?"

Sarcasm dripped off his words like melted cheese.

"Mr. Brazil?"

"It's amazing! You only took thirty years to respond to my call."

Ballard joined him on the top step.

"What call was that, sir?"

"I wanted to talk about my friend. I called many times and they never came and they never called back because they didn't give a shit about John."

Ballard saw a holding area near the front door with bar tables where patrons could drink and congregate while waiting to be seated. It was empty now, too early for a wait for a table. Ballard gestured to the space.

"Can we speak privately over there?"

"Sure, but I have one early bird I need to keep an eye on."

"No problem."

They moved into the waiting corral and Brazil positioned himself so that he could see through the glass windows of the restaurant to a table of four men.

"How long have you been working here?" Ballard asked.

"Almost eight years," Brazil said. "Good people, good food, and I can walk to work."

"I know it's good food. I've eaten here several times."

"Is this where you butter me up and then say the case will never be solved?"

"No, it's not. This is where I tell you I'm going to solve it."

"Sure."

"Look, Nathan, I'm not going to lie to you. A lot of time has gone by. John's parents are dead, one of the original detectives is dead, and the other is retired in Idaho. There are—"

"They never did give a shit anyway. They didn't care."

"Is that based on them not returning your calls?"

"More than that, honey. Not that things are all that different now, but back then they weren't going to jump through hoops for a drug-addicted poof. That's just the way it was."

"You mean a gay man?"

"Poof, fag, queer—whatever you want to call us. LAPD didn't give a shit. Still doesn't."

"To me it's a victim and that's all I see, okay? I inherited this case because it was lost and then it got found. I'm on it now and it doesn't matter to me who John Hilton was or what his lifestyle choices were."

"See, that's what I mean. That's the problem. It isn't a 'life*style*.' And it's not a 'choice.' You're hetero, right?"

"Yes."

"Is that a 'lifestyle choice' or are you just hetero?"

"I get it. My mistake and I appreciate what you're saying. What I'm saying is that it doesn't matter to me what John was or did. Gay or drug addict or both, he didn't deserve what happened and I'm interested, no matter what the people before me were. Okay?"

"Okay. But I have to go check on my table now."

"I'll wait here."

Brazil left the area and went into the restaurant. Ballard watched him take another order for margaritas—it was happy hour—then put in the order at the bar at the back of the restaurant. He came back to Ballard a few moments later. She felt they had gotten the ground rules out of the way and Brazil had had a chance to vent. It was time to get down to business.

"Okay, so how long were you living with John before he was killed?"

"Murdered. I prefer 'murdered' because that's what it was."

"You're right. It was a murder. How long did you live with him?"

"Eleven months. I remember because it was sort of awkward. We lived in this dump in North Hollywood and it was time to sign a new lease. Neither of us wanted to but we were too lazy to look for something else and think about moving all our shit.

Then he got murdered and I couldn't do the rent on my own. I had to move."

"It says in the investigation records that he came to the studio where you were working on the night he was murdered."

"Yes, Archway. I found out later from the guy at the gate."

"And that was unusual for him to come there?"

"Sort of. Not really."

This had stood out to Ballard in the murder book chrono—that it was unusual for Hilton to go to Brazil's workplace. Now she was hearing something different.

"I read a report from the first investigation that had you saying he'd never done that before," she prompted.

"First of all, I didn't know this guy who was interviewing me," Brazil said. "I called him Detective Vitalis—you remember that stuff in the green bottles? And for a while—until they confirmed my alibi—I thought they were going to try to blame me and make it a fag-on-fag crime. So I told him what I told him."

"Which was a lie?"

"No, not a lie. But it wasn't everything, you know? I worked for a company that did craft services. You know, brought all the food and snacks and stuff for whatever production we were on. Sometimes we were at the studio and sometimes we were out filming on location, like on the streets somewhere. And I always told John where we would be and he'd come by and I'd sneak him some food, you know? And that's why he came to the studio that day. He was hungry. He must've had no money and wanted something to eat. But giving my name at the guard shack at Archway wouldn't have worked. It was our first time on that lot and they didn't know me from Adam."

Ballard nodded. It was always good to get the fuller story, but sometimes the more you knew, the more you saw conflicts with other information.

"So, if he had no money for food and tried to come to you, how did he have money to go down to that alley to buy drugs?" she asked.

"I don't know," Brazil said. "Maybe he had something to trade. Maybe he stole something. He did that sort of thing, you know?"

Ballard nodded. It was possible.

"All I know is that if he came to find me it was because he had no money," Brazil said. "I need to go to the bar."

While he was gone, Ballard decided to take the interview in other directions when he got back. This time she had to wait a while as Brazil delivered drinks to his one table, then took their food orders and went back to the kitchen.

"You know, I like you," he said when he returned. "You are not like Detective Vitalis was at all."

"I assume you mean Detective Talis?" Ballard said. "I had a hard time with him too."

"No, it wasn't that. It wasn't because of his name. He had his hair hard-parted on the side and then very slick and in place. I could smell the Vitalis because that's what my father always used."

"Was his name Hunter?"

"Yeah, that's it. Hunter. I remember because there was a bar on the boulevard back then called The Hunter. Their slogan was 'Where the hunter meets the hunted.' Anyway, he was a jerk."

"He's dead."

"Well, he seemed old even back then."

"Were you and John lovers or just roommates?"

"Oh, so we're getting personal."

"Part of the job. Sorry."

"We were both, you could say. Nothing serious but sometimes things would happen."

"Did he have anybody else?"

"Oh, yeah, he had his unattainable fantasy. We all do. "

"Who was his?"

"John went to prison, you know. His parents wouldn't get him a good lawyer and he ended up with a three-year sentence. He fell in love with somebody there who protected him. But that was only there. There are guys who do what they need to do in prison and then on the outside it's a different story. They go from gay love to gay hate. You see it all the time. It's self-denial."

"Did he ever tell you this guy's name?"

"No. I mean, I don't remember if he did. It didn't matter because it was over. His lover got out and went back to straight life."

"But John hung on to the fantasy?"

"Yeah, the dream. He sat around drawing pictures of the guy."

"Pictures?"

"The guy posed for him or something in prison and Johnny was a pretty good artist. It was the one thing he could do well. He was drawing all the time. On napkins, loose papers, anything. He kept a notebook of drawings from when he was in prison."

"Did you ever tell any of this to Detective Vitalis?"

"No, he never called me back after that first interview. When I wasn't useful to him as a suspect, I wasn't useful."

"Is this what you were trying to reach him about? The man in prison?"

"No, I wanted him to call my boss back and say I wasn't a suspect. I got fired because of what he told them—that I would sneak Johnny food every now and then. He told them and I got fired. They thought I was a suspect, and it wasn't fair."

All Ballard could do was nod. She didn't doubt the story for a moment. Hunter and Talis had put together an incomplete murder book on an incomplete investigation. They had been steered away from the truth or turned away on their own. Either way, it was no surprise that they left other victims and casualties in their path.

"Don't be like them," Brazil said.

"I'm not," she said.

22

Ballard got to the station early for her shift and walked into a detective bureau she had never seen so crowded so late in the day. Several dayside detectives were at their desks, working phones and computers. Something had happened. She saw her boss, Lieutenant McAdams, standing by one of the detectives and reading over his shoulder as he typed on a keyboard.

She walked over.

"L-T, what's happening?"

McAdams turned around.

"Ballard, what are you doing in so early?"

"Was going to get an early start. I had some leftover paperwork and wanted to get it in before roll call. Never know what will happen after that."

"Paper on what?"

"Oh, just some follow-up stuff on the crispy critter we had the other night. Arson wanted the photos I took on my phone. And then they never sent me their report. So, I'm asking for that, seeing if they got an ID. What's going on here?"

"We had some hillbilly decide to rob the cash pickup at the In-N-Out on Sunset. Dipshit takes off and realizes he can't get out of the parking lot because the drive-through line's clogging the entrance. He ditches the car and runs up to Hawthorne, where he tries to jack a UPS truck, not knowing the driver's in the back with the packages. The truck takes off, the guy in the back surprises him, they get into a fight for control, and the truck hits three parked cars."

"Wow."

"I'm not done yet. Then this guy jumps out of the truck and is still going, but now he's got the UPS guy and somebody that was in one of the parked cars running after him. He goes north again, tries to cross Hollywood, and is run over by a TMZ tour bus. You know how much paperwork this has generated, Ballard? I've got four guys running OT and two are borrowed from Wilshire. So I hope you weren't planning to hit me up for a greenie on your crispy critter, are you?"

A greenie was an overtime request card.

"No, L-T. No OT."

"Good, because this is going to break the bank, this deployment, and we still have eight days to go."

"Don't worry. You need me to do anything on it?"

She felt she had to offer even though she wanted no part of the case.

"No, we've got it covered," McAdams said. "You just take care of your crispy critter and whatever else comes up tonight. By the way, nothing on a new partner for you yet, but Captain Dean at Wilshire says they can continue to take care of Hollywood Division on the nights you're off."

"Great," Ballard said. "But I don't mind working alone, L-T. I've got patrol backing me up whenever I need it."

She turned away and looked for a desk to use. The one she had been using lately was currently occupied by its dayside owner. She picked a spot farthest away from the other detectives' activity and sat down to work.

Ballard wasn't sure how she felt about McAdams's mention of his efforts to team her with a partner. Her last partner had retired four months earlier and had been on an extended bereavement leave before that. All told, Ballard had already been working alone for seven months. Though the job had always entailed two detectives splitting up seven nights, it had been different these last months truly working by herself. There had been moments of sheer terror, but for the most part she liked it better than having to be with a partner or constantly report every move she was making to him. She liked that the watch commander kept only a loose string on her. And her true supervisor, McAdams, never knew what she was up to for sure.

Ballard realized that the story she had spun for McAdams about the crispy critter had an element of truth to it. She had not received a report from the Fire Department arson team on the man who had died in his tent on Cole Avenue. This prevented her from completing her own report.

She found Nuccio's card in the bottom of her backpack and then opened up her LAPD e-mail account on the desktop computer. She composed and sent Nuccio a message asking for the victim's ID and official cause of death and any other pertinent details, including whether the homeless man's next-of-kin had been located and informed of the death. She was not expecting to hear back from Nuccio until at least the next working day. She knew the arson guys were nine to fivers unless they were called out or were running with a case.

But her cell phone rang a minute after she sent the e-mail.

"Ballard, it's Nuccio."

"I just sent you an e-mail. I need—"

"I read it. That's why I'm calling. You can stand down. RHD is taking it."

"Wait, what?"

"We're calling it a suspicious death after all and that's the protocol. Robbery-Homicide Division handles it."

"What's suspicious about the death?"

"A few things. First of all, the dead guy has some juice, believe it or not. From a rich family down in San Diego. So that's going to sharpen the focus on this."

"What's his name? Who is he?"

"His name is Edison Banks Jr. and his father had a shipyard or something down there and got rich on Navy contracts. He died last year and this kid in the tent inherited a bundle but probably didn't know it. Five years ago, his father got tired of his shit, gave him ten grand in cash and kicked him out of the house. He was twenty. The family never heard from him again. I guess he used up the money and has been up here on the streets ever since. There's a younger brother and now he gets all the dough."

"And you're saying that makes this suspicious?"

"No, I'm saying that makes us want to check all of the boxes on this. And in doing that, it got suspicious."

"How?"

"Two things. One is the autopsy. The blood-alcohol screen was off the chart. Came back with a three-six BAC. That's like triple the drunk driving limit."

"More like quadruple. But he wasn't driving, Nuccio."

"I know that, but this kid is five-eight, a hundred forty pounds, according to the autopsy. That much booze and he wouldn't be driving or anything else. He'd be down for the count."

Ballard didn't bother schooling Nuccio on how blood-alcohol content was not skewed by body size or weight.

"Doesn't matter how drunk he was, he still could've kicked the heater over in his sleep," she said.

"Maybe," Nuccio said. "Except we examined the heater, too. It's got a float valve that cuts off fuel supply to the flame if the device is more than forty-five degrees off level. It's a safety feature. So kicking it over actually puts the flame out. It doesn't start a fire."

"And you tested it?"

"Several times. And it doesn't leak. Only way to spill the fuel is to unscrew the cap and turn it on its side. But the cap was screwed on. So, it's suspicious. This guy's in the tent passed out, somebody for whatever reason crawls into the tent, unscrews the cap, and dumps out the heating oil, screws it back on and gets the hell out. Then lights a match, throws it in, and *whoosh*. Poor guy never knew what hit him. That's the only way it would work and that adds up to suspicious. RHD is taking it by protocol."

Ballard was silent as she considered what Nuccio had described. She saw it like a movie in her mind.

"Who has it at RHD?" she finally asked.

"I don't know," Nuccio said. "I talked to Captain Olivas about it and there's a big powwow tomorrow at eight. I'll find out who he assigned it to then."

Of course, it was Olivas. RHD teams took the big cases. Ballard had been on one of those teams once. Until defending herself against Olivas cost her the job.

"Okay, Nuccio, I'll see you there tomorrow," she said.

"What?" Nuccio said. "No. This was informational only. It's not your case, Ballard. RHD has it, and besides, you don't even know where the meeting is."

"I know that you go to RHD. RHD never comes to you. I'll see you there."

She disconnected the call. She wasn't sure she would go to the meeting—it was her goal in life to never be in the same room with Olivas again—but she needed Nuccio to think she was coming. That would rattle him and it would rattle Olivas when he was told. That's what Ballard wanted.

23

Ballard spent the first hour after roll call trying to get a line on Edison Banks Jr. He had no criminal record and his driver's license had expired three years earlier and not been renewed. Ballard pulled up the DMV photo and estimated it was taken seven years earlier, when the license was issued. It showed a blond-haired surfer type with thin lips and green eyes. Ballard printed it even though she knew that it would probably be useless in terms of showing it to people who might have known Banks in recent years.

Next, she started working the phone, calling shelters, soup kitchens, and homeless outreach centers in the Hollywood area. There weren't many of them and not all of them operated twenty-four hours. She was looking for any sort of connection to Banks that she could have in her back pocket if she crashed the RHD meeting in the morning. She didn't expect to be allowed to stay on the case—that was a given with Olivas the captain in charge—but if she could come up with information that kick-started the investigation or gave it a direction, then her actions on the night of the body's discovery might not be judged so harshly. She knew that Olivas would take any opportunity to second-guess her decisions, and she was vulnerable to criticism on this one: she had passed off what might have been determined to be a homicide to the LAFD arson squad, and that shouldn't have happened. She should have been the one to inform RHD, not the Fire Department.

At the end of an hour she had nothing. Banks had apparently steered clear of places where names and photos are taken in exchange for a bed, a hot meal, or a bar of soap. Or he was using an alias. Either way, he had successfully stayed off the grid. It clearly suggested that Banks had been hiding his trail and didn't want his family to find him.

She grabbed the DMV photo off the printer and a rover from the charging station before heading down the hallway to the watch office. She told Lieutenant Washington that she was going out to conduct a second-level canvass of the area, now that the death had been ruled suspicious.

"Arson deaths go to RHD," Washington said.

"I know," Ballard replied. "There's a meet tomorrow at eight. I just want to finish my report and pass it on. There's a few people out there we missed the other night and now's the time to get them. They scatter at sunup."

Washington asked if she wanted backup and she declined. The presence of uniformed officers would not be conducive to getting information from the denizens of the Hollywood night.

She first cruised around the city park and slowly along Cole to check things out. She saw no activity, except for a few inhabitants of the encampment who were still awake and sitting on the curb or on folding chairs and smoking and drinking by themselves.

At the north end of the park, Ballard saw a group of men sitting under a streetlight. She parked her car across the street from them in front of a prop house and used the rover to call her location in to the watch office. It was a routine practice.

As she got out, she slipped off her suit jacket so the badge on her belt would be readily recognized when she approached the men. Crossing the street, she counted four men sitting together in a small clearing between two tents and a blue tarp lean-to attached to the park's perimeter fence. One of the men spoke up in a raspy whiskey-and cigarette-cured voice before she got to them.

"Why, that's the prettiest po-lice officer I think I ever seen."

The other men laughed and Ballard could tell they weren't feeling any pain at the moment.

"Evening, fellas," she said. "Thanks for the compliment. What's going on tonight?"

"Nothin'," Raspy said.

"We's just havin' an Irish wake for Eddie," said another, who was wearing a black beret.

A third man raised a short dog bottle of vodka to toast the fallen.

"So, you guys knew Edison," Ballard said.

"Yup," said the fourth man.

He appeared to Ballard to be barely twenty years old, his cheeks hardly holding a stubble.

"Were you guys here the other night?" she asked.

"Yeah, but we didn't see nothing till it was all over," said Beret.

"How about before?" Ballard asked. "Did you see Eddie earlier in the night? Was he around?"

"He was around," Raspy said. "Had himself a fiver and he wouldn't share none of it."

"What's a fiver?"

"A whole fifth of the good stuff."

Ballard nodded. Judging by the one man's short dog, she assumed scraping enough change on corners and from passersby to buy a fifth was a rare thing.

"How'd he get the fiver?" she asked.

"He, um, had a guardian angel," said The Kid.

"Someone bought it for him? Did you see who?"

"Nah, just somebody. It's what he said. Said somebody gave him the big boy for nothin'. Didn't have to suck a cock or anything."

"You remember what it was he was drinking?"

"Yeah, Tito's."

"That's tequila?"

"No, vodka. The good stuff."

Ballard pointed to the short dog in the other man's hand.

"Where you guys buy your bottles?"

The man pointed with the bottle down toward Santa Monica Boulevard.

"Mostly over there at Mako's."

Ballard knew the place, an all-night market that primarily sold booze, smokes, rolling papers, pipes, and condoms. Ballard had responded to numerous calls there over her years on the late show. It was a place that drew rip-off artists and assaults like a magnet. Consequently, there were cameras inside and outside the business.

"You think that's where Eddie got his fiver?" she asked.

"Yup," said The Kid.

"Had to be," said Short Dog. "Ain't no other place round here open late."

"You heard about Eddie having trouble with anybody?" she asked.

"Nah, ever'body like Eddie," Short Dog said.

"A gentle soul," Raspy added.

Ballard waited. Nobody volunteered anything about Eddie having trouble.

"Okay, guys, thanks," Ballard said. "Be safe."

"Yup," said The Kid. "Don't want to end up like Eddie."

"Hey, Miss Detective," said Beret. "Why you asking all these questions? Nobody give a shit 'bout Eddie before."

"They do now. Good night, guys."

Ballard got back in her car and drove down to Santa Monica Boulevard. She turned right and went down three blocks to a run-down strip shopping plaza, where Mako's Market was located. The market anchored one end of the plaza and a twenty-four-hour donut shop held down the other end. In between there were two empty businesses, a Subway franchise, and a storefront business that offered one-stop shopping for notary needs, photocopying, and losing weight or quitting cigarettes through hypnosis.

The area patrol car was parked in front of the donut shop,

confirming the cliché. Ballard got out of her car and waved her hand palm down, signaling smooth sailing. Behind the wheel of the patrol car, she could see Rollins, one of the officers who had responded to the fatal fire the other night. He flashed his lights in acknowledgment. Ballard assumed his partner was inside the donut shop.

Mako's was a fortress. The front door had an electronic lock that had to be opened from inside. Once buzzed in, she saw the business was built like a bank in a high-crime neighborhood. The front door led to an anteroom that was ten feet wide and six feet deep. There was nothing in this space except an ATM machine against the wall to the left. Front and center was a stainless-steel counter with a large pass-through drawer and a wall of bulletproof glass rising above it. A steel door with triple locks was to the right of the counter. A man sat on a stool on the other side of the glass. He nodded at Ballard in recognition.

"How's it going, Marko?" she said.

The man leaned forward, pushed a button, and spoke into a microphone.

"All is okay, Officer," he said.

Ballard had heard a story about Marko Linkov having ordered the sign out front many years ago and then accepting the misspelled sign that arrived at half price. She didn't know if it was true.

"You sell Tito's vodka?" Ballard asked.

"Yes, sure," Marko said. "Got it in back."

He started to slip off his stool.

"No, I don't want any," Ballard said. "I just want to know. You sell a bottle of it the other night? Monday night?"

Marko thought about it for a moment and slowly nodded.

"Maybe," he said. "I think so."

"I need to look at your video," Ballard said.

Marko got off the stool.

"Sure thing," he said. "You come in."

He disappeared to his left and Ballard heard the locks on the steel door being opened. She had expected no pushback on her request, no questions about search warrants or other legalities. Marko depended on the police to keep an eye on his business and to respond to his many calls about belligerent or suspicious customers. He knew that if he expected that kind of service it was a two-way street.

Ballard entered and Marko locked the door behind her. She noticed that in addition to the bolt locks he flipped down a metal burglar bar across the door. He wasn't taking chances.

He led her past the display shelves to a back room used for storage and as an office. A computer stood on a small crowded desk that was pushed against a wall. A back door led to the alley behind the plaza; it, too, was steel and equipped with two burglar bars.

"Okay, so…," Marko said.

He didn't finish. He just opened up a screen that was quartered into four camera views, two outside the front, showing the parking lot and the front door of the shop, a third in the alley showing the back door, and the fourth a camera over the ATM in the front room. Ballard saw the patrol car still positioned outside the donut shop. Marko pointed at it.

"Those are good guys," he said. "They hang around, watch out for me."

Ballard still thought the donuts might be the draw but didn't say so.

"Okay, Monday night," she said.

Ballard had no idea when Edison Banks Jr. received the bottle of Tito's his fellow encampment inhabitants saw him with, or how long it would have taken him to consume it. So she asked Marko to start running the playback fast, beginning at dusk on Monday. Every time a customer entered the store he would slow the video to normal speed until Ballard determined that the customer was not purchasing what she was looking for.

Twenty minutes into the playback they got a hit on Tito's vodka but it wasn't what Ballard expected: a Mercedes Benz coupe pulled into the lot and parked in front of Mako's. A woman with long black hair, in stiletto heels and all-black leather pants and jacket, got out and entered the store. Inside, she bought a bottle of Tito's after first withdrawing cash from the ATM. Mako's was a cash-only business.

"Is she a regular?" Ballard asked.

"Her, no," Marko said. "Never seen her. She don't look like a working girl, you know? They different."

"Yeah, they don't drive Mercedes."

Ballard watched as the woman returned to the car, got in, and drove out of the plaza's lot, heading west on Santa Monica—the direction away from the city park where Edison Banks Jr. would burn to death about four hours later. Ballard committed the car's license plate number to memory, which was easy because it was a California vanity plate—14U24ME.

"What is that?" Marko said.

"One for you, two for me," Ballard said.

"Oh. That's good."

"Whose ATM is that?"

"It's mine," Marko said. "I mean, it's a company that has them but they pay me to have it there. I get a cut, you know? It makes me good money because people need the cash when they come in here."

"Right. Can you get records?"

"What records?"

"Of the withdrawals. Like if I wanted to know who she was."

"Mmm, I don't know. You might have to have the legal paper for that. Not my company, you see."

"A search warrant. Okay."

"I mean, if it was up to me, I give you, you know? I always help police. But this guy might not be the same."

"I understand. I have her plate number. I can get it with that."

"Okay. Keep going?"

He pointed to the computer screen.

"Yes, keep going," Ballard said. "We're not even halfway through the night."

A few minutes later in real time and an hour later on the video playback, Ballard saw something that caught her eye. A man in ragged clothes pushed a shopping cart full of bottles and cans up to Mako's, parked it on the sidewalk, and then buzzed to be allowed entrance. He came in and dumped enough change and crumpled bills into the pass-through drawer to purchase a forty-ounce bottle of Old English malt liquor. He then left the store and returned to his cart, securing the full bottle among the bottles and cans he had collected, and started pushing his way out of the lot. He headed east on Santa Monica and Ballard thought she recognized him as one of the onlookers from Monday night after the fire.

It gave her a new idea.

She decided to go find the man who collected the bottles.

24

Ballard caught a call just before end of shift that pulled her away from finishing her report for the RHD meeting on Banks and pushed her into unpaid overtime. It was a he said/he said case on Citrus just south of Fountain. Patrol called her out to referee a violent domestic dispute between two men who shared a one-bedroom, one-bath apartment and had fought over who got to use the shower first before work. They had been drinking and drugging most of the night and the fight began when one of the men took the last clean towel and locked himself in the bathroom. The second man objected and kicked the door open, hitting the first in the face and breaking his nose. The fight then ranged through the small apartment and woke other residents in the building. By the time the police arrived after multiple 911 calls, both men were showing injuries from the altercation and neither was going to work.

The two patrol officers who responded wanted to pass the decision-making off to a detective so they would avoid any future blowback from the case. Ballard arrived and talked to the officers, then to both parties involved. She guessed that the fight wasn't really about a clean towel or the shower but was symptomatic of problems in the men's relationship, whatever that was. Nevertheless, she chose to bag them both, out of protection for them and herself. Domestic disputes were tricky. Calming anger, settling nerves, and then simply backing away might seem to be the most judicious path, but if an hour or a week or a year later the same relationship ends in a killing, the neighbors talk to the news cameras and say the police came out before and did nothing. Better safe now than sorry later. That was the rule and that was why the patrol officers wanted no part of the decision.

Ballard arrested both men and had them transported separately to Hollywood Division jail, where they would be held in adjoining cells. The paperwork involved in booking the two, plus Ballard's need to prepare other documents, pushed her past seven a.m. and the end of shift.

After filing the necessary arrest reports, Ballard took her city car downtown and parked on First Street in front of the PAB. There was no parking there but she was late and her hope was that any traffic officer would recognize the vehicle as a detective ride and leave it unticketed. Besides, she didn't expect to be inside long.

She hooked her backpack over one shoulder and carried a brown paper evidence bag with her. On the fifth floor she entered the Robbery-Homicide Division, realizing that it was the first time she had been back since she involuntarily transferred to Hollywood Division's late show. She scanned the vast room, starting with the captain's office in the back corner. She saw through the glass wall that it was empty. There was no other sign of him—or of Nuccio and Spellman—so she proceeded to the War Room. On the door she saw that the sliding sign was moved to IN USE and knew she had found her party. She knocked once and entered.

The War Room was a 12 x 30 repurposed storage room that held a boardroom-style table and had whiteboards and flat screens on its walls. It was used on task force cases, for meetings involving multiple investigators, or for sensitive cases that should not be discussed in the open squad room.

Captain Robert Olivas was sitting at the head of the long table. To his left were Nuccio and Spellman. To his right were two detectives Ballard recognized as Drucker and Ferlita, both longtime RHD bulls who specialized in burn cases. Drucker had been on the squad so long his nickname was "Scrapyard" because he had replaced two knees, a hip, and a shoulder over time.

"Detective Ballard," Olivas said, his tone even and not projecting any of the enmity she knew he still carried for her.

"Captain," Ballard said, just as evenly.

"Investigator Nuccio told me you might be joining. But I think we have things in hand here and you're not going to be needed on this."

"That's good, because I'm parked out front in a red zone. But before I leave, I thought you might want to see and hear some of the evidence I've collected."

"Evidence, Detective? I was told you left the scene Monday night as soon as you could."

"Not quite like that, but I did leave once the Fire Department said they had things in hand and would contact RHD if anything changed."

She was telling Olivas what her stand would be should he try to raise issues with how she handled the original call. She also guessed that Nuccio and Spellman would not be a problem because they were smart enough not to get in the middle of a police department squabble.

Olivas, a taciturn man with a wide girth, seemed to decide that this one wasn't worth it. It was part of that smooth sailing Amy Dodd had mentioned: Olivas wanted no waves in his final year. Ballard knew this would play well with her real plan for the meeting.

"What have you got?" Olivas asked. "We're not even sure we have a homicide here."

"And that's why you guys down here get the big bucks, right?" Ballard said. "You get to figure it out."

Olivas was finished with the introductory pleasantries.

"Like I said, what have you got, Ballard?"

Now his tone was slipping. Condescension and dislike were taking over. Ballard put the evidence bag on the table.

"I've got this for starters," she said. "An empty fifth of Tito's vodka."

"And how does that fit into this?" Olivas asked.

Ballard pointed to Nuccio.

"Inspector Nuccio told me yesterday that the victim's blood-alcohol content was measured at three-six at the coroner's. That takes a lot of alcohol. I spoke to some of the homeless men who knew the victim and they said that on Monday night Banks was drinking a fifth of Tito's that he wasn't sharing. They said somebody—'a guardian angel'—gave it to him. I recovered the bottle from another homeless man who camps on the same sidewalk and collects bottles and cans for recycling. Chain of custody is for shit but he felt pretty sure he picked up the bottle after Banks chugged the vodka. I figure you might want to take it to latent prints. If you get prints from Banks, it confirms the story. But you might also get the prints of the 'guardian angel,' and that's somebody you want to talk to. That is, if somebody helped get him drunk so they could light him on fire."

Olivas digested that for a few moments before responding.

"Did anybody see this 'guardian angel'?" he asked. "Are we talking man, woman, what?"

"Not the guys I talked to," Ballard said. "But I went down the street to Mako's and they have video of a woman in a Mercedes pulling up and buying a bottle of Tito's about four hours before Banks got burned. That may just be a coincidence but I'll leave that to you guys to figure out."

Olivas looked at his men.

"It's thin," he said. "The whole thing is thin. You men take the bottle and anything else Ballard has. We need to pick up the heater and do our own testing on that. We're going to withhold determination of death until we know what's what. Ballard, you can go. You're off duty now anyway, right?"

"I am," Ballard said. "And I'm out of here. You guys let me know if you need me to go back to the scene for anything tonight."

"That won't be necessary," Olivas said. "We'll handle it from here."

"I just need you to sign off on a summary report on the recovery of the bottle," Ballard said. "So there's a record of chain of custody and no confusion down the line should the bottle of Tito's be significant."

"And to make sure you get the credit," Olivas said.

It was not a question and Ballard was pleased with how Olivas took it.

"We all want proper credit for what we do, don't we?" she said.

"Whatever," Olivas said. "You write it up and I'll sign it."

Ballard unzipped her backpack and removed a file containing two copies of a two-page document. The front page was taken up by a detailed summary of the bottle's origin and the second was the signing page bearing only Olivas's name and rank below a signature line. She placed the documents on the table.

"One for you and one for me," she said.

Olivas signed both documents. Ballard took one and left the other on the table. She put her copy back in its folder and returned it to her backpack.

Ballard threw a mock salute at Olivas, then turned and left the room. On her way out of RHD, she tried to calm herself and control her emotions. It was difficult. Olivas would always be able to get to her. She knew that. He had taken something from her, as other men had in the past. But the others had paid in one way or another: *come-uppance . . . revenge . . . justice* — whatever the term. But not Olivas. Not so far. At best he had been left with a temporary blemish on his reputation that was gone soon enough. Ballard knew she could out-wit and out-investigate him all she wanted, but he would still always have that unnameable thing he had taken from her.

25

After leaving RHD, Ballard went down the hall to the Special Assault Section again. This time Amy Dodd was not in her cubicle, but the station next to it still seemed to be unused. Ballard sat down and logged into the department's computer. She blew out a deep breath and tried to relax now that she was away from her tormentor. She was actually finished for the day, but anxiety was seizing her because of Olivas and what seeing him brought up in her. She had just given up one case and wanted to get back to the other. To keep things moving forward.

She opened her notebook next to the computer and found the page where she had written down the intel she had gathered on Elvin Kidd. She had both the cell number and the landline associated with his business. Connecting to Nexis/Lexis, she ran a search on the numbers and got the service providers, a requirement for a wiretap search warrant. Once she had that, she opened a template for a search warrant application requesting approval of audio surveillance on both phone numbers.

Seeking a wiretap approval was a complicated and difficult process because listening in on personal phone calls starkly conflicted with Fourth Amendment protections against unlawful search and seizure. The probable cause for such an intrusion had to be complete, airtight, and desperate. Complete and airtight because the writer had to lay out in the probable cause statement that the threshold of criminal activity by the target of the surveillance had been easily passed. Desperate because the investigator must also make a convincing argument for the wiretap being the only alternative for advancing the case against the intended target. A wiretap was supposed to be a last-resort measure, and so required a detective to get the written approval of the department. It had to be signed off on by a high-ranking supervisor—like a captain or higher.

It took Ballard an hour to write a seven-page probable cause document that was half boilerplate legalese and half an outline of the case against Kidd. It leaned heavily on information from an LAPD-certified informant named Dennard Dorsey and stated that the wiretap was a last-resort measure because the case was twenty-nine years old and witnesses had died, had faded memories, or could not be located. The document did not mention that Dorsey had not been an active informant in more than a decade or that Kidd had not been active in the Rolling 60s Crips gang for even longer.

As Ballard was proofing the statement on the screen, Amy Dodd arrived at her cubicle.

"Well, this is getting to be a regular thing," she said.

Ballard looked up at her. Dodd looked tired, as though she'd worked a long night on a case. Ballard once again was hit with concern.

"Just in time," she said. "What's the printer code for this unit?"

Dodd said she had to look it up. She sat down at her desk, logged in, then read the unit's printer ID off her screen. Ballard sent the probable cause document to be printed.

"So what's up?" Dodd said from the other side of the partition. "You moving in over there?"

"Writing a search warrant," Ballard said. "I have to take it over to Judge Thornton before he starts court."

"Wiretap?"

"Yeah. Two lines."

Judge Billy Thornton was the Superior Court's wiretap judge, meaning all search warrants for phone surveillance went through him for approval. He also ran a very busy courtroom that usually convened by ten each morning.

Following instructions from Dodd, Ballard went to a break area at the rear of the squad room to fish her document out of the printer. She then came back to her borrowed desk and pulled from her backpack the same file folder she had produced during the War Room meeting with Olivas. She attached the signature page from the chain-of-custody document to the back of the search warrant application and was ready to go.

"I'm out of here," she announced. "You ever want to get together after work, I'm here, Amy. At least until the late show starts."

"Thanks," Dodd said, seeming to pick up on Ballard's worry. "I might take you up on that."

Ballard took the elevator down and then crossed the front plaza toward her car. She checked the windshield and saw no ticket. She decided to double down on her luck and leave the car there. The courthouse was only a block away on Temple; if she was fast and Judge Thornton had not convened court, she could be back to the car in less than a half hour. She quickened her pace.

Judge Billy Thornton was a well-regarded mainstay in the local criminal justice system. He had served both as a public defender and as a deputy district attorney in his early years, before being elected to the bench and holding the position in Department 107 of the Los Angeles Superior Court for more than a quarter century. He had a folksy manner in the courtroom that concealed a sharp legal mind— one reason the presiding judge assigned wiretap search warrants to him. His full name was Clarence William Thornton but he preferred Billy, and his bailiff called it out every time he entered the courtroom: "The Honorable Billy Thornton presiding."

Thanks to the inordinately long wait for an elevator in the fifty-year-old courthouse, Ballard did not get to Department 107 until ten minutes before ten a.m., and she saw that court was about to convene. A man in blue county jail scrubs was at the defense table with his suited attorney sitting next to him. A prosecutor Ballard recognized but could not remember by name was at the other table. They appeared ready to go and the only party missing was the judge on the bench. Ballard pulled back her jacket so the badge on her belt could be seen by the courtroom deputy and went through the gate. She moved around the attorney tables and went to the clerk's station to the right of the judge's bench. A man with a fraying shirt collar looked up at her. The nameplate on his desk said ADAM TRAINOR.

"Hi," Ballard whispered, feigning breathlessness so Trainor would think she had run up the nine flights of steps and take pity. "Is there any chance I can get in to see the judge about a wiretap warrant before he starts court?"

"Oh, boy, we're just waiting on the last juror to get here before starting," Trainor said. "You might have to come back at the lunch break."

"Can you please just ask him? The warrant's only seven pages and most of it's boilerplate stuff he's read a million times. It won't take him long."

"Let me see. What's your name and department?"

"Renée Ballard, LAPD. I'm working a cold case homicide. And there is a time element on this."

Trainor picked up his phone, punched a button, and swiveled on his chair so his back was to Ballard and she would have difficulty hearing the phone call. It didn't matter because it was over in twenty seconds and Ballard expected the answer was no as Trainor swiveled toward her.

But she was wrong.

"You can go back," Trainor said. "He's in his chambers. He's got about ten minutes. The missing juror just called from the garage."

"Not with those elevators," Ballard said.

Trainor opened a half door in the cubicle that allowed Ballard access to the rear door of the courtroom. She walked through a file room and then into a hallway. She had been in judicial chambers on other cases before and knew that this hallway led to a line of offices assigned to the criminal-court judges. She didn't know whether to go right or left until she heard a voice say, "Back here."

It was to the left. She found an open door and saw Judge Billy Thornton standing next to a desk, pulling on his black robe for court.

"Come in," he said.

Ballard entered. His chambers were just like the others she had been in. A desk area and a sitting area surrounded on three sides by shelves containing legal volumes in leather bindings. She assumed it was all for show, since everything was on databases now.

"A cold case, huh?" Thornton said. "How old?"

Ballard spoke as she opened her backpack and pulled out the file.

"Nineteen-ninety," she said. "We have a suspect and want to stimulate a wire, get him talking about the case."

She handed the file to Thornton, who took it behind his desk and sat down. He read through the pages without taking them out of the folder.

"My clerk said there is a time element?" he said.

Ballard wasn't expecting that.

"Uh, well, he's a gang member and we've talked to some others in the gang about the case," she said, improvising all the way. "It could get back to him before we have a chance to go in and stir things up, get him talking on the phone."

Thornton continued reading. Ballard noticed a black-and-white photo of a jazz musician framed on the wall next to the coatrack, where a judge's spare robe hung. Thornton spoke as he appeared to be reading the third page of the document.

"I take wiretap requests very seriously," he said. "It's the ultimate intrusion, listening to somebody's private conversations."

Ballard wasn't sure if she was supposed to respond. She thought maybe Thornton was speaking rhetorically. She answered anyway in a nervous voice.

"We do, too," she said. "We think this is our best chance of clearing the case—that if prompted, he'll check in with his gang associates and admissions of culpability might be made."

She was quoting the document Thornton was reading. He nodded while keeping his eyes down.

"And you want text messaging on the cell phone," he said.

"Yes, sir, we do," Ballard said.

When he got to the sixth page she saw him shake his head once and she began to think he was going to reject the application.

"You say this guy was high up in the gang," Thornton said. "Even back at the time of the killing he was high up. You think he did the actual killing?"

"Uh, we do, yes," Ballard said. "He was in a position to order it done, but because of the possible embarrassment of the situation, we think he did it himself."

She hoped the judge wouldn't ask who "we" constituted, since she was working the case alone at this point. Bosch was out of the department, so he didn't count.

He got to the last page of text, where Ballard knew she was grabbing at straws in support of probable cause.

"This sketchbook mentioned here," the judge said. "Do you have that with you?"

"Yes, sir," Ballard said.

"Let me take a look at it."

"Yes, sir."

Ballard reached into her backpack, pulled out John Hilton's prison sketchbook, and handed it across the desk to Thornton.

"The sketch referred to in the warrant is marked with the Post-it," she said.

She had marked only one drawing because the second drawing was not as clearly recognizable as Kidd. Thornton leafed through the book rather than going directly to the marker. When he finally got there, he studied the full-page drawing for a long moment.

"And you say this is Kidd?" he asked.

"Yes, Your Honor. I have photos of him from that time—mug shots—if you want to see them."

"Yeah, let me take a look."

Ballard returned to the backpack while the judge continued.

"My concern is that you're making a subjective conclusion that, first, this drawing is of Kidd and, second, that the drawing implies some sort of prison romance."

Ballard opened her laptop and pulled up the photos of Kidd taken while he was in Corcoran. She turned the screen to the judge. He leaned in to look closely at the photos.

"You want me to enlarge them?" Ballard asked.

"That's not necessary," the judge said. "I concede that that is Mr. Kidd. What about the romantic relationship? You don't have proof of that, other than to say you can see it in this drawing. Hilton might have just been a good artist."

"I see it in the drawing," Ballard said, maintaining her ground. "Plus you have the victim's roommate confirming that he was gay and that he was fixated on someone. You have the fact that Hilton was murdered in an alley controlled by Kidd at a time when Kidd had cleared out all other gang members. I believe that Hilton was in love with him and what happens in prison stays in prison. Kidd could not have exposure of the relationship undermine his position of authority in the gang. I think it's there, Your Honor."

"I decide that, don't I?" Thornton said.

"Yes, Your Honor."

"Well, your theory is there," Thornton said. "Some of it is supported by probable cause, but as I say, some is assumption, even conjecture."

Ballard didn't respond. She felt like a student being chewed out after school by her teacher. She knew she was going down in flames.

Thornton was going to say she didn't have it, to come back when the probable cause was on solid footing. She watched him flip up the last page to the signature line with Olivas's name on it.

"You're working for Captain Olivas on this?" he asked.

"He's in charge of cold cases," Ballard said.

"And he signed off on this?"

"Yes, sir."

Ballard suddenly felt ill—sick to her stomach. She realized that her deception had sent her down a bad path. She was lying to a superior-court judge. Her enmity for Olivas had led her to carry her subterfuge to a person she had only respect for. She now regretted ever taking the murder book from Bosch.

"Well," Thornton said. "I have to assume he knows what he's doing. I worked cases with him as a prosecutor twenty-five years ago. He knew what he was doing then."

"Yes, sir," Ballard said.

"But I've heard rumors about him. Call it his management style."

Ballard said nothing and Thornton must have realized she wasn't biting on the bait he had thrown into the water. He moved on.

"You're asking for a seven-day wire here," he said. "I'm going to give you seventy-two hours. If you don't have anything by then, I want you off the lines. Shut it down. You understand, Detective?"

"Yes, sir. Seventy-two hours. Thank you."

Thornton went through the process of signing the order she would give to the service providers on Kidd's phones. Ballard wanted him to hurry so she could get out of there before he changed his mind. She was staring at the photo of the musician on the wall but not really seeing it as she thought about the next steps she would take.

"You know who that is?" the judge asked.

Ballard came out of the reverie.

"Uh, no," she said. "I was just wondering."

"The Brute and the Beautiful—that's what they called him,"

Thornton said. "Ben Webster. He could make you cry when he played the tenor sax. But when he drank he got mean. He got violent. I see that story all the time in my courtroom."

Ballard just nodded. Thornton handed her the documents.

"Here's your search warrant," he said.

BOSCH

26

Bosch sat at his dining room table with copies of documents from the Walter Montgomery case broken into six stacks in front of him. In the stacks were all the records of the LAPD investigation of the judge's murder that Mickey Haller had received in discovery prior to trial. Knowing what he did about homicide detectives, prosecutors, and the rules of discovery, Bosch was pretty sure he didn't have everything that had been accumulated during the investigation. But he had enough to at least begin his own.

And Bosch was also sure that he was the only one investigating the matter. Jerry Gustafson, the lead detective, had made it clear when the murder charge against Jeffrey Herstadt was dismissed that he felt the murderer had been set free. To take a new look at his investigation would be to disavow his prior conclusion. The sins of pride and self-righteousness left justice for Judge Montgomery swaying in the wind.

That bothered Bosch to no end.

The six stacks in front of him represented the five tracks of investigation being carried out by Gustafson and his partner, Orlando Reyes, up until they got the DNA hit on Herstadt from the judge's fingernail scrapings. That stopped investigation of anyone other than Herstadt. This was a form of tunnel vision that Bosch had seen before and had probably been guilty of himself when he had been on LAPD homicide duty. With the advent of forensic DNA, he had repeatedly seen science take over investigations. DNA was the panacea. A match turned an investigation into a one-way street, a prosecution into a slam dunk. Gustafson and Reyes dropped all non-Herstadt avenues of investigation once they believed they had their man.

The sixth stack of documents included the case chrono and other ancillary reports on the murder, including the autopsy report and statements from witnesses who were in the park where the deadly attack occurred. The docs in the sixth stack were germane to all five of the other paths of investigation. Bosch had already separated out the documents regarding the Herstadt path and put them aside.

There were also several disks containing video from cameras in the area, including three that were focused on the park. Bosch was aware of these from the Herstadt trial but reviewed them in their entirety first. None of the cameras in the park had caught the actual murder because it had occurred in a blind spot—behind a small building that housed the elevators that carried people to and from the underground parking complex. Other disks turned over in discovery included video from cameras inside the two elevators and the five-floor garage, but these showed no suspects or even elevator riders at the time of the killing.

The park cameras were useful for one thing: they pinpointed the time of the murder. Judge Montgomery was seen walking down steps from Grand Street, where he had just had breakfast. He was trailing twenty feet behind a blond woman, who also was heading toward the courthouse, with what appeared to be a name tag clipped to her blouse. The woman walked behind the elevator building and Montgomery followed. A few seconds later the woman emerged and continued toward the courthouse. But Montgomery never came into camera view again. His attacker had been waiting in the blind. He was stabbed and then the attacker was believed to have used the elevator blind to slip into a stairwell next to the elevators and escape. There were no cameras in the stairwell, and the cameras in the five-floor garage below were either poorly placed, missing, or broken and awaiting replacement. The killer could have easily slipped through the camera net.

By manipulating the video, Gustafson and Reyes had been able to identify the name tag on the woman who had been walking ahead of Montgomery as a juror badge. On the afternoon of the murder, Reyes went to the jury-pool room at the courthouse and found her waiting to be called. He took her to the courthouse cafeteria and interviewed her. She was Laurie Lee Wells, a thirty-three-year-old actress from Sherman Oaks. But her statement, which Bosch read, provided no clues to the murder. She had been wearing Bluetooth earbuds and listening to music on her walk from the parking structure to the courthouse. She did not hear anything occur behind her when she passed by the elevators. The detectives dismissed her value as a witness.

Bosch's starting point was the other tracks of the investigation that Gustafson and Reyes had been on prior to getting the DNA hit on Herstadt. He needed to see if they had been on the right path before the DNA led them astray.

The five tracks involved two cases that were currently on Montgomery's civil docket, one he had recently ruled on, and two from his days in criminal court. The criminal cases entailed convicted defendants who had threatened the judge. The civil cases had large money stakes riding on the judge's ruling or impending ruling.

It had been Bosch's experience that threats made by criminals heading off to prison were mostly hollow. They were the last gasps of people crushed by the system and who had nothing left but the ability to throw empty promises of revenge at those they perceived as their tormentors. Bosch had been threatened many times in his years as a police officer and detective, and not once had the person who issued the remark acted on it.

And so he took up the two tracks involving threats from Montgomery's days on the criminal bench first, not because he believed them to be the best shot but because he wanted to get through them quickly in order to concentrate on the cases involving large sums of money. Money was always the better motive.

He put a live recording of Charles Mingus at Carnegie Hall on the turntable, chosen for the twenty-four-minute version of "C Jam Blues" on side 1. The 1974 concert was up-tempo, high energy, and largely improvisational, and just what Bosch needed for wading through case reports. The concert, including Bosch favorite John Handy on tenor sax, helped put him into the proper groove.

The first threat involved a man sentenced to life without parole for the murder of his ex-girlfriend, who had been abducted and then tortured over a three-day period before perishing from loss of blood. There appeared to be no issue at trial that engaged the judge in any controversial decision against the defense. The suspect, Richard Kirk, had been arrested in possession of the knives and other tools linked forensically to the injuries sustained by the victim. He had also rented the warehouse where the torture-killing had taken place. A month after Kirk was sentenced to prison, the judge received an anonymous letter claiming that he would be eviscerated with a six-inch blade and would "bleed out like a slaughtered pig." It was unsigned but had the hallmarks of Richard Kirk, who had committed much of his torture with a six-inch blade.

While Montgomery had not been eviscerated, he had been stabbed three times in a concentrated area of his torso under his right arm, suggesting a prison-style shanking—three quick thrusts with a blade.

When the threatening letter came in, a sheriff's department investigation was opened and a fingerprint on the stamp attached to the anonymous letter was traced to a legal clerk who worked for Kirk's defense attorney. When confronted, the defense attorney acknowledged taking the letter from Kirk while on a visit with his client to discuss an appeal. He said he never read the letter because it was in a sealed envelope. He simply handed it over to his clerk to mail. The investigation resulted in Kirk being placed in solitary confinement for a year and his attorney being quietly disciplined by the California Bar.

The incident also put Kirk on the radar of the detectives working Montgomery's killing. Reyes requested a list of any prison associates of Kirk's who had been released in the prior year, the theory being that Kirk might have somehow paid an inmate about to be paroled to hit Montgomery. The list included only one man who was paroled to Los Angeles a month before the Montgomery slaying. He was interviewed and alibied through cameras at the halfway house he was required to live in. Gustafson took the investigation no further once Herstadt became their primary suspect.

Bosch got up and flipped the record. The band Mingus had put together went into a song called "Perdido." Bosch picked up the album cover and studied it. There were three photos of Mingus, his big arms around his stand-up bass, but none of the pictures fully revealed his face. In one shot his back was to the camera. It was the first time Bosch had noticed this and it was a curious thing. He went to his record stack and flipped through his other Mingus albums. Almost all of them clearly showed his face, including three where he was lighting or smoking a cigar. He wasn't shy in life or on other album covers. The Carnegie Hall album photos were a mystery.

Bosch went back to work, moving on to the second threat from the criminal side of Montgomery's history as a jurist. This one involved a case where a ruling by Montgomery was reversed on appeal and a new trial ordered because of an error the judge had made in his instructions to the jury.

The defendant was Thomas O'Leary, an attorney who had been convicted of two counts of cocaine possession. According to Gustafson's summary of the case, O'Leary was snared in an undercover operation in which a Sheriff's Department deputy posed as a drug dealer, engaged O'Leary to defend him, and paid for his services three different times with quantities of cocaine. Cameras in an undercover car recorded O'Leary receiving the drugs. At trial

O'Leary conceded that he had received the drugs but put forward an entrapment defense, arguing that he had never previously accepted drugs in payment. He also claimed that the government was targeting him in retribution for his defending high-profile clients in other cases brought by the Sheriff's narcotics unit. O'Leary's contention was that he was not predisposed to break the law in such a way until the undercover deputy persuaded him to.

Part of the entrapment instruction Judge Montgomery gave to the jury was that O'Leary could not be convicted if the jury found that he had not been predisposed to commit the crime in the first incident. He erroneously refused to allow an additional instruction requested by the defense that if O'Leary was not convicted in the first incident then he could not be convicted in the following two because they were essentially the fruit of the first offense.

The jury found O'Leary not guilty of the first charge but convicted him on the second two, and Montgomery sentenced him to eleven years in prison. More than a year passed before the appellate court ruled in O'Leary's favor, ordering him released from prison on bail and to face a new trial. The District Attorney's Office decided not to pursue the case a second time and the charges against O'Leary were dropped. By that time he had been disbarred, and divorced by his wife. He was working as a legal assistant in a law firm. During the final hearing at which the charges were dropped and the case dismissed, O'Leary had lashed out at Montgomery, not specifically threatening him with violence but yelling in court that the judge would pay someday for the mistake that cost O'Leary his career, his marriage, and his life savings.

Gustafson and Reyes investigated O'Leary and checked out his alibi, determining that at the exact time of the murder, his employee ID for the law firm he worked at had registered at the security entrance to the company's building. It wasn't a complete alibi because there was no camera at the entrance. But Gustafson and Reyes did not pursue it further after Herstadt became suspect number one.

Bosch wrote a few notes down on a pad—ideas for how he might follow up on both of these tracks. But his gut told him that neither Kirk nor O'Leary was good for the killing, no matter how angry they were at Montgomery. He wanted to move on to the other three tracks to see if they were more viable.

He got up from the table to walk a bit before diving back in. His knee stiffened when he held it in a sitting position too long. He walked out onto the back deck of his house and checked out the view of the Cahuenga Pass. It was only midafternoon but the freeway down below was slow-moving and clogged in both directions. He realized he had worked straight through the morning. He was hungry but decided to put another hour into the case before going down the hill and getting something that would count as both lunch and dinner.

Back inside, the music had stopped and he went to the record stack to make another selection that would keep his momentum up. He decided to stay with a strong bass quarterbacking the band and started flipping through his Ron Carter albums.

He was interrupted by the doorbell.

27

Ballard was at the door.

"I need your help," she said.

Bosch stepped back and let her enter. He then followed her in, noticing that she had a backpack over her shoulder. As she walked past the dining room table, she looked down at the documents stacked in separate piles.

"Is that the Montgomery case?" she asked.

"Uh, yes," Bosch said. "We got a copy of the murder book in discovery. I'm just looking at the other—"

"Great, so you're working here on it."

"Where else would I—"

"No, that's good. I want you to help me from here."

She seemed nervous, ramped up. Bosch wondered if she had slept since finishing her shift.

"What are we talking about here, Renée?" he asked.

"I need you to monitor a wiretap when I'm not able to," she said. "I have the software on my laptop and I can leave it with you."

Bosch paused to gather his thoughts before replying.

"This is in regard to the Hilton case?" he asked.

"Yes, of course," she said. "Our case. You can work on Montgomery, but when a call or text comes in you'll get an alert on my laptop and you just need to monitor it. It'll be good that you have something else to do while monitoring."

She gestured toward the stacks spread on the table.

"Renée," he said. "Is this a legal tap?"

Ballard laughed.

"Of course," she said. "I got the search warrant signed this morning. Then spent the next two hours getting it set up with the providers—a landline and a cell. Text messages included. Then I went to the tech unit and had the software put on my laptop."

"You went to Billy Thornton with this?" Bosch asked.

"Yes, Department 107. What's wrong, Harry?"

"He wouldn't have signed off on this without an approval from the department. I thought this was a case we were working. Now command staff knows about it?"

"I had a captain sign off on it and he won't be a problem for us."

"Who?"

"Olivas."

"What?"

"Harry, all you need to know is that it's a legit wire. We're good to go."

"Does Billy still have the jazz photo on his wall?"

"Jesus Christ, you don't believe me, do you? Ben Webster, okay? 'The Brute and the Beauty.' Happy?"

"'Beautiful.'"

"What?"

"Webster—they called him 'the Brute and the Beautiful.'"

"Whatever. Are you satisfied?"

"Yeah, okay, I'm satisfied."

"I can't believe you'd think I'd forge a search warrant."

Bosch knew he had to change the subject.

"Well, when did Olivas make captain?"

"Just got the bars."

Bosch knew that Olivas was Ballard's nemesis in the department—and she his. He decided he didn't want to know how she got him to sign off on the warrant. Asking her would risk another rift between them.

"So, it's been a long time since I worked a wiretap," he said instead. "We used to have to go out to the wiretap room in Commerce to listen. You're saying I can monitor it from here?"

"Totally," Ballard said. "It's all on the laptop."

Bosch nodded.

"So, who are we listening to?" he asked.

"Elvin Kidd," Ballard said. "Starting tomorrow. I want to get you set up and comfortable on it, and then after my shift tomorrow morning I'm going to go out to Rialto and shake his tree. Hopefully, he'll get on the phone and call or text to ask his old friends in South L.A. what's going on. We get an admission and we'll take him down."

Bosch nodded again.

"You hungry?" he asked.

"Starving," Ballard said.

"Good. Let's get something to eat and talk this through. When was the last time you slept?"

"I don't remember. But we had a deal, remember?"

"Right."

Bosch drove. They went down the hill, crossed the freeway on Barham and over to the Smoke House by the Warner Brothers studio. Ballard reported that she had not eaten anything since a meal break on her last shift. She ordered a steak, a baked potato, and garlic toast to share. Bosch ordered a salad with grilled chicken. Ballard had brought her backpack into the restaurant and while they waited for their food she updated Bosch on her investigation, detailing her interview with Hilton's former roommate, Nathan Brazil, which confirmed that Hilton was gay and in love with an unattainable man.

"It all leads to Kidd," she said. "He owned that alley and he cleared everybody out, set up the meeting with Hilton, and then executed him."

"And the motive?" Bosch asked.

"Pride. He couldn't have this infatuated kid threatening his reputation. Did you look at the phone records in the murder book when you had it?"

"Yes, but just in a cursory way."

"There were several calls from Hilton's apartment line to a pay-phone number in South Central. It was in a shopping plaza at Slauson and Crenshaw, the heart of Rolling 60s turf. The original investigators didn't do anything with it, thought it was a dealer connection, but I think Hilton was calling Kidd there or trying to reach him, and it was becoming a problem for him."

Bosch sat back and considered her theory as their food arrived. Once the waiter was gone, he summarized.

"Forbidden love," he said. "Lovers in prison, but outside that was a threat to Kidd's position and power. It could get him ousted— maybe even killed."

Ballard nodded.

"Nineteen-ninety?" she said. "That wasn't going to go over on the gang streets."

"That wouldn't go over now," Bosch said. "I heard about this case a few years before I quit where guys on a no-knock search warrant hit a stash house and caught a guy from Grape Street in bed with another guy. They used it to turn him into an inside man in five minutes flat. That was more leverage than holding a five-year sentence over his head. They know they can do the time if necessary, come out and be an operator. But nobody wants a gay rap in the gang. They get that and they're done."

They started to eat, both so hungry that they stopped talking. Bosch ran everything through his filters while silent and spoke when his hunger had been pushed back into its cage.

"So, tomorrow," he said. "How are you going to push his buttons?"

"For one, I hope to catch him at home," Ballard answered, her mouth still full with the last bite of her steak. "He's married now and his business is in his wife's name. When I start mentioning Hilton and their prior relationship, I hope he panics. I doubt the wife knows about his gay relationships. I have the sketchbook. I start showing the drawings and he'll shit a brick."

"But how does that get him on the phone? You're making it between him and her."

"What do you suggest, then?"

"I'm not sure yet. But you have to tie it back to the gang."

"I thought about that, but then I put the risk on Dennard Dorsey. He's in the Rolling 60s module at Men's Central. If Kidd gets the word to somebody in there, Dorsey's toast."

"We need to scheme it some other way. Don't use Dorsey."

"There was another guy in the murder book who worked the street with Dorsey: Vincent Pilkey. But he died a few years back."

"That was after Kidd left South Central, right? Think he'd know that Pilkey's dead?"

Ballard shrugged and attacked the garlic toast.

"Hard to say," she answered. "It could be risky using his name. Kidd might see right through the scam."

"He might," Bosch conceded.

He watched her eat the toast. She looked worn down, like a homeless person who had found a pizza crust in a trash can.

"I assume you're going out there without backup," he said.

"There is none," she said. "This is you and me, and I need you on the phones."

"What if I'm nearby? Someplace with Wi-Fi. There's gotta be a Starbucks near whatever place you're going. Or you can show me how to make my phone a hot spot. Maddie does that."

"It's too risky. You lose signal and you lose any calls that get made. I'll be fine. It's an in-and-out operation. I go in, light the fire, I get out. He—hopefully—starts making calls. Maybe texts."

"We still need to figure out how you light the fire."

"I think I just tell him I work cold cases, was assigned this one, and saw that he was never interviewed back in the day. I let it drop that back then there was a witness who described a shooter that looked a lot like him. He'll deny, deny, I'll leave, and my bet is he gets on the phone to try to find out who this witness is."

Bosch thought about that and decided it could work.

"Okay," he said. "Good."

But he knew that if that was the plan, he needed to say something about Ballard's readiness.

"Look, I know we made a deal and all that, but we're talking about a high-risk move here and you need to be ready," he said. "So, I have to say it: you look tired—and you can't be tired when you do this. I think you should put it off until you're ready."

"I am ready," Ballard protested. "And I can't put it off. It's a seventy-two-hour tap. That's all the judge would give me. It starts as soon as the service providers begin sending the signal—which is supposed to be end of day today. So, we have three days to get this going. We can't put it off."

"Okay, okay. Then you take a sick day tonight so you can sleep."

"I'm not doing that either. I'm needed on the late show and I'm not going to leave them high and dry."

"Okay, then we go back to my house. I have a spare room you can use. You sleep on a bed, not sand, until it's time to go to work tonight."

"No. I have too much to do."

"Then that's too bad. You think this guy is safe because he's supposedly not in the gang anymore. Well, he's not safe—he's dangerous. And I'm not going to monitor anything if I think there's something wrong with the setup."

"Harry, you're overreacting."

"No, I'm not. And right now, the thing I think is wrong is you. Sleep deprivation leads to mistakes, sometimes deadly mistakes, and I'm not going to be part of that."

"Look, I appreciate what you're saying but I'm not your daughter."

"I know you're not, and that has nothing to do with this. But what

I said holds. You use the guest room or you can get Olivas to monitor the tap for you."

"Fine. I'll sleep. But I want to take this garlic toast to go."

"Not a problem."

Bosch looked around for the waiter so he could get the check.

28

While Ballard slept, Bosch went back to the Montgomery case. He kept the music off so as not to disturb her. Not knowing when she might get up, he decided to dive into the shortest stack of documents relating to the three remaining cases he needed to review. These emanated from Judge Montgomery's service in civil court during the last two years of his life.

The shortest stack was actually a hybrid case: it involved the judge in both criminal and civil courts. It started with a murder case in which a man named John Proctor was convicted in an intentional hit-and-run of a woman who had been struck while walking to her car after leaving a Burbank bar, where she had rejected several efforts by Proctor to buy her drinks and start a conversation.

Proctor was represented at trial by an attorney named Clayton Manley. Proctor fired him after the conviction and hired an attorney named George Grayson to handle his appeal. Prior to Proctor's sentencing, Grayson filed a motion for a new trial based on ineffective assistance of counsel. It is a routine gambit to request a new trial based on poor lawyering, though it is rarely successful. But in this case the argument had merit. The motion described several things Manley failed to do in prepping for trial, including exploring a third-party culpability defense based on the fact that the victim was in the midst of a bitter divorce at the time of her death and that her estranged husband had been arrested twice for domestic abuse.

The appeal also included several instances at trial when Manley did not ask pertinent questions of prosecution witnesses or had to be prompted by the judge to object to the prosecutor's witness questioning. Twice during the trial while the jury was not in the courtroom Judge Montgomery hammered Manley for his poor performance, one time directly asking him if he was on any medication that could explain his lack of focus on the case.

Manley worked for the downtown law firm of Michaelson & Mitchell, which had taken on the case and then assigned it to Manley to handle. Though he had handled other criminal matters for the firm, it was his first murder case.

In a one-in-a-hundred decision, Montgomery ordered a new trial, revealing his decision at Proctor's scheduled sentencing. In open court he agreed with Grayson's contention that Manley had blown the case with his inattentiveness and inaction. In canceling the sentencing and ordering a new trial, Montgomery went on record with his view of Manley's performance, castigating the lawyer for his many failures and banning him from handling any future cases in his court.

A reporter from the *Los Angeles Times* was in the courtroom, there to report on the sentencing in a case that had drawn significant media attention because of the nature of the crime. Instead, he left with a story about Manley, which when published the next day included many of Judge Montgomery's harshest quotes. Manley quickly became a courthouse whipping boy, the butt of many lawyer jokes traded in courthouse hallways; he soon even garnered the nickname "UnManley."

At the new trial, the jury found John Proctor not guilty. No one else was ever charged in the killing.

Montgomery then was shifted by the chief judge to civil court and soon enough became embroiled in one himself. Clayton Manley sued the judge for defamation, seeking damages for the "unjust and untrue" statements Montgomery had made in court that were then disseminated by the media. Manley claimed in the filing that

Montgomery had turned him into a courthouse pariah and destroyed his career. Manley said he still worked for Michaelson & Mitchell but was no longer assigned criminal cases and had not appeared in court in any capacity since the Proctor case.

The lawsuit was quickly dismissed on the grounds that a judge's rulings and statements in court were not only protected by the First Amendment right to free speech but sacrosanct for the unbiased and unfettered administration of justice in court. Manley appealed the ruling, but higher courts similarly rejected it twice before he dropped the matter.

That was the end of it, but when Montgomery was murdered a year later his clerk gave the name *Clayton Manley* to detectives asking who the judge's enemies might be. Gustafson and Reyes thought enough of it to investigate, and started by reviewing all matters regarding the Proctor case. They saw enough there to proceed to the next level: Reyes interviewed Manley at his office with his own attorney, William Michaelson, present. Manley provided a solid alibi for the morning of the murder. He was in Hawaii on vacation with his wife at a resort on Lanai. Manley gave the detective copies of his boarding passes, hotel and restaurant receipts, and even photos from his iPhone of him on a fishing charter, taken the day Montgomery was murdered. He also provided copies of e-mails from friends and associates, including Michaelson, who reported the murder to him because they knew he was thousands of miles away in Hawaii.

The interview with Manley had occurred a week before the DNA testing came back with the match to Herstadt. It explained why the Manley stack was the shortest. The detectives apparently accepted Manley's denial of involvement and his alibi.

Still, something about the Manley angle bothered Bosch. There was no mention in the chronological record of the interview with Manley having been set up in advance. In fact, that would have been poor form. Investigators routinely approach subjects without warning. It is better to get extemporaneous answers to questions rather than prepared statements. It's a basic rule of homicide work: don't let them see you coming.

But with no indication in the documents that Reyes gave any prior warning that he was coming to talk to Manley, the attorney was apparently prepared for the interview: he had his own attorney present and alibi documentation ready to be turned over. Bosch wondered if that bothered Reyes or Gustafson. Because it bothered him.

True, Manley had had a protracted dispute with Montgomery, so he could probably assume the police would want to talk to him. That wasn't suspicious to Bosch. Even having a lawyer present didn't raise an eyebrow. It was a law firm, after all. But the detail of the alibi was what bothered Bosch the most. It appeared to be bulletproof, right down to his providing the digital time stamp with the Hawaii photo taken just a few minutes before Montgomery was bladed in L.A. It had been Bosch's experience that an alibi—even a legitimate one—was seldom bulletproof. This one felt to Bosch like a setup. Like maybe Manley knew precisely when he would need an alibi.

Gustafson and Reyes apparently didn't feel the same way. A week later they dropped Manley from consideration when the DNA report landed. Bosch didn't think he would have done so, even with a direct DNA match to another suspect.

He wrote a note on his pad. It was just one word: *Manley*. Bosch was comfortable dropping the first two avenues of investigation he had reviewed, but he felt Manley warranted further follow-up.

Bosch got up from the table and worked the stiffness out of his knee. He grabbed the cane he had leaned into a corner next to the front door and went out for a short walk, up the hill for a block and then back down. The knee got loose and felt pretty strong. He looked forward to retiring the cane completely in a few more days.

When he got back inside the house he found Ballard sitting at the table where he had been working.

"Who's Manley?" she said.

"Just a guy, maybe a suspect," Bosch said. "I thought you were going to sleep longer than a couple hours."

"Didn't need to. I feel refreshed. Two hours on a bed is worth five on the sand."

"When are you going to stop doing that?"

"I don't know. I like being by the water. My father used to say that salt water cures everything."

"There are other ways to accomplish that. You might be 'refreshed' now, but by tomorrow morning you're going to be dragging ass when you go off to confront Kidd."

"I'll be fine. I do this all the time."

"That's not reassuring. We have to work out some kind of signal so I can get you backup if you need it. You going in by yourself is crazy."

"I work every night by myself. This is nothing new."

Bosch shook his head. He still wasn't happy.

"Look," Ballard said, "what I want to do now is show you the software on my laptop so you can monitor everything after I go out there and stir up his shit. I'm going to come by in the morning and leave my laptop with you before going out there."

"You can't just transfer it to my computer?" Bosch asked.

"Not possible. It's proprietary. But it will only take a few minutes to bring you up to date on everything. I know you're old school and never did it this way."

"Just show me."

Bosch cleared space on the table so she could sit next to him. She opened the monitoring program.

"Oh good, we're up," she said. "The tap is in place."

"So the seventy-two-hour clock is already ticking," Bosch said.

"Right. But of course nothing said today is going to be worth a shit, since he doesn't even know he's being investigated."

Ballard showed him how to run the software. She set separate alarm tones for Elvin Kidd's cell and landline, which would sound on the computer any time a call came in or went out. There was a third tone for text messages coming in or going out. She reiterated the rules of listening in. By law the police were forbidden from listening to personal calls. If a call was not specifically about the crime documented in the probable cause statement in the search warrant, the listener had to turn off the speaker but was allowed to check in briefly every thirty seconds to confirm the ongoing phone conversation was personal in nature.

The software recorded only what was live-monitored. Calls not listened to were not recorded. This was why a wiretap required around-the-clock monitoring. It had been at least ten years since Bosch had been involved in a wiretap case. The software was all new but the rules had not changed. He told Ballard that he understood all of that.

"What about the fact that I'm not a cop anymore?" he asked. "What if something good comes in after you shake his tree and I'm sitting here by myself?"

"You're still a reserve with San Fernando PD, aren't you?" Ballard asked.

After leaving the LAPD, Bosch had signed on as a reserve at the tiny city in the Valley's police department to work cold cases. But his tenure there had ended almost a year before, when he was accused of cutting too many corners on cases.

"Well, sort of," he said. "They haven't gotten around to taking my badge because there's still a couple cases I worked on that haven't gotten to court. The prosecutors want me to have a badge and be a reserve when I have to testify. So, technically, yes, I'm a reserve officer but I'm not really doing—"

"Doesn't matter. You have a badge, and a reserve is still a sworn officer. We're good. You can do this."

"Okay."

"So, I'll come by in the morning, leave this with you, and you just leave it on while you do your work. And when you hear any of the alarms just start listening and recording until you know what kind of call it is."

"And you'll call me as soon as you're going in."

"Yes."

"And when you're out. When you're clear."

"Roger that. You don't have to worry."

"Somebody does. What about using a couple Rialto PD uniforms for backup? To wait outside while you're inside."

"If you insist, I will do that."

"I insist."

"Okay, I'll call on my way out there, see if they can spare a car."

"Good."

That made Bosch feel better about everything. He just had to make sure in the morning she did as she said she would.

Ballard was reaching for her laptop to close it, when one of the tones she had programmed sounded.

"Ooh, incoming call," she said. "We get to see how this works."

She moved her hand down to the touch screen and slid the cursor to the Record button. They heard a man's voice answer.

"Hello?"

29

It was a collect call from the Men's Central jail. A robot voice informed the recipient that the call was coming from "D-squared," and that he needed to hit the number 1 button to accept the call and the number 2 button to decline it. The call had come in on Elvin Kidd's cell. He accepted the call.

"Yo, E—that you, n____?"

"What you want, boy? I ain't putting up no bail on you, man. I'm out. You know that."

"No, no, no, my n____. I ain't want nothin'—they got me on a parole hold anyway. I just givin' you a heads-up, man."

"About what?"

Ballard grabbed the pad Bosch had written the name *Manley* on, scribbled a note, and slid it in front of Bosch.

D-squared = Dennard Dorsey. Talked to him Tuesday

Bosch nodded. He understood now who was calling Kidd. Kidd and Dorsey couldn't hear them if Ballard and Bosch talked, but they maintained silence because they wanted not to miss anything.

"It's 'bout that thing in the alley way back when, man. Some cop come in here asking all about that thing that happened with that white boy."

"Asking what?"

"Like was I there and what was going on."

"What you tell 'em?"

"I didn't say shit. I wudn't even there. But I thought, you know, I should tell you they still interested, you know what I mean? Keep your head down, n_____."

"When was this?"

"She came up in here Tuesday. They put me in a room with her."

"She?"

"A lady cop. Kind I'd like to see on my bone, too."

"She got a name?"

"Something like Ballet or something. I didn't properly catch it at the start 'cause I was like, *What you want with me, motherfucker?* But she knew some shit, man. She knew me and V-Dog worked that alley back in the day. You remember him? He died up in Folsom or some shit. It's like one of them cold case things, you know?"

"Who told her about me?"

"I 'on't know. She just got up in my shit and asked about you."

"How'd you get this number?"

"I ain't had no number. I had to call a couple OGs to get it. That's why it took me a couple days to get to you."

"Which OG?"

"Marcel. He had a number for—"

"Okay, dog, don't call me no more. I'm outta the game."

"I know that, but I still thought you'd—"

The call was disconnected by Kidd.

Ballard immediately got up from her seat and started pacing.

"Holy shit," she said. "Dorsey just did what I was going to drive out there and do tomorrow."

"But Kidd didn't give anything up," Bosch cautioned. "He was careful."

"True, but he asked a lot of questions. We got the right guy. It's him and we were fucking lucky the wire got set up already. But now what? Do I still go out there tomorrow?"

"No way. He'll be ready for you and you don't want that."

Ballard nodded while she paced the living room.

"Can you play it again?" Bosch asked.

Ballard came back to the table and replayed the call. Bosch listened closely for anything that might sound like a code passed between the two old gangbangers. But he concluded that Kidd had taken the call out of the blue and there had been no secret message or code imparted. As Dorsey had said, he was simply passing on a warning about a potentially threatening situation.

"What do you think?" Ballard asked.

Bosch thought a moment.

"I think we wait and see if Kidd makes a move," he said.

"But now that he knows about the investigation he may go off-line," Ballard said. "He'll go buy a burner. I would if I were him."

"I could go out and watch him tonight."

"I'm going with you."

"That won't work. It's two hours out there easy with rush hour and you have your shift you said you can't miss. You'd have to turn around almost as soon as we got there. I'll go and you monitor the wire, just in case he's stupid."

The text-message tone sounded from Ballard's laptop.

"Speaking of which," she said.

She pulled up the message. It was outgoing from Kidd's phone.

Need to meet. Dulan's at 1 tomoro. Important!!!!

They both stared at the screen, waiting for a reply.

"You think it's the *Marcel* that Dorsey mentioned?" Ballard asked.

"I don't know," Bosch said. "Probably."

A short reply came through.

I'll be there.

Bosch got up from the table to loosen his knee again.

"I guess if we figure out who Dulan is, we could set up on him tomorrow," he said.

"Dulan's is a soul food kitchen," Ballard said. "Good stuff. But there's at least three of them that I know of in South L.A."

Bosch nodded, impressed by her knowledge.

"Any of them in Rolling 60s turf?" he asked.

"There's one on Crenshaw in the fifties," Ballard said.

"That's probably it. You eat there? Will we stand out if we're in there?"

"You will. But I can pass for high yellow."

It was true. Ballard was mixed race—part Polynesian for sure, though Bosch had never asked about her ancestry.

"So, you inside and me outside," he said. "Not sure I like that."

"They're not going to make a move in a crowded restaurant," Ballard said. "At one o'clock that place will be hopping."

"Then how would you even get close to them to hear anything?"

"I'll figure it out."

"You gotta dress down."

"What? Why?"

"Because of what D-squared told him on the call—that you were a looker."

"Not exactly what he said. But I take the point. I'll go get a couple hours on the beach after work and I'll come dressed down. Don't worry."

"Maybe we should call in the troops. Go to your lieutenant, tell him what you've been doing, get more bodies on this."

"I go in with a homicide and it will be taken off me faster than a pickpocket takes a wallet on the Venice boardwalk."

Bosch nodded. He knew she was right. He pointed to her laptop.

"At work tonight, can you trace that number he texted to, find out who it is?"

"I can try but it's probably a burner."

"I don't know. Kidd's been out of the game. He used his own cell to text—that was a mistake. Out of the game might mean he's got no burner. And people still in the game have burners and change them all the time. But this is a number Kidd had—that he knew. It might be a legit phone."

Ballard nodded.

"Maybe," she said. "I'll see if I can run it down."

Bosch moved to the sliding door and opened it, then stepped out onto the deck. Ballard followed him.

"Amazing view," she said.

"I like it best at night," Bosch said. "The lights and everything. Even makes the freeway look pretty."

Ballard laughed.

"You know, we still don't know why John Jack had this murder book or why he sat on it for twenty years," Bosch said.

Ballard came up to the deck railing next to him. "Does it matter? We have a bead on the doer. And we have opportunity and motive."

"It matters to me," Bosch said. "I want to know."

"I think we'll get there," Ballard said. "We'll figure it out."

Bosch just nodded, but he was doubtful. They—Ballard mostly—had accomplished in a week what John Jack had not been able to do in two decades. Bosch was beginning to subscribe to Ballard's theory that there was something sinister about it—that John Jack Thompson took the murder book because he didn't want the case solved.

And that created a whole new mystery to think about. And a painful one at that.

BALLARD

30

Ballard started her shift at the Watch Three roll call. Nothing had been left in her inbox by day-watch detectives so she went upstairs to roll call to get a take on what was happening out on the street. Lieutenant Washington was holding forth at the podium, another sign that it was shaping up as a slow night. He usually had a sergeant handle roll call while he remained in the watch office monitoring what was happening outside.

Washington called out the teams and their assigned reporting districts.

"Meyer, Shuman: six-A-fifteen."

"Doucette and Torborg: six-A-forty-five."

"Travis and Marshall, you've got forty-nine tonight."

And so on. He announced that State Farm was continuing its stolen-car program, awarding uniform pins to officers who recovered five stolen cars or more during the monthlong campaign. He mentioned that some of the officers in roll call had reached five already and some were stalled at three or four. He wanted shift-wide compliance. Otherwise there was not much out there to talk about. Roll call ended with a warning from the watch commander:

"I know these nights have been slow out there but it will pick up. It always does," Washington said. "I don't want anybody submarining. Remember, this isn't like the old days. I've got your GPS markers on my screen. I see anybody circling the fort, they're going to get the three-one for next DP."

Submarining was a team leaving their assigned patrol area and cruising close to the station so they could return quickly when the shift was over, and the call went out that the first watch teams were down and heading out. Six-A-thirty-one, the patrol area farthest from the station, consisted mostly of East Hollywood, where nuisance calls—homeless and drunk and disorderly—were more frequent. Nobody wanted to work the three-one, especially for a twenty-eight-day deployment period (DP), so it was usually assigned to someone on the watch commander's shit list.

"All right, people," Washington said. "Let's get out there and do good work."

The meeting broke up but Renée stayed seated so she could speak to Washington after the uniformed officers left the room. He saw her waiting and knew the score.

"Ballard, what's up?"

"L-T, you got anything for me?"

"Not yet. You got something going?"

"I got a couple leftover things from last night, a phone number I need to trace. Let me know when I'm needed."

"Roger that, Ballard."

Ballard went back down the stairs and into the detective bureau, where she set up in a corner as usual. She opened her laptop and pulled up the wiretap software on the off chance that Elvin Kidd decided to make a phone call or send a midnight tweet. She knew it was probably a long shot but the clock was ticking on the seventy-two-hour wiretap, so it couldn't hurt to keep the channel open in case she got lucky again.

She set to work tracing the number that Kidd had sent the text to after receiving the jail call from Dennard Dorsey. Her first step was just to run it through a Google database containing a reverse phone directory. That produced nothing. A search on Lexis/Nexis was also fruitless, indicating the number was unlisted. She next signed into the department database and ran a search to see if the number had ever been entered into a crime report or other document collected by the department. This time she got lucky. The number had turned up on a field interview card four years earlier. It had been digitized in the department-wide database and she was able to call it up on the workstation's computer screen.

The field interview was conducted by a South Bureau gang intel team that had stopped to talk to a man loitering outside a closed restaurant at Slauson and Keniston Avenues. Ballard pegged this location as just on the border between Los Angeles and Inglewood — and firmly in Rolling 60s territory. The man's name was Marcel Dupree. He was fifty-one years old and, though he denied membership in a gang, he had a tattoo of the Crips' six-pointed star on the back of his left hand.

According to the FI card, Dupree told the officers who stopped him that he was waiting to be picked up by a girlfriend because he'd had too much to drink. Seeing that no crime had been committed, they filled in an FI card — including cell phone number, home address, birth date, and other details — and left the man where they had found him.

Ballard next entered Marcel Dupree's name into the crime index computer and pulled up a record of numerous arrests and at least two convictions dating back thirty-three years. Dupree had served two prison terms, one for armed robbery and the other for discharging a firearm into an occupied dwelling. What was more important than all of that was that there was a felony warrant out for Dupree for not paying child support. It wasn't much, but Ballard now had something she could try to squeeze him with if necessary.

She spent the next hour pulling up individual arrest reports and more than once found descriptions of Dupree that called him a shot caller in the Rolling 60s Crips. The child support beef had gone to a felony warrant because Dupree owed more than $100,000 in child support to two different women going back three years.

Ballard was excited. She had just connected two of the dots in the

Kidd investigation, and she had something on Dupree she might be able to use to further the investigation. She felt like telling Bosch but guessed he might be asleep. She downloaded the most recent DMV shot of Dupree, which was four years old, along with his last mug shot, which was a decade older. In both he had a perfectly round head and bushy, unkempt hair. Ballard included both photos in a text to Bosch. She wanted him to know what Dupree looked like before they set up their surveillance operation the next day.

She didn't know whether Bosch had a text chime set on his phone but there was no reply after five minutes. She picked up the rover she had taken from a charger at the start of shift and radioed Lieutenant Washington that she was taking a code 7—a meal break—but would have her rover with her as usual. She walked through the station's deserted back lot to her city car and headed out.

There was an all-night taco truck in a parking lot at Sunset and Western. Ballard ate there often and knew Digoberto Rojas, the man who operated it. She liked to practice her Spanish on him, more often than not confusing him with her mix of Spanish and English.

This night he was working alone and Ballard asked him in halting Spanish where his son was. The young man had worked with his father most nights until recently. The last two or three times Ballard had gone to the truck, Digoberto was working alone. This concerned her because it made him a more vulnerable target. They spoke through the truck's counter window as Digoberto made her a pair of shrimp tacos.

"He lazy," Digoberto said. "He want to hang out all day with his *vatos*. Then he say he too tired to come to work."

"You want me to come talk to him," Ballard said, dropping the Spanish. "I will."

"No, is okay."

"Digoberto, I don't like you working out here at night by yourself. It's dangerous working alone."

"What about you? You alone."

"It's different."

She lifted the flap on her jacket to show the gun holstered on her hip. Then she held up the rover.

"I call, my friends come running," she said.

"The police, they protect me," Digoberto said. "Like you."

"We can't be here all the time. I don't want to get a call and find out you got robbed or hurt. If your son won't help you, then find somebody who will. You really need to."

"Okay, okay. Here you are."

He handed her a paper plate through the counter window. Ballard's tacos were on it, wrapped in foil. She handed a ten through the window and Digoberto held his hands up like he was under arrest.

"No, no, for you," he said. "I like you. You bring other police here."

"No, but you need to make a living. That's not fair."

She put the bill down on the counter and refused to take it back. She carried her plate over to a folding table where there were a variety of hot sauces and napkins. She grabbed napkins and a bottle of the mild sauce and went to the communal picnic table that was empty at the moment.

Ballard ate facing Sunset Boulevard and with her back to the taco truck. The tacos were delicious and she didn't bother with the sauce on the second one. Before she was finished, Digoberto came out of the truck through the back door of the kitchen and brought her another taco.

"*Mariscos,*" he said. "You try."

"You're going to make me *el gordo,*" she said. "*Pero gracias.*"

She took a bite of the fish taco and found it to be just as good as the shrimp. But it was milder and she put on hot sauce. Her next bite was better but she never got a third. Her rover squawked and Washington sent her to a traffic stop on Cahuenga beneath the 101 freeway overpass. It was no more than five minutes away. Ballard asked Washington why a detective was needed and he simply said, "You'll see."

Since she had heard no call earlier from patrol or dispatch concerning that location, Ballard knew that whatever it was, they were keeping it off the radio. Plenty of media gypsies in the city listened to police frequencies and responded to anything that might produce a sellable video.

Ballard waved her thanks to Digoberto, who was back in his truck, tossed her plates into a trash can, and got in her car. She took Sunset to Cahuenga and headed north toward the 101. She saw a single patrol car with its roof lights flashing behind an old van that advertised twenty-four-hour rug cleaning on its side panels. Ballard didn't have time to wonder about who would need rug cleaning in the middle of the night. One of the patrol officers who had stopped the van came toward her car, flashlight in hand. It was Rich Meyer, whom she had seen earlier at roll call.

Ballard killed the engine and exited the car.

"Rich, whaddaya got?"

"This guy in the van, he must've gotten off the freeway and pulled under here so that the women he had in the back could take care of business. Me and Shoo come passing through and there's four women squatting on the sidewalk."

"Squatting?"

"Urinating! It looks like human trafficking, but nobody's got ID and nobody's speaking English."

Ballard started toward the van where Meyer's partner, Shuman, was standing with a man and four women, all of them with hands bound behind their back with zip ties. The women wore short dresses and appeared disheveled. They all had dark hair and were clearly Latina. None looked older than twenty.

Ballard pulled her mini-light off her belt and first pointed the beam through the open rear doors of the van. There was a mattress and some ragged blankets strewn across it. A couple of plastic bags were filled with clothes. The van smelled of body odor and desperation.

She moved the light forward and saw a phone in a dashboard cradle. It had a GPS map glowing on it. Moving around the van to the driver's door, she opened it, leaned in, and pulled the phone out of its holder. By tapping the screen she was able to determine the van's intended destination: an address on Etiwanda Street in the Valley. She put the phone in her pocket and went over to where Meyer and Shuman were standing with the detainees.

"Who do we have working tonight that has Spanish?" Ballard asked.

"Uh, Perez is on—she's in the U-boat," Meyer said. "And Basinger is fluent."

Ballard now remembered seeing both officers at roll call. She knew Perez pretty well, plus she thought a woman would be better for interviewing the four females. If she was working the U-boat, which is what they called a single-officer car that only took reports on minor crimes, calling her would not pull her off active patrol. She raised her rover and requested that Officer Perez roll to the scene. Perez came back with a roger and an ETA of eight minutes.

"We should just call ICE and be done with this," Shuman said.

Ballard shook her head.

"No, we're not doing that," she said.

"That's the protocol," Shuman insisted. "They're obviously illegals—we call ICE."

Ballard saw that Shuman had one bar on his uniform sleeve. Five years on the job. She looked at Meyer, who had four bars on his sleeve. He was standing slightly behind Shuman. He rolled his eyes so only Ballard would see. It was a sign that he wasn't going to cause Ballard any grief on this.

"I'm the detective," Ballard said. "I have control of this investigation. We're not calling ICE. If you have a problem with that, Shuman, you can get back in your car and go back out on patrol. I'll handle it from here."

Shuman averted his eyes and shook his head.

"We call ICE, they get sent back and then they do it again," Ballard said. "They go through all the rape and horrors they went through getting here the first time."

"That's not our concern," Shuman said.

"Maybe it should be," Ballard said.

"Hey, Shoo," Meyer said. "I got this here. Why don't you go back to the shop and start the incident report."

The *shop* was the patrol car. Shuman walked off without another word and got in the passenger side of the patrol car. Ballard saw him roughly swing the MDT on its swivel toward him so he could start to type in his incident report.

"I hope he spells my name right," Ballard said.

"I'm sure he will," Meyer said.

Perez got there two minutes early. With her translating, Ballard first questioned the driver, who claimed to know only that he was paid to take the four young women to a party. He said he did not remember where he picked them up or who had paid him. Ballard had Meyer put him in the back of his patrol car and transport him to the Hollywood Station jail, where she would later file paperwork arresting him for human trafficking.

The four women found their voices after the driver was gone from the scene. Through Perez they one by one told stories that were sad and horrible, yet typical of such journeys made by desperate people. They had traveled from Oaxaca, Mexico, and were smuggled across the border in an avocado truck with a secret compartment, each forced to pay for the trip by having sex with several of the men involved. Once across in Calexico they were placed in the van, told they owed thousands of dollars more for the remaining trip, and driven north to Los Angeles. They did not know what awaited them at the address on Etiwanda in the Valley but Ballard did: sexual servitude in gang-operated brothels where they would never break even and would never be missed should they stop earning and their masters decide to bury them in the desert.

After calling for a police tow for the van, Ballard made a call to a battered-woman's clinic in North Hollywood, where she had delivered women before. She spoke to her contact and explained the situation. The woman agreed to take in the four Mexican women and see that they were medically treated and given beds and fresh clothes. In the morning, they would be counseled on their options: returning home voluntarily or seeking asylum based on the threat that the group that procured them would seek to harm them should they go back to Mexico. Neither choice was good. Ballard knew that many hardships awaited the women.

After a flatbed from the police garage arrived to impound the van, Ballard and Perez each took two of the women in their cars to the shelter in North Hollywood.

Ballard did not get back to the station until five a.m. She wrote up the arrest report on the driver of the van, using the name Juan Doe because he still refused to identify himself. That was okay with Ballard. She knew his fingerprint would provide his ID if he had had any previous engagement with U.S. law enforcement. She thought the chances of that were good.

The department had a human trafficking task force operating out of the PAB. Ballard put together a package on the case and put it into the transit box to be delivered downtown first thing. It was one of the few times she didn't mind passing on a case, as late-show protocol dictated. Human trafficking was one of the ugliest crimes she encountered as a detective and it left scars as well as drew up memories of her own past, when she'd been left alone on the streets of Honolulu as a fourteen-year-old.

She left the station at seven a.m. and headed toward her van. She knew she had to be in the Crenshaw District by noon at the latest to be on-site and ready to shadow the meeting between Elvin Kidd and Marcel Dupree. But at the moment she needed the beach. As tired as she was, she wasn't planning to sleep. She needed to get her dog and get out on the water to push herself against the current. To dig deep with the paddle until she had exhausted her body and mind and nothing could get in to haunt her.

BOSCH

31

Bosch had risen early to complete his assessment of the five investigative tracks abandoned in the Montgomery murder case. He wanted to finish before he needed to leave the house to back up Ballard at Dulan's soul food restaurant.

The night before, after Ballard had left, he had reviewed the fourth branch of the investigation and found that it needed follow-up. It revolved around a ruling Judge Montgomery had made in a civil dispute. It started when a Sherman Oaks man named Larry Cassidy began marketing a lunch box that he claimed to have invented. The lunch box had insulated hot and cold compartments, but what made it stand out was its clear plastic window on the inside of the lid; a parent could slip a note or photo behind it for their child to see at school lunchtime.

Sales of the lunch box were moderate until Cassidy's wife, Melanie, started appearing on the Home Shopping Network cable channel to hawk the boxes for $19.95 each. She was going to the HSN studios in Tampa, Florida, twice a month to sell the boxes and was moving thousands of them during each appearance. Cost of manufacture was low and after HSN's cut, the couple were making almost $200,000 a month. That's when Cassidy's ex-wife, Maura Frederick, demanded a share for being the one who designed the box while still married to Cassidy and raising their son, Larry Jr.

Cassidy refused to share even a small percentage of the income generated by the so-called Love for Lunch box and Frederick sued him. He countersued, claiming her suit was a malicious money grab for something she had no right to.

At an evidentiary hearing, Judge Montgomery had both sides proffer their stories on the inspiration for the product's invention. Cassidy provided original drawings dated well after his divorce from Frederick, as well as the patent application he had filed, and receipts from a plastic manufacturer that produced the first mock-ups of the colorful lunch boxes from the design sketches.

Frederick produced only a notarized statement from her son, Larry Jr., now seventeen years old, in which he said he remembered finding notes and cards and drawings from his mother in the Star Wars lunch box he carried to school as a young boy.

Montgomery dismissed Frederick's lawsuit and held for Larry Sr., ruling that while Frederick's actions of long ago certainly might have inspired the Love for Lunch invention, her involvement stopped there; she took on none of the risks or creative aspects in the manufacture and sales of the product. He likened it to someone who used to prop their phone against a book or other object for viewing the screen suing the manufacturer of phone attachments that prop the devices for viewing. Frederick could not be the only parent who ever put a note in a lunch box for their child.

It all seemed cut-and-dried and Bosch initially wondered why the case was included as a potential avenue of investigation in the Montgomery murder. But then he read a report stating that Larry Cassidy Sr. and his new wife, the public face of Love for Lunch, had been found murdered in Tampa, where they had gone to tape an HSN spot. The couple were found shot to death in a rental car in the empty parking lot of a country club, not far from a restaurant where they enjoyed dining while in town. Both had been shot in the back of the head by someone who had been in the back seat of the car. It was not a high-crime district and the assassinations remained unsolved as of the time Montgomery was murdered in Los Angeles.

A copy of a probate filing in the case documents showed that Larry Jr. was the heir to his father and to the money earned by the Love for Lunch business. Larry Jr. still lived in the home of his mother, Maura Frederick.

LAPD detectives Gustafson and Reyes included the case in their list of potential avenues of investigation under the theory that if Frederick was involved in the murder of her ex-husband and his new wife, her anger toward the couple might have also extended to the judge who ruled against her. They made initial efforts to interview Maura Frederick, but those efforts were blocked by an attorney representing Frederick and then dropped altogether when Herstadt was arrested and charged in the judge's murder.

Bosch put the name *Maura Frederick* on his list beneath the name *Clayton Manley.* He thought she should be given a fuller look.

Now, with a mug of morning coffee on the table before him, Bosch took up the final strand of the original investigation. This was the third civil action that had caught the investigators' attention. It again involved a lawsuit and a countersuit. This time the dispute was between a well-known Hollywood actor and his longtime agent. The actor accused the agent of embezzling millions of dollars over his career, and now that that career was on the wane, he wanted a full accounting and the return of everything that was stolen.

A Hollywood dispute would not normally become the stuff of murder investigations, but the actor's lawsuit contained allegations that the agent was a front for an organized-crime family—and that he had used his position in Hollywood to siphon money from clients and launder it through investments in film productions. The actor said he had been threatened with violence by the agent and his associates, including a visit to his home—the address of which was a carefully guarded secret—by a man who said the actor would get acid thrown in his face and his career ruined if he persisted with the lawsuit or attempted to change agents.

In a case that spanned the entire three years that Montgomery occupied his bench in civil court, the judge ultimately ruled in favor of the actor, awarding damages of $7.1 million and voiding the contract between actor and agent. The case was included in the Montgomery murder investigation because at one point in the long proceedings Montgomery reported to court authorities that his wife's pet cat had turned up dead in their front yard by what appeared to be foul play. The animal had been slashed open from front legs to back and did not appear to have injuries that could be attributed to a coyote, even though Montgomery and his wife lived in the Hollywood Hills.

An investigation of the incident pointed toward the dispute between the actor and his agent because of the threats alleged in the action by the actor. But no connection was found between the cat killing and the case, or any other case Montgomery was handling.

Gustafson and Reyes put the case on their list of possibles but carried it no further. Bosch agreed that it was the least likely of the five tracks of potential investigation. Despite the fact that the actor won a rich settlement and the dissolution of his contract with the agent, no harm had come to him in the time since the case was resolved and he had made no complaint of further threats. It seemed unlikely that anyone would go after Montgomery while leaving the actor alone and paying him the awarded judgment.

Bosch was now finished with his review of the murder book and had only two names on his follow-up list: Clayton Manley, the attorney Montgomery had publicly embarrassed, and Maura Frederick, to whom the judge had denied creative and financial rights in the Love for Lunch product.

He wasn't particularly fired up about either one. They bore a further look, but both were long shots and the individuals involved did not nearly reach the level of suspect in Bosch's mind.

And then there were the aspects of the case (and even possible suspects) *not* included in the discovery version of the murder book. Bosch had been on both sides of this. A murder book was the bible.

It was sacred, yet there was something ingrained in every homicide detective to hold back and not give everything you've got to a defense attorney. He had to assume that Gustafson and Reyes had acted in such a way. But knowing that meant nothing. After what Gustafson had said to Bosch in court after the Herstadt case was dismissed, would he be willing to reveal anything else about the case to him? Would Reyes?

Bosch was pretty sure the answer was a resounding no. But he had to make the call or he would never know for sure.

He still remembered the main number at Robbery-Homicide Division by heart. He expected that he always would. He punched it in on his cell phone and when the call went through to the secretary he asked for Detective Lucia Soto. He was immediately connected.

"Lucky Lucy," he said. "It's Bosch."

"Harry," she said, with a smile he could hear in her voice. "A voice from the past."

"Come on, it hasn't been that long, has it?"

"Seems like it."

Soto was Bosch's last partner in the LAPD. It had been more than three years since he had retired, but they had crossed paths several times since.

"So I should be whispering," Soto said. "You're sort of persona non grata around here these days."

"Is that because of the Montgomery case?" Bosch asked.

"You guessed that right."

"That's the reason I'm calling. I've gotta make a run at Gustafson and Reyes. They might have dropped the case because they think they had the right guy. But me, not so much. I'm still working at it and I don't know either one of them. Which one of them do you think would be more receptive to a call from me?"

There was a short silence before Soto responded.

"Hmm," she said. "That's a good question. I think the answer would be neither one of them. But if my life depended on it, I would try Orlando. He's more even and he wasn't lead. Gussy was and he's taken what happened pretty hard. If he had a dartboard at his desk he'd have your photo on it."

"Okay," Bosch said. "Good to know. Do you see Reyes in the squad right now?"

"Uh…yes. He's at his desk."

"What about Gustafson?"

"No. No sign of him."

"You wouldn't have a direct line for Reyes handy, would you?"

"There's always a catch with you, Harry, isn't there?"

"What catch? I'm just looking for a phone number, no big deal."

Soto gave him the number and followed it with a question.

"So, what's it like working for the other side?"

"I'm not working for the other side. I'm doing this thing right now for myself. That's it."

His tone must have been too strident. Soto backed off with the small talk and asked in a perfunctory tone if there was anything else Bosch needed.

"No," Bosch said. "But I appreciate your help. Who you working with these days?"

"I'm with Robbie Robins. You know him?"

"Yeah, he's a good man. Sound detective, reliable. You like him?"

"Yeah, Robbie's okay. I like his style and we've cracked a couple good ones."

"Still working cold cases?"

"As long as they let us. Word is the new chief wants to close down cold case, put more people on the street."

"That would be a shame."

"Tell me about it."

"Well, good luck, Lucia. And thanks."

"Anytime."

They disconnected and Bosch looked at the phone number he had just written down for Detective Orlando Reyes. He didn't think Soto would give him a heads-up about Bosch calling but he decided to call right away.

"Robbery-Homicide Division, Detective Reyes. How can I help you?"

"You can start by not hanging up. This is Harry Bosch."

"Bosch. I *should* hang up. You want my partner, not me."

"I talked to your partner. I want to talk to you now."

"I got nothin' to say to you, man."

"You and Gustafson, you still think you had the right guy?"

"We know we did."

"So you're not working it any longer."

"Case is closed. We didn't get the result we wanted—thanks to you. But the case is CBA."

"So then where's the harm in talking to me?"

"Bosch, I got here after you left but I heard about you. I know you fought the good fight and did some good work. But that's in the past now. You're history and I gotta go."

"Answer one question."

"What?"

"What did you hold back?"

"What are you talking about?"

"In discovery. I got the murder book you two turned over but you held something back. It always happens. What was it?"

"Goodbye, Bosch."

"You know Clayton Manley's alibi was cooked, right?"

There was a pause and Bosch was no longer worried about Reyes hanging up.

"What are you talking about?"

"He knew Montgomery was going to get hit, so he goes to Hawaii and keeps receipts for every penny he spent. Lots of selfies, including one predawn on the charter boat—within an hour of the judge getting hit. That didn't strike you guys as bullshit?"

"Bosch, I'm not talking about the case with you. You want to go after Clayton Manley, have fun. But don't expect us to back you on it. You're on your own."

"What about Maura Frederick? Pretty little wife number two selling Maura's invention and making millions? If that isn't motive, I don't know what is."

Bosch heard Reyes laughing over the phone. Bosch had been trying to get a rise out of him with his provocative statements, but he wasn't expecting laughter.

"You think it's funny?" Bosch said. "You're letting her get away with murder."

"I guess this is what happens when you don't have a badge no more," Reyes said. "Check your computer, Bosch. Google it. Tampa PD cleared that murder a month ago and Maura Frederick had nothing to do with it. You owe me, man. I just saved you some big-time embarrassment."

Bosch seethed with humiliation. He should have checked the Florida case for an update before throwing it in Reyes's face. He managed to gather himself and throw back something else.

"No, Reyes, you still owe me," Bosch said. "I saved you from convicting an innocent man."

"Bullshit, Bosch," Reyes said. "A killer walks free because of what you and that asshole lawyer Haller have done. But it doesn't matter because we're done here."

Reyes disconnected and Bosch was left holding a dead phone to his ear.

32

Bosch got up from the table and went into the kitchen to make more coffee. He was still stinging from the rebuke Reyes had hit him with. He had no doubt about his actions regarding Jeffrey Herstadt, but it stung when a representative of the police department he had invested three decades of his life in dismissed him so harshly.

A killer walks free because of you.

Those words hurt enough for Bosch to want to take another look at his actions to see if he had taken a wrong turn somewhere.

He checked his watch. He had an hour before he needed to get on the road to meet with Ballard. She had sent a message setting a rendezvous point at a gas station before she would go into Dulan's to spy on the meeting between Elvin Kidd and Marcel Dupree.

Bosch refilled his cup and went back to the dining room table. He decided he would do exactly what Reyes suggested: he would Google the Tampa case and get the latest update.

Before he got the chance, his cell phone buzzed. It was Mickey Haller.

"About that thing we talked about at lunch during the trial," he said, "when do you want to do the video?"

Bosch's mind was so deep into his review of the Montgomery investigation that he had no idea what Haller was talking about.

"What video?" he asked.

"Remember, CML?" Haller said. "Chronic myeloid leukemia? I

want to take a video deposition with you and get rolling on that, send out a demand letter with the video."

Now Bosch remembered.

"Uh, it's gotta wait a bit," he said.

"Why is that?" Haller said. "I mean, you came to me with it. You know, make sure Maddie is covered. Now it's gotta wait?"

"Just a bit. I have two different cases I'm working. I don't have time to sit for a video. Give me about a week."

Bosch thought of something as he mentioned the cases.

"It's your life," Haller said. "I'm here when you're ready."

"Hey, listen," Bosch said. "I don't know if this will happen but I might end up going to see another lawyer. Not because I want to hire him but I want him to think I do. I might mention this case—the CML thing—and he might ask why I chose him. All right if I tell him you recommended him? Then if he checks with you, you cover for me and let me know."

"I don't know what the fuck you're talking about."

"It's complicated. His name is Clayton Manley. All you need to do if he calls is say yes, you recommended him to me."

"*Clayton Manley*—why is that name familiar?"

"He was an early-on suspect in the Montgomery killing."

"Oh, yeah. I knew it. You're working that case, aren't you? You think Manley's the killer?"

Bosch was now regretting having brought up the half-formed idea.

"I'm reviewing the murder book—at least what you got in discovery," he said. "I may want to size up Manley with a ruse. That's where you would come in."

"The case is over, Harry," he said. "We won!"

"*You* won, but the case isn't over. I have it directly from the LAPD that they aren't doing anything with it because they still say it was Herstadt. It's *case closed* over there and that means nobody's doing a damn thing to find the real killer."

"Except you now. You're a dog with a bone, Bosch."

"Whatever. Are we good on the Manley thing? In case it happens?"

"We're good. Just don't hire him for real."

"Don't worry. I won't."

They disconnected and Bosch got back to his Google search. He quickly found and pulled up a story from the *Tampa Bay Times* on the arrest of two suspects in the killing of Larry and Melanie Cassidy.

Two Arrested in Palma Ceia Murders
By Alex White, Staff Writer

Two men were arrested Thursday in the double slaying of a California couple who were found shot to death execution-style in a car parked at the Palma Ceia Country Club last February.

At a press conference at the Tampa Police Department, Chief Richard "Red" Pittman announced the arrests of Gabriel Cardozo and Donald Fields in the slayings of Larry and Melanie Cassidy on February 18. Both men are being held without bail pending arraignment on the charges.

Pittman said the killings were motivated by money. Larry Cassidy was known to have been carrying at least $42,000 in cash that he had won earlier that day at the Hard Rock Resort & Casino. Pittman said the suspects abducted the couple in their own car and had them drive to a darkened corner of the empty parking lot of the Palma Ceia Country Club, which is closed on Mondays. They forced Larry Cassidy to turn over the cash he was carrying as well as jewelry both victims were wearing. It was believed that Cardozo then executed the couple with shots to the back of the head.

"It was cold-blooded," Pittman said. "They got what they wanted—the money and jewelry—but then they killed them anyway. It was heartless. The indications from the crime scene are that the victims put up no resistance."

Pittman said Cardozo was believed to have been the shooter. The police chief praised the work of Detectives Julio Muniz and

George Companioni in bringing the case to closure. According to Pittman, the two detectives solved the case by painstakingly back-tracing the movements of the doomed couple throughout the days before the murders.

Muniz and Companioni learned that the Cassidy couple had arrived from Los Angeles on Sunday, Feb. 17, for an appearance by Melanie Cassidy on the Home Shopping Network scheduled for the following Tuesday afternoon. Melanie Cassidy regularly hosted a sales segment regarding a unique student lunch box that she and her husband had created. The two had been to Tampa on several prior occasions and routinely stayed at the Hard Rock because they enjoyed the casino. They were also regulars at Bern's Steakhouse.

Pittman stated that the Hard Rock security team was fully cooperative with the investigation. Muniz and Companioni were able to use casino surveillance cameras to trace the couple's movements during the day of the killings. They were seen gambling and winning a jackpot on one of the progressive play tables, meaning that a community pot continually grows in value as gamblers from all connected tables play. Certain winning hands draw a percentage of winnings from the progressive pot. Larry Cassidy won a $42,000 jackpot and cashed in the casino check he received after the win.

Pittman said they also observed two men in the casino watching the couple's movements after the jackpot win. The two men, later identified as Cardozo and Fields, were traced by the detectives as well. It is believed, according to the investigators, that they followed the Cassidy couple when they left the casino to celebrate their winnings during a dinner at Bern's. In an earlier report, the *Times* spoke with James Braswell, who served the couple. He said the couple were regulars but that Monday night they were more celebratory than usual, buying a bottle of expensive champagne and even sharing it with a couple at a nearby table.

Pittman said that after dinner the couple left the restaurant and drove toward Bayshore Boulevard on their way back to their hotel. At the red light at Howard Avenue and Bayshore, they were rear-ended by the car behind them. When Larry Cassidy got out to check for damage to his rental car, he was confronted by Cardozo, who showed he had a handgun in his belt. He ordered Cassidy back into his car and then got into the back seat behind him. The Cassidy car then proceeded to Palma Ceia on MacDill Avenue, with Fields following in the suspects' car. The killings occurred shortly after the car was parked.

Cardozo and Fields were identified through a facial recognition program used to analyze the Hard Rock surveillance videos. The process took more than two weeks and was conducted by the Florida Department of Law Enforcement. The suspects were then traced to separate apartments in Tampa Heights, where they were living under false names and paying cash for rent.

A team of officers directed by Lt. Greg Stout, of the Special Operations Unit, made simultaneous raids on the apartments early Thursday, and both men were arrested without incident. Stout said at the press conference that a gun believed to have been the murder weapon was found hidden in Cardozo's apartment.

"We have no doubt that these are the right guys," Stout said.

Muniz and Companioni appeared at the press conference but did not address the media. When contacted by phone later, Companioni said, "This guy, Cardozo, is a piece of [expletive] and that's all I have to say."

The suspects are scheduled to be arraigned tomorrow at the Hillsborough County Courthouse.

Bosch read through the story a second time and came away as convinced as the Tampa police apparently were. Reading between the lines, he guessed that Fields had flipped and was hoping to avoid a murder charge by laying the killings squarely on his partner,

Cardozo. It seemed obvious that someone was talking or they would not have had the details about the fender bender and the abduction at the traffic light.

Other stories followed in the weeks after the arrest story, but Bosch didn't need to read them. What he knew already scratched Maura Frederick off his list.

But Clayton Manley was still on it, and Orlando Reyes had not said anything about him when he rejected talking to Bosch earlier.

Bosch grabbed his phone and hit Redial. This time he decided on a different tack with Reyes.

The unsuspecting detective answered promptly.

"Robbery-Homicide Division, Detective Reyes. How can I help you?"

"You can start by telling me why you dropped Clayton Manley."

"Bosch? Bosch, I told you, I'm not talking to you."

"I checked out Tampa and you were right: Maura Frederick is in the clear. But that was just a deflection, Reyes. You need to tell me why you dropped off Manley or you're going to have to tell it to a judge."

"What the fuck are you talking about? Are you crazy?"

"There's something missing about Clayton Manley from the murder book, something not in discovery, and if I put that idea in Haller's ear he's going to run with it and he's going to drag you and your dumbshit partner into court to talk about it with the judge."

"You're the dumbshit, Bosch. There's nothing. We got the DNA hit on that nutjob and that was it. Game over. We didn't need to do anything else on Manley."

"It's in the chronology, Reyes. Actually, it's what's *not* in the chrono. The interview with Manley came a week before the DNA hit, but there's nothing on Manley in the chrono that week after you talked to him. You aren't going to convince me—or Haller or the judge—that you did nothing on Manley that week. He was a solid suspect. At least a person of interest. So what happened? What did you leave out of discovery? What happened the week before the DNA came back?"

Reyes said nothing—and that was when Bosch knew he had struck a nerve. His bluff was on the nose. Gustafson and Reyes had taken the Manley angle another step but had left it out of the discovery version of the murder book they handed over to the defense.

"Talk to me, Reyes," Bosch said. "I can contain it. You don't and you get Haller up your ass. If he smells any money in this he'll sue you, the department, the city—it'll blow up and you get blown up with it. You want that? You're new to RHD. You think they'll keep you around if you get tainted with this?"

He waited and Reyes finally broke.

"Okay, listen, Bosch," he began. "Detective to detective, I'll give you something and you do whatever the fuck you want with it. But it won't add up to anything because your nutjob was the guy. He fucking did it."

"Just give it to me," Bosch said.

"You have to protect me. No Haller, no fucking lawyers."

"No Haller, no lawyers."

"Okay, the only thing we left out of discovery was that we started out with Manley by running down every lawyer in that firm."

"Michaelson and Mitchell."

"Right, every lawyer. We wanted to see who we were dealing with, what other clients they were representing. It's a big powerful law firm and we had to step carefully. We put all the lawyer names in the county courts computer and got all their cases in the last ten years. It was a lot. But we got one hit of interest."

"Which was?"

"About five years ago Michaelson and Mitchell represented Dominick Butino. Got him off on a weapons beef—witness changed his story. And that was it. Then the DNA came in on Herstadt and we dropped it. It didn't mean anything anyway."

Bosch knew the name. Dominick "Batman" Butino was a reputed

organized-crime figure from Las Vegas who had business interests in Los Angeles. Bosch now knew exactly what Gustafson and Reyes had done. They had DNA directly linking Herstadt to the Montgomery killing. They weren't going to put something in discovery—a certified mobster—that would allow the defense to create any sort of jury distraction.

They didn't want Haller building a potential third-party-culpability case by pointing to a lawyer who had threatened and sued Montgomery, and whose firm represented a notorious organized-crime figure. Butino's nickname did not come from the superhero but from his alleged use of a baseball bat to collect money owed to him.

It was a classic anti-discovery move by the cops. And it may have inadvertently hidden the real killer.

"Which lawyer?" Bosch asked.

"What?" Reyes said.

"Which lawyer in the firm represented Butino?"

"William Michaelson."

A founding partner. Bosch wrote it down.

"So, you never talked to Manley about this?" he asked.

"Didn't need to," Reyes said.

"Did he ever know he was being looked at, that he was a suspect?"

"No, because he wasn't a suspect. He was a person of interest for about five minutes. You're acting like we dropped the ball on this but we didn't. We had a DNA match, a suspect documented to have been in the vicinity, and then we had a confession. You think for one second we were going to spend another minute on Clayton Manley? Think again, Bosch."

Bosch had what he needed but couldn't end the call without throwing something back at Reyes.

"You know what, Reyes, you were right about what you said before," he said. "A killer is out there walking free. But not because of anything I did."

He disconnected the call.

BALLARD

33

Ballard met Bosch at a gas station on Crenshaw four blocks from Dulan's. She was driving her van and Bosch was in his Cherokee. She had loaded her paddleboard inside the van to avoid being conspicuous. They pulled up side by side, driver's window to driver's window. Bosch had dressed as a detective, right down to his sport coat and tie. Ballard had dressed down and was wearing a Dodgers cap and a sweatshirt and jeans. Her hair was still damp from the shower after paddling.

"What's our plan?" Ballard asked.

"I thought you had the plan," Bosch said.

She laughed.

"Actually, I caught an all-night case last night and didn't have much time to scheme," she said. "I do have good news, though."

"What's that?" Bosch asked.

"Marcel Dupree hasn't paid child support in three years and a judge wants to talk to him about it. He's got a felony warrant."

"That helps."

"So what do you think we should do?"

"You've been in there before? What's the setup?"

"One time. I read somewhere they had the best fried chicken in the city. And peach cobbler. So, I went to see. It's like a counter—you go down the line, order what you want, then take it on a tray and find a place to sit. They have an overflow room that will probably be in use at one today, end of the lunch hour."

"We need a signal. In case you need me. We've got no radios."

"I brought my rover in case we want to hook Dupree up after."

She handed the radio across to Bosch.

"You keep it in case something goes really sideways and you need to call it in. You remember the codes?"

"Of course. Code three—officer needs help. But what if things don't go sideways? What are we doing?"

"Well, I'm going in by myself. Most people by themselves look at their cell phones. I'll text you a running play-by-play and a code three if I need you to call in the troops."

Bosch thought about things before speaking next.

"Once you're in there and have your phone out, text me a hello so I know we have a clear signal," he said. "But my question is what are you hoping to accomplish in there? You think you're going to overhear their conversation, just get a look at Kidd, what?"

"Yeah, I want to get a look at him," Ballard said. "And if I'm lucky and I'm close, I may hear something. I'll put my phone on Record but I know that's a long shot. I want to see if he's panicked, and if he is then maybe we take it to the next step and really spook him to see what he does. We can also squeeze Dupree."

"When?"

"Maybe right after lunch. You're dressed up like a detective and I'm undercover. Maybe we call South Bureau, get a couple unies to pull him over, and then we take him back to South Bureau and borrow a room."

"How close are the tables in there?"

"Not that close. They wouldn't have picked the place if they knew people were sitting on top of each other."

Bosch nodded.

"Okay, let's see what happens," he said. "Don't forget to text me so I know we have a signal."

"It's just a first step," Ballard said. "I want to see who we're dealing with here."

"Okay, be safe."

"You too."

Ballard drove off. She checked the dashboard clock and saw it was 12:45. She made a U-turn on Crenshaw and headed back toward the restaurant. It was busy and there was no parking directly in front of the establishment. She parked at the curb half a block away and texted Bosch before getting out of the van.

Going in.

She got out, slinging her backpack strap over her shoulder, and walked to the restaurant. Her gun and handcuffs were in the pack.

She entered Dulan's at exactly one p.m. and was immediately hit with the smell of good food. It suddenly occurred to her that to complete her undercover picture she was going to have to eat. She looked around. Every table in the front room of the restaurant was taken and there was a line of people waiting to go down the hot line and get their food. Acting like she was looking for a friend, she checked out the overflow room to the right. There were empty tables here. She stopped short when she saw a man sitting by himself at a four-top. He was texting on his phone. She was sure it was Marcel Dupree. The round head but now with braids instead of unkempt. He had no food or drink in front of him. He was totally dressed in Crips blue, right down to the flat-billed Dodgers cap. It looked like he was waiting for Elvin Kidd before ordering.

The room was long, with a row of four-top tables running down the right side and deuces running down the left. The table across the aisle from Dupree's four-top was already taken by a couple. The next deuce down was taken as well, but the third was open. Ballard realized that by sitting there she could have a full view of whoever sat across the table from Dupree.

She walked down the aisle, passing Dupree, and to the open table. Hanging her backpack over the back of the chair, she dropped her van keys on the table and turned to the four-top across the aisle, where three young women sat.

"Excuse me, do you mind watching my stuff while I go get food?" she asked. "I won't be long. The line isn't bad."

"Sure, no problem," one of the women said. "Take your time."

"I'll be quick."

"No worries."

She went back into the main dining room and got in line. While she waited she kept her eyes on the door to see if Kidd would enter. She looked away for just a moment, to text Bosch that only Dupree was in the building. Bosch responded, saying he had left the gas station and had moved closer to the restaurant. He asked if she was close to Dupree, and Ballard responded.

I got a table close enough to watch.

Bosch's return came immediately.

Just be careful.

Ballard didn't respond. It was her turn to order. She asked for fried chicken, collard greens, and peach cobbler. She wanted enough food to keep her at the table for as long as Dupree and Kidd were at theirs. After paying, she took her tray to the next room and saw that Dupree was now facing another black man at his table. The shaved scalp told her it was likely Kidd. She had not seen him enter the restaurant and guessed there might be a rear entrance. She carried her food tray past them and to her table, where she sat at a diagonal to the man meeting Dupree.

Ballard stole a casual glance and confirmed that it was Kidd. She took her phone out and held it at an angle so it would appear she was looking at something on the screen or taking a selfie, and started taking a video of Dupree and Kidd.

After a few seconds she stopped the video and texted it to Bosch. His response came quick.

No CLOSER!

And she sent him one back.

Roger that!

She started the video again but didn't hold the phone consistently in one spot or it could be a giveaway. She ate her food and continued to act like she was reading e-mails, at times placing the phone flat on the table, at other times holding it up as if to look closely at something on the screen. The whole time she was recording.

Because of the distance between the two tables, Ballard could make out very little of what was said by Kidd and nothing of what was said by Dupree. The men were speaking in low tones, and only now and then could a word or two be heard from Kidd. It was clear by his demeanor, however, that Kidd was agitated if not angry about something. At one point he poked a finger down hard on the table and Ballard clearly heard him say, "I am not fucking around."

He said it in a controlled and angry tone that carried through the sounds of dining, conversation, and overhead music in the room.

At that point Ballard had propped her phone against a sugar caddy on the table. The phone was tilted so it would look like she was reading or watching something, but it provided a low-angle recording of Kidd. She just hoped it picked up the audio.

Kidd lowered his voice again and continued speaking to Dupree. Then, seemingly in mid-sentence, Kidd got up from the table and started walking toward Ballard.

She quickly realized that if he saw the screen of her phone, he would know she was recording his meeting with Dupree. She grabbed the phone and cleared the screen just as Kidd got to her table.

He walked by her.

She waited, wanting to turn to see where he was going, but not willing to risk it.

Then she saw Dupree rise and head up the aisle to the main room and the front door of the restaurant. She saw him stuff an envelope in the side pocket of his sweatpants as he walked.

Ballard let a long five seconds go by before she turned to look behind her. Kidd was nowhere to be seen. There was a rear hallway with a restroom sign. She quickly texted Bosch.

Elvin has left the building. Dupree coming out front.
Blue sweats, dodgers cap, stay with him.

Ballard got up and went in the direction Kidd had gone. There were three doors at the end of the rear hallway: two restrooms and a rear exit. She pushed the third door open a few inches and saw nothing. She went wider and saw a white pickup truck with the KIDD CONSTRUCTION sign on the door going down the alley. She turned around and hurried back to the front of the restaurant, calling Bosch as she went.

"*Elvin has left the building*—really?" he said.

"I thought it was cute," Ballard said. "Where's Dupree?"

"He's sitting in a car on the street, making a call. Where's Kidd?"

"I think he's heading back to Rialto."

"Did you get anything?"

"I'm not sure. I got close but they were whispering. I'll tell you one thing, though, Kidd was angry. I could tell."

Ballard slowed her pace so that when she stepped out of the restaurant, she would look nonchalant.

"What's our move?" Bosch asked.

"Stay on Dupree," Ballard said. "I want to get to my van and see what I got on my phone."

"Roger that."

"I think Kidd gave Dupree something. I want to see if I got it."

"You were videoing?"

"Trying to. Let me check and I'll hit you back."

She disconnected and ten seconds later was at her van.

She sat and watched the video she had taken. The playback was jumpy but she had Kidd on the screen and Dupree in side profile at times. Even with the volume on Max she could not make out what was said until Kidd's outburst—"I am not fucking around"—came through loud and clear.

She then watched as Kidd got up from the table and started walking toward the camera. His body partially obscured the angle, and the frame jostled as Ballard grabbed the phone to kill the camera. A split second before the recording ended, Kidd cleared enough of the frame to reveal the table he had just left. A white envelope was lying on the red-and-white-checked tablecloth at the spot he had vacated. It looked like a folded napkin for a place setting.

The video ended but Ballard knew that Dupree had then picked the envelope up.

She called Bosch back.

"I think Kidd gave Dupree some money. He left an envelope on the table and Dupree took it."

"Money for what?"

"Let's ask him."

34

Ballard called the detective commander at South Bureau, explained who she was, and asked whether there was a free interview room she could borrow to talk to a local. The lieutenant said that all interview rooms were free at the moment and she was welcome to take her pick. She called Bosch back and said they were all set.

"Only one problem," Bosch said.

"What's that?" Ballard asked.

"I'm not a cop. They're not going to let me waltz in there with you and a custody."

"Come on, Harry—if anybody says *cop,* it's you. But can you leave your cane in the car?"

"I didn't even bring it."

"Good, then we're in business. Where are you? I want my rover so I can call in a traffic stop on Dupree."

"I see your van. I'll meet you there."

"Dupree's still not moving?"

"Still on the phone. And I can see it's a flip."

"A burner. Perfect. I wonder what he's up to."

"We should have someone on the wire."

"But we don't, and besides, I doubt he's talking to Kidd. He just left him. They already talked."

"Roger that."

Ballard waited, and soon enough Bosch pulled up beside her and handed her the rover through the window. She called for a patrol unit to meet her at the corner where Dupree was still parked.

It was twenty minutes before a patrol unit shook loose of another call and arrived. All the while Dupree remained in his car, working his phone. Ballard flagged down the patrol car, badge in hand, and leaned down to look in at the two officers inside.

"Hey. Ballard, Hollywood Division."

The patrol car's driver did the talking. He wore short sleeves but had three hash marks tattooed on his left forearm. A veteran street copper who was serious about it. The other uni was a black woman who didn't look old enough to have more than a few years on the job.

"You guys know Marcel Dupree, Rolling 60s?"

Both shook their heads.

"Okay, well, that's him parked up the block in the black Chrysler 300 with the low profile. You see what I'm talking about?"

The driver's name tag said DEVLIN. Ballard could guess what nicknames he had garnered over the years.

"Got it," he said.

"Okay, he's wanted on a child support warrant," Ballard said. "That's our in. Arrest him, take him to South Bureau, and put him in a room. I'll take it from there."

"Weapons?"

"I don't know. I just saw him outside the car and he didn't look like he was carrying. But he has a weapons record and he might have a piece in the car. I'm actually hoping so. Then we'd have something to really work with. He's also got a burner he's talking on right now. I want that."

"You got it. Now?"

"Go get him. Be careful. Oh, and one other thing: when you pull him out, don't let him close the car door."

"Roger that."

Ballard stepped back and the patrol car took off. She quickly went to her van, where Bosch was waiting. They got in and she pulled into traffic. She made a U-turn that brought a chorus of angry honks. She hit the flashers and sped down the street until she pulled in behind the patrol car. It had parked off the rear side of Dupree's Chrysler at an angle that would make it difficult for him to flee in his car without hitting either the patrol car or the vehicle parked in front of him.

Devlin was standing at the driver's door, speaking to Dupree through the open window. His partner was on the other side of the car in a ready stance, her hand on her holstered weapon.

Ballard and Bosch stayed in the van and watched, ready if needed.

"You carrying, Harry?" Ballard asked.

"Nope," Bosch said.

"If you need it, I've got a backup under the dash behind the glove box. You just have to reach up under there."

"Nice. Roger that."

But Devlin persuaded Dupree to step out of the car and put his hands on the roof. His partner came around the car and stood by the rear passenger door as Devlin moved in and cuffed Dupree, taking one hand off the roof at a time. He then searched his pockets, putting the burner phone, a wallet, and a white envelope on the roof as he found them.

Several people honked their horns as they drove by the scene, apparently protesting another arrest of a black man by a white officer.

Dupree himself did not seem to protest anything. As far as Ballard could tell, he had said nothing since stepping out of the car. She watched as he was walked to the rear door of the patrol car and placed in the back seat.

With the suspect secured, Ballard and Bosch emerged from the van and approached the Chrysler, the driver's door still open.

"If he has a gun in there, it will be within reach of the driver's seat," Bosch said. "But you should search, not me."

"I will," Ballard said.

But first she went over to Devlin and his partner.

"Take him to South and put him in a room at the D-bureau," she said. "I talked to Lieutenant Randizi and he cleared it. We'll check the car and lock it up, then we'll get over there."

"Roger that," Devlin said. "Pleasure doing business with you."

"Thanks for the help."

The two unies got in their car and took off with Dupree. Ballard went to the Chrysler, snapping on gloves as she approached.

"You worried about a warrant?" Bosch asked.

"No," Ballard said. "Driver left his door open and has a past record of gun violence. If there is a weapon in here, we have a public safety issue. I think that qualifies as a 'search incidental to a lawful arrest.'"

She was quoting from a legal opinion that allowed vehicle searches if public safety was an issue.

Ballard leaned into the driver's seat through the open door. The first thing she checked was the center-console storage compartment, but there was no weapon. She leaned farther in and checked the glove box. Nothing.

She lowered herself and reached under the driver's seat. There was nothing on the floor. She reached up blindly into the springs and electronic controls of the seat and her hand found an object that felt like the grip of a handgun.

"Got something," she announced to Bosch.

She pulled hard and could feel tape coming free. She brought a small handgun out from beneath the seat, black tape still attached to it.

"Now we're talking," she said.

She put the gun on the roof of the car with the other property found on Dupree's person. She picked up the phone and thumbed it open. On the screen she saw that Dupree had missed a call from a 213 number that looked vaguely familiar to her. It had come in just a few minutes before, while Dupree was being arrested. She took out her own phone and called the number. It connected right away to a recording that said it was a Los Angeles County number that did not accept incoming calls.

"What is it?" Bosch asked.

He had come up next to her.

"Dupree just missed a call from a county line that doesn't accept incoming calls," Ballard said. "Only calls going out."

"Men's Central," Bosch said. "Somebody was calling him from jail."

Ballard nodded. It sounded right. The phone didn't appear to be password protected. Ballard wanted to know whom Dupree had been talking to before his arrest, but she did not want to risk the case by looking through the phone's previous-call list without a warrant.

"What's in the envelope?" Bosch asked.

Ballard closed the phone and put it back on the car's roof. She then took up the envelope. It was not sealed. She opened it and thumbed through the stack of currency inside.

"Thirty one-hundred-dollar bills," she said. "Kidd was paying Dupree—"

"To hit someone," Bosch said. "You need to call Men's Central and get Dennard Dorsey in protective custody as soon as possible. Call right now."

Ballard tossed the envelope back on the roof of the car and pulled her phone again. She called the Men's Central number she had stored on her phone for when she wanted to set up an inmate interview. It was the only number she had.

She got lucky. Deputy Valens answered the call.

"Valens, this is Ballard. I was in there a couple days ago to talk to a guy in the Crips module named Dennard Dorsey. You remember?"

"Uh, yeah, I remember. We don't get many looking like you in here."

Ballard ignored the comment. This was an emergency.

"Listen to me," she said. "That conversation sparked something and you need to grab Dorsey and put him in protective custody. Nobody can get near him. You got that?"

"Well, yes, but I need an order from command for that. I can't just—"

"Valens, you're not listening. This is about to go down now. A hit was put on Dorsey and it could happen any minute. I don't care what you need to do, just get him out of that module or he's going to get whacked."

"Okay, okay, let me see what I can do. Maybe I'll move him into the visiting room and tell him you're coming back. Meantime, I'll work on a transfer."

"Good. Do it. I'll call you back when I know more."

Ballard disconnected and looked at Bosch.

"They're going to secure him, one way or another," she said. "I'll call back in a bit to make sure."

"Good," Bosch said. "Now let's see what Dupree has to say about it."

35

Ballard and Bosch let Dupree marinate in an interview room at South Bureau while they drank coffee and schemed out how Ballard would handle the interview. They had agreed that it had to be her. Bosch had no police powers. If the interview became part of a court case, it could collapse things if revealed that Dupree was interviewed by someone other than an active-duty law enforcement officer.

They agreed that Ballard would sit across from Dupree with her cell phone on her thigh so she could look down and see any messages from Bosch, who would watch the interview in real time from the detective bureau's video room.

An hour after Dupree had been placed in the room, Ballard entered. She and Bosch had just been informed by Deputy Valens at Men's Central that Dennard Dorsey was safe and in protective isolation away from the Crip tank. He had also told them that a review of recordings off the two pay phones in the tank revealed that an inmate named Clinton Townes had placed a collect call at the exact time of the missed incoming call registered on Dupree's burner.

Ballard was confident that she had all she needed to flip Dupree. She entered the interview room with a rights waiver form and a large evidence envelope containing the smaller envelope of cash recovered in Dupree's arrest.

Dupree's hands were cuffed behind him to a chair anchored to the floor. The room was ripe with his body odor, a sign that he was nervous—as anybody held in custody would be.

"What the fuck is this?" he said. "You hold me in here like this for fucking child support?"

"Not quite, Marcel," Ballard said. "We pulled you in on the child support thing, but this isn't about that and I'm pretty sure you know it."

It suddenly dawned on Dupree that he recognized Ballard.

"You," he said. "I seen you at Dulan's."

"That's right," Ballard said as she pulled out her chair and sat down across the table from him. "I didn't hear everything you and Kidd talked about. But I heard a lot."

"Nah, you didn't hear shit. We were tight."

Ballard took her phone off her belt and held it up to show him.

"I got it all on here," she said. "Our tech unit can do amazing things with audio. Even bring up whispers. So we're going to see about that, but it doesn't really matter."

She put the phone down on her thigh where he couldn't see its screen.

"I'm here to explain to you what your situation is and how I can help you and you can help yourself," she said. "But Marcel, for me to do that you have to waive your rights and talk to me."

"I don't talk to the po-lice," Dupree said. "And I don't waive nothin'."

This was good. He did not say the magic words—*I want a lawyer*—and until he did, she could work on convincing him that it was in his best interest to talk to her.

"Marcel, you're fucked. We found the gun in your car."

"I don't know nothin' about a gun."

"Nine-millimeter Smith and Wesson? Satin finish? I'd bring it in to show you but it's against the rules."

"Never seen no gun like that."

"Except it was tucked up under the seat you were sitting in when you got popped a couple hours ago. So you can go with the never-seen-it-before claim, but it's going to go down in flames—and you're a twice-convicted felon, Marcel. That means five years back in a cage just for possession of a firearm."

She let that sink in for a moment. Dupree shook his head woefully.

"You people planted it," he said.

"That'll work about as well as I-never-seen-it-before," Ballard said. "Be smart, Marcel. Listen to what I can do for you."

"Fuck. Go ahead."

"I can help you with this. I can even make it go away. But it's a trade, Marcel. I need you to cooperate with me or we shut this down here and now and I file the gun charge and whatever else I can come up with. That's the choice here."

She waited. He said nothing. She started reciting the Miranda rights warning. He interrupted.

"Okay, okay, I'll talk to you. But I want it in writing."

"Let me finish and then you have to sign the waiver."

She started the warning from the beginning. She didn't want any lawyer down the line to complain of improper advisement. When she was finished, she asked if he was right- or left-handed.

"Right."

"Okay, I'll take the cuff off your right hand and you sign. You get froggy with me and there are four guys watching this on the other side of that door. You try to hurt me and they will definitely hurt you in a way you'll never recover from. Do you understand?"

"Yeah, I get it. Come on, let's just do this. Let me sign the motherfuckin' paper."

Ballard set the waiver form and a pen down in front of Dupree. She then got up and moved behind him, uncuffed his right wrist, and snapped the open cuff closed around the middle bar of the chair's backrest. She stayed behind him.

"Go ahead and sign, then bring your hand back here."

Dupree signed the document and did as instructed. Ballard

reversed the process and recuffed him, then went back to her seat. She returned her cell phone to her thigh.

"Now *you* sign a paper," Dupree said. "Says you drop the gun charge for my help."

Ballard shook her head.

"You haven't given me any help," she said. "You help me and I'll get the D.A.'s Office to put it in writing. That's the deal. Yes or no? I'm running out of patience with you."

Dupree shook his head.

"I know I'm fucked," he said. "Just ask your questions."

"Okay, good," Ballard said. "I'll start by letting you know we had Elvin Kidd on a wiretap, Marcel—all his phone calls and texts. We got the text to you where he set up the meeting today at Dulan's. We have you meeting with him there and we have this."

She opened the evidence envelope and slid out the envelope full of cash.

"He hired you to hit somebody at Men's Central and you agreed to arrange it. Now that is conspiracy to commit murder on top of the gun charge. So, you are in a bottomless hole here that you are never climbing out of unless you give us something we like better than you. You understand? That's how this works."

"What do you want?"

"Tell me the story. Tell me who Kidd wanted hit and why. I need a name to stop it from happening. Because if it's too late, then it's too late for you. No deals. You're done."

"A guy named D-squared."

"That doesn't help me. Who is D-squared?"

"I don't even know his first name. His last name is Dorsey. Like the high school."

"Your call in the car outside Dulan's. You set this in motion, didn't you?"

"Nah, I was just calling a friend."

"Clinton Townes? Was that your friend?"

"What the fuck?"

"I told you. We had this wired from the start. We knew about Dorsey and we knew about Townes. But it's still conspiracy to commit murder and that makes your gun charge look like a walk in the park. Conspiracy to commit jumps you up to life without, Marcel. You know that, right?"

"Motherfuckers, you played me."

"That's right—and now you've got one path to the light, Marcel. It's called *substantial assistance*. That's you giving me everything. Everything you know. And you can start by telling me why Elvin Kidd wanted D-squared hit."

Dupree shook his head.

"I don't know—he didn't say," he said. "He just said he wanted him taken care of."

Ballard leaned across the table.

"Elvin Kidd is retired," she said. "He's out of the game. He's running a fucking construction company in Rialto. You don't run a hit on one of your own in Men's Central for three thousand dollars without a damn good reason. So if you want to help yourself here, you'll answer the question: What did he tell you?"

Dupree's eyes were cast down at the table. The dread he was feeling was almost palpable. Ballard was looking at a man realizing that life as he had known it was gone. He was now a fifty-one-year-old snitch and would forever be an outcast in the world he knew. He was a violent criminal but Ballard felt empathy for him. He had been born into a dog-eat-dog world, and now he was the meal.

"He say this guy crossed him from way back and now he's causing problems," Dupree said. "That's all. Look, I'd tell you if I knew. I'm cooperating but I don't know. He wanted him hit, he paid the money, and with an OG like Kidd, I don't ask no questions."

"Then why was he mad at you at Dulan's? He raised his voice."

"He mad 'cause I gave out his number so D-squared could talk to him. I thought it was legit because D used to be his boy on the blocks, back in the day. I thought they maybe still have business together or something. I didn't know. I fucked up and gave him the number. E-K was mad about that."

"So what was the call in the car after Dulan's?"

"I had to set it up, you know. Get the word to my boy Townes."

Ballard knew that while there were pay phones that allowed inmates to call out from their modules at Men's Central, no one could simply call in. But it was well documented that gangs used various methods of getting messages into the jail. Mothers, wives, girlfriends, and lawyers of incarcerated gangsters often carried gang business inside. But the call Dupree got from Townes seemed to have come too quickly for that method. Townes appeared to have gotten the message to call Dupree within thirty minutes of the meeting at Dulan's. There had long been rumors of gangs using jail deputies to get messages inside—deputies motivated by threat or extortion or just plain greed.

"How'd you get the word inside?" Ballard asked.

"A guy I know. He take the message for me."

"Come on, Marcel. What guy? Who did you call?"

"I thought this was about Dorsey."

"It's about everything. Who got the message to Townes?"

Ballard felt her phone buzz on her thigh and looked down to read the text from Bosch.

Don't waste time on this. It'll be on the phone. Move on.

Ballard was annoyed because she knew Bosch was right. A search warrant for the phone would produce the number or numbers Dupree had called after Dulan's, and that would likely lead to the message carrier. She needed to move the story on to Elvin Kidd.

"Okay, never mind who you called," she said. "Tell me about Townes. He's the hitter inside?"

Dupree shrugged. He didn't want to verbally acknowledge it.

"Yes or no, Marcel?" Ballard pressed.

"Yeah, he does a piece of work now and then," Dupree said.

"Do you have to get approval from a higher-up to do something like this? You call somebody for approval to hit Dorsey?"

"I tell some people but it wasn't like 'approval.' Just to let them know we had a piece of business and Kidd was paying. Look, you going to take care of me on this, right? Like you said."

"I'll tell the D.A. you've given 'substantial assistance to the investigation.'"

"That ain't shit. We had a deal."

"If we get Kidd, 'substantial assistance' will mean a lot."

"I'm going to need witness protection after this."

"That will be on the table."

Ballard felt another vibration on her thigh and looked down at her phone.

Tell him we want him to call Kidd, say the job is done.

Ballard nodded. It was a good idea. They had the wire up on Kidd for another two days and they could legitimately record the call. It might or might not draw an admission about the Hilton case, but it could sew up the conspiracy-to-commit-murder case. Ballard understood that sometimes you know a suspect is good for one crime but you settle for getting him for another.

"There's one more thing we're going to need you to do, Marcel," she said. "We're going to set up a phone call between you and Kidd. You're going to tell him that Dorsey is dead, and we're going to see what he says. And you're going to ask him why he wanted him hit in the first place."

"Nah, I'm not doin' that," Dupree said. "Not till I got something in writing on 'substantial assistance.'"

"You're making a mistake, Marcel. You bring in the D.A. now to write that up and they're going to bring in a lawyer for you and the whole thing will blow up bigger than we can handle on this level. We miss our chance to do this with Kidd and it's 'Fuck you, Marcel Dupree.' That's the opposite of 'substantial assistance.' I'll charge you with conspiracy to commit murder for hire and go home happy with just that."

Dupree said nothing.

"This room stinks," Ballard said. "I'm going to go out and get some fresh air. When I come back, you tell me whether you want us to make a case against you or Elvin Kidd."

Ballard got up, pocketed her phone and picked up the envelopes, then started around the table toward the door.

"Okay, I'll do it," Dupree said.

Ballard looked back at him and nodded.

"Okay, we'll set it up."

36

Ballard rolled out of work at six a.m. on Saturday morning after an uneventful shift on Watch Three. She had spent most of the night writing a detailed summary of the events that took place the day before on the Hilton investigation. This was a report she wasn't turning in to anyone yet. She was operating completely off the reservation on the Hilton case with the hope that it would be easier to ask for forgiveness than permission—especially if she bagged Elvin Kidd. In that case, the summary report might be needed at a moment's notice.

After leaving the station, she drove out to Venice and did a short paddle through the morning mist, with Lola sitting on the board's nose like the figurehead on the prow of an old ship. After getting cleaned up, she waited until 8:30 to make a call, hoping she would not be waking anybody up.

When Ballard had worked at RHD, everybody had a go-to in every part of the casework: a go-to forensic tech, a go-to judge for warrants, a go-to prosecutor for advice and for filing charges on the wobblers—the cases that took some fortitude and imagination to pursue in court. Ballard's go-to at the District Attorney's Office had always been Selma Robinson, a solid and fearless deputy D.A. in the Major Crimes Unit who preferred the challenge cases over the gimmes.

Because the nature of the midnight beat was to turn cases over to other detectives in the morning, Ballard had gone to the D.A.'s Office few times in the four years she had been assigned to the late show. In fact, she was not sure the cell number she was calling for Selma Robinson was still good.

But it was. Robinson answered in a sharp, alert voice, and it was clear she had kept Ballard's cell on her contacts list.

"Renée? Wow. Are you okay?"

"Yes, I'm fine. I didn't wake you?"

"No, I've been up for a while. What's up? It's good to hear your voice, girl."

"You too. I've got a case. I want to talk to you about it if you have some time. I'm living in Venice now. I could come your way, maybe buy you breakfast. I know this is straight out of the blue but—"

"No, it's fine. I was just about to get something. Where do you want to meet?"

Ballard knew Robinson lived in Santa Monica on one of the college streets.

"How about Little Ruby's?" she asked.

The restaurant was just off Ocean Boulevard in Santa Monica and just about equidistant for both of them. It was also dog-friendly.

"I'll be there by nine," Robinson said.

"Bring your earbuds," Ballard said. "There's some wiretap material."

"Will do. You're bringing Lola, I hope."

"I think she'd love to see you."

Ballard got to the restaurant first and found a spot in a corner that would give them some privacy to review the case. Lola went under the table and lay down, but then immediately jumped up when Robinson arrived and Lola remembered her old friend.

Robinson was tall and thin and Ballard had never known her to keep her hair in anything but a short Afro that was stylish and saved her time every morning while getting ready for battle in the courts. She was at least a decade older than Ballard and her first name had a deep history, her parents having met during the historic civil rights march from Selma to Montgomery, Alabama.

Ballard and Robinson hugged briefly but the prosecutor fawned over Lola for a full minute before sitting and getting down to the business of breakfast and crime.

"So like I said on the phone, I'm working on a case," Ballard began. "And I want to know if I have it or not."

"Well, then let's hear it," Robinson said. "Pretend I'm in my office and you've come over to file. Convince me."

As succinctly as she could, Ballard presented the Hilton case, going over the details of the murder and then the long period the case spent gathering dust in a retired detective's home study. She then moved into the investigation conducted in more recent days, and how it finally focused on Elvin Kidd and Ballard's theory about the true motive for the killing. She revealed that she had flipped Marcel Dupree, stopped a murder from occurring in Men's Central, and extracted a confession that could take Kidd off the streets for good. But what she wanted was to close the Hilton case, and with Dupree's cooperation, she believed she was close. She asked Robinson to listen to the ninety-second wiretapped phone conversation set up between Dupree and Kidd late the afternoon before, assuring her that the wiretap had been authorized by Judge Billy Thornton.

One complication Ballard mentioned in introducing the wiretap was that the men on the call sounded very similar in tone and used similar street slang. Ballard repeated in her introduction to the play-back that the first voice belonged to Dupree and the second voice was Kidd's. Robinson put in her earbuds and plugged into Ballard's computer. Ballard opened the wiretap software and played the phone call. At the same time, she gave the prosecutor a copy of a transcript she had produced during her work shift.

Dupree: Yo.

Kidd: Dog.

Dupree: That thing we were talking about? All done.

Kidd: It is?

Dupree: Motherfucker's gone to gangsta's paradise.

Kidd: I ain't hear nothin'.

Dupree: And you prolly won't out there in Rialto. The sheriffs don't be puttin' out press releases on convicts gettin' killed in jail and all. That don't look good. But you want, you can check it, my n____.

Kidd: How's that?

Dupree: Call up the coroner. They gotta have him over there by now. Also, I hear they gonna put him out for a full gangsta's funeral in a few days. You could come over, see him in the box for yourself.

Kidd: Nah, I ain't doin' that.

Dupree: I get it, seeing that you put the motherfucker in the box.

Kidd: Don't be sayin' that shit, n ____.

Dupree: Sorry, cuz. Anyway, it's done. We good now?

Kidd: We good.

Dupree: You ever going to tell me the reason? I mean, that n____ was your boy back in the day. Now it come to this.

Kidd: He was putting pressure on me, man, that's all.

Dupree: Pressure for what?

Kidd: A piece of work I had to handle back then. A white boy who owed too much money.

Dupree: Huh. And he was bringing that up now?

Kidd: He told me five-oh came round visiting him up at Bauchet and asking 'bout that thing. He then gets my number off you and calls me up. I can tell he's on the make. He going to be trouble for me.

Dupree: Well, not anymore.

Kidd: Not anymore. I thank you, my brother.

Dupree: No thing.
Kidd: I'll check you.
Dupree: Later, dog.

Robinson pulled out her earbuds when the call was over. Ballard held her hand up to stop her from asking any questions.

"Hold on a second," Ballard said. "There's another call. He does try to confirm Dorsey's death and we had that set up with the coroner's office."

The next call was from Elvin Kidd to the Los Angeles County Medical Examiner's Office, where he spoke to a coroner's investigator named Chris Mercer. Ballard handed Robinson a second transcript and told her to put her buds back in. She then played the second recording.

Mercer: Office of the Medical Examiner, how can I help you?
Kidd: I'm trying to find out if a friend of mine is there. He supposedly got killed.
Mercer: Do you have the name?
Kidd: Yes, it's *Dorsey* for the last name. And *Dennard* with a *D* like *dog* for the first.
Mercer: Can you spell both names, please?
Kidd: D-E-N-N-A-R-D D-O-R-S-E-Y.
Mercer: Yes, we have him here. Are you next-of-kin?
Kidd: Uh, no. Just a friend. Does it say there how he died?
Mercer: The autopsy has not been scheduled. I only know that he passed while in custody at the Men's Central jail. There will be an investigation and we will conduct the autopsy next week. You could call back for more information then. Do you know who his next-of-kin might be?
Kidd: No, I don't know that. Thank you.

After hearing the call to the M.E., Robinson asked to hear the first call again. Ballard watched her as she listened. Robinson nodded at certain points as though checking things off a list. She then pulled her earbuds out again.

"The code-switching is interesting," the prosecutor said. "He sounds like two different people on the two calls. All gangster on the call with Dupree, then light and bright with the coroner's office."

"Yeah, he knew how to play it," Ballard said. "So what do you think?"

Before Robinson could answer, a waitress arrived at the table. They both ordered coffees and avocado toast. After the waitress was gone, Ballard watched Robinson lean forward on the table, furrowing her brow and wrinkling the otherwise smooth, mocha-brown skin of her forehead.

"I always have to look at a case from the defense point of view," she said. "What are the weaknesses that could be exploited at trial? I think the conspiracy to commit is a slam dunk. We'll convict on that no problem. That extra call to the Medical Examiner was genius. I can't wait to play that to a jury and have the defense try to explain it."

"Good," Ballard said. "And on the Hilton murder?"

"Well, on the murder, he never says outright, 'I killed the guy.' He says he handled a 'piece of work,' which in some quarters is a euphemism for murder. He also says 'white boy' but doesn't mention anybody by name."

"But when you add in the conspiracy, it's obvious he wanted to kill Dorsey to keep the cover on Hilton."

"Obvious to you and me, but possibly not to a jury. Also, if you have one charge that's a dunker and one that has issues, you drop the wobbler and go with the sure thing. You don't want to show weakness to a jury. So I know you don't want to hear this, but right now, I would only file the conspiracy. I would make the reason for the conspiracy the Hilton murder and put it out there, but I would not ask the jury to decide a verdict on that. I would say, 'Give me a conspiracy-to-commit verdict,' and this guy goes away for good anyway. I know that's not the answer you wanted."

Disappointed, Ballard closed her laptop and leaned back in her chair.

"Well, shit," she said.

"Have you gone back to Dorsey since he was pulled out of the Crip tank?" Robinson asked.

"No, should I?"

"You said he wasn't helpful before, but maybe if he knows that his old boss Kidd put a hit out on him, he might change his tune. And maybe he knows something he's held back."

Ballard nodded. She realized she should have thought of that.

"Good idea," she said.

"What is Dupree's status?" Robinson asked.

"Right now he's in holding at South Bureau. He's looking for a substantial-assistance deal. We have till Monday morning to charge him."

"You'd better take good care of him. If Kidd finds out Dorsey's alive, he'll know he's been set up."

"I know. We have him on keep-away status."

"By the way, who's 'we'?"

"My regular partner's out on leave. This whole thing was actually brought to me by a retired homicide guy named Bosch. He got the Hilton murder book from John Jack Thompson's widow after his funeral."

"Harry Bosch, I remember him. I didn't know he retired."

"Yeah, but he's got reserve powers through San Fernando PD."

"Be careful with that. That could be an issue if he has to testify to anything you can't be a witness to."

"We talked about that. We know."

"What about Kidd? Are you going to bring him in for a conversation?"

"We were thinking that was our last move."

Robinson nodded thoughtfully.

"Well, when you're ready, bring this back to me," she finally said. "I'd love to try this case. On Monday, come see me and I'll file the case on Dupree and work out the cooperation agreement. Does he have a lawyer?"

"Not yet," Ballard said.

"Once he lawyers up, I'll make the deal."

"Okay."

"And good luck with Dorsey."

"As soon as we finish breakfast, I'm going downtown to see him again."

As if on cue, the waitress came and put down their coffees and plates of avocado toast. She also had a dog biscuit for Lola.

37

They brought Dorsey to see her in the same interview room at Men's Central. He had to be pushed into the room by Deputy Valens when he saw it was Ballard waiting for him.

"You set me up, bitch!" he said. "I ain't talking to you."

Ballard waited until Valens finished cuffing him to his chair and left the interview room.

"I set you up?" she said then. "How's that?"

"All I know is, you drag me in here, next thing I know I'm in solitary with a snitch jacket," Dorsey said. "Now people out to kill me."

"Well, people are out to kill you but it isn't because of me."

"That's some bullshit right there. I was doing fine till you come see me."

"No, you were doing fine until you called Elvin Kidd. That's where your trouble started, Dennard."

"The fuck you talking about, girl?"

"We had Elvin up on a wire. We heard your call and then, guess what? We have him setting up the hit. On you."

"You runnin' a bullshit game now."

"Am I, Dennard?"

Ballard opened her laptop on the table.

"Let me walk you through it," she said. "Then, if you think it's a game, I'll tell them to put you back with your friends in the module. So you can feel safe and at home."

She opened up the file that contained the recordings of calls made to and from Elvin Kidd's phones.

"So the first thing you need to know is that we had a phone tap on Kidd," she said. "So when you called to warn him about me asking questions, we got the whole conversation down on tape."

She started playing the first recording and waited for Dorsey to recognize his own voice and Kidd's. He unconsciously leaned forward and turned his head as if to hear the recording better. Ballard then cut it off.

"That ain't legal," Dorsey said.

"Yes, it is," Ballard said. "Approved by a superior-court judge. Now, let me just jump ahead to the important part for you to hear."

She moved the recording forward a minute to the part where Kidd asked Dorsey who gave him his number and Dorsey revealed that it had been Marcel Dupree. She turned the playback off again.

"So you tell Kidd that Marcel Dupree gave you his number and what does Kidd do? He hangs up on you and then sends a text to Marcel saying he wants a meet."

Ballard now held up her phone and showed Dorsey a freeze-frame that clearly depicted Kidd, with Dupree in profile, sitting at the table at Dulan's.

"I took this picture yesterday when they met at Dulan's," Ballard said. "You know the place down on Crenshaw? At that meeting Kidd gave Marcel three thousand dollars. What do you think that was for, Dennard?"

"I suppose you're gonna tell me," Dorsey said.

"It was to set you up for a hit in Men's Central. To have you whacked by one of your fellow Crips. You know Clinton Townes, right?"

Dorsey shook his head, as if he was trying to keep the information Ballard was laying on him from getting inside his ears.

"You're just spinning stories here," he said.

"That's why we had you pulled out of the tank, Dennard," Ballard said. "To save your life. Then we picked up Marcel and flipped him as easy as a pancake. Got him to call Kidd back and tell him it was all taken care of and you weren't going to be a problem. Take a listen."

Ballard cued up the scripted call between Dupree and Kidd and played it in its entirety. She sat back and watched Dorsey's face as he came to realize his own people had turned against him. Ballard knew how he felt, having once been betrayed by her partner, her boss, and the department itself.

"And wait, I've got one more," she said after. "Kidd even called the Medical Examiner's Office to make sure your cold dead body was there, waiting to be cut up in autopsy."

She played the last recording. Dorsey closed his eyes and shook his head.

"Mother*fucker,*" he said.

Ballard closed the laptop but kept her phone on the table. It was recording the conversation. She stared at Dorsey, who was now staring down at the table, his eyes filling with hate.

"So…," she said. "Elvin Kidd wanted you dead and now thinks you *are* dead. You want him to get away with that? Or do you want to tell me what you really know about what happened in that alley where that white boy got murdered?"

Dorsey looked up at her silently. She knew he was an inch away from breaking.

"You help me, I can help you," she said. "I just came from talking to a prosecutor. She wants Kidd for the murder. She'll talk to your parole officer, see about getting your violation lifted."

"You were supposed to do that," Dorsey said.

"I was going to, but having a prosecutor do it is money. But that doesn't happen unless you help me out here."

"Like I tol' you before, he told us to stay out the alley that day. Next thing I know, there was a murder back in there and police shut down our operations. We found a different location on the other side of the freeway."

"And that was that? You never spoke to Kidd about it, never asked any questions again? I don't believe that."

"I did ask him. He told me some shit."

"What shit, Dennard? This is the moment where you either help or hurt yourself. What did Elvin Kidd say?"

"He said he had to take care of this white kid he knew from when he was away."

"Away? What does that mean?"

"Prison. They were up there in Corcoran together and he said the kid owed him money from up there for protection."

"Did he mention the kid's name?"

"Nope. He just said he wouldn't pay what he owed so he arranged the meet and cleared us all out. Then the kid got shot."

"And you assumed Elvin Kidd shot him."

"Yeah, why not? It was his alley. He controlled everything. Nobody got shot there without his okay or him doin' it his own self."

Ballard nodded. It was not a direct confession from Kidd to Dorsey but it was close, and she thought it would be good enough for Selma Robinson. Then Dorsey, unprompted, added icing to the cake.

"When we had to move locations because the heat was on with the killing, I looked it up in the paper," he said. "I only found one thing but I remember the kid got shot had a name like a hotel. *Hilton* or *Hyatt* or some shit like that. And so I wondered if'n he had all that hotel money, how come he didn't just pay what he owed. He was stupid. He shoulda paid and then he'd be alive."

Dorsey had just pulled it all together. Ballard was elated. She picked up her phone, ended the recording, and put it in her pocket. She wished it were Monday and Selma Robinson was at the Hall of Justice. She wanted to go there right now and file a murder charge against Elvin Kidd.

BOSCH

38

The suede couch in the waiting area at Michaelson & Mitchell was so comfortable that Bosch nearly nodded off. It was Monday morning but he still had not recovered enough sleep from his all-night surveillance of his daughter's house the Saturday before. Nothing had happened and there had been no sign of the midnight stalker, but Bosch had kept a caffeine-stoked vigil throughout the night. He tried to make up the sleep on Sunday but thoughts about the Montgomery case kept him from even taking a nap. Now here he was, about to meet with Clayton Manley, and he felt like sinking into the waiting-room couch.

Finally, after fifteen minutes, he was collected by the young man from the reception desk. He led Bosch around a grand circular stair-case, then down a long hallway past frosted-glass doors that had the lead partners' names on them, and finally to the last office on the hall. He entered a large room with a desk, a sitting area, and a glass wall that looked down on Angels Flight from sixteen floors up.

Clayton Manley stood up from behind the desk. He was nearing forty, with dark hair but gray showing in his sideburns. He wore a light gray suit, a white shirt, and a blue tie.

"Mr. Bosch, come in," he said. "Please sit down."

He extended his hand across the desk and Bosch shook it before taking one of the club chairs in front of the desk.

"Now, my associate said you are looking for an attorney for a possible wrongful-death suit, is that correct?" Manley asked.

"Yes," Bosch said. "I need a lawyer. I talked to one and he didn't think he was up to it. So now I'm here, talking to you."

"Was it a loved one?"

"Excuse me?"

"The decedent who was the victim of the wrongful death."

"Oh, no, that would be me. I'm the victim."

Manley laughed, then saw there was no smile on Bosch's face. He stopped laughing and cleared his throat.

"Mr. Bosch, I don't understand," he said.

"Well, clearly I'm not dead," Bosch said. "But I've got a diagnosis of leukemia and I got it on the job. I want to sue them and get money for my daughter."

"How did this happen? Where did you work?"

"I was an LAPD homicide detective for over thirty years. I retired four years ago. I was forced out, actually, and I sued the department back then for trying to take away my pension. Part of the settlement put a cap on my health insurance, so this thing I've got could bankrupt me and leave nothing for my daughter."

Manley had shown no visible reaction to Bosch's mention that he had been an LAPD detective.

"So how did you get leukemia on the job?" Manley said. "And I guess the better question is, how do you prove it?"

"Easy," Bosch said. "There was a murder case and a large quantity of cesium was stolen from a hospital. The stuff they use in minute quantities to treat cancer. Only here, the amount missing was not minute. It was everything the hospital had and I ended up being the one who recovered it. I found it in a truck but didn't know it was there until I was exposed to it. I was checked out at the hospital and had X-rays and checkups for it for five years. Now I have leukemia, and there's no way it's not related to that exposure."

"And this is all documented? In case files and so forth?"

"Everything. There are the records from the murder investigation, the hospital, and the arbitration on my exit. We can get all of that. Plus, the hospital made sweeping security changes after that—which to me is an admission of responsibility."

"Of course it is. Now, I hate to ask this, but you said this was a wrongful-death case. What exactly is your diagnosis and prognosis?"

"I just got the diagnosis. I was tired all the time and just not feeling right, so I went in and they did some tests and I was told I have it. I'm about to start chemo, but you never know. It's going to get me in the end."

"But they didn't give you a time estimate or anything like that?"

"No, not yet. But I want to get this going because, like I said, you never know."

"I understand."

"Mr. Manley, these are tough people—the lawyers the city's got. I've fought them before. I went back to that attorney for this and he didn't seem real motivated because of the fight it would involve. So I need to know if this is something you can do. If you want to do it."

"I'm not afraid of a fight, Mr. Bosch. Or should I call you Detective Bosch?"

"*Mister* is good."

"Well, Mr. Bosch, as I said, I'm not afraid of a fight and this firm isn't either. We also have very powerful connections at our disposal. We like to say we can get anything done. Anything."

"Well, if this works out, there are a few other people I wouldn't mind doing something about."

"Who was your previous attorney?"

"A guy named Michael Haller. A one-man operation. People call him Mickey."

"I think he's the one they made a movie about—he works out of his car."

"Yeah, well, ever since he got famous, he doesn't take on the hard cases anymore. He didn't want this one."

"And he told you to come to me?"

"Yeah, he said you."

"I don't know him. Did he tell you why he recommended me?"

"Not really. He just said you'd stand up to the department."

"Well, that was kind of him. I will stand up to the department. I'll want to get whatever records you and Mr. Haller have on the pension arbitration. Anything related to the medical issue."

"Not a—"

Suddenly a bird slammed into the glass to Manley's right. He jumped in his seat. Bosch saw the stunned bird—it looked like a crow—fall from sight. He had read a story in the *Times* about the mirrored towers on Bunker Hill being bird magnets. He got up and walked to the glass. He looked down into the plaza fronting the upper station of Angels Flight. There was no sign of the bird.

Manley joined him at the window.

"That's the third time this year," he said.

"Really?" Bosch said. "Why don't they do something about it?"

"Can't. The mirroring is on the outside of the glass."

Manley returned to his seat behind his desk and Bosch went back to the club seat.

"What is the name of the doctor you're seeing for this?" Manley asked.

"Dr. Gandle," Bosch said. "He's an oncologist at Cedars."

"You'll have to call his office and tell them to release documents regarding your case to me."

"Not a problem. One thing we haven't talked about is your fee. I'm on the pension and that's it."

"Well, there are two ways we can go about doing this. You can pay me by the hour. My rate is four-fifty per billable hour. Or we can work out a prorated commission fee. You pay nothing and the firm takes a percentage of any money awarded or negotiated. The percentage would start at thirty and the more money recovered, the lower it goes."

"I'd probably do the percentage."

"Okay, in that case, I would take the case to the management board and they would discuss the merits and then decide if we accept the case."

"And how long does that take?"

"A day or two. The board meets Tuesdays and Thursdays."

"Okay."

"With what you've told me, I don't think it will be a problem. And I can assure you we are the right firm to represent you. We will bend over backward to serve you and to successfully handle your case. I guarantee it."

"Good to know."

Bosch stood up and so did Manley.

"The sooner you get me your files, the sooner the board will make a decision," Manley said. "Then we'll get this started."

"Thanks," Bosch said. "I'll get it all together and be in touch."

He found his own way out, passing by the closed doors of both Mitchell and Michaelson, and wondering if he had accomplished anything by bracing Manley. One thing he had noticed was that there was nothing of a personal nature in his office: no photos of family or even of himself shaking hands with people of note. Bosch would have thought it was a borrowed office if Manley hadn't mentioned that the bird collision was the third this year.

Outside the building, Bosch stood in the plaza, where office workers were sitting at tables eating late breakfasts or early lunches from a variety of shops and restaurants on the bottom level. He checked the perimeter of the building and didn't see the fallen bird. He wondered whether it had somehow survived and flown off before impact, or whether the building had a fast-moving maintenance team that cleaned up debris every time a bird hit the building and dropped into the plaza.

Bosch crossed the plaza to the Angels Flight funicular, bought a ticket, and rode one of the ancient train cars down to Hill Street. The ride was bumpy and jarring, and he remembered working a case long ago in which two people had been murdered on the mini-railroad. He crossed Hill and went into the Grand Central Market, where he ordered a turkey sandwich from Wexler's Deli.

He took the sandwich and a bottle of water to the communal seating area and found a table. As he ate, he sent a text to his daughter, knowing that it had a better chance of being answered than a phone call. His riffing about her and the lawsuit with Manley had reminded him that he wanted to see her. Spending Saturday nights secretly watching her house was not enough. He needed to see her and hear her voice.

> Mads, need to go down to Norwalk to pull a record for a case. That's halfway to you. Want to get coffee or dinner?

Ballard had called Bosch on Sunday from Ventura, where she was visiting the grandmother who had raised her during most of her teenage years. The update on the Hilton case was that Ballard had gone to see a prosecutor who was ready to file on Elvin Kidd. There was a list of things Selma Robinson wanted covered on the case to shore it up on all sides. Among those was Hilton's birth certificate. Robinson wanted no surprises and no missing pieces of the puzzle when she took the case to court.

Bosch didn't expect that his text to his daughter would be answered quickly. She was almost never prompt in her replies. Even though she was inseparable from her phone and therefore got his messages in a timely fashion—even if she was in class— she always seemed to deliberate at length over his communications before responding.

But this time he was wrong. She hit him back before he was finished with his sandwich.

> That might work. But I have a class 7–9. Early dinner okay?

Bosch sent back a message saying any time was a good time and that he would head south after lunch, take care of his business in Norwalk, then get to a coffee shop near Chapman University and be ready to meet whenever she was ready.

In answer, he got a thumbs-up.

He dumped his trash in a can and took the bottle of water with him back to his car.

39

Bosch descended the steps of the county records building in Nor-walk with his head down and his thoughts so far away that he walked by the horde of document doctors without even noticing them waving application forms at him or offering translation help. He continued into the parking lot and toward his Jeep.

He pulled his phone to call Ballard, but it buzzed in his hand with a call from her before he got the chance.

"Guess what?" she said by way of a greeting.

"What?" Bosch replied.

"The D.A.'s Office just charged Elvin Kidd with counts of murder and conspiracy to commit murder. We fucking did it, Harry!"

"More like you did it. Did you pick him up yet?"

"No, probably tomorrow. It's sealed for now. You want to be in on it?"

"I don't think I should be part of that. Could make things complicated, me not having a badge. But you're not going out there alone, right?"

"No, Harry, I'm not that reckless. I'm going to see if SWAT can spare a few guys. I'll also have to call in Rialto PD because it's their turf."

"Sounds like a plan."

"So, where are you?"

"On my way down to see my daughter. I'll be back up tonight."

"Any chance you can go by Norwalk? I still haven't gotten anything from Sacramento and it's on Selma's follow-up list. We need Hilton's birth certificate."

Bosch pulled the documents out of his inside coat pocket. He unfolded them on the center console.

"I just walked out. Had to show my San Fernando star to get access. I traced Hilton through his mother. Her maiden name was Charles but she was never married before she married his stepfather."

"Donald Hilton."

"Right."

"So, she was an unwed mother."

"Right. So I looked through births under her name and found a birth that matched the DOB on John Hilton's driver's license. It was him. And the father was listed as John Jack Thompson."

Ballard had a delayed reaction.

"Holy shit," she finally said.

"Yeah," Bosch said. "Holy shit."

"Oh my god, this means he sat on his own child's murder case! He stole the book so no one else could work it, then didn't work it himself. How could he do that?"

They were both silent for a long moment. Bosch returned to the thoughts that had preoccupied him as he left the records building: the gut punch of knowing his mentor had acted so unethically and had put pride ahead of finding justice for his own child.

"This explains Hunter and Talis," Ballard said. "They found out and then took a dive on the case to save Thompson from being embarrassed by public knowledge in the department that his son was—take your pick—a drug addict, an ex-con, and a gay man in love with a black gangbanger."

Bosch didn't respond. Ballard had nailed it. The only thing she had left out was the possibility that Thompson's actions may have been an effort to protect his wife from that knowledge too. Bosch also thought about what Thompson had told him that time about not bringing a child into the world. It made him wonder if he had known about Hilton before his death or learned of his son only when Hunter and Talis brought the news.

"I'm going to call Talis back," Ballard said. "I'm going to tell him I know why he and his partner took a dive. See what he has to say then."

"I know what he'll say," Bosch responded. "He'll say it was a different time and the victim was a no-count. They weren't going to ruin John Jack's marriage or reputation by hanging all this on the clothesline for the world to see."

"Yeah, well, fuck that. There is no valid reason for this."

"No, there isn't. Just be careful about going back to Talis."

"Why should I? Don't tell me you're sticking up for that old-school bullshit."

"No, I'm not. I'm just thinking about the case. Selma Robinson might have to bring him down to testify. You don't want to turn him into a hostile witness for the prosecution."

"Right. I didn't think about that. And sorry about that 'old-school' crack, Harry. I know you're not like that."

"Good."

They were both quiet again for a long moment before Bosch spoke.

"So who do you think redacted the report in the murder book?" he asked. "And why?"

"Talis will never own up to it now," Ballard said. "But my guess is they interviewed Hilton's mother and stepfather, were told the real father was Thompson, and put it in the report. They inform Thompson and he asks them to wipe all mention of it out of the murder book. You know—professional courtesy, scumbag to scumbag."

Bosch thought that was a harsh assessment, even while feeling that what John Jack had done to his own son was unforgivable.

"Or it was in the book all along and Thompson did it after he stole it," Ballard added. "Maybe that was why he stole it. To make sure any mention of the biological father's identity was removed or redacted."

"Then why not just throw the book away or destroy it?" Bosch asked. "Then there would be no chance any of this would ever come to surface."

"We'll never know about that. He died with that secret."

"I'm hoping there was still enough detective in him to think someone would get the book after he was gone and look into the case."

"That someone being you."

Bosch was silent.

"You know what I wonder?" Ballard said. "Whether Thompson even knew about the kid before the murder. You have an unwed mother. Did she tell him? Or did she just go off and have the kid and put his name on the birth certificate? Maybe Thompson never knew till Talis and Hunter came around on the case and asked him about it."

"It's a possibility," Bosch said.

More silence followed as both detectives contemplated the angles on this part of the case. Bosch knew there were always unanswered questions in every murder, every investigation. Those who were naive called them loose ends, but they were never loose. They stuck with him, clinging to him as he moved on, sometimes waking him up in the night. But they were never loose and he could never get free of them.

"Okay, I'm gonna go," Bosch finally said. "My kid's only free till seven and I want to get down there."

"Okay, Harry," Ballard said. "I forgot to ask. Did you go down there Saturday night?"

"I did. It was all clear."

"Well, I guess that's good."

"Yeah. So let me know how it goes tomorrow with Kidd. Think he'll talk?"

"I don't know. You?"

"I think he's one of those guys who will waive but then won't say a thing of value and will try to work you to see what you've got on him."

"Probably. I'll be ready for that."

"And don't forget his wife. She either knows everything or doesn't know anything, and either way you might be able to work some good stuff out of her."

"I'll remember that."

"I had this case once. Arrested the guy on an old one-eighty-seven and at the preliminary the judge held him over but said the evidence was so thin he was going to set a low bail till the trial. So the guy makes bail and proceeds to do everything he can to delay the trial: he fires lawyers right and left, and every new guy asks the judge for more prep time. It goes on and on like that."

"Enjoy your freedom as long as you can."

"Right. I mean, why not if you're out and about on bail? So enjoying his freedom includes meeting this woman and marrying her, apparently never telling her, 'Oh by the way, baby, someday, eventually, I have to go on trial for murder.' So—"

"No! You're kidding?"

"No, this is what he did. I found out after. And so finally, four years into all of these delays, the judge has had enough, says no more delays, and the guy finally goes to trial. But he's still out on bail and he had a shirt-and-tie job—he was like a Realtor or something. So every day he put on his suit and tie at home and told his wife he was going to work, but he was really going to his own murder trial and keeping it a secret from her. He was hoping he'd get a *Not Guilty* and she would never know."

"What happened?"

"Guilty. Bail revoked on the spot and he's taken away to jail. Can you imagine that? You get a collect call from your husband at the county jail and he says, 'Honey, I won't be home for dinner—I just got convicted of murder.'"

Ballard started laughing.

"Men are devious," Bosch said.

"No," Ballard said. "Everybody's devious."

"But I always wish I'd known the wife had been kept in the dark. Because I think I could have used that. You know—talked to her, enlightened her, maybe gotten her on my side, and who knows what would've come out. It's a funny story but I always thought I should've known."

"Okay, Harry, I'll remember that. Safe travels and tell your daughter hello."

"Will do. Happy hunting tomorrow."

Bosch got back over to the 5 freeway and continued south. The amusement of the story he had told Ballard wore off and soon he was thinking about John Jack Thompson, what he had done, and his possible motives. It felt like such a betrayal to Bosch. The man who mentored him—who instilled in him the belief that every case deserved his best, that everybody counted or nobody counted—that man had submarined a case involving his own blood.

The only saving grace of the moment was that he was going to see his own daughter. Whether he got five minutes with her or fifty, he knew that she would pull him out of darkness, and he would be renewed and able to move on.

Bosch got to Old Towne in the city of Orange at 4:15 p.m. and drove around the Circle twice before finding a parking spot. He went into the Urth Café and ordered a coffee. He texted Maddie his location and said they could meet there or anywhere else she wanted. She texted back that she would let him know as soon as she was free from the meeting she was having with other students regarding a joint psychology project.

Bosch had brought his laptop in with him, as well as a file containing all the reports from the Montgomery murder book that referenced the short-lived Clayton Manley tangent. He tried to escape thoughts of John Jack Thompson by piggybacking on the coffee shop's Wi-Fi and calling up stories on the case involving Dominick Butino. He found three stories that had run in the *Times* and he read them now to refresh his memory.

The first story was about Butino's arrest in Hollywood for assault and mayhem after an attack on a man in the back of a catering truck parked outside an independent studio on Lillian Street. Police at the time said the man who operated the truck, which provided meals for film and TV crews, owed Butino money because he had financed the purchase of the truck. The story said that the man was attacked with a baseball bat and that Butino also went on a rampage inside the catering truck, using the bat to destroy several pieces of food-prep equipment. The victim, who was identified in the story as Angel Hopkins, was listed in critical-but-stable condition at Cedars Sinai Medical Center, with a fractured skull, a ruptured eardrum, and a broken arm.

According to the story, Butino was arrested when an off-duty police officer providing security at the studio on Lillian walked to the truck to purchase coffee and found the suspect standing outside the back door of the truck, wiping blood off a baseball bat with a kitchen apron. Hopkins was then found unconscious on the floor of the truck's kitchen.

The second story was a follow-up published the next day that identified Butino, of Las Vegas, as a suspected member of a Chicago-based organized-crime family known simply as the Outfit. It also said he was known as "Batman" in organized-crime circles because of his prowess with the black baseball bat he was known to carry when collecting money as part of the Outfit's loan-sharking operations.

The third story came three months later and it was about the District Attorney's Office dropping all charges against Butino during the trial, when Angel Hopkins refused to testify against him. The prosecutor explained to reporters that despite the officer who happened on the scene being willing to tell his part of the story, the case could not move forward without the victim telling jurors what happened, who did it, and why. Butino's attorney, William Michaelson, was quoted in the story as saying the whole thing was a misunderstanding and misidentification of his client. Michaelson praised the justice system for a just result in a case that had brought his client undue publicity and stress.

It was obvious to Bosch that Hopkins had been intimidated or paid off by Batman or his associates, maybe even his lawyers.

Bosch saw a few other mentions on Google of Butino being involved in activities in Las Vegas. One story was about a campaign donation he had made to a mayoral candidate being returned by the candidate because of Butino's background. The story quoted the candidate as saying, "I don't want any money from Batman."

Another story was simply a name check in which the mobster was mentioned as being in front-row attendance at a boxing match at the MGM Grand.

A third story was the most recent and was about a federal RICO investigation into the corrupt practices of a Las Vegas company that provided linens for several casino resorts on the Strip. Butino was mentioned as a minority owner of the linen and laundry company.

Next Bosch moved to the California Bar website and searched the name William Michaelson to see if any disciplinary actions had been taken against the attorney. He found only one: it had occurred four years earlier, when Michaelson was censured in a case where he took a meeting with a prospective client in a contract dispute. The woman later complained to the bar that Michaelson listened to her outline her side of the dispute for forty minutes before saying he was not interested in taking the case. She later found out that he was already engaged by the defendant she intended to sue and had taken the meeting with her in order to get inside information on the opposition.

It was a sneaky move, and while the bar went easy on Michaelson, it told Bosch a lot about his character and ethics. Michaelson was a lead partner in the firm. What did that say about the other partners and associates who worked for him? What did that say about Manley, who was just one door farther down the hallway at the firm?

"Hey, Daddo."

Bosch looked up as his daughter slipped into the chair across the table from him. His eyes lit up. He felt the hurt of having learned about John Jack Thompson and everything else slip away.

40

Maddie slipped her backpack under the table in front of her.

"Is this okay?" Bosch asked. "I thought you were going to text me."

"Yeah, but I love this place," Maddie said. "Usually, you can't get a table."

"I must've hit it at the right time."

"What are you working on?"

Bosch closed his laptop.

"I was looking up a lawyer on the California Bar," he said. "Wanted to know if anybody had dinged him with a complaint."

"Uncle Mickey?" Maddie asked.

"No, no, not him. Another guy."

"Are you working on a case?"

"Yeah. Actually two of them. One with Renée Ballard—who says hello, by the way—and one sort of on my own."

"Daddo, you're supposed to be retired."

"I know but I want to keep moving."

"How's your knee?"

"It's pretty good. Today I went out without the cane. All day."

"Is that okay with the doctor?"

"He didn't want me to use it at all. He's a hard-liner. So how's school?"

"Boring. But did you hear the big news? They caught that guy Saturday night."

"You mean the creeper?"

"Yeah, he broke into the wrong house. It's on the *Orange County Register* website. Same thing—a house of girls. He snuck in, only he didn't know one of the girls had her boyfriend staying over. The boyfriend catches him in the house, beats the crap out of him, then calls the cops."

"And he's good for the other two?"

"The police haven't called us, but they told the *Register* they would be doing the DNA stuff, seeing if he was connected. But they said the MO was the same. *Modus operandi*—I love saying those words."

Bosch nodded.

"Do you know where the house was?" he asked. "Was it near yours?"

"No, it was in the neighborhood on the other side of the school."

"Well, great, I'm glad they caught the guy. You and your roommates should be able to sleep better now."

"Yeah, we will."

Bosch intended to call his contact at the Orange Police Department on his drive back up to L.A. to find out more about the arrest. But he was elated by the news. He was acting reserved because he didn't want his daughter to know how truly unnerving the situation had been for him. He decided to move on to other subject matter with her.

"So, what's the psych project you're all doing?"

"Oh, just a dumb thing on how social media influences people. Nothing groundbreaking. We have to write up a survey and then spread out and find people on campus to take it. Ten questions about FOMO."

She pronounced the last word *foe-moe*.

"What is 'foe-moe'?" Bosch asked.

"Dad, come on," Maddie said. "Fear Of Missing Out."

"Got it. So, you want something to eat or drink? You have to go up to the counter. I'll hold the table."

He reached into his pocket for some cash.

"I'll pay with my card," Maddie said. "Do you want something?"

"Are you getting food?" Bosch asked.

"I'm going to get something."

"Then get me a chicken-salad sandwich if they have it. And another coffee. Black. Let me give you some cash."

"No, I have it."

She got up from the table and headed to the counter. He was constantly amused by how she always wanted to pay herself with her credit card, when the credit-card bill came to him anyway.

He watched her order from a young man who most likely was a fellow student. She smiled and he smiled and Bosch began to think there was a previous connection.

She came back to the table with two coffees, one with cream.

"You have to study tonight?" Bosch asked.

"Actually, no," Maddie said. "I have class seven to nine and then some of us are going to the D."

Bosch knew that the D was a bar called the District favored by students over twenty-one. Maddie was one of them. The reminder of that prompted Bosch's next question.

"So which way are you leaning today? For after graduation."

"You're not going to like it, but law school."

"Why do you think I won't like that?"

"I know you want me to be a cop. Plus it means more school and you already spent a ton of money sending me here."

"No, how many times have we had this talk? I want you to do what you want to do. In fact, the law is safer and you'd make more money. Law school is great, and don't worry about the costs. I have it covered. And I didn't spend a ton of money sending you here. Your scholarships covered most of it. So it's the other way around. You saved me money."

"But what if I end up like Uncle Mickey—*defending the damned,* as you like to say?"

Bosch drank some of his fresh coffee as a delaying tactic.

"That would be your choice," he said after putting the cup down. "But I hope you'd at least look at the other side of it. I could set you up if you wanted to talk to some people in the D.A.'s Office."

"Maybe someday you and I could be a team. You hook 'em and I cook 'em."

"That sounds like fishing."

"Speaking of fishing, is that what you came down to ask me about?"

Bosch drank more coffee before answering. He caught a further break when the handsome lad from the counter delivered their food and Maddie over-thanked him. Bosch looked at her plate. It seemed like everybody was eating avocado toast lately. It looked awful to him.

"Is that dinner?" he asked.

"A snack," Maddie said. "I'll eat at the D. The guy with the grill outside has the best veggie dogs. It's probably the thing I'll miss most about this place."

"So if it's law school, not here?"

"I want to get back to L.A. Uncle Mickey went to Southwestern up there. I think I could get in. It's a good feeder school for the public defender's office."

Before Bosch could react to that, the handsome server came back to the table and asked Maddie if she liked her toast. Maddie enthusiastically approved and he went back behind the counter. He hadn't bothered to ask Bosch how his sandwich was.

"So that guy, you know him?" Bosch asked.

"We had a class together last year," Maddie said. "He's cute."

"I think he thinks you're cute."

"And I think you're changing the subject."

"Can't I just come down and hang with my daughter a little bit, drink coffee, eat a sandwich, and learn new words like *foe-moe?*"

"It's an acronym, not a word: *F-O-M-O.* What's really going on, Dad?"

"Okay, okay. I wanted to tell you something. It's not a big deal but you always get mad when you think I intentionally don't tell you things. I think it's called *FOLO*—Fear Of Being Left Out."

"That doesn't make sense. Plus *FOLO* is already taken: that's Fear Of Losing Out. So what's the news? Are you getting married or something?"

"No, I'm not getting married."

"Then what?"

"You remember how I used to have to get chest X-rays because of that case I had where radioactive material was found?"

"Yes, and then you stopped when they said you had a clean bill of health."

The concern was growing in her eyes. Bosch loved her for that.

"Well, now I have a very mild form of leukemia that is highly treatable and is being treated, and I'm only telling you this because I know you would scream at me if you found out later."

Maddie didn't respond. She looked down at her coffee and her eyes shifted back and forth as if she was reading instructions on what to say and how to act.

"It's not a big thing, Mads. In fact, it's just a pill. One pill I take in the morning."

"Do you have to do chemo and all of that?"

"No, I'm serious. It's just a pill. That is the chemo. They say I just take this and I'll be okay. I wanted to tell you because your uncle Mickey is going to bat for me on this and he's going to try to get some money for it. It happened when I was on the job and I don't want to lose everything I have set up for you because of it. So he said it could make some news, and that's what I wanted to avoid—you reading about it online somewhere and then being upset with me for not telling you. But, really, everything is fine."

She reached across the table and put her hand on top of his.

"Dad."

He turned his hand over so he could hold her fingers.

"You have to eat your snack," he said. "Whatever that is."

"I don't feel like eating now," she said.

He didn't either. He hated scaring her.

"You believe me, right?" he asked. "This is like a formality. I wanted you to hear it from me."

"They should pay. They should pay you a lot of money."

Bosch laughed.

"I think you should go to law school," he said.

She didn't see the humor in that. She kept her eyes down.

"Hey, if you don't feel like eating that, let's take it to go and then go over to that ice-cream place you like, where they cold brew it, or whatever it's called."

"Dad, I'm not a little girl. You can't make everything right with ice cream."

"So, lesson learned. I should have just shut up and hoped you never found out."

"No, it's not that. I'm allowed to feel this way. I love you."

"And I love you, and that's what I'm trying to say: I'm going to be around for a long while. I'm going to send you to law school and then I'm going to sit in the back of courtrooms and watch you send bad people away."

He waited for a reaction. A smile or a smirk, but he got nothing.

"Please," he said. "Let's not worry about this anymore. Okay?"

"Okay," Maddie said. "Let's go get that ice cream."

"Good. Let's go."

She waved the cute guy over and asked him for to-go boxes.

An hour later Bosch had dropped his daughter back at her car and was heading north on the 5 freeway toward L.A. It had been a double-whammy of a day: John Jack Thompson injecting pain and uncertainty into his life, then Bosch doing the same to his daughter and feeling like some sort of criminal for it.

The bottom line was that he was still having a hard time with Thompson. Bosch was almost seventy years old and he had seen some of the worst things people can do to each other, yet something done decades ago and long before his knowledge of it had sent him reeling. He wondered if it was a side effect of the pills he was taking each morning. The doctor had warned there could be mood swings.

On top of all that, he realized he was experiencing FOMO: he wanted to be there when Ballard took down Elvin Kidd for killing John Jack Thompson's son. Not because he wanted to see the arrest itself—Bosch had never taken particular joy in putting the cuffs on killers. But he wanted to be there for the son. The victim. John Hilton's own father apparently didn't care who had killed him, but Bosch did and he wanted to be there. Everybody counted or nobody counted. It might have been a hollow idea to Thompson. But it wasn't to Bosch.

BALLARD

41

Ballard had her earbuds in and was listening to a playlist she had put together for building an edge and keeping it. She was squeezed between two large Special Ops officers in the back of a black SUV. It was seven a.m. and they were on the 10 freeway heading out to Rialto to take down Elvin Kidd.

Two SUVs, nine officers, plus one already in an observation post outside Kidd's home in Rialto. The plan was to make the arrest when Kidd emerged from his house to go to work. Going into the residence of an ex-gang member was never a good plan; they would wait for Kidd to step out. The last report from the man in the OP had been that the suspect's truck and attached equipment trailer were backed into the driveway. No movement or light had been reported inside the house.

The arrest plan had been approved by the Special Ops lieutenant, who was in the lead SUV. Ballard's role was as observer and then arresting officer. She would step in after Kidd was in custody and read the man his rights.

In the second SUV the men had carried on a conversation as though Ballard was not among them. The dialogue crisscrossed in front of her without so much as a *What do you think?* or a *Where do you come from?* thrown Ballard's way. It was just nervous chatter and Ballard knew everybody had different ways of getting ready for battle. She put her earbuds in and listened to Muse and Black

Pumas, Death Cab, and others. Disparate songs that all built and held an edge for her.

Ballard saw the driver talking into a rover and pulled out her buds.

"What's up, Griffin?" she asked.

"Lights on in the house," Griffin said.

"How far out are we?"

"ETA twenty minutes."

"We need to step it up. This guy might be ready to boogie. Can we go to code three on the freeway?"

Griffin relayed the request by radio to Lieutenant Gonzalez in the lead SUV and soon they were moving toward Rialto under lights and sirens at ninety miles per hour.

She put the earbuds back in and listened to the propulsive words and beat of "Dig Down" by Muse.

> *We must find a way*
> *We have entered the fray*

Twelve minutes later, they were three blocks from Kidd's home at a meeting point with a couple of Rialto patrol officers called in by courtesy and procedure. Gonzalez and the other SUV team were in position a block from the other side of the suspect's house. They were waiting for the call from the OP on Kidd emerging before making a move. Ballard had pulled her buds out for good in the middle of "Dark Side" by Bishop Briggs. She was ready to go. She hooked an earpiece attached to her rover on her ear and tuned the radio to the simplex channel the team was using.

Three minutes later they got the call from the OP. Ballard didn't know if he was in a vehicle, a tree, or the roof of a neighbor's house, but he was reporting that a black male matching Elvin Kidd's description was outside the house putting a toolbox into the back of the equipment trailer. He was getting ready to go.

The next radio call placed him at the truck's door, opening it with a key. Ballard then heard Gonzalez's voice ordering everyone in. The SUV she was in lurched forward, slamming her back against her seat. Tires squealed as it made the right turn and then the vehicle picked up speed as adrenaline coursed through her bloodstream. The other SUV was point. Through the windshield, Ballard saw it arrive on scene first and pull across the pickup truck's exit path from the driveway. Only a second behind, the second SUV pulled up on the front lawn, blocking the only other potential angle of escape.

A lot of adrenalized shouting occurred as the Special Ops team emerged from the vehicles with weapons drawn and pointed them at the unsuspecting man in the pickup truck.

"Police! Show me your hands! Show me your hands!"

As previously planned and ordered by Gonzalez, Ballard stayed behind in the SUV, waiting for the call that Kidd had been secured and all was clear. But even turning sideways, she did not have a clear view of the pickup's front cab through the open door of the SUV. She knew that this was the moment where anything could happen. Any sudden or furtive movement, any sound, even a radio squawk, might set off a barrage of gunfire. She decided not to wait for Gonzalez's call—she had objected to staying behind from the start. She climbed out of the SUV on the safe side. She drew her weapon and moved around the back of the vehicle. She had a ballistic vest strapped on over her clothes.

She moved around the SUV until she had an angle on the front of the pickup. She saw Kidd inside, palms on top of the wheel, fingers up. It looked like he was surrendering.

The cacophony of voices gave way to the single voice of Gonzalez, who ordered Kidd to get out of the truck and walk backward toward the officers. It seemed like minutes, but it took only seconds. Kidd was grabbed by two officers, put on the ground, and cuffed. They then stood him up, leaned him forward over the hood of his truck, and searched him.

"What is this?" Kidd protested. "You come to my home and do this shit?"

Ballard heard her name over the radio earpiece, her cue that it was safe for her to move in and speak to Kidd. She holstered her weapon and walked to the pickup. She was surprised by the pitch of her own voice as the adrenaline held her vocal cords tight; at least to herself, she sounded like a little boy.

"Elvin Kidd, you are under arrest for murder and conspiracy to commit murder. You have the right to remain silent. Anything you say can and will be used against you in a court of law. You have the right to an attorney. If you cannot afford an attorney, one will be provided for you. Do you understand these rights as I have recited them to you?"

Kidd turned his head to look at her.

"Murder?" he said. "Who'd I murder?"

"Do you understand your rights, Mr. Kidd?" Ballard said. "I can't talk to you until you answer."

"Yeah, yeah, I understand my fucking rights. Who you all sayin' I killed?"

"John Hilton. Remember him?"

"I don't know who the fuck you're talking about."

Ballard had anticipated such a deflection. She also anticipated that this might be her only moment to confront Kidd. He would most likely demand a lawyer and she would never get close to him again. She would also soon be yanked off the case because all of her off-the-reservation actions would come to light with his arrest. It was not the right place to do what she was about to do, but to her, it was now or never. She pulled her mini-recorder from her back pocket and hit the Play button. The recording of the wiretap between Kidd and Marcel Dupree was cued to a particular moment. Kidd heard his own voice come from the device:

A piece of work I had to handle back then. A white boy who owed too much money.

Ballard clicked off the recorder and studied Kidd's reaction. She could see the wheels grinding, then coming to a halt at the phone call he had received from Dupree. She could tell he knew he had just experienced his last moments of freedom.

"We're going to take you back to L.A. now," Ballard said. "And you'll get a chance to talk to me if—"

She was interrupted by a voice in her ear. The man in the observation post.

"Somebody's coming out. Black female, white bathrobe. She's got…I think…gun! Gun! Gun!"

Everyone reacted. Weapons were drawn and the Special Ops guys all turned toward the front of the house. Through the narrow space between the two black SUVs, Ballard saw the woman on the stone walk leading from the front door to the driveway. She wore an over-size robe—probably her husband's—that had allowed her to conceal a handgun in the sleeve. It was up and out now, and she was yelling.

"You can't take him!"

Her eyes then fell on Ballard, who stood there as an open target in the clearing between the two SUVs and the pickup. Ballard held the recorder in her hand instead of her gun.

Ballard saw the woman's arm come up. It almost seemed to be in slow motion. But then the movement stopped, the angle of the gun still down. Then the side of her head exploded in blood and tissue before Ballard even heard the shot come from a distance. She knew it had come from the OP.

The woman's knees bent forward and she collapsed on her back on the stone path her husband had likely installed himself at their house.

Officers rushed forward to secure the gun and check on the woman. Ballard instinctively took a step in that direction as well and then remembered Kidd. She turned back to him, but he was gone.

Ballard ran out to the street and saw Kidd running, hands still cuffed behind his back. She took off after him, yelling to the others.

"We've got a runner!"

Kidd was fast for a man his age wearing construction boots and running with his arms behind his back. But Ballard closed on him before the end of the block and was able to grab the chain between his cuffs and pull him to a stop.

Now she pulled her gun and held it at the side of her thigh.

"Did you kill her?" Kidd said breathlessly. "Did you mother-fuckers kill her?"

Ballard was out of breath herself. She tried to gulp in air before responding. She felt sweat popping on her neck and scalp. One of the SUVs was barreling down the street toward them. She knew they would grab him now and these would possibly be her last moments with Kidd.

"If we killed her, it's on you, Elvin," she said. "It's all on you."

42

The killing of Cynthia Kidd had brought out the Critical Incident Vehicle, which was a thirty-two-foot RV repurposed as a mobile incident command and interview center. The CIV was parked two doors down from the Kidd home. The street was taped off at both ends of the block, with members of the media standing vigil at the closest point. The physical and forensic investigation continued at the house while all officers involved in the morning's incident were debriefed by detectives from the Force Investigation Division in the second room of the CIV, the room dubbed "the Box" because of its perfectly square dimensions.

FID detectives interviewed the Special Ops officers one by one about the arrest gone sideways, and Ballard was listed as last to be questioned. Each officer had a union defense representative at their side, because they all knew that the outcome of the shooting investigation could determine their career paths. There was a somber silence hanging over everything. A highly trained SWAT team had killed the wife of a suspect under arrest. It was a colossal failure of tactics. Added to that, the dead woman was black and this would invariably draw massive public scrutiny and protest. It would invariably lead to rumors that the victim had been unarmed and simply gunned down. The true story—as bad as it was on its own—would be bent to the needs of those with agendas or axes to grind in the public forum. Everybody on scene knew this and it resulted in a blanket of dread descending over the proceedings on the residential street in Rialto.

It was almost three hours after the shooting before Ballard was finally interviewed. The session with an FID detective named Kathryn Meloni lasted twenty-six minutes and was largely focused on the tactics Ballard had used during the Kidd arrest and the tactics she had observed being used by the arrest team. Ballard's defense rep, Teresa Hohman, happened to have been in Ballard's academy class, where they competed closely in all the physical challenges for top female recruit but always had beers and cheers at the academy club after. It was that bond that had prompted Ballard to ask her to be her rep.

Up until the final minutes of the questioning, Ballard believed she had given no answer that could come back on her or the Special Ops team in terms of mistakes or poor tactics. Then Meloni hit her with a trap question.

"At what point did you hear Lieutenant Gonzalez or anyone else order someone to either watch or guard the front door?" she asked.

Ballard took several seconds to compose her answer. Hohman whispered in her ear that there was no good response, but that she had to answer.

"There was a lot of yelling," Ballard finally said. "Screaming at Elvin Kidd in the truck. I was concentrating on him and my role in the arrest. So I didn't hear that particular order when it was given."

"Are you saying that there was an order and you just didn't hear it?" Meloni asked. "Or was it that there was no order given?"

Ballard shook her head.

"See, I can't answer that one way or the other," she said. "I had a laser focus on what I was doing and needed to be doing. That's how we're trained. I followed my training."

"Going back now to the planning meeting prior to the operation," Meloni said. "Did you tell Lieutenant Gonzalez that the suspect was married?"

"I did."

"Did you tell him or members of the team that the wife could be expected to be in the home?"

"I think we all knew, making the arrest so early in the morning, that we could expect her to be on scene. In the house."

"Thank you, Detective. That's it for now."

She reached over to turn the recorder off but then stopped and turned back to Ballard.

"One more thing," she said. "Do you believe that killing Mrs. Kidd may have saved the lives of officers today?"

This time Ballard didn't pause.

"Absolutely, yes," she said. "I mean, we were all wearing vests and those guys had ballistic helmets and so forth, so you can never be sure. But I was standing there in the open in front of the pickup and she could have shot me. Then for a moment she hesitated and got hit herself."

"If she hesitated, do you think she was not intending to fire her weapon?" Meloni asked.

"No, it wasn't that. She was going to shoot. I could feel it. But she hesitated because I was between her and her husband—until he took off running, that is. I think she thought that if she shot and missed me, she might hit him. So that's when she hesitated. Then she got hit and maybe that saved my life."

"Thank you, Detective Ballard."

"Sure."

"If you don't mind staying in the room, your captain wants to come in and speak to you next."

"My captain?"

"Captain Olivas. You were working this case for him, correct?"

"Oh, yes, correct. Sorry, I'm still a little shaken up."

"Understandable. I'll send him in."

Ballard was surprised that Olivas was on scene. They were more than an hour away from the city and she hadn't expected him to be involved in the FID investigation at all. Her mind raced and she began to feel dread at the realization that Olivas must have been informed about the case that had led to Elvin Kidd. He knew what she had done.

"He told me he wanted to speak to you alone," Hohman said. "Is that okay?"

She and Teresa still met for beers from time to time, even though their paths in the department were quite different. Ballard had previously told Hohman of her history with Olivas.

"Or I can stay," she said.

"No," Ballard said. "I'm okay. You can send him in."

The truth was Ballard didn't want a witness to what might come out or happen next, even if that witness was her own friend and defense rep.

After Teresa left, Olivas entered the CIV, walked through the outer room and into the Box. He silently took a seat across the table from Ballard. He stared at her for a moment before speaking.

"I know how you did it," he said.

"Did what?" Ballard said.

"Got my signature on the wiretap warrant."

Ballard knew there was no use denying the truth. That wasn't the right move here.

"And?"

"And I'm willing to play along."

"Why?"

"Because I've got a year until I'm out. I don't need another fight with you and, right now, this is another feather in my cap. We took down a murderer, cleared a thirty-year-old case."

"We?"

"That'll be how it plays. We both win. You keep your badge, I look good. What's not to like about that?"

"I guess that woman who got her head blown off might find something not to like."

"People do stupid things in high-stress situations. Gangbanger's wife? There will be no blowback on this one. Internally, at least. There will be protests and Black Lives Matter and all of that. But internally she doesn't matter in this equation. She's collateral damage. What I'm saying, Ballard, is that I could take you down for this. Take your badge. But I'm not. I'm going to give you credit for this. And you give me credit right back."

Ballard knew what was happening. The command staff of the department was known to watch out for their own. Olivas was angling for one more promotion before he pulled the pin on his career.

"You want to make deputy chief, don't you?" she said. "Going out on a DC's pension, that would be sweet. Add a corporate security job to that and you'll be rolling in the green, huh? Living on the beach."

City pensions were based on salary at the time of retirement. There was a long history in the department of promotions within command ranks just prior to retirement—with city taxpayers footing the bill. There was also a history of punitive demotions among rank-and-file members that lowered their pensions and payouts. Ballard suddenly flashed on the legal fight Harry Bosch had engaged in after his retirement. She didn't know all the details, but she knew the department had tried to fuck him over.

"My business is my business," Olivas said. "All we need right now is to agree on a course of action."

"How do I know you won't try to fuck me over in the end?" Ballard said.

"I thought you would ask that. So this is what we do: once the smoke clears here, we go back to L.A. and hold a press conference— you and me—and we tell the story. That's your edge. Once it's public record, it would look bad for me to turn around and do something against you before I leave. Understand?"

Ballard found the idea of being part of a press conference with her oppressor and nemesis revolting.

"I'll pass on the press conference," she said. "But I'll share credit with you and keep my badge. And I don't need an edge. If you do try to come back on me in any way before you quit, I'll tell the world about this dirty little deal and you'll go out as a lieutenant instead of a deputy chief. Understand?"

Ballard reached down to her thigh and picked up her phone. She brought it up and put it down on the table. The recording app was open on the screen. The elapsed time on the file being recorded was over thirty-one minutes.

"Rule number one," she said. "If IA or FID records an interview with you, you record it yourself. To be safe. I just sort of forgot to turn it off."

Ballard watched the skin around Olivas's eyes tighten as anger charged his blood.

"Relax, Captain," she said. "It makes us both look bad. I can't hurt you without you hurting me. That's the point, you see?"

"Ballard," Olivas said, "I always knew there was something I liked about you besides your looks. You're a devious bitch and I like that. Always have."

She knew that he thought the words would hurt and distract her. He made a swipe at the phone but she was ready and grabbed it off the table, his hand brushing over hers. She stood up, her chair falling back against the aluminum wall.

"You want to fight me for it?" she asked. "I've gotten strong since you did what you did to me. I will kick your fucking ass."

Olivas remained seated. He held his hands up, palms out.

"Easy, Ballard," he said. "Easy. This is crazy. I'm good with what we said. The deal."

The door to the CIV opened and Teresa Hohman looked in, drawn by the clattering of the chair against the vehicle's thin wall.

"Everything okay in here?" she asked.

"We're fine," Olivas said.

Hohman looked at Ballard. She wasn't taking Olivas's word for it. Ballard nodded, and only then did Hohman step back and close the door.

Ballard looked back at Olivas.

"So we have a deal?" she asked.

"I said yes," he said.

Ballard turned off the recording app and put her phone in her pocket.

"Except now I want something else," she said. "A couple of things, actually."

"Jesus Christ," Olivas said. "What?"

"If Elvin Kidd decides to talk, I do the interview."

"Not a problem—but he'll never give it up. That'll get him killed inside. I already heard he told FID to pound fucking sand when they tried to question him about his own wife getting killed. No interview. He wants a lawyer."

"I'm just saying: my case, my interview—if there is one."

"Fine. What's the other thing?"

"The arson case. Put me back on it."

"I can't just—"

"It was a midnight crime, you need a midnight detective. That's what you say and what you do. You tell the others on the case that there's a briefing tomorrow at eight to bring me up to date."

"Okay, fine. But it's still run out of RHD and my guys are lead."

"Fine. Then I think we're done here."

"And I want the summary report on this on my desk before that meeting."

"Not a problem."

She turned toward the door. Olivas spoke to her as she was stepping out.

"You watch yourself, Ballard."

She looked back in at him. It was an impotent threat. She smiled at him without humor.

"You do that too, Captain," she said.

43

It took Ballard most of her shift after roll call that night to write up the final summary report on the Hilton case. It had to be complete but carefully worded on three fronts. One was to keep Harry Bosch in the clear, and the second was to include Olivas in a way that would be acceptable under lines of command and protocol. The third front was actually the most difficult. She had left her direct supervisor, Lieutenant McAdams, in the dark through the entire investigation. Her saying in the report that she had been operating under the direction of Captain Olivas covered a lot of things but did nothing to lessen the damage that her actions would do to her relationship with McAdams. She knew that she was going to have to sit down with him sooner rather than later and try to smooth things over. It would not be a pleasant conversation.

Her only break came when she got up from the computer to change her focus and relax her eyes. She took her cruiser and went over to the taco truck to pick up some food to go.

Digoberto was once again working alone. But at the moment at least he was busy with a line of nightingales—three young women and two men—fresh out of a club that had just closed at four a.m. Ballard waited her turn and listened to their insipid chatter about the scene they had just left. Ballard hoped there would be some fresh shrimp left by the time she ordered.

When one of the men noticed the badge peeking through her

coat on her belt, their talk dropped to whispers, and then by group consent they offered Ballard the front of the line, since she was obviously working and they weren't sure what to order. She took them up on the kind offer and got her shrimp tacos, answering routine questions from the group as she waited for Digoberto to put her order together.

"Are you on a case or something?" one of the women asked.

"Always," Ballard said. "I work graveyard—what they call the late show because there's always something going on in Hollywood."

"Wow, like what is the case you're on right now?"

"Uh, it's about a young guy—about your age. He was in the wrong place at the wrong time. He got shot in an alley where they sell drugs."

"Shot dead?"

"Yeah, dead."

"That's crazy!"

"A lot of crazy stuff happens around here. You all should be careful. Bad things happen to good people. So stick together, get home safe."

"Yes, Officer."

"It's Detective, actually."

She brought the food back to the station in a take-out box, passing a shirtless and fully tattooed man cuffed to the lockdown bench in the back hallway. At her borrowed work space she continued writing her report while eating, careful not to drop crumbs into the keyboard and draw a complaint from the desk's daytime owner. The foil wrapping had kept everything warm and the shrimp ceviche tacos had not lost their flavor on the ride back.

At dawn she printed out three copies of her report: one for Lieutenant McAdams, which she put in his inbox along with a note asking for a private meeting; one for herself, which went into her backpack; and the third for Captain Olivas. She put it into a fresh file folder and carried it with her as she headed across the parking lot to her cruiser.

Her phone buzzed almost as soon as she pulled out of the Holly-wood Division parking lot to head downtown. It was Bosch.

"So I have to read about the Kidd case in the *L.A. Times?*"

"I'm so sorry. I've just been running crazy and then I wasn't going to call you in the middle of the night. I just left the station and was about to try you."

"I'm sure of that."

"I was."

"So they killed his wife."

"Awful. I know. But it was her or us. Truly."

"They going to get dinged for that? Are you?"

"I don't know. They fucked up. Nobody was watching the door. Then she came out and it went sideways. I think I'm in the clear because I was just a ride-along, but those guys are probably all getting letters."

Bosch would know she meant a letter of reprimand in their personnel files.

"At least you're all right," he said.

"Harry, I think she was about to shoot me," Ballard said. "Then she got hit."

"Well, then they had the right man in the OP."

"Still. We had locked eyes. When it happened, she was looking at me, I was looking at her. Then…"

"You can't dwell on it. She made a choice. It was the wrong one. Is Kidd talking?"

"He lawyered up and isn't talking. I think he thinks he can sue the city for his wife and get enough money for a big-time lawyer—maybe your boy, Haller."

"I doubt that. He doesn't voluntarily take murder cases anymore."

"Got it."

"So, should I expect a call about my involvement in the Hilton case?"

"I don't think so. I just finished the report and left you out of it. I said the widow found the murder book after her husband's death and contacted a friend to turn it in. Your name is nowhere in the report. You shouldn't have any problem at all."

"Good to know."

Ballard drove down the ramp off Sunset onto the 101. The freeway was crowded and moving slow.

"I'm taking it down to Olivas right now," she said. "I have a meeting at PAB anyway."

"Meeting on what?" Bosch asked.

"That arson-murder I worked the other night. I'm back on it. They need a midnight detective to help work it. And that's me."

"Sounds like they're finally getting smart down there."

"We can only hope."

"That's Olivas, right? One of his cases."

"He's the captain, yes, but I'll be working with a couple detectives and the LAFD arson guys. So, what are you doing?"

"Montgomery. I have something in play. We'll see how it— hey, I almost forgot, that guy down in Orange I told you about that was creeping the houses where female students lived? They bagged him."

"Fantastic! How?"

"He creeped a house Saturday night but didn't know a boyfriend was staying over. He caught the guy, trimmed him up a little bit, then called the police."

"Good deal."

"Last night I called one of the OPD guys on it—the guy I gave the heads-up to about me watching over Maddie's place. He said the guy had a camera with an infrared lens. He had photos of the girls sleeping in their beds."

"That's fucked up. That guy should go away and the key should get lost. He's on a path, you know what I mean?"

"And that's the issue. No matter how twisted this is, right now they have him for burglary of an occupied dwelling. That's it until the DNA comes back on the other hot prowls. But meantime, their worry is he'll bail out and disappear."

"Shit. Well, who is he? A student?"

"Yeah, he goes to the school. They think he followed girls from the campus to their houses and then came back to creep the places and take his pictures."

"I hope they put a rush on the DNA."

"They did. And my guy's going to let me know if he makes bail. The arraignment's this morning and they have a D.A. who's going to ask the judge to go high on the bail."

"Did your daughter ever know that you were going down there on Saturday nights and watching her house?"

"Not exactly. It only would have worried her more."

"Yeah, I get that."

They ended the conversation after that. Ballard bailed from the freeway at Alvarado and took First Street the rest of the way into downtown. She was early for her meeting and early for most of the staff at the PAB. She had her pick of parking in the garage beneath the police headquarters.

She ended up on the Robbery-Homicide Division floor twenty minutes before the meeting time set by Olivas. Rather than go into the squad room and have to endure small talk with people she knew were predisposed not to like her, she walked up and down the hallway outside, looking at the framed posters that charted the history of the division. When she had worked for RHD, she had never taken the time to do so. The division was started fifty years earlier after the investigation into the assassination of Robert Kennedy revealed the need for an elite team of investigators to handle the most complex, serious, and sensitive cases—politically or media-wise—that came up.

She walked by posters displaying photos and narratives on cases ranging from the Manson murders to the Hillside Stranglers to the Night Stalker and the Grim Sleeper—cases that became known around the world and that helped cement the reputation of the

LAPD. They also established the city as a place where anything could happen—anything bad.

There was no doubt an esprit de corps that came with an assignment to the RHD, but Ballard, being a woman, never felt fully a part of it, and that had always bothered her. Now it was a plus, because she didn't miss what she'd never had.

She heard talking from the elevator alcove and looked down the hallway to see Nuccio and Spellman, the arson guys from the Fire Department, cross the hall and go through the main door to RHD. They, too, were early—unless Olivas had given them a different start time for the meeting.

Ballard stepped through another door, which led into the opposite end of the squad room. She headed down the main aisle, passing more historical posters and some movie posters until she reached the Homicide Special unit and the War Room. She entered, hoping that Nuccio and Spellman were the first to arrive and that she could talk to them before Olivas and his men got there.

But it didn't work out that way. She knocked once and entered the War Room, only to find the same five men who had been there last time sitting in exactly the same positions. That included Olivas. They were in mid-discussion, which ceased the moment she opened the door. Since everybody was at least fifteen minutes early, Ballard took that as confirmation that Olivas had given the men an earlier start time, perhaps to discuss what to do about her inclusion in the case before she arrived. She assumed that would largely mean Olivas directing the other investigators to keep her at arm's length. It would be something she needed to redirect.

"Ballard," Olivas said. "Have a seat."

He pointed to a seat at the end of the rectangular table. It would put her opposite him, with the two LAFD guys to her right and the two RHD guys, Drucker and Ferlita, to her left. On the table was a murder book with very few pages in it and a few other files, one of them thicker than the murder book.

"We were just talking about you and how we're going to work this," Olivas said.

"Really?" Ballard said. "Before I got here—nice. Any conclusions?"

"Well, for starters, we know we have you out there in Hollywood working the late show, so trolling for witnesses is still important. I know you did a couple sweeps out there already, but people in that world come and go. It would be good to hit that strip again."

"Anything else?"

"Well, we were just getting started."

"Well, could we start then with an update on where we are on the investigation? What happened with the bottle I gave you guys?"

"Good idea. Scrapyard, why don't you summarize where things are?"

Drucker looked surprised that he had drawn the request from Olivas. He opened a file on the table in front of him and reviewed a few things in it, probably to gather his thoughts, before speaking.

"Okay, on the bottle," he said. "We took it into latents as suggested and they did get a twelve-point match to a thumbprint off the victim, Edison Banks. So we are good there. We went out last night to find the bottle collector you got it from, to reinterview him and see if there was anything else to glean from him now that we have confirmation on the bottle. Unfortunately, we didn't find him and—"

"What time were you out there?" Ballard asked.

"About eight," Drucker said. "We looked around for an hour, couldn't find him."

"I don't think he gets back to his squat till later," Ballard said. "I'll find him tonight."

"That would be great," Drucker said.

There was an awkwardness to the conversation, an acknowledgment that the men were doing what they should have done from the start—bringing in the expert on the dark hours of Hollywood.

"Were there other prints on the bottle?" Ballard asked.

Drucker flipped a page of the report in front of him.

"Yes," he said. "We got a palm print. We matched it to the liquor license belonging to Marko Linkov, who operates the Mako store where we believe the bottle was originally sold. We spoke to him and watched the video you told us about. So we are up to speed there."

"So it was the woman in the video?" Ballard said.

"We traced her plate — 'one for you, two for me' — and it turns out that plate was stolen off a same-make and -model Mercedes earlier that day. Our working conclusion is that the woman bought the bottle and gave it to our victim. Whether that was part of the plan to kill him, we don't know. We have so far not been able to identify her."

"What about the ATM? She got cash from there."

"She used a counterfeit card with a legit number and PIN belonging to a seventy-two-year-old man living in Las Vegas, Nevada."

"Did the ATM have a camera? Did you get a clear shot of her?"

"You watched the store video," Ferlita said. "She put her hand over the camera. She knew just where it was."

"No picture," Drucker added.

Ballard did not respond. She sat back in her chair and considered all the new information. The complexity of the mystery woman's actions was very suspicious and raised more questions.

"I don't get it," she finally said.

"Get what?" Olivas asked.

"I'm assuming this woman is the suspect," she said. "Stolen plate, stolen ATM card. But for what reason? Why didn't she buy the bottle somewhere else, where it would never be connected?"

"Who knows?" Nuccio said.

"It's like she wanted to be seen but not identified," Ballard said. "There's a psychology there."

"Fuck her psychology," Drucker said. "We just need to find her."

"I'm just saying, if we understand her, maybe it helps find her," Ballard said.

"Whatever," Drucker said.

Ballard let him have his moment before pressing on.

"Okay, what else?" she said.

"Isn't that enough?" Ferlita said. "We've had the case two days and most of that was spent catching up to you."

"And you wouldn't have what you have if not for me," Ballard said. "What about the victim and the probate case? Is that a copy of the file?"

She pointed to the thick file on the table next to Drucker.

"It is," he said. "We've gone through it a couple times and haven't found anything that links up to this. One of those cases where you feel it in your gut but there's no evidence of anything."

"Can I take that, then?" Ballard asked. "I'll give it a read while I'm in the car tonight watching for the bottle man. Then I'll be as up to date on this as everybody else."

Drucker turned to Olivas for approval.

"Of course," Olivas said. "We'll make you a copy. Knock yourself out."

"Has anybody talked to the Banks family?" Ballard asked.

"We're going down to San Diego today to interview the brother," Drucker said.

"Want to come?" Ferlita asked, a baiting tone in his voice.

"I'll pass," Ballard said. "I'm sure you two can handle it."

BOSCH

44

Bosch spent Wednesday morning gathering files for a follow-up meeting scheduled with Clayton Manley. The attorney had called the day before and reported that the firm's litigation committee had agreed to take on Bosch's case on a commission basis. Bosch pulled all the records that he had kept from the missing-cesium case from a box where he stored documents from the most important cases of his career — most solved, some not.

He then picked up his phone, made a call, and left a message canceling a physical therapy session for his knee that had been scheduled for that morning. He knew his therapist would take the cancellation out on him when he arrived for the next session. He could already feel the pain from that.

When his phone buzzed two minutes later he guessed it would be his therapist saying he would be charged for the session anyway, since he had canceled on the day of. But the call turned out to be Mickey Haller.

"Your boy the clay man called like you said he would."

"Who?"

"Clayton Manley. His e-mail is 'clayman at Michaelson & Mitchell.' He asked me to send the pension stuff 'cause he's taking on your wrongful-death case. You told him you were actually dying?"

"I may have, yes. So you're cooperating? He left me a message wanting to meet today. This must be why."

"You told me to cooperate, I'm cooperating. You're not going to let him file something, are you?"

"It won't get that far. I'm just trying to get inside that place."

"And you're not telling me why?"

Bosch got a call-waiting beep. He checked his screen and saw it was Ballard.

"You don't need to know yet," he told Haller. "And I have a call coming in that I should take. I'll check in about all of this later."

"All right, bro—"

Bosch clicked over to the other call. It sounded like Ballard was in a car.

"Renée."

"Harry, what do you have going today? I want to talk to you about something. Another case."

"I have an eleven o'clock meeting downtown. After that I have time. Are you headed to the beach now?"

"Yes, but I'll sleep a few hours and then we can meet after your thing. How about lunch?"

"Musso's just hit a hundred years old."

"Perfect. What time?"

"Let's make it one-thirty in case my thing runs long. You'll get more sleep."

"See you there."

She disconnected and Bosch went back to work on his own case, putting together a carefully constructed file he would give Clayton Manley. He left the house at ten and headed toward his downtown appointment, knowing from his call with Manley the day before that he was in play at Michaelson & Mitchell.

Bosch had noted four things during his earlier visit to Manley. One was that in a firm that had at least two floors of lawyers, Manley's office, as remote as it seemed to be at the end of the hallway, was just doors away from the offices of the firm's two founding partners. There had to be a reason for that, especially in light of the embarrassing run-in Manley had had with Judge Montgomery. That kind of public chastisement and humiliation would usually result in an order to clear out your desk and be gone by the end of the day. Instead, Manley maintained a position close to the firm's top two seats of power.

The second thing he had noticed was that Manley apparently did not have a personal secretary or a clerk—at least not one sitting outside his office. There was no law firm staff at all in that hallway. Harry assumed that the doors he had passed to the offices of Mitchell and Michaelson led to large suites, each with its own set of clerks and secretaries guarding the entrances to the throne rooms. There had to be a reason Manley had none of that, but Bosch was more interested in how that could affect his plans for the meeting at eleven.

The last two things Bosch had noted during his first visit were that Manley's office appeared to have neither a private bathroom nor a printer in plain view. His conclusion was that Manley most likely relied on a secretarial or law-clerk pool somewhere else in the offices, as well as a printer used by lesser members of the firm.

Not until he was on the 101 heading south did he remember he was supposed to call Mickey Haller back. He put his cell phone on speaker when he made the call. His Jeep had been manufactured about two decades before there was anything known as Bluetooth.

"Bosch, you dog."

"Sorry about cutting you off before."

"No problem and you didn't have to call back. I said my piece."

"Well, I wanted to ask you something. Did Manley ask you why you recommended him to me?"

"Matter of fact, he did."

"And?"

"I can barely hear you, man. You need to get a car that's quiet on the inside and has a digital sound system."

"I'll think about it. What did you tell Manley about recommending him to me?"

"I told him that what you wanted to do was really outside my wheelhouse. I also told him I thought he got a bad shake from Judge Montgomery that time. I said there is no call to embarrass a fellow lawyer, no matter what the cause. So I sent you over there because it looked like a case that could get him some positive attention. All that good?"

"All that was perfect."

"I don't know exactly what you're up to, bro, but I hope you aren't going to dump me for this guy. Because the truth is, I could run circles around him—backward."

"I know that, *bro,* and that's not the play. We'll be back on track soon. Just trust me with this."

"I had the file from the pension case messengered over to him. Make sure when all is said and done that I get it back."

"Will do."

Twenty minutes later Bosch was on the suede couch in the waiting room at Michaelson & Mitchell. He had a file full of documents on his lap. He had gotten there early so he could again take the measure of the place, check faces of lawyers and personnel, see who was going up and down the winding staircase. He opened his phone, pulled up the general number of the law firm, and waited.

There was a buzz and the young man behind the reception counter took a call. Bosch heard him say, "I'll walk him back."

The receptionist removed his telephone headset and started around the counter. Bosch pushed the Call button on his phone.

"I'll take you back now," the young man said. "Would you like a bottle of water or something else?"

"No, I'm good," Bosch said.

Bosch got up to follow. Almost immediately there was the sound of the phone buzzing at the reception desk. The receptionist looked back at his station, a pained expression on his face.

"I know the way," Bosch said. "I can make it on my own."

"Oh, thank you," the young man said.

He peeled off to go back to the phone and Bosch rounded the staircase and headed down the hall to Clayton Manley's office. He pulled out his phone and ended the call.

The offices with names on the doors were all on the left side. These were on the outside of the building, with windows overlooking Bunker Hill. There were two unmarked doors on the right side of the hallway. As Bosch headed toward Manley's office, he opened each of these, knowing that if he surprised someone in an office he could just say he was lost. But the first room was a small break room with a coffee maker and a half-size, under-counter refrigerator with a glass door displaying designer waters and sodas.

He moved to the next room down and found a supply room with a large copy machine next to a bank of shelves containing paper, envelopes, and files. There was also an emergency exit door.

Bosch quickly stepped in and assessed the printer. He made the easiest move to disable it, reaching behind it and unplugging the power cord. The cooling fan and digital screen went dead.

He quickly returned to the hallway, walked down to Manley's office, and knocked once politely on the door before entering. Manley stood up behind his desk.

"Mr. Bosch, come on in."

"Thank you. I brought the documents you asked for—from the radiation case."

"Have a seat and let me just send this e-mail. It's actually to Mr. Haller, thanking him for the docs he sent relating to your pension arbitration."

"Okay, good. How was he to deal with?"

Manley typed a few words onto his screen and hit the Send button.

"Mr. Haller?" he asked. "He was fine. Seemed pleased to help. Why? Was there something I missed?"

"No, no, I just didn't know whether he was second-guessing, you know, passing on the case."

"I don't think so. He seemed eager to help and messengered over everything he had. Let me see what you have there. I also have a contract and power of attorney for you to sign."

Bosch handed the file across the desk. It was almost an inch thick and he had padded it with non-pertinent reports from the case in which he had gotten dosed with cesium years before. Manley made a cursory flip through the file, stopping once to look at one of the documents that had randomly caught his attention.

"This is great stuff," he finally said. "It will be very helpful. We just need to formalize our agreement that I'm representing you on a commission basis and I will take it from here. You'll have the power and might of this entire firm behind you. We'll sue the bastards."

Manley smiled at the final cliché.

"Uh, that's great," Bosch said. "But...you can call me paranoid but I don't want to leave that file here. It's the only evidence I have of what happened to me. Is there any chance you could make copies and I keep the originals?"

"I don't see why not," Manley said without hesitation. "Let me give you the contract to read over and sign and I'll go get this copied."

"Sounds good."

Manley looked around on his desk until he found a thin file. He opened it and handed Bosch a three-page agreement under the *Michaelson & Mitchell* letterhead. He then pulled a pen out of a holder on his desk and put it down in front of Bosch.

"And I'll be right back," Manley said.

"I'll be here," Bosch said.

"Can I get you something? Water? Soda? Coffee?"

"Uh, no, I'm fine."

Manley got up from his desk and left the office with Bosch's file. He left the door to the room open a foot. Bosch quickly got up and went to the door to watch Manley go down the hall to the copy room. He listened while Manley loaded the stack of documents, then cursed when he realized the machine was dead.

Now was the moment. Bosch knew that Manley would either come back to his office, inform Bosch of the copy trouble, and summon a clerk to do the copying, or he would go off further into the office complex in search of another copier.

Bosch saw Manley emerge from the copy room, head down and focused on the documents he was carrying. He quickly went back to his seat in front of the desk. He was holding and reading the contract when Manley stuck his head in the door.

"We're having trouble with the copier over on this side," he said. "It will take me a few extra minutes to get this done. You okay?"

"No worries," Bosch said. "I'm fine."

"And nothing to drink?"

"Nothing, thanks."

Bosch held up the contract as if to say it would keep him busy.

"Back soon," Manley said.

Manley left and Bosch heard his footsteps going down the hall. He quickly got up, quietly closed the door to the office, and went back to the desk, this time going behind it to Manley's seat. He checked his watch first to time Manley's absence, then did a quick survey of the top of the desk. Nothing caught his eye, but the computer screen was still active.

He looked at the desktop on the screen and saw a variety of files and documents, including one that said BOSCH STUFF. He opened it and found that it contained notes from his first meeting with Manley. He read these quickly and determined it was an accurate accounting of their conversation. He closed the file and looked at the labeling of others on the desktop. He saw nothing that drew his attention.

He checked his watch and then rolled the chair back from the desk so he could get quicker access to the keyed file drawers on either side of the footwell. One of them had the key in the lock. Bosch turned it and opened the drawer. It contained file folders of different colors, most likely color-coded in some way. He walked his fingers through them to the files labeled with *M* names, but found no file on Montgomery.

He checked his watch. Manley had been gone two minutes already. He pulled the key out of the drawer and used it to unlock the other one. He went through the same procedure here and this time found a file marked MONTGOMERY. He pulled it quickly and flipped through it. It was as thick as the file he had given Manley to copy. It appeared to be documents from Manley's ill-fated defamation lawsuit against the judge—the face-saving measure that had been destined to fail from the beginning.

Bosch noticed that the inside flap of the file had several hand-written names, numbers, and e-mails on it. With no time to think about what these might mean, he pulled out his phone and took a photo of the inside flap and the table-of-contents page opposite. He then closed the file and slid it back into the drawer. He closed and locked the drawer and transferred the key back to its original position.

He checked his watch. Three and a half minutes had gone by. Bosch had given Manley over a hundred pages to copy, and had placed in the middle of the package two pages that were stapled together and would cause a delay if they jammed a copier. But Bosch couldn't count on that. He thought he had two minutes more at the most.

He went back to the computer and pulled up Manley's e-mail account. Bosch's eyes ran down the list of senders and then the words in the subject boxes. Nothing was of interest. He did an e-mail search of the name *Montgomery* by subject but no messages came up.

He then closed the e-mail page and went back to the home screen. In the Finder application he searched the name *Montgomery* again, this time coming up with a folder. He quickly opened it and found it contained nine files. He checked his watch. There was no way he could risk looking through them all. Most were simply labeled MONTGOMERY plus a date. All the dates were before the date of the defamation suit, so Bosch took these to be prep files. But one file was titled differently: it said simply TRANSFER.

Bosch opened TRANSFER and it contained only a thirteen-digit number, followed by the initials *G.C.* and nothing else. The mystery of it intrigued him. He took a photo of it as well.

As Bosch closed the folder, he heard the *ding* of a new e-mail from the computer. He opened Manley's e-mail account and saw that the new message had an address that included the name *Michaelson* and the subject header *Your new "client."*

Bosch knew he was out of time, and that if he opened the e-mail it would be marked as read. It could tip Manley to what he had been doing. But the quote marks around the word *client* got the best of him. He opened the e-mail. It was from Manley's boss, William Michaelson.

You fool. Your client is working on the Montgomery case. Stop all activity with him. Now.

Bosch was stunned. Without thinking more than a second about it, he deleted the message. He then went to the Trash folder and deleted it from there as well. He closed the e-mail account, moved the desk chair back into place, and crossed to the door to reopen it. Just as he swung the door in a foot, Manley arrived with the file and his copies of the documents.

"Going somewhere?" he asked.

"Yeah, to look for you," Bosch said.

"Sorry, the machine jammed. Took longer than I thought. Here are your originals."

He handed Bosch a stack of documents. He held the copies in his other hand and headed toward his desk.

"Did you sign the contract?"

"Just about to."

"Everything in order?"

"Seems so."

Bosch came back to the desk but didn't sit down. He took the pen off the table and scribbled a signature on the contract. It wasn't his name but it was hard to tell what name it was.

Manley moved around behind his desk and was about to sit down.

"Have a seat," he said.

"Actually, I have another appointment, so I need to go," Bosch said. "After you've looked at all of that stuff, why don't you just give me a call and let's discuss next steps?"

"Oh, I thought we had more time. I wanted to talk about bringing in a video team and going through the story with you."

"You mean in case I die before we get to court?"

"Actually, it's just the latest vogue in negotiations: have the victim tell his own story instead of the lawyer. When you have a good story—like you do—it gives them a real taste of what to expect in court. But we'll set that up for next time. Let me walk you out."

"No worries," Bosch said. "I know my way out."

A few moments later Bosch was headed down the hallway. As he passed the door that said WILLIAM MICHAELSON on the frosted glass, it opened and a man was standing there. He looked to be about sixty years old, with a graying fringe of hair and the paunch of a relaxed and successful businessman. He stared at Bosch as he went by. And Bosch stared right back at him.

45

The Musso & Frank Grill had outlasted them all in Hollywood and still packed them in for lunch and dinner every day in its two high-ceilinged rooms. It had an old-world elegance and charm that never changed, and a menu that kept that spirit as well. Most of its waiters were ancient, its martinis were burning cold and came with a sidecar on ice, and its sourdough bread was the best south of San Francisco.

Ballard was already seated in a semicircular booth in the "new room," which was only seventy-four years old compared with the hundred-year-old "old room." She had documents from a file spread in front of her and it reminded Bosch of how he had reviewed the Montgomery file. Bosch slid into the booth from her left.

"Hey."

"Oh, hey. Let me clear some of this stuff out of the way."

"It's okay. It's good to spread a case out, see what you got."

"I know. I love it. But we've got to eat eventually."

She stacked the reports in a crosshatch pattern so that the distinct piles she had been making wouldn't get mixed up. She then put it all down next to her on the banquette.

"I thought you wanted to tell me about your case," Bosch said.

"I do," Ballard said. "But let's eat first. I also want to hear about what you've been so busy with."

"Probably not anymore. I think I just blew it."

"What? What do you mean?"

"I have a guy—a Bunker Hill lawyer. I think there's a chance he had Montgomery hit. His alibi is just too perfect and there are a couple other things that don't jibe. So I posed as a client and went in to see him, and they figured it out this morning. His boss did. So that's the end of that angle."

"What will you do now?"

"Don't know yet. But just the fact that they got on to me about it makes me think I'm on the right track. I have to come up with something else."

A waiter in a red half-jacket came over. He put down plates of bread and butter and asked if they were ready to order. Bosch didn't need a menu and Ballard had one in front of her.

"I wish it was tomorrow," Bosch said.

"How come?" Ballard asked.

"Thursday is chicken pot pie day."

"Ooh."

"I'll have the sand dabs and an iced tea."

The waiter wrote it down and then looked at Ballard.

"Are they good, the sand dabs?" Ballard asked Bosch.

"Not really," Bosch said. "That's why I ordered them."

Ballard laughed and ordered the sand dabs and the waiter walked away.

"What are sand dabs?" Ballard asked.

"Really?" Bosch said. "It's fish. Little ones that they bread and fry. Squeeze some lemon on them. You'll like them."

"What's the lawyer's motive—on your case?"

"Pride. Montgomery embarrassed him in open court, banned him from his courtroom for incompetence. The *Times* picked up on it and it went from there. He hit the judge with a half-assed defamation suit that got thrown out and made more news, which only put his reputation further down the toilet. His name is *Manley*. People started calling him *UnManley*."

"And he's still at a Bunker Hill law firm?"

"Yeah, his firm stuck with him. I think he's gotta be related to somebody. He's probably Michaelson's son-in-law or something. They have him in a back office down a hallway where the big shots can keep an eye on him."

"Wait a minute, 'Michaelson'? Who is that?"

"He's the one who found out I was working on the Montgomery case. Cofounder of the firm, Michaelson & Mitchell."

"Holy shit!"

"Yeah, I sort of saw an e-mail where he told my suspect what I was up to."

"I don't mean about that. I mean about this."

She pulled the documents she had been working on back up onto the table and started separating the individual stacks. She leafed through one of the stacks until she found what she was looking for and handed it to Bosch. It was a legal motion with a court date stamp on it. Bosch wasn't sure what he was looking for until Ballard tapped the top of the page and he saw the law firm letterhead: *Michaelson & Mitchell.*

"What is this?" he asked.

"It's my case," Ballard said. "My crispy critter from the other night. The coroner identified him and it turned out he was worth a small fortune. But he was a homeless drunk and probably didn't know it. That was a motion filed by Michaelson & Mitchell last year trying to kick him out of the family trust because he had been MIA for like five years. His brother wanted him out of the money and hired Michaelson & Mitchell to get it done."

Bosch read the front page of the stapled document.

"This is San Diego," he said. "Why would the brother hire an L.A. firm?"

"I don't know," Ballard said. "Maybe they have an office down there. But it's Michaelson whose name is on the pleading. It's all over the case file I got from Olivas."

"Did the brother get what he wanted?"

"No, that's the point: he didn't win. And a year later the missing brother gets melted in his tent with a rigged kerosene heater."

Ballard spent the next ten minutes walking Bosch through the murder of Edison Banks Jr. All the while, Bosch tried to wrap himself around the fact that the Michaelson & Mitchell law firm was involved in both of their cases. Bosch didn't believe in coincidences but he knew they happened. And here two detectives working different cases had just found a link between them. If that wasn't a coincidence, he didn't know what was.

When Ballard finished her summary, Bosch keyed in on one aspect of the case she had mentioned.

"This woman who bought the bottle of vodka," he said. "No ID on her or the car?"

"Not so far. The car's plate was stolen and the ATM card she used was bogus—stolen from Vegas."

"And no photo."

"Nothing clear. I have the store's video on my laptop if you want to see."

"Yes."

Ballard pulled her laptop out of her backpack and opened it on the table. She brought up the video, started playing it, and turned the screen so Bosch could see it. He watched the woman park her car and enter, use the ATM, buy the bottle of vodka, and then leave. He noticed a height scale on the frame of the store's door. With the stilettos, the woman was almost five-ten on the scale.

Her height may have been discernible but her face was never clearly seen on the video. But Bosch watched her mannerisms and the way she walked when she went back to the Mercedes. He knew that she could have been wearing all manner of disguises, from a wig to hip padding, but the way someone walked was usually always the same. The woman had a short stride that may have been dictated by her stiletto heels and skintight leather pants, but there was something else.

Bosch moved the cursor to the Rewind arrow on the screen and backed up the video so he could watch her get out of the Mercedes and enter the store. Her moving toward the camera gave another angle on her gait.

"She's slightly intoed," Bosch said. "On the left."

"What?" Ballard asked.

Bosch reversed the video again and turned the screen back to Ballard before hitting the Play button. He leaned over to see the screen and narrate.

"Watch her walk," he said. "Her left leg is slightly intoed. You can tell by the front point of those shoes. It's pointing inward."

"Like pigeon-toed," Ballard said.

"Doctors call it *intoed*. My daughter had it but she grew out of it. But not everybody does. This woman—it's only on her left. You see it?"

"Yes, barely. So what's it get us? Maybe she was faking it to fool observant investigators like you."

"I don't think so."

Now Bosch went into his briefcase and pulled out his laptop. While it was booting up, the waiter brought him an iced tea. Ballard stayed with just water.

"Okay, look at this," Bosch said.

He pulled up the surveillance video from Grand Park and started playing it. He turned the screen to Ballard.

"This is the morning Judge Montgomery got murdered," he said. "This is him coming down the steps on his way to the courthouse. Check out the woman walking ahead of him. That's Laurie Lee Wells."

They watched silently for a few moments. The woman was dressed in a white blouse and tan slacks. She had blond hair, a thin build, and was wearing what looked like flats or sandals.

Bosch continued his narration.

"They both go behind the elevator building," he said. "Her first, then him. She comes out but he doesn't. He was stabbed three times. She keeps going to the courthouse."

"She's intoed," Ballard said. "I see it. On her left side."

The condition was more clearly seen when the woman turned and started walking directly toward the courthouse and the camera.

"One blond-haired, one black-haired," Ballard said. "You think it's the same woman?"

"Same walk in both videos," Bosch said. "Yeah, I do."

"What do we have here?"

"Well, we have two different cases with the same law firm involved. A law firm with an attorney who had a grudge against Judge Montgomery. A law firm also representing the brother who had at least a legal grudge against Edison Banks. On top of that, this firm has represented a known organized-crime figure from Las Vegas—where, by the way, the woman in black's ATM number was stolen from."

"Who?"

"A guy named Dominick Butino, an enforcer known as 'Batman,' but not because he likes comic books and superheroes. And remember that Clayton Manley—the lawyer Montgomery threw out of his courtroom—is still at the firm. They have him hidden away under the watchful eyes of the founding partners. But when you have a lawyer who fucks up like that and brings shame to your firm, what do you usually do?"

"Cut ties."

"Exactly. Get rid of him. But they don't do that."

"Why?"

"Because he knows something. He knows something that could bring the house down."

"So what you're getting at here is that this law firm set up these hits. Manley was part of it and they don't want him running around loose," Ballard said.

"We have no evidence of that, but, yeah, that's exactly what I'm thinking."

"A female hit man they probably connected with through their organized-crime clientele."

"Woman."

"What?"

"Hit woman."

The waiter brought their sand dabs and Bosch and Ballard didn't speak until he was gone.

"Didn't the original detectives on Montgomery track that woman down?" Ballard asked. "Looks like she was wearing a juror badge."

"They went to the jury pool and talked to her," Bosch said. "She said she didn't see anything."

"And they just believed her?"

"She told them she was wearing earbuds and listening to music. She didn't hear the judge get attacked behind her. They bought it, dropped her right there."

"But also, wouldn't she have had blood on her? You said the judge was stabbed three times and she's wearing a white blouse."

"You'd think so, but this was a pro hit. Montgomery was stabbed three times under the right arm. In a wound cluster the size of a half dollar. The blade cut the axillary artery—one of the three main bleeders in the body. It's a perfect spot because the arterial spray is contained under the arm. The assassin walks away clean. The victim bleeds out."

"How do you know so much about this?"

Bosch shrugged.

"I had training when I was in the army."

"Do I want to hear why?"

"No, you don't."

"So then what do we do now about this hit *woman*?"

"We go find her."

46

The first move they made was to find out whether Laurie Lee Wells was Laurie Lee Wells. Bosch had pulled the witness report on Wells out of the murder book files and shared it with Ballard. The report was written by Orlando Reyes, who had conducted the interview. It said he had routinely run Wells's name through the NCIS database and had found no criminal record. This was expected; L.A. County did not allow people with criminal records to serve on juries. No follow-up was noted in the report.

Ballard and Bosch drove up to the Valley and the address on the report after finishing their sand dabs. With Bosch driving, Ballard looked up Laurie Lee Wells on IMDb and other entertainment databases and determined that there was a legitimate actress with the name who had had limited success in guest appearances on various television shows over the past years.

"You know there's a TV show on HBO about a hit man who wants to become an actor?" Ballard said.

"I don't have HBO," Bosch said.

"I watch it at my grandmother's. Anyway, Laurie Lee Wells was on it."

"So?"

"So it's weird. The show is about a hit man wanting to be an actor. It's a dark comedy. And here we have an actress who might *be* a hit woman."

"This isn't dark comedy. And I doubt Laurie Lee Wells the actress is the Laurie Lee Wells we're looking for. Once we confirm that, we need to figure out how and why her identity was taken and used by our suspect."

"Roger that."

Laurie Lee Wells the actress lived in a condominium on Dickens Street in Sherman Oaks. It was a security building, so they had to make first contact through an intercom at the gate—never the best way to do it. Ballard had the badge, so she handled the introduction. Wells was home and agreed to see the two investigators. But then she did not buzz the gate unlocked for nearly three minutes, and Bosch guessed she was cleaning up—hiding or flushing illegal substances.

Finally, the gate buzzed and they entered. They took an elevator to the fourth floor and found a woman waiting by an open door. She resembled the driver's license photo they had pulled up earlier. But Bosch realized immediately she was not the woman they had studied on the videos. She was too short. This woman was barely five feet tall; even four-inch stilettos would not make her as tall as the woman who hit the five-ten mark on the door of Mako's.

"Laurie?" Ballard said.

She wanted to keep the interview friendly, not adversarial, and going with first names was prudent.

"That's me," Wells said.

"Hi, I'm Renée and this is my partner, Harry," Ballard said.

Wells smiled but looked a long time at Bosch, not able to hide her surprise at his age and the fact that he wasn't doing the talking.

"Come on in," she said. "I hate to say this because I've actually played this part in a TV show, but 'What's this about?'"

"Well, we're hoping you can help us," Ballard said. "Can we sit down?"

"Oh, sure. Sorry."

Wells pointed to the living room, which had a couch and two chairs clustered around a fireplace with fake logs in it.

"Thank you," Ballard said. "Let's get the preliminaries out of the way. You are Laurie Lee Wells, DOB February twenty-third, 1987, correct?"

"That's me," Wells said.

"Have you been on jury duty any time in the last five years?"

Wells furrowed her brow. It was a question from left field.

"I can't—I don't think so," she said. "The last time was a long time ago."

"Definitely not last year?" Ballard asked.

"No, definitely not for a long time. What does it—"

"Were you interviewed last year by two LAPD detectives investigating a murder?"

"What? What is this? Should I call a lawyer or something?"

"You don't need a lawyer. We think someone was impersonating you."

"Oh, well, yes—that's been going on for almost two years now."

Ballard paused and sent a glance toward Bosch. Now they were the ones thrown a curveball.

"What do you mean by that?" Ballard finally asked.

"Someone stole my ID and has been impersonating me for two years," Wells said. "They even filed my taxes last year and got my return, and it's like nobody can do anything about it. They ran up so much debt I'll never be able to buy a car or get a loan. I have to stay here because I already own it, but now my credit is shit and nobody will believe it's not me. I tried to buy a car and they said no way, even though I had letters from the credit-card companies."

"That's terrible," Ballard said.

"Do you know how your identity was stolen?" Bosch asked.

"When I went to Vegas," Wells said. "My wallet got stolen when I was at a show. Like pickpocketed or something."

"How do you know it happened there?" Bosch asked.

Wells's face turned red with embarrassment.

"Because I was at one of those shows where men are the dancers," she said. "I had to pay to go in—it was a bachelorette party—and then when I wanted to get my wallet out to give a tip to the dancers, it was gone. So it happened there."

"And you reported it to the LVPD?" Ballard asked.

"I did, but nothing ever happened," Wells said. "I never got anything back, and then somebody started applying for credit cards in my name and I'm fucked for the rest of my life. Excuse my language."

"Do you happen to have a copy of the crime report?" Ballard asked.

"I've got a ton of copies because I have to send one to explain things every time I get ripped off," Wells said. "Hold on."

She got up and went out of the room. Ballard and Bosch were left to stare at each other.

"Vegas," Ballard said.

Bosch nodded.

Wells soon came back and gave Ballard a copy of the two-page crime report she had filed in Las Vegas.

"Thank you," Ballard said. "We won't take too much more of your time but can I ask, are you getting regular reports on the usage of your name by the identity thief?"

"Not all the time, but the detective will call me every now and then and tell me what the thief is up to," Wells said.

"What detective is that?" Ballard asked.

"Detective Kenworth with Vegas Metro Police," Wells said. "He's the only one I've ever dealt with."

"'Ken...worth,'" Ballard said. "Is that two names or one?"

"One. I don't remember his first name. I think it's on the report."

"Well, what did he tell you was going on? Was it just local purchases?"

"No, she moved around. It was travel and hotels and restaurants. She kept applying for new cards because as soon as we got a fraud alert we'd shut it down. But then a month later she'd have another card."

"What an awful story," Ballard said.

"And all because of a bachelorette party too," Wells said.

"Do you remember the name of the place where this happened?" Bosch asked. "Was it at a casino?"

"No, it wasn't a casino," Wells said. "It was called Devil's Den and it was usually a strip bar for men. I mean, the dancers were women—but on Sunday nights it's *for* women."

"Okay," Ballard said.

"Do you vote?" Bosch asked.

It was another question out of the blue but Wells answered.

"I know I should," she said. "But it doesn't seem to matter in California."

"So you're not registered to vote," Bosch said.

"Not really," Wells answered. "But why do you ask me that? What does it have to do with—"

"We think the person who stole your ID may have impersonated you during jury duty," Bosch said. "You have to be registered to vote to be included in the jury pool. She may have registered to vote as you and then gotten picked for jury duty."

"God, I wonder if she made me a Republican or a Democrat."

Back in the car Bosch and Ballard talked it out before making their next move.

"We need to get the address off her voter registration," Bosch said. "It will tell us where the jury notice would have gone."

"I can handle that," Ballard said. "But what are we thinking here? This whole setup—this hit—relied on the killer getting a jury summons? That seems...I don't know. Like a long shot, if you ask me."

"Yes, but maybe not as long as you think. My daughter got a jury summons less than two months after she registered to vote. It's supposed to be random selection. But every time they pull out a new pool of jurors, they winnow out those who have recently served, or who haven't responded to summons in the past and have been referred for action. So the new voter has a better chance than others to get the call."

Ballard nodded in a way that showed she was unconvinced.

"We also don't know how long this was planned or how it was planned," Bosch continued. "Laurie gets her wallet stolen last year and maybe they applied for the full setup. A voter registration card could be useful in a scam as a second ID. The thief could have had this idea for a long time and then things fell into place."

"We have to find out whether there's a connection between Devil's Den and Batman Butino."

"And talk to the detective with Metro Vegas. See how much he tracked this."

"Maybe he got photos or video of the phony Laurie Lee Wells," said Ballard. "What else?"

"We need to talk to Orlando Reyes," Bosch said. "He interviewed her."

"That's what I don't get. She killed the judge and then just reported for jury duty? Why? Why didn't she get the hell out of there?"

"To complete the job."

"What does that mean?"

"To complete the cover. If she had walked in one door of the courthouse and out the other, they would have known it was her. She stayed around so Reyes could find her, interview her, and move on."

"It's like buying the Tito's vodka. She could have done it anywhere, but she bought it two blocks from where Banks was murdered— and at a place she knew had cameras that we would eventually get to. I said this to Olivas and the others. There is a psychology there. She's a show-off. I think she gets off on hiding in plain sight. I don't know why but it's there."

Bosch nodded. He believed Ballard was correct in her assessment.

"It will be interesting to hear Reyes's take on her," he said.

"I thought those guys weren't talking to you," Ballard said. "Maybe I should take Reyes."

"No. You do and the case gets grabbed by them and RHD. Let me do it. When I explain that this could end up being very embarrassing for him, I think he'll agree to meet me off campus and talk."

"Perfect. You take him and I'll work on the other stuff."

"You sure?"

"Yes, my badge gives me better access on all of it. You take Reyes, I'll take the rest."

Bosch started the Jeep so he could get her back to her own car in Hollywood.

"And we also need to figure out how to approach Clayton Manley," he said as he pulled away from the curb.

"I thought you said he was onto you," Ballard said. "You're not thinking about going back in there posing as a client, are you?"

"No, that's burned. But if I can get Manley somewhere by himself, I might be able to lay it on the line for him and make him see that his options are dwindling."

"I'd like to be there for that."

"I want you there showing off your badge and gun. Then he'll know his ass is hanging out there in the wind."

"The times you were with him in his office…"

"Yeah?"

"You didn't do anything I need to know about, right? Nothing that could cause blowback on the case?"

Bosch thought about what he should tell her. About what he did and what could be proved that he did.

"The only thing I did was read an e-mail that came up on his screen," he finally said. "I told you this before. It was when he left the room to make copies. I heard a *ding* and looked at his e-mail and it was from his boss, Michaelson, calling him a fool for letting a fox into the henhouse. That sort of thing."

"And you're the fox."

"I'm the fox."

"And that's it?"

"Well, then I deleted it."

"You deleted the message?"

"Yeah, I didn't want to risk him reading it while I was there in the office. I had to get out before he found out."

"Okay, you never told me this, right?"

"Right."

"And, really, that was all you did?"

Bosch thought about the photographs he had taken with his phone in Manley's office. He decided to keep those to himself. For now.

"That was it."

"Good."

47

On the way back to Hollywood to drop Ballard at her car, Bosch called Reyes on his direct number at RHD and put it on speakerphone.

"Robbery-Homicide, Reyes."

"Reyes, this is the luckiest call you ever took."

"Who is—Bosch? Is this Bosch? I'm hanging up."

"You do and you can read about it in the paper."

"What the fuck are you talking about now? Am I on a speaker?"

"I'm driving so you're on the speaker. And I'm talking about the real killer of Judge Montgomery. It's going to come out soon, and you can look like you were a part of it or you and your partner can look like the ones who flat-out got it wrong—which is not far from the truth, Reyes."

"Bosch, I'm not playing your games. I—"

"Not a game, Orlando. This is your chance to fix the fuckup. Meet me at the pink benches near the elevators in Grand Park in an hour."

"No way. In an hour, I'm going home. Beat the traffic."

"Then remember when the shit hits the fan that I was the one who gave you a shot at being part of this. One hour. Be there or beat the traffic. I don't really care. I was once in the squad, Reyes, and I wanted to give you a courtesy. *Adios.*"

Bosch disconnected.

"You think he'll show?" Ballard asked.

"Yeah, he'll show," Bosch said. "When I talked to him before, I think he kind of sensed this was no CBA. I think he was bullied by his partner. That happens."

"I know."

Bosch looked over at her and then back to the road.

"You talking about me?" he asked.

"No, of course not," she said. "Besides, we're not partners. Officially."

"We clear this case and it may come out. What we've been doing."

"I don't know. Olivas put me on the Banks case. I connected it to you and this. I don't see any blowback. Especially now that I have Olivas on a leash."

Bosch smiled. Ballard had told him about the conversation she'd had with Olivas in the CIV. She thought the deal she had made and the recording she had as a backup gave her the upper hand.

"You really think you have that guy on a leash, huh?"

"Not really. But you know what I mean. He doesn't want any waves. He wants a nice flat surface that he can paddle away on in a year. He causes me grief and I'm going to turn it right back on him. He knows that."

"You've got the world wired."

"For now. But nothing lasts forever."

She had parked her cruiser on the street near Musso's and Bosch pulled in behind it.

"What will you do now?" he asked.

"Go to the station, grab a few hours' sleep in the cot room before going to roll call."

"Back in the day, when I was at Hollywood Division, we called it the Honeymoon Suite."

"They still do—at least some of the old-school guys. Some things about the department will never change."

Bosch thought she was referring to something deeper than the nap room at the station.

"Okay, I'll hold off calling you after I get with Reyes," he said. "You call me when you wake up."

"Will do," Ballard said.

She got out of the car and he drove on. Thirty minutes later he was sitting on the pink bench second closest to the elevator building in Grand Park. The closest bench was occupied by a vagrant who was lying with his head propped up on a dirty duffel bag and reading a paperback with the cover torn off. Bosch did not know if Reyes knew what he looked like but he doubted that he would be mistaken for the man reading.

Ten minutes past the designated meeting time, Bosch was about to give up on Reyes. He was seated on the bench at an angle that gave him an open view of anyone walking across the park from the direction of the Police Administration Building. But nobody was coming. Bosch leaned forward to push himself up and not put stress on his knee when he heard his name spoken from behind. He didn't turn. He waited and a man in a suit came around the bench from behind him. Bosch noted the uneven drape of the suit jacket over the hips and knew the man was carrying. He was mid-thirties and completely bald on top, with a monk's fringe around the sides.

"Reyes?"

"That's right."

The man sat down on the bench.

"I almost went to the guy over there with the book," Reyes said. "But I figured you had a little more dignity than that."

"That's funny, Orlando," Bosch responded.

"So, what can I do for you, Bosch? I have to get out to Duarte and traffic's going to be a motherfucker."

Bosch pointed toward the elevator building. They were at an angle similar to that seen from the camera on the courthouse facade behind them. They could not see the place where Judge Montgomery had been fatally stabbed.

"Tell me about the juror," Bosch said.

"Who?" Reyes said. "What juror?"

"The witness. Laurie Lee Wells. Your name is on the report. You interviewed her."

"Is that what this is about? Forget it, we're not going to go over every step of the investigation. She was a waste of time and now you're wasting my time. I'm going home."

Reyes stood up to leave.

"Sit down, Orlando," Bosch said. "She was the killer and you missed it. Sit down and I'll tell you about it."

Reyes stayed standing. He pointed down at Bosch.

"Bullshit," he said. "You're just looking for absolution. You got the real killer kicked free and now you're grabbing at straws. That woman didn't see anything, didn't hear anything. She was listening to Guns N' Roses, Bosch. Turned up loud."

"That's a nice detail," Bosch said. "It wasn't in your report. Neither was anything about checking her out."

"I checked her out. She was clean."

"You mean you ran her name. But if you had gone to her apartment and knocked on her door, you would have seen that the real Laurie Lee Wells of Dickens Street, Sherman Oaks, was not the Laurie Lee Wells you interviewed. You got duped, Orlando. Sit down and we can exchange information. I'll tell you about it."

Reyes was hesitant, even jumpy. It was as if one foot wanted to head toward Duarte and the other wanted to go to the bench. Bosch threw his final argument at him.

"Do you know that the supposed juror you talked to is suspect number one on another RHD case? The crispy critter they picked up the other night. That was a hit disguised as something else. Just like Montgomery."

Reyes finally sat down.

"Okay, Bosch, let's hear it. And it better be good."

"No, it doesn't work that way. You talk to me first. I want to know about the interview. How you found her, where you talked to her. You talk to me, then I talk to you."

Reyes shook his head, annoyed that he had to go first. But then he started telling the story.

"Simple. We collected video, then we watched the video. We saw the woman and identified the jury tag. I forget what Gussy was doing but I came over on my own. We didn't have a name, obviously, so I asked to look around the jury assembly room. Nobody matched her. The jury clerk told me they had sent three groups up to courtrooms for jury selection that day. I checked those out, too, and still didn't see her. I knew she couldn't already be on a case because she was coming in too early for that. On the tape, I mean. Trials don't start till ten each day. She's on the tape before eight."

"So how'd you find her?"

"The jury clerk told me to check out the cafeteria next to the jury assembly room. I did and there she was. Drinking coffee and reading a book. The blond hair stood out, you know? I knew it was her."

"So you approach?"

"Yes, I badged her, told her about the murder and that she was on the video. I wanted to take her back to the PAB for the interview but she said she was on a jury panel and wanted to stay at the cafeteria. I talked to her there."

"You didn't record it?"

"No, if she turned out to be a witness of value, I would have gone the whole nine yards with her. But she wasn't. I learned that pretty quick when it was clear she didn't know what had happened twenty feet behind her. She had on the earbuds, remember?"

"Yes, Guns N' Roses. Did you check her ID?"

"I didn't look at her license, if that's what you mean. But I knew the jury clerk would have all of that if we needed it. Look, Bosch, it's your turn now. Tell me what you think you have and what you think you know."

"One more question. Once you spoke to her and got her name, did you go to the jury clerk and confirm that she was a real juror?"

"Why would I do that, Bosch?"

"So the answer is no. You found her sitting in the cafeteria but you didn't make sure she was legitimately there as a juror."

"I didn't have to. She didn't see anything, she didn't hear anything, she was of no use to me as a witness. Now, are you going to tell me what you think you know about her, or not?"

"I know the real Laurie Lee Wells who lives at the address you put in the report was never called for jury duty at the time of the murder and was not the woman in the video."

"Fuck me. And you tie the woman in the video to that lawyer Montgomery had the problem with?"

"Working on that. That lawyer's firm represents a party who may be involved in an arson-murder, and the same woman is on video in the vicinity of that killing. I think she's a hitter who works for somebody that law firm represents. There are more connections—mainly through Las Vegas—and we're working on them as well."

"Who is 'we,' Bosch? Don't tell me you brought that lawyer Haller into this."

"No, not him. But you don't need to know who I'm working with. You need to sit tight until I put all of this together and then *we* will bring it to you. That okay with you, Orlando?"

"Bosch, you don't even—"

He was interrupted by a buzzing from his pocket. He pulled out his phone and looked at a text. He was about to type a response when he got a call on the phone and took it. He held a hand up to Bosch to keep him from speaking. He listened to the caller and then asked one question: "When?" He listened some more before saying, "Okay, I'm heading there now. Pick me up out front."

He disconnected the call and stood up.

"I gotta go, Bosch," he said. "And it looks like you're a day late and a dollar short."

"What are you talking about?" Bosch asked.

"Clayton Manley just took a dive off an office tower in Bunker Hill. He's splattered all over California Plaza."

Bosch was momentarily stunned. Then for a quick moment he thought about the crow that had hit the mirrored glass in Manley's office and then fallen down the side of the building.

"How do they know it was him?" he asked.

"Because he sent an adios e-mail to the whole firm," Reyes said. "Then he went up and jumped."

Reyes turned and walked away, heading back to the PAB to catch a ride with his partner.

BALLARD

48

Instead of sleeping, Ballard called the Las Vegas Metro number off the police report Laurie Lee Wells had provided. But she was surprised when the voice that answered said "OCI."

Every law enforcement agency had its own glossary of acronyms, abbreviations, and shorthand references to specialized units, offices, and locations. Harry Bosch had once joked that the LAPD had a full-time unit dedicated to coming up with acronyms for its various units. But Ballard knew that generally *OC* meant *Organized Crime,* and what gave her pause was that the Wells report dealt with the theft of a wallet.

"OCI, can I help you?" the voice repeated.

"Uh, yes, I'm looking for Detective Tom Kenworth?" Ballard said.

"Please hold."

She waited.

"Kenworth."

"Detective, this is Detective Renée Ballard, Los Angeles Police Department. I'm calling because I'm wondering if you can help me with some information regarding a homicide case I'm investigating."

"A homicide in L.A.? How can we help you from over here in Las Vegas?"

"You took a report last year from a woman named Laurie Lee Wells. Do you remember that name?"

"Laurie Lee Wells. Laurie Lee Wells. Uh, no, not really. Is she your victim?"

"No, she's fine."

"Your suspect?"

"No, Detective. Her wallet was stolen in Vegas at a place called the Devil's Den and that resulted in her identity being stolen. Does any of this ring a bell yet?"

There was a long pause before Kenworth responded.

"Can I get your name again?"

"Renée Ballard."

"And you said Hollywood."

"Yes, Hollywood Division."

"Okay, I'm going to call you back in about five minutes, okay?"

"I really need to get some information. This is a homicide."

"I know that, and I will call you back. Five minutes."

"Okay, I'll give you my direct number."

"No, I don't want your direct number. If you're legit, I'll find you. Talk to you in five."

He disconnected before Ballard could say anything else.

Ballard put the phone down and started to wait. She understood what Kenworth was doing—making sure he was talking to a real cop on a real case. She reread the Metro police report Laurie Lee Wells had given her. Less than a minute later she heard her name over the station intercom telling her she had a call on line 2. It was Kenworth.

"Sorry about that," he said. "Can't be too careful these days."

"You're working organized crime, I get it," Ballard said. "So, who stole Laurie Lee Wells's identity?"

"Well, hold on a second, Detective Ballard. Why don't we start with you telling me what you're working on? Who's dead and how did Laurie Lee Wells's name come into it?"

Ballard knew that if she went first, Kenworth would control the flow of information going both ways. But it felt as though she had no choice. His callback and cagey manner told her that Kenworth wasn't going to give until he got.

"We actually have two murders, one last year and the other last week," she said. "Our victim last year was a superior-court judge who was stabbed while walking to the courthouse. Our victim last week was burned alive. So far, we've come up with two connections: the same law firm represented players likely involved in each of these seemingly unrelated cases—and then there's the woman."

"The woman?" Kenworth asked.

"We've got the same woman on video in the immediate vicinity of each crime scene. She's wearing different wigs and clothing but it's the same woman. In the first case, the judge's murder, she was even corralled as a possible witness and identified herself to police as Laurie Lee Wells, giving the correct address of the Laurie Lee Wells who had her wallet and identity stolen in Las Vegas last year. Problem is, we went to that address and spoke to the real Laurie Lee Wells, and she's not the woman on the video. She told us about what happened in Vegas and that's what brings me to you."

There was silence from Kenworth.

"You still there?" Ballard prompted.

"I'm here," Kenworth said. "I was thinking. These videos, you have a clear shot of the woman?"

"Not really. She was clever about that. But we identified her by her walk."

"Her walk."

"She's intoed. You can see it in both videos. Does that mean anything to you?"

"'Intoed'? Nope. I don't even know what it means."

"Okay, then what can you tell me about the Laurie Lee Wells case? Have you identified the woman who took her identity? You work in organized crime. I have to assume her case has been folded into something bigger."

"Well, we have some organized groups here who engage in identity theft on a large scale, so a lot of that comes through our office. But with the Wells case we took it because it fit with a location we've been looking at."

"The Devil's Den."

Kenworth was silent, pointedly not confirming Ballard's supposition.

"Okay, if you don't want to talk about the Devil's Den, then let's talk about Batman," Ballard said.

"'Batman'?"

"Come on, Kenworth. Dominick Butino."

"That's the first time you've mentioned him. How is he part of this?"

"The law firm that connects all of this also repped Butino on a case over here. They won it. Let me just ask you, Detective, since you're in OCI—have you ever heard of a woman hitter, maybe working for Butino or the Outfit?"

As was becoming routine, Kenworth didn't answer right away. He seemed to have to carefully weigh every piece of information he eventually gave Ballard.

"It's not that hard a question," Ballard finally said. "You either have or you haven't. Your hesitation suggests you have."

"Well, yeah," Kenworth said. "But it's more rumor than anything else. We've picked up intel here and there about a woman who handles contracts for the Outfit."

"What are the rumors?"

"We had a guy—a connected guy—come out here from Miami. He ended up dead in his suite at the Cleopatra. The casino surveillance cams showed him going up with a woman. The scene looked like a suicide—he sucked down a bullet. But the more we looked into it, the more we think it was a hit. But that was nine months ago and we haven't gotten anywhere with it. It's gone cold."

"Sounds like our girl. I'd like to see the video."

Kenworth gave that his usual pause.

"I'll show you mine if you show me yours," Ballard prompted. "We can help each other here. If it's the same woman, we have something big. Give me your e-mail and I'll send you what we've got. You send me what you have. This is what cooperating police agencies do."

"I think that will be all right," Kenworth finally said. "But we don't have her face. In a city of cameras, she seemed to know where every one of them was placed."

"Same here. What's your e-mail? I'll send you the first video. You send me back yours and then I'll send you our second. Deal?"

"Deal."

After disconnecting, Ballard uploaded the video from Mako's that showed the suspect buying the bottle of Tito's and using the ATM. On the e-mail to Kenworth, she wrote *Black Widow* in the subject line because that was the name Ballard had come up with for the dark-haired, darkly dressed version of the suspected killer.

Kenworth carried his telephone manners into his e-mail etiquette: after a half hour, Ballard had received nothing in return from the Las Vegas detective. She was beginning to feel she had been ripped off and was about to call him when a return e-mail came in with the *Black Widow* subject line. It had two videos labeled CLEO1 and CLEO2 attached. The only message in the e-mail said: "The car in Cleo2 was stolen, set on fire in Summerland."

Ballard downloaded and watched the videos.

The first was a camera trail that showed a man in a Jimmy Buffett shirt playing blackjack at a high-roller table at the Cleopatra. Ballard assumed he was the victim-to-be. The woman sitting next to him was not playing any hands. She had long and full blond hair that appeared to be a wig. Its thick bangs acted like a visor, shielding her downward-tilted face from camera capture.

The man cashed in his chips, then the camera angles changed as the couple left the table and headed to the elevator reserved for tower suites. The woman kept her head down and away from any camera. She carried what appeared to be a large white overnight bag slung over one of her shoulders and she was wearing black parachute pants and a halter top. The last capture shown on the video was the couple in the elevator, the 42 button on the panel glowing as they rode up. The time stamp on the elevator shot showed them getting off on the forty-second floor at 01:12:54 and then the video ended.

Ballard went to CLEO2. This video began with the elevator camera and a time stamp of 01:34:31 and showed a woman getting aboard on the forty-second floor. She was wearing a wide-brimmed hat that totally obscured her face. Only a small fringe of black hair could be seen going down her back. She was wearing black slacks, blouse, and sandals. The overnight bag strapped over her shoulder was black but had the same dimensions as the one seen in the CLEO1 video.

The woman got off the elevator at the casino level and the cameras followed her through the vast gaming space and out the doors to a parking garage. She walked down a parking aisle, got into a silver Porsche SUV, and drove away.

Thanks to Kenworth's message, Ballard knew the fate of the Porsche.

Ballard reversed the video and watched the woman walk down the parking aisle again. She noted the gait was slightly intoed.

"Black Widow," Ballard whispered.

Making good on her deal, she uploaded the video from Grand Park and sent it to Kenworth with a message:

It's the same woman in your videos. Three 187s now. We need to talk.

After sending it, she realized *187* might not be the penal code number for murder in Nevada. She also realized that not only did Vegas Metro and LAPD need to talk, but LAPD needed to talk among themselves. The case had reached a point where she needed to bring Olivas up to date and put the need for interagency cooperation with Vegas on his plate.

But before she did that she had to tell her own partner.

Ballard called Bosch and he picked up immediately. But his voice was drowned out by the background noise of traffic and a blaring siren. She managed to hear him yell, "Hold on."

She waited as he apparently rolled up the windows of his car and put in earbuds.

"Renée?"

"Harry, where are you? What's going on?"

"Heading to Bunker Hill behind an RA. Clayton Manley just went down thirty-two floors without an elevator."

"Oh, shit. He jumped?"

"That's what they're saying. Who knows? RHD is taking it. Gustafson and Reyes. I'm heading there, see what I can find out."

"Listen, Harry, be careful. This thing is coming together. I've been talking to Vegas Metro. They have a case over there, a murder. They sent video and it's our girl. The Black Widow."

"That's what they call her?"

"No, actually, I called her that when I sent them our videos."

"What's the case over there?"

"Mob-related. Some OC guy from Miami checked into the Cleopatra but didn't check out. It was a suicide setup—like he swallowed a bullet. But they have him on video going up to the room with the Black Widow. Then she comes down, different wig, different look. But she has the walk. It's her. I'm sure."

There was a silence, but with Bosch, Ballard was used to it.

"Fake suicide," he finally said.

"Like with Manley," Ballard said. "But why is RHD taking it if it's a suicide—supposedly?"

"I don't know. Maybe what I've been telling Reyes made them put Manley back on their radar. I was in the middle of telling him how they'd missed Manley when he got the call. Anyway, I'm pulling in. I'm going to see if I can get up to the firm."

"Harry, she could be up there. Or at least still in the vicinity."

"I know."

"Well, if they felt the need to get rid of Manley, they might feel the same about you. You're the one who went in there and stirred things up."

"I know."

"So don't go in. Just wait for me there. I'm on my way."

BOSCH

49

Bosch pulled to the curb just past the art museum on Grand. He unlocked the glove compartment and took out two things: a small six-shot pistol in a belt-clip holster and an old LAPD ID tag he was supposed to have turned in upon his retirement but claimed he had lost.

He now clipped the gun to his belt and put the ID in his coat pocket. He put the Jeep's flashers on and got out. Walking past the museum toward California Plaza, he saw Gustafson and Reyes standing at the open trunk of their unmarked car, getting out equipment they would need for their investigation. Bosch cut a path to them. Gustafson saw him coming.

"What are you doing here, Bosch?" he said. "You're not LAPD, you're not wanted."

"You guys wouldn't even be here if it weren't for me," Bosch said. "You would be—"

"For the record, Bosch, I still think you are full of shit," Gustafson said. "So you can go now. Bye-bye."

Gustafson slammed the trunk of the car to underline Bosch's dismissal.

"You're not listening to me," Bosch said. "This is no suicide and the hitter could still be in that building."

"Right. Orlando just told me all about your lady hitter. That's a good one."

"Then why are you here, Gustafson? Since when does RHD roll on suicides?"

"This guy takes a dive, his name comes up in our case, we get the call. A waste of my fucking time."

Gustafson walked by him and headed toward the scene in the plaza. Reyes dutifully followed and didn't say a word to Bosch.

Bosch watched them go and then surveyed the area. There was a crowd at the far end of the building, where Bosch could see men in security uniforms creating a perimeter around a blue canvas tarp that had been used to cover the body of Clayton Manley. The EMTs from the rescue ambulance were heading that way, and Gustafson and Reyes weren't far behind them. Even from a distance Bosch could see that the blue tarp was just a few feet from the building.

There was nothing routine about suicides, but Bosch knew from his years on the job that jumpers usually propelled themselves away from the structure they dropped from. There were always the "step-offs," but that method was not as precise or as final as the jump-off. Buildings often had architectural parapets, window-washing scaffolds, awnings, and other features that could interfere with a straight drop. The last thing a suicidal individual wanted was to have a fall broken and to bounce down the side of a building, possibly being left at the bottom alive.

Bosch deviated from the path the others were taking and headed toward the building's entrance. As he went, he surveyed California Plaza. It was surrounded on three sides by office towers. The one he was heading toward was the tallest but Bosch assumed that cameras somewhere in the plaza would have captured Manley's fall. From them it might be possible to determine whether he had been conscious when he fell.

He reached into his pocket as he approached the revolving glass doors at the lobby entrance, pulled out his old ID, and clipped it to the breast pocket of his jacket. He knew that the plan now was to keep moving and not stop long enough for anyone to read the date on it.

Once he passed through the door, he saw the round security desk with a sign saying that visitors must show ID before being allowed to go up. Bosch strode toward it confidently. A man and a woman sat behind the counter, both wearing blue blazers with name tags.

"Detective Bosch, LAPD," he said. "Have any of my colleagues asked about visitors today to Michaelson & Mitchell on the sixteenth floor?"

"Not yet," the woman said. Her name tag said RACHEL.

Bosch leaned over the counter as if to look down at the screen in front of Rachel. He put his elbow on the marble top and drew his hand up to his chin as if contemplating her answer. This allowed him to block her view of his ID tag with his forearm.

"Can we take a look, then?" he said. "All visitors to the firm."

Rachel started typing. The angle Bosch had on her screen was too sharp and he could not see what she was doing.

"I can only tell you who was put on the visitor list this morning," Rachel said.

"That's fine," Bosch said. "Would it say which lawyer in the firm they were visiting?"

"Yes, I can provide that if needed."

"Thank you."

"This is about the suicide?"

"We're not calling it a suicide yet. We need to investigate it and that's why we want to see who came up to the firm today."

Bosch turned and looked through the glass walls of the lobby. He did not have a view of the death scene but felt he was only a few moves ahead of Gustafson and Reyes. One of them would be going up to the firm soon.

"Okay, I have it here," Rachel said.

"Is that something you can print out for me?" Bosch asked.

"Not a problem."

"Thanks."

Rachel moved down the counter to a printer and took two pages out of the tray. She handed them to Bosch, who took them as he walked around the counter toward the elevators.

"I'm going up to sixteen," he said.

"Wait," Rachel said.

Bosch froze.

"What?" he asked.

"You need a visitor card to get to the elevators," Rachel said.

Bosch had forgotten that the elevator lobby was protected by electronic turnstiles. Rachel programmed a card and handed it to him.

"Here you go, Detective. Just put it into the slot at the turnstile."

"Thank you. How do I get access to the roof?"

"You can get to thirty-two, but from there you have to take the maintenance stairwell up. It's supposed to be locked but I guess today it wasn't."

"How do employees get up to their offices?"

"They enter the underground parking on Hill Street, take an elevator to this level, then everybody goes through the turnstiles. Employees get permanent cards."

"Okay, thanks."

"Be careful up there."

Bosch decided to go to the roof first. As he rode the elevator up, he tried to think in terms of how the Black Widow did it. She had somehow lured Manley to the roof and then pushed him off, or incapacitated him and pushed him off. The question was how she got him up there. Forcing him at gunpoint to walk through the law firm and take an elevator up would have been too risky. Just the chance that someone could be on the elevator would seem to scratch that as a possibility. But somehow, she had gotten Manley up there.

As the elevator ascended, he looked for the first time at the printout he had received at the security desk. He knew, of course, that the

Black Widow could have arrived as an employee or with an employee, but nevertheless he studied the names of the seventeen visitors on the list. None of them was Laurie Lee Wells. That would have been too easy. But only four were women, none were visiting Manley, and only one was visiting either Michaelson or Mitchell. That name was Sonja Soquin, who had arrived at 2:55 p.m. for a three o'clock appointment with Michaelson. Calculating from the time Reyes got the call while sitting with Bosch, he estimated that Manley had fallen from the building to his death sometime between 3:50 and 4:00 p.m.

The elevator opened and Bosch stepped out. He looked up and down the hall and saw a uniformed officer standing in front of an open door Bosch assumed was the maintenance entrance to the roof. He walked that way.

"Anybody gone up yet?" he asked.

"Not yet," the officer said. "It might be a crime scene."

As Bosch got closer he saw that the officer's name tag said OHLMAN.

"I'm going up," Bosch said.

The officer hesitated while eyeing Bosch's ID tag. But Bosch turned as if to look back down the hallway.

"This is the only way up?" he asked.

"Yes, sir," Ohlman said. "The door was open when I got up here."

"Okay, let me take a look. My partner, Reyes, will be up soon. Tell him I'm up top."

"Yes, sir."

Ohlman stepped aside and Bosch entered a large maintenance room that had an iron staircase going up to the roof.

Bosch took the stairs slowly, favoring his surgically repaired knee. It was at least thirty steps. When he got to the top he leaned against a steel railing to catch his breath for a moment and then pushed through a door.

A murder of crows flew into the air as the metal door was taken by the wind and banged sharply against the wall. Bosch stepped out. The view was magnificent. To the west he could see the sun beginning to dip toward the Pacific, the orange ball reflecting on a blue-black surface at least twenty miles away.

He walked toward the far edge, where the building curved and which he judged was the point Manley had dropped from. He walked slowly and scanned the ground, moving first across a helicopter pad and then an expanse of gravel on tar. An LAPD helicopter was circling above. Heavy wind buffeted his body, a reminder not to get too near the edge.

Under his feet he could feel that the tar had softened in the direct sunlight of the day.

The door slammed behind him and he whirled around, his hand going to his hip.

There was no one.

The wind.

A two-foot-high parapet ran along the edge of the building. It had a metal endcap containing the lighting strip that outlined the edges of the building in blue at night. The mirrored tower looked generic by day but was a standout on the downtown skyline after sundown.

Near the edge he saw a disturbance in the gravel—a three-foot-long deviation where gravel had been raked off the tar. He lowered himself, bracing his new knee with his hand as he dropped into a baseball catcher's stance. He studied the marking and decided it could have been a drag mark or a slide mark that occurred during a struggle. But it appeared to have occurred recently: the tar had not been grayed by exposure to the sun and smog, as it had been in other places.

A helicopter made a loud pass overhead. Bosch did not look up. He studied what he was sure was a mark left by Clayton Manley before he went over the edge and down to the hard ground like a broken crow.

50

There was another police officer standing guard in the reception area on the sixteenth floor. His name tag said FRENCH.

"Any of my guys up here yet?" Bosch asked.

"Not yet," the officer said.

"You're keeping people from leaving?"

"That's right."

"When did you get here?"

"We were code seven at the food court across the street. We got here pretty quick after the call. Maybe twenty-five minutes ago."

"We?"

"My partner's upstairs. The firm has elevators on the second level too."

"Okay, I need to go back to the victim's office."

"Yes, sir."

Bosch walked past the suede couch and started around the staircase but then thought of something and returned to the officer.

"Officer French, did anybody try to leave while you've been here?"

"Just a couple people, sir."

"Who?"

"I didn't get names. I wasn't told to do that."

"Male or female?"

"Two guys, they said they had to go to court. I told them we'd get them cleared as soon as possible. They said they'd call the courtroom to notify them."

"Okay, thanks."

Bosch headed around the stairway again. He was convinced that the Black Widow had come and gone. He moved quietly down the hall. The door to Michaelson's office was closed but the door to Mitchell's office was open, and as Bosch passed he saw an older man with graying hair standing at the floor-to-ceiling window looking down into the plaza.

The door to Clayton Manley's office was closed as well. Bosch leaned his ear against it and listened for conversation but heard nothing. He pulled his jacket sleeve over his palm and pushed the handle down to open the door.

The office was empty. He walked in and closed the door, then stepped to the side of the door and took in the room as a whole. He checked the floor first and saw no indentations in the carpet or anything else that drew suspicion or interest. Scanning the rest of the room, he saw no signs that a struggle had taken place.

He got up and moved behind the desk, using the cuff of his coat again to hit the space bar on the computer. The screen came alive but was password protected. Continuing with the cuff over his hand, he opened drawers in the desk, finding nothing of note until he got to the first of the bottom file drawers. The key was still in the lock. He managed to turn it with his sleeve and there on top of several files were the documents Bosch had given Manley that morning. Bosch saw that there were several notes written in the margins of the top sheet.

Just as he lifted the documents out of the drawer, the door to the office swung open and the man Bosch had seen at the window in Mitchell's office was standing there. He was taller than Bosch had realized from the previous glimpse. Sharp shoulders, thick in the middle but not fat. Forty years before, he could have been an offensive lineman.

"Who are you?" he said. "Are you the police? You have no right to be going through an attorney's documents, dead or alive. This is outrageous behavior."

Bosch knew there was no good answer or bluff to the questions. He was in a jam. The only thing he apparently had going for him was that Mitchell—if it was Mitchell—didn't recognize him. This made Bosch jump to the possibility that Mitchell was unaware and isolated from the nefarious actions of his own law firm.

"I said, who the hell do you think you are, coming in here and going through privileged information?" the man demanded.

Bosch decided his only defense was offense.

He pulled the ID tag off his jacket, held it out, then shoved it into his jacket pocket.

"I was a cop but not anymore," he said. "And I'm not randomly going through Manley's files. I came for my own files. He's dead and I want my stuff back."

"Then what you do is hire a new attorney and he requests the files as your representative," the man said. "You don't break and enter an office and steal documents out of a drawer."

"I didn't break in. I walked in. And I'm not stealing what is already mine."

"What is your name?"

"Bosch."

The name made no discernible impact on the man in the doorway, further supporting Bosch's assumption.

"I had an appointment with Manley," Bosch said. "I came in to sign papers and I find out he's splattered all over the plaza down there. I want my file and I want the documents I gave him and I want to be out of here."

"I told you, it doesn't work that way," the man said. "You take nothing from this room. Do you understand?"

Bosch decided on a different tack.

"You're Mitchell, right?"

"Samuel Mitchell. I cofounded this firm twenty-four years ago. I am chairman and managing partner."

"Managing partner. That means you collect the money but aren't involved in the cases, right?"

"Sir, I am not going to talk to you about my job or this firm."

"And so you probably didn't know what Manley and your partner Michaelson were up to. You didn't know about the woman?"

"The woman? What woman? Who are you talking about?"

"Sonja Soquin. Laurie Lee Wells. The Black Widow—whatever they called her. The woman they used to get things done when there was no other way—legally—to do it."

"You're not making sense to me and I want you to leave. Now. The police are coming up here any moment."

"I know. And that's not a good thing for you, Samuel. It's going to unravel everything. Where is she? Where is Sonja Soquin?"

"I don't know who or what you're talking about."

"I'm talking about the woman they used to kill Judge Montgomery for what he did to Manley in court. The woman they used to kill Edison Banks Jr. so he would not be a threat to the shipping fortune of one of your biggest clients. The woman they used who knows how many other times before that."

Mitchell looked like he had been hit with a bucket of cold water. His face stiffened. His eyes opened wide and an understanding of things came to them. Bosch judged it to be sincere. Genuine surprise, then a terrible understanding.

He shook his head and recovered.

"Sir," he said. "I am asking you to leave this office right—"

There was a metal *snap* and a thumping sound. They overlapped in the way a drummer will hit the snare and pump the bass at the same moment. The top of Mitchell's carefully combed hair popped up and Bosch heard the bullet hit the coffered ceiling. Mitchell then dropped hard onto his knees, his eyes now blank, unseeing. He was dead before he pitched forward, going down face-first to the floor without putting out a hand to break the fall.

Bosch looked at the open door behind his body. He expected Michaelson to step in but it was the Black Widow. Down at her side she carried a black steel automatic with a suppressor attached. She had the dark wig on and black clothing.

Bosch bent his elbows and raised his hands to show he was no threat. He hoped that the metallic sound of the shot and Mitchell's body dropping might bring the officer from the waiting area. Or maybe Gustafson and Reyes would finally arrive and save the day.

Bosch nodded at the body.

"I guess the Manley suicide isn't going to sell now," he said.

She didn't take the bait at first. She just looked at him with what was either a sneer or a crooked smile. Like an actress Bosch had always liked over the years. Oddly, he started thinking about the movies she had been in: *Diner, Sea of Love,* the one where she was a detective working a serial case and—

"Why did you do this?" the woman said. "You're not even a cop."

"I don't know," Bosch said. "Once a cop, always a cop, I guess."

"You should've stayed away from it."

Bosch detected a slight accent but couldn't place it. Eastern Europe, he guessed. He knew she was going to shoot him now and there was no way he could get to his own gun in time.

"Why didn't you leave—after Manley?" he asked. "You should have been long gone."

"I did," she said. "I was clear. But then I saw you. I came back for you. The job was Manley and you. You just saved me a lot of time."

Bosch put it together: Michaelson was cleaning up a mess. No matter what hold Manley had had on him and the firm, he had finally outstayed his welcome by letting the fox into the henhouse. He had to go—and so did the fox.

"What about Mitchell?" Bosch asked. "Was he a freebie?"

"No, he was just in the way," the woman said. "But I can make it work. You'll get credit for him too."

Bosch nodded.

"I get it," he said. "Angry ex-cop goes on a rampage. Throws his lawyer off the roof, kills the founding partner. It won't work. I was with a cop when you threw Manley over the edge."

She made a gesture with the gun.

"It's the best I can do under the circumstances," she said. "I'll be gone when they figure it out."

She steadied her aim and Bosch knew this was it. He suddenly thought of Tyrone Power dying while fighting a fake duel and doing what he loved. And John Jack Thompson going to his grave with a terrible secret. He wasn't ready to go either way.

"Let me ask you one question," he said.

"Hurry," she said.

"How'd you get him up there? Manley. How'd you get him to the roof?"

She gave the crooked smile again before answering. Bosch saw her aim drop again.

"That was easy," she said. "I told him you were coming for him and that we had a helicopter waiting for him on the roof. I said we were going to Vegas, where he was getting a new name and a new life. I told him Mr. Michaelson had set it all up."

"And he believed you," Bosch said.

"That was his mistake," she said. "We purged his computer and he sent an e-mail to the firm saying goodbye. Once we were up there, the rest was easy. Just like this."

BALLARD

51

Ballard came out of the elevator and immediately saw the uniformed police officer standing in a waiting area to the left. She walked directly to him, pulling her jacket back to show her badge. She saw his name was *French*.

"I'm looking for a guy—sixties, mustache, looks like a cop," she said.

"There was a guy like that but he had a legit ID," French said.

"Where is he?"

French pointed.

"He went around the stairs," he said.

"Okay," Ballard said.

She walked to the reception desk, where a young man was playing solitaire on his phone.

"Where is Clayton Manley's office?"

"You go around the stairs and it's the last office at the end of the hall past Mr. Michaelson's and Mr. Mitchell's offices. I can take you back."

"No, you stay here. I'll find it."

Ballard moved quickly toward the curving staircase and the hall. As she entered the passageway she saw the first two doors on the left closed, but the last door was open and she heard voices. One belonged to a woman and the other, unmistakably, to Harry Bosch.

She quietly drew her weapon and held it in two hands in front of her as she moved down the hallway and closer to the open door. She strained to listen.

"That was his mistake," the woman said. "We purged his computer and he sent an e-mail to the firm saying goodbye. Once we were up there, the rest was easy. Just like this."

Ballard came to the door and saw a woman standing with her back to her. Dark hair, dark clothes. She thought: *Black Widow.* Beyond her was a man facedown on the floor. Gray hair but not like Bosch's.

The woman was raising a weapon with a sound suppressor attached.

"You move, you die," Ballard said.

The woman froze, her arm straight but the weapon only halfway up to firing position.

"Drop the weapon and let me see both hands," Ballard ordered. "Now!"

The woman remained frozen and Ballard knew she was going to have to shoot her.

"Last chance. Drop...the...weapon."

Ballard raised her arms slightly so she could sight down the barrel of her pistol. She would cut the woman's cords with a shot to the back of the neck.

The woman opened her gun hand and the weight of the barrel with the suppressor dropped the muzzle downward as the handle came up.

"I've got a hair trigger on this," she said. "I drop it, it could go off. I'm going to lower it to the ground."

"Slowly," Ballard said. "Harry?"

"I'm here," Bosch said from the right.

"You carrying?"

"Have it on her right now."

"Good."

The woman in the room started to bend her knees and flex down.

Ballard followed her with the aim of her gun, holding her breath the whole time until the weapon was dropped the last few inches.

"All right, stand up," Ballard ordered. "Move to the window and put your palms flat on the glass."

The woman did as instructed, stepping to the floor-to-ceiling glass panel and then raising and placing her hands against it.

"You got her?" Ballard asked.

"I've got her," Bosch said.

He raised his aim to assure Ballard he had the woman firmly in his sights. Ballard holstered her weapon and moved in to search the woman.

"Do you have any other weapons on you?"

"Just the one on the floor."

"I'm going to search you now. If I find another weapon on you it's going to be a problem."

"You won't."

Ballard moved forward and used her foot to push the woman's legs apart. She then began a pat-down that started low with the legs before moving up.

"Do you have to do that?" the woman asked.

"With you, yes," Ballard said.

"And I bet you like it."

"Part of the job."

Finished with the search, Ballard put her hand on the woman's back to hold her in place. She then pulled her cuffs off her belt.

"Okay, one at a time," she said. "I want you to bring your hand down from the glass and behind your back. Your right first."

Ballard reached up and grabbed the right wrist as it was coming down and started bringing it behind the Black Widow's back. But the woman turned as if being pivoted by Ballard. Ballard tried to stop it.

"No—"

Ballard saw it before she felt it. In the woman's hand was an open folding knife with a blade curved like a horn. All matte black except for the edge of the blade that had been sharpened to a shine. The woman brought it up and into Ballard's left armpit and then put her other arm around her neck in a V hold. She was now behind Ballard and using her as a shield. Ballard saw Bosch holding his weapon, looking for a clean shot that wasn't there.

"I sliced a bleeder under her arm," the woman said. "She's got three minutes and she'll bleed out. You put the gun down. I walk out of here. She lives."

"Take the shot, Harry," Ballard said.

The woman adjusted herself behind Ballard to improve her shielding. Ballard could feel her breath on the back of her neck. She could feel blood running over her ribs and down her side.

"Two and a half minutes," the woman said.

"There's a cop out front," Bosch said.

"And there's an exit to the stairs in the copy room. We're almost at two minutes."

Bosch remembered seeing the emergency exit door. He signaled with the gun toward the door.

"Go," he said.

"Gun," the woman said.

Bosch put his gun down on the desk.

"Harry, no," Ballard managed to say in a whisper.

She then felt herself being dragged toward the office door.

"Get back against the bookshelf," the woman ordered.

Bosch raised his hands and moved back. Ballard was dragged toward the door.

"You're going to have a choice now," the woman said. "Save her or go after me."

Ballard felt the woman's grip release and she fell back against the doorframe and then slid down to a sitting position.

Bosch came quickly around the desk to her. His hands immediately went inside her jacket to her belt and pulled off the radio. He knew how to use it.

"Officer down! Need immediate medical on sixteenth floor of California Plaza West. Office of Clayton Manley. Repeat, officer down. Officer stabbed, losing blood, needs immediate medical."

He put the rover on the floor and then opened Ballard's jacket to get a look at the knife wound.

"Harry...I'm okay, go after her."

"I'm going to lay you on your right side so the wound is on the high side. You're going to be all right. I'll compress the wound."

"No, go."

Bosch ignored her. As he gently put her down on her side he heard footsteps running in the hallway. Officer French appeared in the doorway.

"French," Bosch yelled. "Get the EMTs. There's a team down in the plaza. Get them up here, now. Then put out a broadcast. A woman, thirties, white, black hair, all black clothing, armed and dangerous. She went into the exit stairs. She's trying to get out of the building."

French didn't move. He seemed frozen by what he was seeing.

"Go!" Bosch yelled.

French disappeared. Ballard looked up from the floor to Bosch. She felt her clock running out. For some reason, she smiled. She barely heard Bosch talking to her.

"Stay with me, Renée. I'm going to use your arm to compress the wound. It's gonna hurt."

Holding her by the elbow, he shifted her arm up so that he could hold her biceps down on the wound. It didn't hurt at all and that made her smile.

"Harry..."

"Don't talk. Don't waste your energy. Just stay with me, Renée. Stay with me."

BALLARD AND BOSCH

52

Ballard couldn't seem to move on the bed without setting off searing pain that ran like branches of lightning over the left side of her body. She was being treated at White Memorial in Boyle Heights. It was the second morning after the events at California Plaza and she was out of the intensive care unit. The Black Widow had only nicked her axillary artery with her curving blade, but nevertheless Ballard had suffered a major loss of blood. The EMTs had contained it and then an ER doctor had sutured her damaged blood vessels in a four-hour surgery. It was just that now her left arm felt like it had been strapped to her body with bungee cords and any little movement set off pain like she had never felt in her life.

"Stop moving."

She turned her head to see Bosch enter the room.

"Easier said than done," she said. "Did you have trouble getting in this time?"

"No," Bosch said. "I'm finally on the Approved list."

"I told them you were my uncle."

"I'll take that over *grandfather*."

"I should've thought of that. So, what's the news? She's still in the wind?"

Bosch sat down on a chair next to the bed. There was a table to his left crowded with flower vases and stuffed animals and cards.

"The Black Widow's in the wind," he said. "But at least they know who they're looking for. They got a print off one of the cartridges in the gun she left and IDed her—they think. Turns out the FBI's been looking for her for a while for some wet work she did in Miami."

"They have her name?"

"Catarina Cava."

"What's that, Italian?"

"No, Cuban, actually."

"How did she get hooked up with Batman?"

"You forget, I'm not part of the club anymore. People from your department aren't telling me jack. What I know I got from a fed who interviewed me and is part of the task force they're putting together on this. The bureau, Vegas Metro, LAPD. He told me Butino and his people picked up on her when they had a piece of work that was mutually beneficial. Then she became his go-to. Which in turn brought her to the attention of Michaelson & Mitchell."

"They have Michaelson?"

"Yeah, they grabbed him at Van Nuys Airport. He was about to take a private jet to Grand Cayman. Now he's trying to deal his way out, laying everything off on Manley. Of course, Manley's dead and his computer was purged before he went off the roof. But I told them what Cava told me: that Michaelson set up the hit on Manley and me."

"Well, I hope they put Michaelson away for a hundred years."

"It's a dance. He'll eventually realize he has to reveal all if he wants any shot at a break."

"Does your FBI source have any idea about what Manley's hold was on Michaelson? Like why they didn't get rid of him sooner?"

"They just assume he knew too much. They believe they're going to find other cases where Michaelson used Cava. Judge Montgomery wasn't the first hit. In fact, that may have been a rogue operation— Manley making use of their in-house hitter without Michaelson's approval. But what was he going to do? Fire him? He knew too much. Michaelson was probably going to wait for Herstadt to be convicted, the case to die down a little bit, and then he would make his move on Manley."

"But you came along and sped it all up."

"Something like that."

Bosch absentmindedly picked up a stuffed dog that had been sent to Ballard with a get-well-soon card.

"That's from my friend Selma Robinson," Ballard said. "The deputy D.A. on the Hilton case."

"Nice," Bosch said.

He put the dog back. Ballard looked at the crowded table. It seemed odd to receive bouquets and get-well cards after being slashed with an assassin's blade—there was no specialty card for that from Hallmark. But the table and just about every other horizontal surface in the room seemed to be covered with flowers, cards, stuffed animals, or something else from well-wishers, most of them fellow cops. It was an odd contradiction to receive so much attention and so many get-wells from a department she thought had turned its back on her long ago. The doctor told her that more than thirty cops had showed up the night of her surgery to donate blood for her. He gave her a list of names. Many were from the late show but most were complete strangers to her. When she read the names, a tear had gone down her cheek.

Bosch seemed to understand the currents that were going through her. He gave her a moment before asking, "So, Olivas been by?"

"Yes, actually," Ballard said. "This morning. Probably felt he had to."

"He's had a good week."

"Damn right. First he gets credit on the Hilton case. Now all of this. He's going to clear Montgomery, Banks, and Manley. The guy's going four for four."

"That's a hell of an average. All because of you."

"And you."

"Maybe it'll get you off the late show."

"No, I don't want that. I'd still never work for him. Olivas. And if not RHD, where am I going to go? Besides, after midnight is when it all happens in this town. I like the dark hours. As soon as they let me, I'm going back."

Bosch smiled and nodded. He had known that would be her answer.

"What about you?" Ballard asked. "What are you going to do now?"

"Today's my day for visiting," Bosch said. "I'm going to go see Margaret Thompson next."

Ballard nodded.

"Are you going to tell her about John Hilton?" she asked.

"I don't know," Bosch said. "Not sure she needs to know all that."

"Maybe she already does."

"Maybe. But I doubt it. I don't think she would have called me in the first place if she'd known. I don't think she would have done that to me, you know? Led me to finding out about him."

Bosch was silent after that and Ballard waited a moment before speaking.

"I'm sorry," she said. "I know he was important to you. And to have this…truth come out…"

"Yeah, well…," Bosch said. "True heroes are hard to come by, I guess."

They were silent another moment and Bosch wanted to change the subject.

"When I went there last, to her house," he said, "you know, to look through his office—before we knew why he took the murder book…anyway, I found a box in his closet where he kept old cases. Not full murder books, but copies of some chronos, reports, and summaries from old cases."

"That he had worked?" Ballard asked.

"Yeah, from his own cases. And there was one—it was a sixty-day summary from a case I had worked with him. This girl rode her bike under the Hollywood freeway...and then she disappeared. A few days later she was found dead. Murdered. And we never cleared it."

"What was her name?"

"Sarah Freelander."

"When was the murder?"

"Nineteen eighty-two."

"Wow, that's old. And never solved?"

Bosch shook his head.

"I'm going to ask Margaret for that box," he said.

Ballard could tell that Bosch's eyes were seeing the case from long ago. Then he seemed to come back to the present. He brightened and smiled at her.

"Okay, then," he said. "I guess I'll let you rest. Any idea when you'll be out of here?"

"They're just worried about infection now," Ballard said. "Otherwise, it's all good. So I think they're going to watch it another day and then let me go. Two days at the most."

"Then I'll be back tomorrow. You need anything?"

"I'm good. Unless you want to go take my dog for a walk."

Bosch paused.

"I didn't think so," Ballard said, smiling.

"I'm not really good with animals," Bosch said. "I mean, did you want—"

"Don't worry about it. Selma has been checking on her and taking her out."

"Then good. That's perfect."

Bosch stood up, squeezed her right hand, and then headed toward the door.

"Sarah Freelander," Ballard said.

Bosch stopped and turned around.

"If you work that case, I work it with you."

Bosch nodded.

"Yeah," Bosch said. "That's a deal."

He started to leave the room. Ballard stopped him again.

"Actually, Harry, I need one more thing from you."

He came back to the bed.

"What?"

"Can you take a picture of all the flowers and stuffed animals? I want to remember all of this."

"Sure."

Bosch pulled his phone and stepped to one side so he could get the whole display of good wishes in the frame.

"You want to be in it?" he asked.

"God, no," Ballard said.

Bosch took three shots from slightly different angles, then opened the camera app on the phone to select the best shot to send her. As he clicked on the "All Photos" option, he saw the shot he had taken while searching Clayton Manley's office. He had forgotten about it in all the activity that had occurred later. It was a photo of a document on Manley's computer before it had been purged.

The document was named TRANSFER and contained only a thirteen-digit number followed by the letters *G.C.* Bosch realized now that *G.C.* might stand for *Grand Cayman*.

"Harry, something wrong?" Ballard asked.

"Uh, no," Bosch said. "Something's right."

EPILOGUE

She always sat facing the door. She always came as soon as they opened at 11 so she could get her *café con leche* and Cuban toast before he arrived. This time was no different. It was early, before the lunch rush at El Tinajon. Otherwise they wouldn't make the Cuban toast. It wasn't on the menu—you had to ask for it.

In her peripheral vision she saw a woman come from the kitchen and she thought it was Marta with her toast. But it wasn't. The woman sat down across from her, and there was a familiarity about her.

"Batman's not coming," she said.

Now Cava recognized her.

"You lived," she said.

Ballard nodded.

"He gave me up, didn't he?" Cava said.

"No," Ballard said. "Batman's not talking. It was Michaelson."

"Michaelson…"

She seemed genuinely surprised.

"Grand Cayman was the nexus," Ballard said. "He was headed there when they grabbed him. Then we found your offshore account there—thanks to Harry Bosch. That led to the feds finding his at the same bank. Once the feds got to his money, the game was over. He gave everybody up just so he could keep enough to take care of his family."

"Family first," Cava said.

"And he told us how to find you."

"The only mistakes I have ever made came from trusting men."

"They can let you down. Some of them."

Cava nodded. Ballard watched her hands.

"Don't move your hands," she said. "You're under arrest."

Those last three words were the cue. Soon, members of the task force—FBI, Vegas Metro, LAPD—came down the back hallway and through the kitchen and the front door, weapons drawn, no chances taken with the Black Widow.

Ballard stood up and backed away from the table. Men moved in on Cava, took her by the arms, held her tightly, and searched her. They found the curved knife in the homemade forearm scabbard that Ballard had missed that day four weeks earlier. They found a pistol in the purse she had put down on the floor.

As she was being cuffed, Cava kept her eyes on Ballard. She smiled slightly when she was led away from the table and toward the front door. There was a van waiting to transport her to the bureau's Las Vegas field office. It took off as soon as the side door was slammed shut.

"Way to go, Renée."

It was Kenworth from Vegas Metro. He moved behind her and took the recorder off her belt as she detached the mini-microphone from inside the opening of her blouse. She pulled the wire up and out and handed it to him.

"She didn't really give up anything," Ballard said.

"She exhibited knowledge of the conspiracy and crimes," Kenworth said. "That's what the prosecutor will say. And I say: *good job*."

"I have to make a call now."

She pulled her phone and hit one of the names on her list of favorites as she stepped into the rear hall for privacy.

"Harry, we got her."

"No hitches?"

"No hitches. She even had the knife. It was in this elastic strap on her forearm. I just missed it that day."

"Anybody would have."

"Maybe."

"So, she talk to you? Say anything?"

"She said you can never trust men."

"Word to the wise, I guess. How do you feel?"

"I feel good. But she sort of smiled at me when they were taking her out of here. Like she was saying this isn't over."

"What else could she do? Anyway, she gave me that smile too."

"It was weird, though."

"Vegas is weird. When are you coming back?"

"I'll go to the bureau's field office and see what they need from me. Then I'll head back as soon as I'm clear."

"Good. Let me know."

"You working on Freelander?"

"Yeah, and I found the guy. The one she said no to. He's still around."

"Don't do anything until I get back."

"Roger that."

ACKNOWLEDGMENTS

The author had the help of many in the writing of this book. They include Rick Jackson, Mitzi Roberts, Tim Marcia, and David Lambkin on the law enforcement side and Daniel Daly and Roger Mills on the legal side.

With regard to researching and editing I wish to thank Asya Muchnick, Linda Connelly, Jane Davis, Heather Rizzo, Terrill Lee Lankford, Dennis Wojciechowski, John Houghton, Henrik Bastin, Pamela Marshall, and Allan Fallow.

Many thanks to all.

Author's Note: The steps a law enforcement agency must take to obtain a court-approved wiretap are many. They were shortened for dramatic purposes in this novel.

ABOUT THE AUTHOR

Michael Connelly is the author of thirty-three novels, including the #1 *New York Times* bestsellers *The Night Fire, Dark Sacred Night, Two Kinds of Truth*, and *The Late Show*. His books, which include the Harry Bosch series, the Lincoln Lawyer series, and the Renée Ballard series, have sold more than seventy-four million copies worldwide. Connelly is the creator and host of the *Murder Book* true-crime podcast and is the executive producer of the Amazon Studios original series *Bosch*, starring Titus Welliver. A former newspaper reporter, he has won numerous awards for his journalism and his novels. He spends his time in California and Florida.

THE HERO OF
THE POET
AND *THE SCARECROW*
IS BACK!

JACK MCEVOY, THE JOURNALIST WHO NEVER

BACKS DOWN, TRACKS A SERIAL KILLER WHO

HAS BEEN OPERATING UNDER THE RADAR—

UNTIL NOW.

FAIR WARNING

AVAILABLE MAY 2020

Please turn the page for a preview.

1

had called the story "The King of Con Artists." At least that was my headline. I typed it up top but was pretty sure it would get changed because it would be an overstepping of my bounds as a reporter to turn a story in with a headline. The headlines and the decks below them were the purview of the editor and I could already hear Myron Levin chiding, "Does the editor rewrite your ledes or call up the subjects of your pieces to ask additional questions? No, he doesn't. He stays in his lane and that means you need to stay in yours."

Being that Myron was the editor he was speaking of in third person, it would be hard to come back with any sort of defense. But I sent the story in with the suggested headline anyway because it was perfect. The story was about the dark netherworld of the debt collection business—$600 million a year of it siphoned off in scams—and the rule at *Fair Warning* was to bring every fraud down to a face, either the predator's or the prey's, the victim or the victimizer. Make every story personal. And this time it was the predator. Arthur Hathaway, the King of Con Artists, was the best of the best. At sixty-two years old, he had worked every con imaginable in a life of crime centered in Los Angeles, from selling fake gold bars to setting up phony disaster-relief websites. Right now, he ran a racket convincing people they owed money that they didn't really owe, and getting them to pay it. And he was so good at it that junior swindlers were paying him for lessons on Mondays and Wednesdays at a defunct acting studio in Van Nuys. I had infiltrated as one of his students and learned all I could. Now it was time to write the story and use Arthur to expose an industry that bilked millions and millions each year from everybody from little old ladies with dwindling bank accounts to young professionals already deep in the red with college loans. They all fell victim and sent their money because Arthur Hathaway convinced them to send it. And now he was teaching eleven future con men and one undercover reporter how to do it for fifty bucks a head twice a week. The swindler school itself might be his greatest con of all. The guy was truly a king with a psychopath's complete lack of guilt. I also had reporting in the story on the victims whose bank accounts he had cleaned out and whose lives he had ruined.

Myron had already sold the story as a co-project to the *Los Angeles Times,* and that guaranteed it would be seen and the Los Angeles Police Department would have to take notice. King Arthur's reign would soon be over and his roundtable of junior con men would be rounded up as well.

I read the story a final time and sent it to Myron, copying William Marchand, the attorney who reviewed all *Fair Warning* stories pro bono. We didn't put anything up on the website that was not legally bulletproof. *Fair Warning* was a five-person operation if you counted the reporter in Washington, DC, who worked out of her home. One "wrong story" spawning a winning lawsuit or forced settlement would put us out of business, and then I'd be what I had been at least twice before in my career: a reporter with no place to go.

I got up from my cubby to tell Myron the story was finally in, but he was in his own cubby talking on the phone, and I could tell as I approached that he was on a fundraising call. Myron was founder, editor, reporter, and chief fundraiser for *Fair Warning.* It was an internet news site with no paywall. There was a donate button at the bottom page of every story and sometimes at the top, but Myron was always looking for the great white whale that would sponsor us and turn us from beggars into choosers—at least for a while.

"There really is no entity doing what we are doing—tough watchdog journalism for the consumer," Myron told each prospective donor. "And with the current administration's philosophy of deregulation and limiting oversight, there is nobody out there looking out for the little guy. Look, I get it, there are donations you could make that might give you a more visible bang for your buck. Twenty-five dollars a month keeps a kid fed and clothed in Appalachia. I get that. It makes you feel good. But you donate to *Fair Warning*, and what you are supporting is a team of reporters dedicated to—"

I heard "the pitch" several times a day, day in and day out. I also attended the Sunday salons where Myron and board members spoke to potential high-level donors, and I mingled with them afterward, mentioning the stories I was working on. I had some extra cachet at these gatherings as the author of two bestselling books, though it was never mentioned that it had been more than ten years since I had published anything. I knew the spiel was important and vital to my own paycheck—not that I was getting anywhere close to a living wage for Los Angeles—but I had heard it so many times in my four years at *Fair Warning* that I could recite it in my sleep. Backwards.

Myron stopped to listen to his potential investor and muted the phone before looking up at me.

"You in?" he asked.

"Just sent it," I said. "Also to Bill."

"Okay, I'll read it tonight and we can talk tomorrow if I have anything."

"It's good to go. Even has a great headline on it. You just need to write the deck."

"You better be—"

He took his phone off mute so he could respond to a question. I gave him a salute and headed toward the door, stopping by Emily Atwater's cubicle on my way out to say goodbye. She was the only other staffer in the office at the moment.

"Cheers," she said in her crisp British accent.

We worked out of an office in a typical two-story plaza in Studio City. The first level was all retail and food, while the second floor was walk-in businesses like car insurance, manicure/pedicure, yoga, and acupuncture. Except us. *Fair Warning* wasn't a walk-in business, but the office came cheap because it was located above a marijuana dispensary and the venting in the building was such that it brought the aroma of fresh product inside our office on a 24/7 basis. Myron took the place on a heavily discounted basis.

The plaza was L-shaped and had an underground parking garage with five assigned spaces for *Fair Warning* employees and visitors. That was a major perk. Parking in the city was always an issue. And sheltered parking was an even bigger perk for me because this was sunny California and I rarely put the top up on my Jeep.

I had bought the Wrangler new with the advance on my last book, and the odometer served as a reminder to me of how long it had been since I was buying new cars and riding bestseller lists. I checked it as I fired up the engine. I had strayed 122,172 miles from the path I had once been on.

2

I lived in Sherman Oaks on Kester Avenue by the 101 freeway. It was a 1980s Cape Cod–style apartment building consisting of twenty-four townhomes that formed a rectangle enclosing a court-yard with a community pool and barbecue area. It, too, had parking underneath.

Most of the apartment buildings on Kester had names such as the Capri and Oak Crest and the like. My building stood nameless. I had moved in only a year before, after selling the condo I had bought with that same book advance. The royalty checks had been getting smaller and smaller each year and I was in the midst of reordering my life to live within the paychecks from *Fair Warning*. It was a difficult transition.

As I waited on the sloping driveway for the garage gate to lift, I noticed two men in suits standing at the call box at the pedestrian gate to the complex. One was white and middle fifties, the other a couple of decades younger and Asian. A little kick of wind opened the Asian man's jacket and I got a glimpse of the badge on his belt.

I drove down into the garage and kept my eyes on the rearview. I saw them follow me down the slope and in. I pulled into my assigned space and killed the engine. By the time I grabbed my backpack and got out, they were behind the Jeep and waiting.

"Jack McEvoy?"

He had gotten the name right but had pronounced it wrong. *Mick-a-voy.*

Yes, McEvoy," I said, getting it right. *Mack-a-voy.* "What's going on?"

"I'm Detective Mattson, LAPD," the older of the two said. "This is my partner, Detective Sakai. We need to ask you a few questions."

Mattson opened his jacket to show that he, too, had a badge, and the gun to go with it.

"Okay," I said. "About what?"

"Can we go up to your place?" Mattson asked. "Something more private than a garage?"

He gestured to the space around them as if there were people listening from all quarters, but the garage was empty.

"I guess so," I said. "Follow me. I usually take the stairs up but if you guys want the elevator, it's down at that end."

I pointed to the end of the garage. My Jeep was parked in the middle and right across from the stairs leading up to the center courtyard.

"Stairs are good," Mattson said.

I headed that way and the detectives followed. The whole way to my apartment door I was trying to think in terms of my work. What had I done that would draw the attention of the LAPD? While the reporters at *Fair Warning* have a lot of freedom to pursue stories, there is a general division of labor, and criminal scams and schemes were part of my turf along with internet-related reporting.

I began to wonder if my Arthur Hathaway story had run across a criminal investigation of the swindler and if this would be a request from Mattson and Sakai to hold the story back. But as soon as I thought of that possibility, I dismissed it. If that were the case, they would have come to my office, not my home. And it probably would have started with a phone call, not an in-person show-up.

"What unit are you from?" I asked as we crossed the courtyard toward apartment 7 on the other side of the pool.

"We work downtown," Mattson said, being coy, while his partner was being silent.

"What crime unit, I mean," I said.

"Robbery-Homicide Division," Mattson said.

I didn't write about LAPD per se, but ten years ago I did. I knew that the elite squads worked out of the downtown headquarters, and RHD, as it was called, was the elite of the elite.

"So then what are we talking about here?" I said. "Robbery or homicide?"

"Let's go inside before we start talking," Mattson said.

I got to my front door. His nonanswer seemed to push the answer toward homicide. My keys were in my hand. Before unlocking the door, I turned and looked at the two men standing behind me.

"My brother was a homicide detective," I said.

"Really?" Mattson said.

"LAPD?" Sakai asked, his first words.

"No," I said. "Out in Denver."

"Good on him," Mattson said. "He's retired?"

"Not exactly," I said. "He was killed in the line of duty."

"I'm sorry to hear that," Mattson said.

I nodded and turned back to the door to unlock it. I wasn't sure why I had blurted that out about my brother. It was not something I usually shared. People who knew my books knew it but it wasn't something I mentioned in day-to-day conversation. It had happened a long time ago in what seemed like another life.

I got the door open and we entered. I flicked on the light. I had one of the smallest units in the complex. The bottom floor was an open plan with a living room flowing into a small dining area and then the kitchen beyond it, separated only by a counter with a sink. Along the right wall was a set of stairs leading up to a loft, which was my bedroom. There was a full bath up there and a half bath on the first floor beneath the stairs. Less than a thousand square feet in total. The place was neat and orderly but that was only because it was starkly furnished and featured little in the way of personal touches. I had turned the dining room table into a work area. A printer sat at the head of the table. Everything was set for me to go to work on my next book and it had been that way since I moved in.

"Nice place. You been here long?" Mattson asked.

"About a year," I said. "Can I ask what this—"

"Why don't you have a seat on the couch there."

Mattson pointed to the couch that was positioned for watching the flat screen on the wall over the gas fireplace I never used.

There were two other chairs across a coffee table, but like the couch they were threadbare and worn, having spent decades in my prior homes. The decline of my fortunes was reflected in my housing and transportation. I wondered if Mattson and Sakai knew anything about that.

Mattson looked at the two chairs and chose the one that looked cleanest and sat down. Sakai, the stoic, remained standing.

"So, Jack," Mattson said. "We're working a homicide and your name came up in the investigation and that's why we're here. We have—"

"Who got killed?" I asked.

"A woman named Christina Portrero. You know that name?"

I spun it through all the circuits on high speed and came back with a blank.

"No, I don't think so. How did my name—"

"She went by Tina most of the time. Does that help?"

Once more through the circuits. The name hit. Hearing the full name coming from two homicide detectives had unnerved me and knocked an obvious name out of my head.

"Oh, wait, yeah, I knew a Tina—Tina Portrero."

"But you just said you didn't know the name."

"I know. It just, you know, out of the blue it didn't connect. But yes, we met once and that was it."

Mattson turned and nodded to his partner. Sakai moved forward and held his phone out to me. On the screen was a photo of a woman with dark hair and even darker eyes. She looked midthirties but I knew she was midforties. I nodded.

"That's her," I said.

"Good," Mattson said. "How'd you meet?"

"Down the street here. There's a restaurant called Marmalade. I moved here from Hollywood, didn't really know anyone and was trying to get to know the neighborhood. I'd walk down there for a drink every now and then because I didn't have to worry about driving. I met her there."

"When was this?"

"I can't pinpoint the exact date but it was after I moved in here. So about a year ago. Probably a Friday night. That's when I would usually go down there."

"Did you have sex with her?"

I should have expected the question but it hit me out of the blue.

"That's none of your business," I said. "It was a year ago."

"I'll take that as a yes," Mattson said. "Did you come back here?"

I understood that Mattson and Sakai obviously knew more about the circumstances of Tina Portrero's murder than I did. But the questions about what happened between us a year ago seemed overly important to them.

"This is crazy," I said. "I was with her one time and nothing ever came of it after. Why are you asking me these questions?"

"Because we are investigating her murder," Mattson said. "We need to know everything we can know about her and her activities. It doesn't matter how long ago. So I will ask you again: Was Tina Portrero ever in this apartment?"

I threw my hands up in a gesture of surrender.

"Yes," I said. "More than a year ago."

"She stay over?" Mattson asked.

"No, she stayed a couple hours, then got an Uber."

Mattson didn't immediately ask a follow-up. He studied me for a long moment, as if trying to decide how to proceed.

"Would you have any of her property in this apartment?" he asked.

"No," I protested. "What property?"

He ignored my question and came back with his own.

"Where were you last Wednesday night?"

"You're kidding, right?"

"No, we're not."

"What time Wednesday night?"

"Let's say between ten and midnight."

I knew I had been at Arthur Hathaway's seminar on how to rip people off until the 10 p.m. start of that window. But I also knew that it was a seminar for con artists and therefore didn't really exist. If these detectives tried to check out that part of my alibi, they either would not be able to confirm the seminar even existed or would be unable to find anyone to confirm I was there because that would be acknowledging that they were there. They would not want to do this. Especially after the story I just turned in was published.

"Uh, I was in my car from about ten to ten-twenty and then after that I was here."

"Alone?"

"Yes. Look, this is crazy. I was with her one night a year ago and then neither of us kept in contact. It was a no-go for both of us. You understand?"

"You sure about that? Both of you?"

"I'm sure. I never called her, she never called me. And I never saw her at Marmalade again."

"How'd that make you feel?"

I laughed uneasily. "How did what make me feel?"

"Her not calling you back after?"

"Did you hear what I said? I didn't call her and she didn't call me. It was mutual. It just wasn't going to go anywhere."

"Was she drunk that night?"

"Drunk, no. We had a couple of drinks there. I paid the tab."

"What about back here? More drinks or right up to the loft?"

Mattson pointed upstairs.

"No more drinks here," I said.

"And everything was consensual?" Mattson said.

I stood up. I'd had enough.

"Look, I've answered your questions," I said. "And you're wasting your time."

"We'll decide if we're wasting our time," Mattson said. "We are almost finished here and I would appreciate it if you would sit back down, Mr. McEvoy."

He pronounced my name wrong again, probably intentionally.

I sat back down.

"Look, I'm a journalist," I said. "I've covered crime—I've written books about murderers. I know what you are doing, trying to knock me off my game so I'll make some kind of an admission. But it's not going to happen, because I don't know anything about this. So could you please—"

"We know who you are," Mattson said. "You think we would come out here without knowing who we're dealing with? You're the *Velvet Coffin* guy, and just for the record, I worked with Jesse Franceur. He was a friend and what happened to him and with him was bullshit."

There it was. The cause of the enmity that was dripping off Mattson like sap off a maple.

"*Velvet Coffin* closed down four years ago," I said. "Mostly because of the Franceur story—which was one-hundred percent accurate. There was no way of knowing he would do what he did. Anyway, I work someplace else now and write consumer protection stories."

"Good for you. Can we get back to Tina Portrero?"

"There is nothing to get back to."

"How old are you?"

"What's that got to do with anything?"

"You seem kind of old for her. For Tina."

"She was an attractive woman and older than she looked. I think she said she was forty-two when I met her that night."

"But that's the point, right? She was older than she looked. You, a guy in your fifties, moving in on a lady you thought was in her thirties. Kind of creepy, you ask me."

I felt my face turning red with embarrassment and indignation.

"For the record, I didn't 'move in on' her," I said. "She picked up her drink and came down the bar to me. That's how it started."

"Good for you," Mattson said sarcastically. "Must've made your ego stand at attention. So let's go back to Wednesday. Where were you coming from during those twenty minutes you said you were in the car driving home that night?"

"It was a work meeting," I said.

"With people that we could talk to and verify if we need to?"

"Yes."

"Good. So tell us again about you and Tina."

I could tell what he was doing. Jumping around with his questions, trying to keep me off balance. I covered cops for almost two decades for two different newspapers and the *Velvet Coffin* blog. I knew how it worked. Any slight discrepancy in the retelling of the story and they would have what they needed.

"No, I already told you everything. You want anything more from me, then you have to give information."

The detectives were silent, apparently deciding whether to deal. I jumped in with the first question that came to mind.

"How did she die?" I asked.

"She had her neck snapped," Mattson said.

"Atlanto-occipital dislocation," Sakai said.

"What the hell does that mean?" I asked.

"It basically means internal decapitation," Mattson said. "Somebody—somebody strong or with some kind of tool—did a one-eighty on her neck. It was a bad way to go."

I felt a deep pressure begin to grow in my chest. I did not know Tina Portrero beyond the one evening I was with her, but I couldn't get the image of her—refreshed by the photo shown by Sakai—being killed in such a horrible manner out of my mind.

"It's like that movie *The Exorcist*," Mattson said. "Remember that? With the possessed girl's head twisting around."

That didn't help things.

"Anyway," Mattson continued. "The killer had the decency to turn Tina back right afterward. Put her in her bed. But there were stretch marks on her neck."

I knew he was just trying to get a reaction out of me. Maybe he was also trying to see if I wouldn't react.

"Okay, look," I said. "I didn't have anything to do with this and can't help you with your investigation. So if there are no other questions, I would like—"

"There are more questions, Jack," Mattson said sternly. "We are only getting started with this investigation."

"Then, what? What else do you want to know from me?"

"Well, you being a reporter and all, do you know what 'digital stalking' is?"

"You mean like social media and tracking people through that?"

"I'm asking questions. You're supposed to answer them."

"Well, you have to be more specific, then."

"Well, Tina told a good friend of hers that she was being digitally stalked. When her friend asked what that meant, Tina said a guy she had dated knew things about her he should not have known. She said it was like he knew all about her before they even met. And this was a guy she said she met in a bar."

"I met her in a bar a year ago. This whole thing is—wait a minute. How did you even know to come here to talk to me?"

"She had your name. In her contacts. And she had your books on the night table."

I couldn't remember whether I had discussed my books with Tina the night I met her. But since we had ended up at my apartment, I believed that it was likely that I had.

"And on the basis of that, you come here like I'm a suspect?"

"Calm down, Jack. You know how we work. We are conducting a thorough investigation. So let's go back to the stalking. For the record, was that you she was talking about with the stalking?"

"No, it wasn't me."

"Good to hear. Now, last question for now: Would you be willing to voluntarily give us a saliva sample for DNA analysis?"

The question came out of the blue and internally startled me. I hesitated. I jumped to thinking about the law and my rights and totally skipped over the fact that I had committed no crime and therefore my DNA in any form from semen to skin residue could not be found at any crime scene from last Wednesday.

"Is that a no?" Mattson asked.

I came out of the reverie and realized that my DNA was my quickest way off their radar.

"Actually, it's a yes," I said. "When do you want to do it?"

"How about right now?"

Mattson looked at his partner. Sakai reached inside his suit coat and pulled out two six-inch test tubes with red rubber caps attached to a long-ended cotton swab contained inside the glass. I realized then that most likely the sole purpose of their visit was to get my DNA. They had something, the killer's DNA. They, too, knew that it would be the quickest way to determine whether I had any involvement in the murder.

Well, that was fine with me. They were going to be disappointed by the results.

"Let's do it," I said.

3

As soon as the detectives left, I pulled my laptop out of my backpack, went online, and searched the name Christina Portrero. I got two hits, both on the *Los Angeles Times* site. The first was just a mention on the newspaper's homicide blog, where every murder in the county was duly recorded. This report was early in the case and had few details other than the fact that Portrero was found dead in her bed during a wellness check by police after she did not show up for work and did not respond to calls or messaging through social media. The report said foul play was suspected but the cause of death had not yet been determined.

I was a religious reader of the blog and realized I had read the story and scanned through it without recognizing the name Christina Portrero as the Tina Portrero I had met one night the year before. The use of the formal first name had not clicked in my memory circuits. I wondered what I would have done if I had recognized her as the woman I had met. Would I have called the police to mention my experience, my knowledge that she on at least one occasion had gone to a bar herself and had picked me for a one-night stand?

The second hit in the *Times* was a fuller story that ran the same photo Detective Sakai had shown me. Dark hair, dark eyes, looking younger than she was. I had completely missed seeing this story, because I would have recognized the photo. The story said Portrero worked as a personal assistant to a film producer named Shane

Sherzer. This I thought was interesting because a year earlier when we had met, she was doing something else in the film business. She was a freelance reader who provided "coverage" of scripts and books for a variety of producers and agents in Hollywood. I remembered her explaining that she read material submitted to her clients for possible development as films and TV shows. She then summarized the scripts and books and checked off on a form the kind of project they were: comedy, drama, young adult, historical, crime, etc.

She concluded each report with her personal take on the potential project, recommending a hard pass or further consideration by higher-ups in the client's company. I also remembered that she told me that the job often required her to visit production companies located at the major studios in town—Paramount, Warner Brothers, Universal—and that it was very exciting because on occasion she saw major movie stars walking freely between the offices and stages and the commissary.

The *Times* story included quotes from a woman named Lisa Hill who was described as Portrero's best friend. She told the newspaper that Tina led an active social life and had recently straightened out her life after suffering from some addiction issues. Hill did not reveal what these issues were and probably wasn't even asked. It seemed to have little to do with who had killed Portrero by twisting her neck 180 degrees.

Neither of the *Times* posts mentioned the exact cause of death that was described to me in grim detail by the detectives. The second, fuller story said only that Portrero had suffered a broken neck. Maybe it had been decided by *Times* editors not to put the fuller details into the story, or maybe they had not been told. The information on the crime in both posts was attributed to the generic "police said." Neither detective Mattson nor Sakai was mentioned by name.

It took me a couple attempts to spell *atlanto-occipital dislocation* correctly so that I could search it on Google. Several hits came up, most of which were on medical sites that explained what it was and how it was most often seen in traumatic vehicle accidents involving high-speed collisions.

The Wikipedia citation summed it up best:

> **Atlanto-occipital dislocation (AOD), orthopedic decapitation,** or **internal decapitation** describes ligamentous separation of the spinal column from the skull base. It is possible for a human to survive such an injury; however, only 30% of cases do not result in immediate death. Common etiology for such injuries is sudden and severe deceleration leading to a whiplash-like mechanism.

The word *mechanism* in that description began to haunt me. Mattson said someone strong or with some kind of tool had powerfully twisted Tina Portrero's neck. I now wondered if there had been any markings on her head or body that indicated a tool had been used.

The Google search brought up a few citations of AOD as cause of death in auto accidents. One in Atlanta and another in Dallas. The most recent in Seattle. All were deemed accident-related, and there was no citation for AOD being the cause of death in a murder case.

I needed to do a deeper dive. When I was working for the *Velvet Coffin*, I had once drawn an assignment to write a story about a convention of coroners from around the world. They had all convened in downtown Los Angeles, and my editor wanted a feature on what coroners talk about at conventions. The editor who assigned me the piece wanted war stories and the gallows humor exhibited by the people who deal in death and dead bodies day in and day out. I wrote the story but in reporting it learned of a website primarily used by medical examiners as a resource spot for posing questions to other coroners when faced with unusual circumstances involving a death.

The site was called causesofdeath.net and it was password protected, but because it was available to coroners around the world, the password was mentioned on much of the literature handed out at the convention. I had entered the site a few times over the years since I attended the convention just to poke around and see what was happening and of current interest on the discussion board. But I had never posted anything until now. I worded my post so that I was not falsely holding myself out as a medical examiner, but I wasn't exactly saying that I wasn't, either.

> Hey all. We have a homicide case here at LA with atlanto-occipital dislocation—female victim, 44 yoa. Anybody seen AOD before in homicide? Looking for etiology, tool marks, derma marks, etc. Any help is welcome. Hope to see all at next IAME con. Have not been since it was here in the City of Angels. Cheers, @MELA

The post was carefully worded. The shorthand to suggest intimacy. YOA for years of age, AOD the abbreviation for atlanto-occipital dislocation. The mention of the International Association of Medical Examiners convention was legit because I was there. But it would help readers of the post believe I was a working coroner. I knew it edged ethical considerations but I wasn't acting on this as a reporter. At least not yet. I was acting as an interested party. The cops had come and collected my DNA and all but said I was a suspect. I needed information and this might be one means of getting it. I knew it was a shot in the dark but it was one worth taking. I would check the site in a day or two to see if I had any takers.

Next on my list was Linda Hill. She was quoted in the *Times* story as a close friend of Portrero's. For her, I switched hats—from potential suspect to journalist. After the routine efforts to get a phone number for her turned up nothing, I reached out to her—or at least who I thought was her—with private messages to her Facebook page, which appeared dormant, and on her Instagram account as well.

> Hi, I am a journalist working on something on the Tina Portrero case. I saw your name in the Times story. I am sorry for your

loss. I would like to talk to you. Are you willing to talk about
your friend?

I included my name and cell number on each message but also
knew that Hill could reach back to me through those social media
outlets as well. Like the message on the IAME board, it would be a
waiting game.

Before shutting down my efforts, I checked back on causes
ofdeath.net to see if my fishing expedition had attracted any bites.
It had not. I then went back into Google and started reading up on
digital stalking or cyberstalking, as it was more commonly referred
to. Most of what was out there didn't jibe with what Mattson had
described. Cyberstalking most often involved victims being harassed
by someone they knew in at least a peripheral way. But Mattson had
specifically said that Tina Portrero had complained to a friend—
most likely Lisa Hill—that she had gone on a date with a man who
seemed to know things about her he shouldn't have known.

With that quote in mind, I set out to learn all I could about Tina
Portrero myself. I quickly realized I might already have an advantage
over the mystery man who had set off alarms with her. When I went
down the usual checklist of social media apps, I remembered that I
was already her friend on Facebook and a follower on Instagram.
We had exchanged these connections the night we had met. Then
afterward, when no second date grew out of the initial meeting,
neither of us had bothered to unfriend or block the other. This I
had to admit was vanity—everybody likes to pad their numbers, not
subtract from them. Higher numbers equal higher popularity. It was
all bullshit but it was the way it was.

Tina's Facebook page had not been very active and appeared to
be used primarily as a means of keeping in touch with family. I
remembered when we had met that she said her family was from
Chicago. There were several posts spread over the last year from
people with her same last name. These were routine messages and

photos. There were also several cat and dog videos posted by her or to her.

I moved on, going from Facebook to Instagram and seeing that Tina was far more active here, routinely posting selfies and other photos of herself engaged in various activities with friends or by herself. Many had captions that identified the locations and people in the shot. I went back through the feed several months. Tina had been to Maui once and Las Vegas twice during that time. There were shots of her with various men and women, and multiple photos of her at clubs and bars and house parties. It was clear from these that her drink of choice was an Aperol Spritz.

I have to admit that even though I knew she was dead, I felt envious as I reviewed her recent life in photos and saw how full and active it was. My life was nothing in comparison and I fell into morbid thoughts about her upcoming funeral, where invariably her friends and others would say she had lived life to the fullest. The same could not be said about me.

I tried to shake off the feelings of inadequacy, reminding myself that social media was not a reflection of real life. It was life exaggerated. I moved on and the only post I found of real interest was a photo and caption from four months earlier that showed Tina and another woman in her early thirties. They had their arms around each other. The caption Tina had written said: "Finally tracked down my half sis Taylor. She's a blast and a half!!!!!"

It was hard to tell from the post whether Taylor was a half sister who was elusive and therefore had to be tracked down, or whether Taylor had been previously unknown to Tina. The one thing that was clear was that the two women definitely looked like they were related. Both had the same high forehead and attached earlobes, dark eyes, and dark hair. The genetic connection between the women was readily apparent.

I searched to see if there was a Taylor Portrero on Instagram or Facebook but drew a blank. It appeared that if Tina and Taylor were half sisters, they had different last names. This could have occurred through marriage but it also could simply mean they had different fathers.

After my survey of social media ended, I went into full reporter mode and used a variety of search engines to look for other references to Christina Portrero. I was soon able to find the side of her not celebrated on social media. She had a DUI arrest on her record as well as an arrest for possession of a controlled substance—that being MDMA, more commonly referred to as Molly, a drug that increases the activity of neurotransmitters in the brain and causes mood-elevating effects. The arrests resulted in two stints in court-ordered rehab and probation, which she completed in order to have the judge expunge her record of convictions. Both arrests occurred more than five years before. Even so, it seemed to me that MDMA was a young person's drug, and with her arrest occurring in 2014, Tina was then still in her late thirties. That struck me as odd and I wondered if the drug had been planted in her possession. Because the case had been adjudicated and expunged, those details were beyond my grasp.

I was still online, looking for more details about the dead woman, when my phone buzzed and the screen showed a blocked number.

I took the call.

"This is Lisa Hill."

"Oh, good. Thank you for calling me."

"You said you wanted to do a story. For who?"

"Well, I work for an online publication called *Fair Warning*. You might not have heard of it but our stories are picked up by newspapers like the *Washington Post* and the *L.A. Times* all the time. We have a first-look agreement with NBC News as well."

I heard her typing on a keyboard and knew she was going to the site. It made me think she was smart and nobody's fool. There was silence for a moment as I guessed she was looking at the *Fair Warning* home page.

"And you're on here?" she finally said.

"Yes," I said. "You can click on the link where it says staff in that red banner and it will take you to our profiles. I'm the last one. The most recent hire."

I heard the click while I was giving the direction. More silence followed.

"How old are you?" she asked. "You look older than everybody but the owner."

"You mean the editor," I said. "Well, I worked with him at the *L.A. Times* and went with him to this new venture."

"And you're here in L.A.?"

"Yes, we are based here. Studio City."

"I don't get it. Why does a site like this for consumers care about Tina getting murdered?"

That was the question I was ready for.

"Part of my beat is cybersecurity," I said. "And I have sources in the LAPD and they know I am interested in cyberstalking because that gets into the area of consumer security. That's how I heard about Tina. I talked to the detectives on the case—Mattson and Sakai— and they told me that she had complained to friends that she felt some guy she had dated or met was digitally stalking her—that was the phrase the detectives used."

"They gave you my name?" Hill asked.

"No, they wouldn't give out a witness's name. I—"

"I'm not a witness. I didn't see anything."

"Sorry, I didn't mean it that way. From the investigation stand-point, they consider anybody that they talk to in the case a witness. I know you don't have any immediate knowledge of the case. I saw your name in the *Times* story and that's why I reached out."

I heard more typing before she responded. I wondered if she was checking on me further by typing an email to Myron, who was at the top of the *Fair Warning* staff page and listed as founder, publisher, and editor in chief.

"Did you used to work for something called *Velvet Coffin?*" she asked.

"Yes, before I came to *Fair Warning*," I said. "It was locally based investigative reporting."

"It says you went to jail for sixty-three days."

"I was protecting a source. I wouldn't give up the name of a source. The federal government wanted it."

"What happened?"

"After days the source came forward on her own and I was released because the feds got what they wanted."

"What happened to her?"

"She was fired for leaking information to me."

"Oh, man."

"Yeah. Can I ask you a question?"

"Yes."

"I'm curious. How did the *Times* find you?"

"I once dated someone who works there in the Sports section. He's on my Instagram and saw the photo I posted after Tina died, and he told the reporter that he knew somebody who knew the dead girl."

Sometimes it takes a break like that. I'd had more than a few of those in my career.

"Got it," I said. "So, can I ask you, then, are you the one who told the detectives about the cyberstalking?"

"They asked me about anything unusual with her lately and I couldn't really think of anything except some asshole she went out with a few months ago seemed like he knew too much about her, you know?"

"Knew too much how?"

"Well, she didn't really say a lot. She just said she met this guy at a bar and it was supposed to be some rando hookup but that it felt like a setup. Like they were having drinks and he said stuff that made her realize he already knew who she was and things about her and it was really fucking creepy and she just got the hell out of there."

I was having trouble tracking the steps of the story so I tried to break it down into pieces.

"Okay, so what was the name of the place where they met?" I asked.

"I don't know but she liked to go to places up in the Valley," Hill said. "Places on Ventura. She said the men up there weren't so pushy. And I think it had something to do with her age."

"How so?"

"She was getting older. The guys in the clubs in Hollywood, West Hollywood, they're all younger or looking for younger."

"Right. Did you tell the police that about her preferring the Valley?"

"Yeah."

I had met Tina in a restaurant bar on Ventura. I was beginning to understand the interest in me that Mattson and Sakai had.

"She lived near the Sunset Strip, right?" I asked.

"Yes," Hill said. "Just up the hill. Near the old Spago's."

"So would she drive over the hill to the Valley?"

"No, never. She got a DUI a while back and she stopped driving when she went out. She used Uber and Lyft."

I assumed that Mattson and Sakai had gotten Tina's Uber and Lyft records. They would help identify the bars she frequented and be a bounty in determining her other movements. I recalled that she had ordered a car from her cell on the night we had met at a bar on Ventura Boulevard.

"And so, getting back to the stalking thing," I said. "She just went to the club on her own and met this guy, or was it prearranged like through a dating app or something?"

"No, she was doing her thing," Hill said. "She just went there to get a buzz on and hear music, maybe meet a guy. Then she sort of bumped into this guy at the bar. From her standpoint it was random, or it was supposed to be."

It seemed to me that Tina's habit of going alone to bars to maybe meet a guy was an engagement in risky behavior. I held no old-fashioned beliefs about women. They were free to go wherever and do what they wanted. And I was not going anywhere near the idea that a victim is responsible for what happens to her. But I did have an angle on Tina now as a risk-taker. Add that to alcohol and the prior possession and most likely the use of mood-elevating drugs, and she was someone who no doubt engaged in risky behavior. Going to bars where men were less pushy was not enough of a safety edge. Not by a long shot.

"Okay, so they meet at the place and start talking and having drinks at the bar," I said. "And she had never seen him before."

"Exactly," Hill said.

"And did she tell you what he specifically said that creeped her out?"

"Not really. She just said, 'He knew me. He knew me.' It was like he somehow let it slip that he knew her and it wasn't random at all."

"Did she say whether he was already there when she got to the club or came in after?"

"She didn't say. Hold on, I have another call."

She didn't wait for my response. She clicked over to the other call and I waited, thinking about the incident in the club. Then, when Hill came back on the line her tone and words were completely different. She was harsh and angry.

"You motherfucker. You scumbag. You're the guy."

"What? What are you—"

"That was Detective Mattson. I emailed him. He said you're not working a story and I should stay away from you. You knew her. You knew Tina and now you're a suspect. You fucking asshole."

"No, wait. I'm not a suspect. Yes, I met Tina once but I'm not the guy from the—"

"Don't come fucking near me!"

She disconnected the call.

"Shit!"

I felt like I had been punched in the gut, and my face burned with humiliation over the subterfuge I had used. I had lied to Lisa Hill. I wasn't even sure why or what I was doing. The visit from the detectives had tipped me into a rabbit hole and I didn't know whether I was following it as a reporter or somebody infatuated with a dead woman I had met only one time.

I had lied to the detectives as well. The truth was I liked the Tina Portrero I had met at Marmalade. And I wanted more of her. I wanted to see her again but she had rejected me and easily moved on.

That night she had ordered a car and left. I asked for a return engagement and she had said no.

"I think you're too straight for me," she said.

"What does that mean?" I asked.

"That it wouldn't work."

"Why?"

"Nothing personal. I just don't think you're my type. Tonight was great, but for the long haul, I mean."

"Well, then, what is your type?"

It was such a lame response. She just smiled and said her car was arriving. She went through the door and I never saw her again.

Now she was dead and I was either fixated on her or the rejection or both. My life had somehow changed since the moment the two detectives had come to me in the garage. I was down the rabbit hole now and I sensed that what was ahead of me in this place was only darkness and trouble.

Five years ago I had lost everything. My job and the woman who had shot me in the heart with her love. I had blown it. I had not taken care of the most precious thing I had. I had put myself and a story ahead of everything else. True, I had come through dark waters. I had killed men and nearly been killed. I had ended up in jail because of a commitment to my job and its principles, and because deep down I knew she would sacrifice herself to save me. When it all fell apart, my self-imposed penance was to leave everything behind and turn myself in a different direction. For a long time before, I had said death was my beat. Now, with Christina Portrero, I knew it still was.